A Dream
Of Shadows

A Dream
Of Shadows

A Novel of Reincarnation

Diana M. DeLuca

For Aletha
with thanks for your
support and wise words —
Sid was lucky to work with you

Diana M. DeLuca
January, 2016

Seafield House Publications

Centennial, Colorado

A Dream of Shadows: A Novel of Reincarnation

Seafield House Publications

Centennial, Colorado

seafieldpubs@aol.com

ISBN 978-0-9960934-0-8

Library of Congress Control Number:

2014907506

This is a work of fiction. All of the characters, names, incidents, organizations, and dialogue in this novel are either the products of the author's imagination or are used fictitiously.

Printed in the United States of America

Publication managed by Superior Book Productions

www.SuperiorBookProductions.com

For Vincent Charles DeLuca

Preface

As much as we may have learned about death, it is still our greatest mystery. It is also one of our greatest fears, built into the very way we talk about it. We describe death as a defeat, a loss, and an enemy, and most organized religions promise ways to overcome it. But what if death were merely the start of the greatest journey of our lives? What if all the promises were just distractions to finding the reason we were born? Socrates claimed that the unexamined life is not worth living. Perhaps it's also possible that the unexamined death is not worth dying.

A Dream of Shadows is based loosely on my own experience with deaths in my family, but it is also based on the life of Aonio Paleario, a renowned Renaissance intellectual, famous for his beautiful speaking voice and oratorical skill. He was executed for heresy in 1570 because of his determination to pursue truth independently. I have taken many liberties with his story and with the times he lived in, however, so while Paleario deserves to be better known, this is neither a biography nor a history of his age.

Special thanks are due to the first readers of the draft of this novel: Kimi Mann, Lynn King, Pat Harrop, Irwin Kirk, Sid Scott, Hiroshi Kato, Deborah Stetser, Marty Pisano, George Sweanor, and Sidney Bronstein. Their words of encouragement and criticism were vitally important in shaping the story's outline. Thanks are also due to Tyler Tichelaar for valuable suggestions on the novel's structure and Roz Hurley, whose graceful artwork figures prominently on the cover. I also need to issue special thanks to the congregation of St Thomas in Abiquiú in New Mexico who allowed me to observe their prayer rituals, and to the people of Portobello, Columbia, whose devotion to the figure of the Nazareno, otherwise known as the Black Christ, in the Iglesia de San Felipe helped me to understand the attraction and power of being part of a community of believers.

I want also to thank the late Professor Bruce Stillians of the University of Hawaii's Department of English who conveyed to me, his student, his love of complexity and precision. Despite the advice and kindness of these readers, all inelegancies and inaccuracies are, of course, my own.

I hope this book will generate discussion about the interrelation of the world, the nature of personal spirituality, and the wonder of death. As the main character concludes, none of us has the right to consider ourselves inconsequential.

Introduction

Bill Del Vecchio, 2:00 p.m.

*I*LIE IN *my bed in an old house where the wind bears the memories of the millions of lives lived on this planet before mine. I am about to make my transition into that wind, and soon I too will be just someone who once lived here. Still, that passage into the unknown does not bother me as much as knowing I leave with no idea of why I was here or what my life was about.*

If I were going to find answers, I know I should have started asking long ago—long before time carried me to the inevitable irrelevance faced by old men. We live in a world ruled by usefulness and productivity, things that have no meaning for me anymore. But I do have a question: How useful can someone be as he faces death?

I understand why people don't talk about old age and death. A youthful world expects everything to be fixed. That's why plastic surgeons exist—to nip and tuck old age away. I don't blame people who do this. Looking your age means the indignity of being called "dear" in the shops, having people assume you are living on a "fixed income," or being the old folks to whom neighborhood children deliver cookies at Christmas so they can learn charity.

I also don't blame the young for emphasizing the present. I never believed I would shrivel into nothingness. Grow old? Me? How could I? I disliked old people with their endless talk about the past and their disapproval of the present because it wasn't the world they grew up in. I remember promising myself I wouldn't become one of them—hunched over and shuffling, with straw-dry, grey hair cut tight against my skull.

I spent my twenties and thirties in complete denial. I went into my forties certain I would beat entropy, the law of physics that says everything decays over time. But by my fifties, it dawned on me my will might not be enough to make my body immortal. Over the following ten years, I watched the craggy deterioration of my face, gravity's effect on my body, and the emergence of various complaints I'd laughed at before. My God, I thought, I'm decrepit. I've become a tattered coat upon a stick. Except I wasn't. Not really. Not until a lifetime of smoking caught up with me. I suppose I should have expected it and not just because I chose to smoke. My doctor once looked at me with drooping beagles' eyes and told me if I lived long enough, I was going to get cancer of something.

They found the tumor in my lungs by accident. I caught a cold, it went into pneumonia, they took an x-ray, and there it was. By then we had moved to Denver to be near our son who had left California a number of years before. I think I must have been unconsciously looking for meaning even then because the idea of the West appealed to me. The mountains and land seemed a likely avenue to some sort of awakening, but you have to be open to be ready for it, and I recognize now that I wasn't.

One thing I did learn, though, was the limit to medicine. A surgeon's optimistic assessment never comes with an accuracy meter. "We got it all" seems to mean we hope we did, but only time will tell. In my case, the doctors quoted the odds while the patient, me, had to take my chances.

I don't think I'm afraid of dying, but I know I am afraid of death. Dying is the transition while death is the finality. My biggest fear about dying is pain, which can be dealt with. My biggest fear about death is lack of meaning and there's no pill for that. Death is the final summation, the words spoken over you at the end. Not that I want any kind of funeral, and I don't want to know what others say about me. I've heard eulogies that made me wonder if I was listening to the right one. Did a god walk among us and I not know it?

What I mean is the finality of death in a culture valuing eternal youth— or at least as much as cosmetic surgery can provide. As a species, we seem to have forgotten how to move on—if ever we knew. Perhaps our fear of letting go is why we have churches on almost every corner. I've never found this abundance comforting, nor, it seems does anyone else except for completing some sort of a to-do list: Attend church, check. Take care of afterlife: check. Meaning and purpose? Just have faith. But faith in what?

None of my rambling thoughts seems very helpful to me right now, but what am I supposed to be thinking about as death creeps up on me? There's no point in thinking about the future when there isn't going to be one. The present's unattractive with its physical problems and sickness. That leaves only the past, but what do you do if, like me, you didn't like it when you lived it?

As I see it, the biggest trouble with the past is that it offers object lessons when we can't do anything about it. Why be born if all we end up with is a list of mistaken things we did when we were too young to know any better? Still, if I must think about the past, I suppose it could be useful for being honest about myself. For me, this isn't going to be easy. I would have to admit that I was an insignificant spear-bearer on a stage calling for heroes, that the world would be the same had I never taken up its space, and that my life appears to have had no purpose other than the selfish one of existing. I would despair of all this if I weren't already dying.

Even in my darkest moments, though, I cannot give up a shred of stubborn hope. I want to believe there is some purpose to all of this. What is life? What is death? What is real and what's not? The religious say the purpose of life is to worship God. Are we then merely slaves to a cosmic ego?

Others say our purpose is to procreate the next generation of successors to our own miserable selves, train our replacements so to speak. But if that's the case, why live beyond forty? Why live into an old age that serves no obvious purpose except to use up medical resources?

I've always said there's nothing beyond the void, the same one that existed for us before we were born: a sort of darkness we left and will return to. But if this is true then life is meaningless. It is as bleak as dried grasses beaten down by the north wind in a landscape of frozen tundra. I can't accept that idea although I have no evidence for anything more.

Like everyone else born on a small planet endlessly circulating a sun destined one day to go dark, I am bound by my notions of a beginning and an end: life had to start somewhere and it must be headed somewhere. That's a human trait for you: yearning for something while not believing in its possibility, a great existential irony if I ever heard one. But can I be blamed for wishing for something or someone to explain to me what my life was all about before I leave it?

Chapter 1

Denver, Colorado, December 14

THE DEL VECCHIO'S house sat on the bluffs above Denver, a rambling ranch-style, set on an old five-acre horse property. The front windows looked out on a circular, gravel drive that filled with puddles during the snowmelt. The back windows looked out over the Denver skyline far below, past the barn and down to a cottonwood tree, standing alone and out of place on the scrubby back acreage eaten down by the horses.

In this upper part of the city, the relentless wind swooped down from the foothills, driving people indoors to avoid summer thunderstorms and confounding them with ground blizzards during the winter. What the winds did not scour, they blew away, leaving behind a fine layer of dust on houses, cars, people, and animals.

Inside, the house was basically one long hallway that went the length of the building and from which all the other rooms opened. The living area was loosely organized into places to talk and eat without much regard for formality. This was a house of a particular place and time and those who came later, like the family currently living here, could only learn but never live its history.

The del Vecchios, William, his wife, Anna, and their cat came to this house to be near their son, Michael, a pilot who flew out of an airport north of Denver. They were part of a large group migration from California, prompted by a failing economy on the West Coast. By sheer numbers, these new Westerners tempered Colorado's conservative politics and bolstered the economy. Those who prospered from their presence welcomed them. Those who looked back with nostalgia saw them as a threat to a passing way of life. And they were right. But it was also true of the del Vecchios. Two years after moving into the old ranch house, gathering together horses, sheep, and goats, William "Bill" del Vecchio developed lung cancer, had surgery that could not cure it, and started on the slippery slope to death.

As impending deaths usually do, Bill's illness affected family dynamics, mainly confirming entrenched family fault lines. If this was the del Vecchio family, it was tradition not to talk about serious things. Michael's relationship with his father remained distant. Anna still tried to keep the peace. Bill sailed above family problems by ignoring them.

This family division of behavior might have continued unchanged had not Bill's care been assumed by the local hospice. It was then that Marion came into their lives as Bill's caseworker. On her first visit, when she asked how the family was coping, she was more than startled to learn that her patient had forbidden anyone to tell his elderly mother in Los Angeles about his being near death. Foreseeing trouble ahead, she recognized the need to rectify the situation and set out to do it.

"I know this is difficult," Marion told Anna forthrightly, "but Bill can go anytime. We need to talk about this situation with his mother."

When Anna looked doubtful, Marion sat down with her and unfolded a three-panel piece of paper on a coffee table. She smoothed the creases where the paper had been folded and ran her fingers down the columns as if she were searching a telephone directory.

"Here are the signs of impending death," she said. "Bill's been lucky to live a full life until now, but his breathing is becoming irregular, his blood pressure is erratic, and his heart is racing. These are the classic signs. I want you and the rest of the family ready, so Bill's mother needs to know." She stressed the last six words.

Instead of answering, Anna let her eyes slide to the Christmas tree where the cat had knocked down the ornaments and pulled off the tinsel. To her, the disarray was emblematic of her life. She'd made a promise to her dying husband, and she still wanted to keep it.

Marion was not discouraged by Anna's response. She'd been in the death business a long time; her body had thickened from eating at night to stay awake until death arrived, usually at dawn. She didn't know why. All she knew was that the last few hours of life were as challenging as birth, yet they were treated as a mere by-product of living: be born and you will die, the truism people didn't think about until forced to. She knew that Anna del Vecchio might not be ready, but death was.

"I understand it's difficult to go against Bill's wishes," Marion said, "but his mother has to know sooner or later. Why don't you call her now and save a very difficult conversation later on. This would be a good time."

Marion studied Anna as she waited for her reply. Her patient's wife was in her mid-fifties, dressed in a wrinkled green T-shirt bearing the words "Colorado Horse Rescue" and jeans that looked as if she'd slept in them. She didn't look frightened, only tired and discouraged. Marion knew there must be something she was missing. Perhaps it would help if she could get Anna to talk about her life with her husband.

"Why don't you tell me about Bill? How did you meet?"

Anna looked up in surprise. "I was a student at UCLA. He was a radio announcer on a classical music station. I'd phone up occasionally and ask him to play particular pieces. I thought he had a beautiful voice."

"Was his mother in the picture then? How did everyone get on?"

"He was living at home. He said his father had left the family and he was helping her out. It sounded noble in a way. But I soon learned that someone was always angry in his family, and they wouldn't speak to one another for years. Bill's mother never welcomed me."

"How about your own family? How did they feel about you and Bill?"

"Just my mother. She said Bill was old enough to be my father. But there were only thirteen years between us. My mother grew to accept Bill with time."

"And Bill and your son?"

"Michael and Bill aren't as close as I hoped they would be."

"Does your son get on with Bill's mother?"

"With Carolina?" Anna thought about it. "Michael saw her on holidays when we went out there to visit. I suppose they're all right with one another. Carolina's trouble is with me, not my son."

Marion pounced. "Where is your son now? Would he be willing to make the call for you?"

Anna looked at Marion blankly. She hadn't thought about asking Michael. Involuntarily, she glanced down the back hallway where he was staying in the small guest room, the last one at the end. "I don't know," she admitted. "Michael moved in this morning. He's been on the phone since then getting other pilots to take over his runs. He said he'd stay here until it's all over, but I know if he doesn't fly he doesn't get paid."

"But would he be willing to call her? It's good when everyone in the family takes some responsibility. Why don't you ask him?"

Anna thought for a few minutes, shrugged, and then walked slowly down the hallway. A pause, a door opened, a murmur of conversation, and two sets of footsteps came back down the long passage past Bill's open doorway.

"Is he dead?" Michael asked.

"Not yet," Marion said. "That's not it. Your mother and I have been talking about what needs to be done. It's a difficult time, but someone needs to phone your grandmother and tell her about your dad. Will you do it?"

Michael sat uneasily on a chair at the end of the coffee table. He knew that telling Carolina her son was dying would produce a maelstrom of invective and accusation.

"I don't know how she'll take it, hearing it from me. We're not that close."

"Someone has to do this," Marion encouraged him. "Your grandmother needs to hear this from someone in the family."

"I've never done anything like this before," Michael admitted. "I don't know how to do it. How much time do I have?" He glanced at his mother, but she didn't meet his eyes.

"Let's not wait any longer," Marion urged. She had picked up the subtle suggestion he might be willing. "I can help you find the way to tell her if you want."

Michael squared his shoulders. He felt as if he were fifteen whenever he entered his parents' house, and he'd never understood why everyone operated in it with such repressed, polite anger.

"What do I say?" he said finally. "She'll ask questions I can't answer."

"Just be honest," Marion replied. "Tell her your father is in the final stages of lung cancer and you have been asked to call her. You can say he is under hospice care and is in and out of consciousness."

"Then what?" Michael imagined awkward, reproachful silences he would feel obliged to fill by saying the first stupid thing coming into his head. Talk about being fifteen again.

"Think this through, Michael. She'll likely ask you how long he's been ill, whether he's in pain, and what happens next. You can answer those questions, can't you?"

Michael thought for a moment. Damn this family. He wondered if he could distract his grandmother by focusing on the immediate situation rather than the causes and motives leading up to it.

"Can she talk to him? What if she asks?"

"Tell her she can speak to him if he's conscious. I'm sure he'd like to talk to her as well. Tell her you believe he was trying to save her from worry and this has been sudden. Try to ease the shock for her."

Michael doubted Carolina would believe they were thinking of her. Realistically, he knew she would suspect the worst, and this time she might be right. She wouldn't believe that not telling her was Bill's idea. Not her son. It had to be a plot hatched by Anna and Michael. She'd think they hated her so much that they deliberately kept a dying man away from his mother. Still, this was his father's decision, and his father never did things unintentionally. Michael walked back down the hall of windows until the door to the guest room closed quietly behind him.

"What happens now to Bill?" Anna asked. She wanted to cry but could not.

Marion reopened the roadmap to death. "I'll leave this for you to read. One by one his systems will continue shutting down. He'll alternate between being cold and running a fever. Your job will be to keep him comfortable. I think he must be hanging on by sheer force of will. I'm surprised that he hasn't decided to let go before this."

"That's Bill." Anna managed to give a small smile. "He always wanted to be in charge."

"Now, is there something you want to do? You need to take care of yourself as well. I can stay with him and give you a break. Perhaps you'd like to take a shower before I leave?"

Anna shook her head. It didn't seem the time to think about herself. "Will he wake up?" she asked instead.

"If he's in pain. You know what to do when that happens. I'm leaving you a full bottle of morphine." Marion held the little bottle up to the light and tapped it with her finger. She read the lines on the bottle and recorded the result in her narcotics log. "Give him a dropper full under his tongue as needed."

Anna looked warily at the bottle. She didn't feel prepared for this. If he had wanted to talk about his life and feelings, she had the tools and training, but not for a terrible silence that left her no focus for her own fears and with little to contribute. She envied Marion who knew what to do.

"What happens if I overdose him? Should I keep a written record of what he's given?"

"Follow the directions and you'll be fine. The cancer will cause his death, not you. You're doing all you can to help him."

"What's happening to him right now? Can he hear us?" Could Bill have overheard their plans to tell Carolina against his wishes? She knew they were intervening in his death, going against what he said he wanted. But did Bill really mean to throw his family into such confusion?

"Hearing is the last thing to go, so even if he appears to be asleep it's quite possible he's hearing you."

"He'd hear music then?" Anna knew it would bring him peace if anything could.

"Playing music is a good idea if he's always enjoyed it."

Marion was glad if Anna could find something to occupy her. People forget many things about a death but not their own participation. Anna would remember playing music for her dying husband just as Michael would remember calling his grandmother, whether he wanted to or not.

"Try to remind him of happy things. Talk to him. He'll hear you. There's no need to break the connection. I'll wait to see how Michael's done with his grandmother, and I'll be back first thing in the morning unless you call me sooner."

They heard the sound of a door closing and the sound of Michael returning from his mission. He looked drawn and suddenly exhausted.

"I told her. She was shocked and started crying. She says she'll call back when she's able to talk. She wants to come here, but she needs someone to travel with her. She says she's going to try making arrangements to fly here tonight. She wants to know why nobody told her."

"What did you tell her?" Anna asked.

"I said I didn't know. I had to keep saying it. How am I to know if he's spiritually ready for death? If he's had last rites. Or the burial plans."

"Let's sit down and talk about this," Marion said. "You need to be on the same page and supporting one another. Michael, you did a good thing in talking to your grandmother. It was an important and very difficult job you did for your family. We need you to continue. Will you be the person who keeps her informed?"

Michael nodded unhappily. He had little choice since Carolina had already started the blaming process and did not wish to speak to Anna. He knew he would be the one who called when his father died and the one who listened to Carolina's anger and grief, all the more acute because she hadn't known.

"Anna, is there someone else who can stay with you and help?"

"Carole said she'd come. Bill asked for her."

Michael frowned slightly but said nothing.

"Is she a family member?"

"No," Anna replied. "She's a neighbor. But she and Bill are close, and Bill wanted her to be with us."

"Michael, you don't look happy about this," Marion observed.

"I'm not unhappy, just confused. We dated for a year or so and then broke up. I don't really understand what she has to do with this. But if that's what he wants, that's fine."

"Your mother needs all the help she can get right now. If Carole can help your father, it's a good thing. Can you be OK with it?"

"Sure, why not?" Michael looked awkward. "It's up to him."

"When will she get here?" Marion asked.

"Any minute, I think," Anna said. "She had to come from work."

"How old is Bill's mother? Is her health good enough to make the trip?" Marion was determined to remain pragmatic.

"She's in her late eighties with heart trouble," Anna explained. "She'd have to fly from the West Coast and would need wheelchair assistance along with someone to travel with her. We'd all be better off if she doesn't try."

"Let's say she does. Can you accommodate her if she gets here?"

"I'll sleep on the couch and Carolina and whoever is with her can have the second bedroom with the two beds. Perhaps Michael could go out to the airport to get them."

Michael did not refuse. Anna imagined the ride back from the airport would be one of the worst experiences of his life. Carolina's arrival would be one of the worst of hers.

"Just as long as you have a plan. I'm going to stay here with you until Carole comes. I'll just need to make a phone call." Marion went into the kitchen and left mother and son alone.

Anna looked curiously at Michael. She could see Bill in his narrow face and her own family in his dark brown hair and muscular build. Bill's hair was Sicilian blue-black, curled in waves like Michael's, but his skin was ruddy. Bill's father came from Salerno, and she remembered being told how the sun kisses the Mezzogiorno, the lower lands of the Italian peninsula, making its people dark. Anna had only seen a picture of the man, and no one talked about him. Michael had her fair complexion, or maybe Bill's mother gave him the lighter coloring. Carolina's family was from northern Italy, more German than Italian, and she had blue eyes and fair hair. She was born on the East Coast, but her mother sent her back to Italy for her education, perhaps not trusting the new world to train her daughter. This may have contributed to the family's lack of closeness. Before her mother died alone, ignored by her children, she told Carolina bitterly that her turn would come. "You watch," she said. "You'll die alone, just like me. No one's gonna want you either."

"This whole situation isn't right," Michael said with another frown.

Anna did not reply immediately. She knew Bill must have expected his mother would turn her anger on Anna. Did he care? Did he think Anna wouldn't mind? Did he prefer not to deal with Carolina's anger himself? Anna would never know.

"I think your father thought it would be easier."

"For him," Michael said bitterly. He walked back down to his room, refusing to allow his mother to see his pain.

Anna shook her head as she watched him leave. She assumed that Bill's closeness to Carole was the problem. But Carole was never just a neighbor to Bill. She was the daughter Bill never had. There was immediate recognition between them when they met. Both were nonconformists, full of easy laughter at the pretensions of what they called The Others. It didn't take Anna long to realize they considered her among them. It was different between Bill and Michael. They had little in common to begin with and both were too stubborn to accommodate the other. It was unsettling. Perhaps the best of all possible worlds out in the West wasn't so wonderful after all.

"Is Michael OK with Carole coming here or am I imagining things?" Marion asked as she came back from the telephone in the kitchen.

"I'm not sure," Anna replied grimly. "But we'll make do."

They heard the sound of a car parking under the Russian olives beside the driveway just as Marion was packing up her things.

"How is he?" Carole asked as she burst through the front door. She filled the room with energy and the moment. Her blonde hair glistened as if she had just washed it.

"He's failing," Marion replied. "He may not make it through the night."

"Michael told Carolina," Anna blurted out.

"He did? How did you get him to do it?" Carole's eyebrows rose and she paused for a moment in taking off her coat.

"I didn't. Marion asked him to." Anna conceded the point.

"Good thing. It needed to be done. How did she take it?" Carole hung her coat over a chair in the space they called the dining room and came over to sit on the sofa. She stared at Anna, waiting for the details.

"She's trying to get a flight from LA to come here." Anna pursed her lips at the impracticality of an infirm, elderly woman flying across the country.

"Gutsy," Carole said, "but not a good idea, is it?"

"Bill wouldn't like it. But I give her credit for wanting to come." Since Michael had been the one to tell Carolina about Bill's cancer, Anna could afford a marginal tolerance.

Marion interrupted gently before the two women become too engrossed in discussing the distant Carolina.

"I need to visit another family, but I want to be sure you are all right before I leave. I'd like to go over what's been settled. You have enough morphine to keep Bill comfortable until I come back. The catheter is working properly, and I've changed the bag. Michael's in charge of communication with his grandmother. Hospice is responsible for Bill's care—you have the hotline number. If there's any change call right away. Someone is always on duty, and I will be here in a few minutes. Do not call 911. I'll check in a little later to see how things are going. Please call anytime if you have questions."

They listened to the nurse's car crunch over the frosty gravel and out to the road. Anna felt grateful for Carole's presence. It was times like this that she was sorry that Michael and Carole had not stayed together.

"She said Bill would enjoy music."

"Well," Carole said briskly. "Why don't you get on with it? OK if we get some coffee started. It could be a long night. Get the music on first, though."

Anna sat on the floor in front of the stereo. She rifled through the cassettes looking for the pieces she knew Bill had loved over the years. As she laid them on the carpet and turned on the player she felt she was counting the years of their marriage. They were too poor at the beginning to afford anything top-rate. Their collection gradually improved when they didn't have to shop exclusively in bargain bins. Now it was a music library befitting a man who once hosted a classical music radio program. She tried to choose the best recordings of his favorite pieces and put on a Brahms symphony. The majestic music filled the room and spilled over into the bedroom next door where Bill could hear it.

Perhaps in response to the new sounds, Bill groaned and became restless. Carole picked up the morphine bottle from the coffee table.

"How often does he get this?"

"As needed," Anna replied.

"I'd say he could use some. How much?"

"The directions say to fill the stopper to the line and put it under his tongue."

They went into the bedroom and lifted Bill gently to open his mouth and put the drug under his tongue. "Here's some joy juice for you," Carole said.

They laid him back and straightened out the sheets around him. His eyes raked the ceiling and closed. He seemed to drift back to sleep.

"So Michael had to tell Carolina." Carole's face was a mixture of surprise and respect as they went back into the kitchen and she took out the coffee maker.

"It was difficult. No one expected anything else." Anna pulled down the coffee cups.

"I wouldn't have wanted to do it either. Bill should have told her." Carole measured the coffee and water into the pot, waited for the first burble, and then sat down at the kitchen table to watch.

"Bit late now." Anna's tone implied she did not care for a discussion regarding her role in supporting Bill's decisions.

"Do you think she'll come?"

"If she can find someone to come with her. But it's not a good idea, at least I don't think so." Anna tried to keep her voice neutral. The phone rang and startled them.

"I'll get it," Carole said as she picked up the kitchen's wall phone. She listened for a few moments and put her hand over the mouthpiece. "It's Carolina asking for Michael."

"He's in the guest room."

Carole walked down the hall, knocked on Michael's door, and relayed the message. She returned and hung up the receiver.

"How long do you plan to stay?" Anna asked.

"As long as Bill needs me. I've arranged to take time off work, and I told Richard he'd have to fend for himself for a few days. He said no problem. I'm sure he hasn't forgotten how to be a bachelor. He was one long enough before we married. How are you holding up?"

"All right, I suppose. I'm doing what hospice says to do."

"Have you thought about what you'll do afterwards?"

"I not ready to think about the future. Hospice told me not to make major changes for a year unless I absolutely have to. I'm focused on just getting through the moment."

"Well, there's reality here. This is an old house and the acres and animals are a lot to keep up. Caregiving is a role, not a life definition. It's something you do, but there's always a termination point. You have to plan for when it ends."

Anna bent down to shake cat food into a bowl. "Where's Sam?" she said to no one in particular when there was no sign of the cat.

"I saw him in Bill's room," Carole said. "Leave him alone. He'll come when he's hungry."

"Maybe so," Anna replied, but then she walked down the hall to look in her husband's room. The large white and tabby cat was curled up on the bed tucked tightly against Bill's side. "Sam? Dinner?" she asked gently. The cat lifted his head and looked at her with green, knowing eyes but stayed where he was. "All right," she said, "come when you're ready." The cat put his head down again.

Carole frowned as she waited for Anna. She stirred her coffee. They would both need the caffeine if they were to be on watch all night.

Michael's door opened and he came down the hall. "She's not coming. Her doctor says she shouldn't and none of her friends are willing to travel with her. There are Catholic things she wants done. I don't know what's she's talking about, but she's insistent. Says you should call her and she'll give you the list. Otherwise, have a priest call her and she'll tell him. She was upset when I said there wasn't a crucifix over the bed."

"OK," choked Anna. "I'll try to figure out what she's talking about. Maybe I can make a donation to the Church and have a priest stop by. Bill hasn't been to church for years, but maybe he'd like it."

"Hello, Michael," Carole said pointedly. "How have you been? Still flying out of Jefferson Airport?"

Michael nodded curtly. "Still doing art?"

"Always," she said.

"What's Michael going to do afterwards?" Carole asked abruptly after Michael returned to his room.

"What do you mean?"

"He's flying cargo loads out to small towns. Potatoes to Podunk. With all his qualifications, he ought to be flying big time. Commercial jets. Not many people are that qualified to both fly and repair aircraft. He's never lived up to his potential."

"I think he's happy with his life," Anna said.

"No, he's not," Carole said definitively.

"I don't know then." Anna realized Bill must have discussed intimate family matters with Carole. "Michael will be fine," she added conclusively.

"Do you know why Bill left it to you both to tell his mother?"

Anna looked out of the kitchen window at the expanse of land behind the house and considered her reply. "It had to do with the past," she replied evasively, not knowing what else to say. How could she admit that despite over thirty years of marriage, Bill had kept things from her, things he probably had told Carole.

"The past? You can blame the past for everything."

"Bill's family never talked about things," Anna replied grimly.

What Anna did not say was how she was starting to see Bill as an enigma who kept secret who he was even from those closest to him. Why did he refuse to tell his mother? Why was it so hard for him to be a father? What was he thinking as he knocked on death's door? She didn't know.

3:00 p.m.

I'VE BEEN DEALING *with a strange vision lately. I've been seeing what looks like a deep crevice partially hidden by quartz-flecked, granite outcroppings. I can't see beyond its blackness, but somehow I know there is a cavern behind it. What would be inside that cavern is anyone's guess.*

My mother would expect saints and incense, but that's her view of the afterlife; in my case, if there is anything, it would probably be dungeons and gremlins with pitchforks.

I don't discount the possible connection between the crevice and the morphine they've been giving me, yet the crevice seems more real than hallucination. When I open my eyes, I am in my bedroom with Anna, hovering around me. When I close them, there is the crevice. I don't know if I am expected to push my way in, but I know I'm not about to. If I wait, the crevice shimmers like an after-image and fades, even though I suspect its disappearance is only temporary.

I don't know how much longer I will to be allowed my resistance. All I know is I am not ready to submit even if my pride is illusory. In my darker moments, I imagine life's scorn. Your vaunted free will? It's only as much as we grant you. All you have is the larger progression of the human experiment. Our experiment. You and your kind can be wiped out tomorrow. We've done it before, and the dinosaurs were much larger than you. Yes, I hear life's sneer, and I know a dying man can hardly expect or even hope that life will explain itself to him and conform to his idea of making sense. But knowing that only makes me cling more tightly to what I have left of it.

Beyond Anna, my only reality is the cat, Sam. He jumps on my bed and snuggles against me, leaving only to use his box and eat before he jumps back up with a polite meow to tell me he is returning and asking if I missed him. Strangely enough, I do. He stares at me with his penetrating green eyes before he curls himself into a ball and takes his place. There's something reassuring about his warmth and pressure against my legs. As long as I can feel him, I know I am still alive.

When I first learned about my illness, I denied it. For one ridiculous week, I walked on the treadmill as if getting back into shape would cure me. When that didn't work, I became frustrated and yelled at Anna. She was hurt but I was beyond caring. Irrationally, I became jealous of people who knew they would wake up in the morning. I particularly resented the feeling people were waiting for me to give up, make a choice, or ask some existential question.

Now in the face of the indignities of death and dying, defiance seems pointless, even though I am still not ready. This morning, out of pride and obstinacy, I refused to use the bedpan. Pushing Anna away, I hung my legs over the side of the bed and tried to stand. The rebellion worked for a few moments, until my legs buckled and she had to lift me back. Then, to make things worse, I couldn't pee. Anna finally asked the hospice nurse to come insert a catheter. I felt humbled needing help with such a basic human function and wondered if diapers—the final humiliation—were next, but I was grateful for the relief. The nurse set up the tubing, pulled the bedclothes up around me, and patted my shoulder as she left.

Keeping things to myself has been my protection, but even I can see how it will affect Anna when she finds the book I was writing. She'll find the manuscript tucked away behind the books on the shelf, in the same place where I hid my cigarettes. Yes, I should have quit smoking once the cancer was diagnosed. But I couldn't see how quitting at this late stage was going to make any difference. So I didn't. A lifetime's habit is not so easily ended.

I take a deep breath to clear my mind. Family things are too tangled for me—too many people with their issues and too many evasions. The morphine Anna places under my tongue is simpler and more interesting. It gives me an initial rush followed by a sensation of falling. Then I feel warm and things move in slow motion while parts of me become numb. The pain goes away, but the drug leaves my mind jumbled. Sometimes I think I'm lucid; other times I think I'm imagining things. Time has no meaning for me and I remember events with the wrong people in them, seeing Anna, for example, in a memory of events from long before I met her.

I never believed in an afterlife, despite what my mother's priests tried to drill into me about purgatory and salvation. You die and then it's over— that's what I've always said. But it means I have no vision for death or any way to understand and deal with it—perhaps because I've tried to live my life detached from meaning. How ironic those words sound coming from a man fighting to keep a connection to life even if it's just to a collection bag under the bed. Perhaps the crevice and whatever lies behind it have been given to me as my vision. If I walk into that darkness on my own time, then perhaps I have some control after all. At least that would be interesting.

Listen to me. Here I am trying to dictate the terms of my death again. They're not going to like me much on the other side of whatever is out there. Still, I haven't lost all my faculties yet. In fact, I still can hear. My other senses are gone or going, but my hearing is better than it has been in years. I can hear Anna and the nurse, although not everything they're saying. It doesn't matter anymore what they're deciding.

Carole is right. She always is because she calls things as she sees them. Her honesty is what attracted me. She's the truth-teller and we both look at the world as an immediate place. Anna, on the other hand, thinks in metaphors—everything has to be connected to something else, like those philosophers she read while she was in graduate school. Too many scholars, too many ideas, too many theories—it made my head spin, and I couldn't see where it made life any better to think that much. Carole is right about Michael. He should have built a major career long ago. He's that brilliant, but he's stuck somewhere in the ordinary, waiting for something to happen to him. But then aren't we all waiting for something? I'm waiting for death. Anna is waiting for me to die. But then what? I wonder what her life will be like once I'm gone.

There's the crevice again. I sense its impatience. Without wanting to, I feel myself pulled into what looks like a vortex, a spiraling mass of cloud that envelops me and drags me forward. I lose myself in the power of its presence. When the motion stops, I realize I have been taken through the crevice and into whatever lies behind it.

. . .

At first, I can see nothing except for a pinprick of light flashing on the rough wall in front of me. As I watch, the light grows larger until it becomes like a window. I frown in concentration and try to look through it, but all I can see at first is a foggy light. Eventually, I think I can make out what looks like a rainy scene of a house and hills and trees. Meanwhile the window keeps expanding until it has become a doorway. That alarms me and I try to back away from it only to feel something pushing me forward. Again, I try to pull back, but then I am propelled firmly through the door and into a landscape of wet and mist.

. . .

I am on a low hill looking up at an isolated stone building that stands at the end of a track lined with cypress trees. It is flanked by what appear to be farm buildings and fenced areas for carts and livestock. The house looks grey under the pressing rain clouds, although in the distance, I can see the weather clearing and the sun starting to turn the clouds from grey to gold.

Across the valley, I can see a small town perched precariously on the top of a hill. It has steeples, towers, and stone houses crammed together along a ridgeline. It looks as if it belongs in the Renaissance paintings that Anna studied, the kind where the artist is working out perspective and depth in the landscapes. Is this Italy? I close my eyes, but that doesn't help because when I open them, I'm still there. I feel as if I am in a dream where nothing makes sense and time does not exist. Now I am annoyed: if this is a game, I don't know the rules or for what I am playing. Resentfully, I look behind me for the opening, but is has not reappeared and I sense it will not. Whatever has brought me here intends me to stay. With no other obvious options, I move farther into the scene and approach the buildings.

The main house has two floors of undistinguished earth-colored stone cut by evenly spaced windows on both floors, a small covered porch with *stone arches, and a slightly pitched roof of orange tile. I see a dry fountain in the courtyard; I watch as rain drips down the fruit and nymphs sculpted around its basin. The house appears solid although not luxurious. On a bright, warm day, one might generously describe it as having great potential, but today it looks forlorn.*

I watch as a white cat with tabby stripes just like Sam's darts around the fountain and passes right in front of me. He has caught something as I can see a tail hanging from his mouth. He doesn't pay me the slightest attention, even though he almost runs over my feet. Somewhere in the distance I hear a goat bleating and the rattle of stable doors as horses move around restlessly. I hear one stamp its foot. It must be nearing time for its dinner.

Most of the house's windows are shuttered, but one is open on the ground floor. As I approach it to peer through the thick bottle-glass, the impossible happens: the downstairs walls pull apart like theater scenery and I feel myself propelled into the house. Once inside, I find myself in a dark, wood-paneled room lit by candles and heated by logs in a stone fireplace. Behind me the walls glide silently closed.

There are people here, but no one looks at me or seems to have noticed anything. I'm not even sure what has happened myself. One moment I am in my bed, then I am in a cavern, and now I am in somebody's else house somewhere in time. I stand irresolutely off to one side, waiting to be spotted and accused, but again no one notices me. When a woman bearing dishes passes me with no comment, it dawns on me that I must be invisible—free to look around, listen, and perhaps learn why I have been brought here.

Chapter 2

Colle de Val D'Elsa, near Siena, Italy, May 1567

THE DOG LAY on a straw-filled pallet to the side of the wood fire burning in a carved stone fireplace. The grape leaves, angels, and animals carved into the stonework meant nothing to him. He was interested only in the warmth generated by the fire. He was an old dog, fifteen years now, with grizzled jaw, droopy eyelids, and hip bones protruding where his brown hair had worn thin. He had lived with the family since puppyhood and he knew them well.

There was the loud-voiced woman in the kitchen who shouted at him but often threw him an unexpected scrap of meat from her cooking; his mouth sucked open and his jaw snapped shut as he caught it. He knew the children, the boy who rolled on the grass with him but became increasingly unkind until the dog learned to avoid him, and the two little girls who tried to ride him. They were all grown up now and he was grown old. He knew the sharp voice of the woman whose words "Bruno. Out," meant he should slink away before calamity struck. He knew the man who accompanied his master on his travels; he'd run round the cart as they loaded it up, barking out his protest at their leaving until he was yelled at for disturbing the horse. But most of all, he knew the man who took him on long, wonderful walks where he could chase rabbits, roll in smelly things, and lope in the sunshine for the sheer joy of being a dog.

Now he lay on the pallet, half-dozing. From time to time, his eyes opened, revealing a half moon of white along his lower lids. He had sensed something he couldn't place, so he looked anxiously from person to person, but they were all there. Whatever it was that disturbed him seemed to pose no danger, so he put down his head and went back to sleep.

Two women and a young girl sat on a wooden bench facing the fireplace but some distance back from it. The bench had a high back and sides and was padded inside with olive-green fabric. It was high enough off the ground for the ladies to use footstools while the little girl could swing her legs without bothering the carved apples and grapes on the frieze around the bottom of the bench.

One of the women, dressed in the dark, high-necked clothes of household authority, was Bruno's sharp-tongued woman, Marietta Paleario. Marietta's hair was tied back severely and she bore herself very upright as much from personal discipline as from the straight back of the bench. The second woman was her daughter, Caterina, one of the girls who had played with Bruno when she was young. She was married now and had already given her husband two children: the little girl now learning from her grandmother how to tat, and the hoped-for son and heir, three months old, lying in a carved wooden cradle on the floor beside his mother.

Behind the women, leaning over the back of the bench and watching as her mother guided her granddaughter's small fingers in making loops and knots, was the youngest daughter, Beatrice, hardly grown out of adolescence. She looked thoughtful and was listening carefully to what was happening around her. From time to time, she ran her hand lovingly down the soft fabric of her dress, suggesting she was not long beyond wearing hand-me-downs from her older sister.

Three men stood next to the fireplace, in the warmest spot, holding wine goblets painted with the crest of the city of Salerno. Marietta had ordered these from a famous glassworks to recall that Prince Ferrante of Salerno had offered his support to her husband not only because of his distinguished scholarship but because of what the prince said was their shared family line. Marietta liked the idea that the Paleario family was of noble origin. She hoped her husband, Aonio, appreciated her efforts to maintain their social standards.

Bruno's master, Aonio Paleario, white-haired now, was one of the men at the fireplace. He stood with his long, dark vest drawn tightly round him as if his slender frame were perpetually cold. The old man's craggy, narrow face, dark eyebrows, penetrating eyes, distinctive nose, and clipped beard made him look dignified but also reserved. On the other side of the fireplace was his more fashionable son, Fedro, the one the family dog had learned to avoid. Fedro was stocky, with dark, tightly curled hair and coarser features. His hooded eyes were set close into a broad face, and to look into them was to look into black unfathomable pools. In between the two Paleario men was a rotund priest with his back to the fire. The priest was flapping his vestments to warm his buttocks while delivering a pompous, self-important waterfall of words.

"The best music is at Santa Maria Novella in Florence," the priest pronounced authoritatively to father and son. "The choir has improved immeasurably with the new cappelmeister. Of course, Duke Cosimo authorized new hymnals in 1560, which undoubtedly helped. No one could read the old ones anymore. Too much candle wax and smoke. I thought the new lace on the choir gowns was nice, but the priest needs to do something about his biretta. It looked shabby."

"Now, Fra Pietro," Fedro said to the priest, "so far you have described only peripherals." Fedro used the ironic tone of the provocateur looking to see what reaction he could arouse. He smiled slightly as he knew the priest could not resist the bait. "It seems to me...."

"Peripherals!" Fra Pietro did not allow Fedro to finish his thought.

His face flushed up to his cropped grey hair, his eyebrows rose in a quizzical arch, and his double chin shook. "Fedro, my fine young friend, those they assuredly are not. We are talking about ritual in the Catholic Church. Observance is no minor matter. The Council of Trent settled all matters of faith. It is our duty to believe and follow the Church teachings."

"But, sir," Fedro objected in mock seriousness, only to have the priest break in once more.

"No, Fedro, these are not minor concerns."

"I was going to say, sir, that I wondered if God were not present just as much in shabby surroundings as in the grandest?"

"Spoken like a contentious lawyer!" A saliva bubble gathered at the edge of the priest's mouth. "This is not a matter of God's presence, Fedro. It is a matter of observing the Church's duty to God. The other month I went to Mass at the duomo in Siena. When the communicant bent to flick the imps away from under the altar, I was struck by the beauty of his hands. It echoed the beauty of the ritual and made his movements a statement of belief in God. Your father should certainly understand what I am talking about. It is the matter of the relation between ritual and belief."

After this outburst of piety, the priest suddenly stopped and shook his finger. "Fedro, you're a rascal. You catch me every time, don't you? I should know better by now." The priest relaxed his shoulders and took a sip of his wine.

Fedro laughed and turned toward his father. "Is Fra Pietro correct?" he asked Aonio with mock innocence. "Where do you stand on this matter of ritual beauty and prayer?"

"Yes, indeed, Aonio," said Fra Pietro with suddenly attentive eyes and pointed interest. "Fedro is quite right. Where do you stand on this issue of ritual and personal belief?"

Aonio's jaw set. Because of his scholarship and reputation, he had been examined twice by the Inquisition. These examinations were serious affairs and he had found them physically and mentally draining. He had talked himself out of trouble each time, but now he felt too old to do it again. A bland and orthodox answer was needed to deprive Fra Pietro of something to report to his superior, the Bishop of Colle.

"I find both belief and ritual are beautiful and necessary," Aonio said. "Ritual without belief is vapid, but belief must be presented in a way it can be shared."

It was a good answer. It said nothing. But Aonio was disturbed and not a little frightened. Couldn't Fedro see the danger? Fra Pietro was trying to learn whether Aonio was a reformer who thought believers should talk directly to God without Church intercession. Aonio knew he was right to be fearful; his supporters were growing old and some had died. One of these days he would be left friendless and then the wolves would fall on him.

If Fedro understood his father's predicament, he gave no sign. His cold eyes looked merely amused. "Would you say, then, a service at Florence where the priest flicks imps away with less grace has the same value as one in Siena with the priest of the beautiful hands?" He looked directly at his father.

"There are many types of beauty, Fedro," Aonio replied sternly, his eyes trying to warn his son not to continue the discussion. "There is also the beauty of sincerity and humility. You should know that. I am sure both priests are equally devout and thus equally beautiful."

Fedro frowned, twirled the stem of his wine glass, and looked at the fire. His father had just made him look a fool by telling him he was shallow. Distinctions of language and meaning mattered in an academic household. It reminded Fedro that despite his own growing reputation, he would never escape the shadow of a famous father. The only consolation he could feel was that the priest had not recognized the subtlety of the put down.

Fedro was right. The exchange had gone over Fra Pietro's head. Armed with ignorance, fueled by wine, and fired with ambition, the priest welcomed the chance to have an exchange with such a famous scholar as Aonio Paleario, an encounter he could retell entirely to his own credit. Also to his own advantage. If he could report even a hint of heresy, and if the Bishop of Colle were pleased with the information, he might be recommended for a better position in Rome.

"Come, come, Aonio," said Fra Pietro impatiently, "you have not answered the question. Where do you stand on the place of ritual in the Catholic Church?"

Aonio answered carefully. "Once I was asked by a student to conduct a debate on the nature of salvation. I told him this was not a topic for debate but for faith. I consider ritual within the Church to be a similar topic, one best deferred to those such as Fra Pietro who are better qualified to deal with it."

"There," snorted Fra Pietro, "evasion and diplomacy hand in hand. What more is to be expected from the University of Milan's famous professor of debate and eloquence?"

If the priest pretended to be frustrated that Aonio had turned a question into a disquisition on something else entirely, his reaction was only for show. He may not have learned enough to hang Aonio this time, but the evening was not a complete waste. The dinner was good and he was already planning to appropriate Aonio's words as his own whenever the occasion arose. The priest turned around to face the fire, put his wine glass on the mantle, and rubbed his hands.

Bruno let out a faint whimper and his legs twitched as if he were running in his dreams. Everyone stopped to look at him.

"That dog shouldn't be in here," Marietta said stiffly. "He should be out where he belongs."

Bruno was instantly startled awake at the word out. Resignedly, he pushed himself up on his front paws and struggled to get his back legs under him so he could stand up and slink into the kitchen. Maybe the woman out there would let him lie down near her stove. His first attempt was futile. He fell back on the pallet.

"That's all right, Bruno," Aonio called to him. "Stay where you are, boy."

Bruno recognized the word stay. Poised on his front paws again, his hindquarters still bent beneath him, he looked indecisive, but when no one said anything more, he chose to obey the more comforting command and settled back down with a thump.

"He should be outside," Marietta repeated.

"Let him be, Wife" Aonio replied. "It's cold and wet outside, and I'm sure Ceciliana is busy cooking and doesn't want him underfoot in the kitchen. He's old like some of us here and deserves comfort. I hope someone is kind enough to give me a warm pallet by the fire when I am too old to move. Come to think of it, I'm probably old enough now to have earned it."

"Would you think your life unhappy if you did not have such comfort at the end?" Fra Pietro asked.

"I already consider my life happy for the things I have been able to study and the people I have known. A warm pallet at the end would be nice but would make no real difference. One cannot allow one small portion to dominate the experience of an entire lifetime. Happiness lies in remembering the good things."

"Then you consider Bruno to be happy despite his age and infirmity?" the priest asked.

"We all grow old," Aonio said with a smile. "I would say that if Bruno had a sentient soul, he would say that while the warm hearth is a nice place for him to be, it does not make him any more or less happy. He lived a virtuous life, doing very well what is asked of any dog. I am sure he dreams now of the things that gave him pleasure when he was younger and finds happiness in remembering them."

Aonio was about to add that he saw a lot of himself in the dog, when Fra Pietro changed the subject abruptly. Aonio smiled again. Fra Pietro found it difficult to let anyone else talk. *Ecce homo interruptus.* The priest did not remain silent unless he was learning something useful. Aonio wondered if God ever before had made such a transparent man and then called him to serve the Church.

Fra Pietro turned to Marietta. "How are you and your charming daughters?" he asked. Since he had baptized each of Marietta's babies and buried two of them, he felt he should show some interest in their welfare.

"We're well." Marietta replied for them all. To this point, she had sat quietly, modeling prudence, sobriety, and virtue for her daughters. Her frowns were designed to train her daughters to become ornaments to their social station, so, in keeping with her theories of appropriate female behavior, all the Paleario women had remained silent.

Fra Pietro approved of Marietta. He knew her family, the Guidottis of Colle, who were supportive of the Church. They traded in wool and corn and had done well, permitting them to buy a substantial villa in town. Marietta looked a lot like her late mother, another virtuous woman who came to daily prayers and never missed Mass. They had buried her ten years ago alongside her husband in the family crypt, under a large statue of an angel pointing to heaven. The local joke was that the angel was warning God to keep the money flowing because business was all the Guidottis ever talked about. They were a handsome family who aged well, and Marietta, in particular, looked younger than being in her late fifties. Her blonde hair was still full, her blue eyes were sharp, and her fingers easily twisted string as she taught the little girl how to make lace.

"You have fine lace there," Fra Pietro said genially to the little girl. The child looked up uncertainly and smiled. Fra Pietro liked the way Marietta kept her children and grandchildren under control. He wished every parent did so.

"My girls are talented. I took great pains to teach them." Marietta's voice was Tuscan, clipped and distinct as she made her vowels. She made sure that her children never allowed a lazy drag of vowels as Ceciliana sometimes did or dropped their verb endings like the peasants in the south. It would not do to raise children who sounded as if they had been dragged up in poverty. Marietta gestured to the blonde woman beside her. "Our eldest girl, Caterina, is the cleverest. She's an artist. Her needlework is superb."

"That's good. That's good." Pietro interrupted without enthusiasm.

Marietta was not to be deterred from completing her thought. She glanced disapprovingly at the girl behind her. "Beatrice could do as well as Caterina if she applied herself. She sews a seam straight enough but she's careless with it. She'll need to learn quickly now she's fifteen. It's time to think about a husband for her."

Pietro did not bother to reply. Beatrice, on the other hand, frowned and looked at her father. Her reaction was the result of her mother's recent insistence that she needed to know what men carried between their legs and how they used it. Any desire Beatrice might have had for a husband rapidly vanished as Marietta described in graphic detail her first night as a bride. It turned into pure distaste when Marietta got caught up in the moment and described her confinements. Beatrice slipped away as soon as she could and went to Ceciliana for comfort. "Is it all so horrible?' she asked. Ceciliana didn't dispute the accounts but just laughed and said that it wasn't all paying for Adam and Eve's sins. In fact, it could be great fun. "Just get a good-looking husband who knows what he's doing," she said, "and don't get too caught up in those books of yours."

"You're a fine example to your children," Fra Pietro said finally to Marietta who was clearly waiting for some approval from him. "They should be grateful for all you have done for them." He managed to smile beneficently as if he were looking down at her in church.

Fra Pietro was looking far down the road as he spoke. If the Church seized the Paleario estates, as they usually did for convicted heretics, all family property would be sold at auction. There would be bargains and perhaps a bribe to the auctioneer would bring him Aonio's wooden traveling desk. Closed up and lifted off its carved wooden base, the desk looked like a large wooden packing box with rings on each end for lifting it onto a cart. But when it was opened and the front folded down to rest on pull-out supports, there was an ample writing surface, built-in, finely carved drawers, and cupboards more than adequate for papers and writing equipment. Fra Pietro liked the carved angels and animals on the drawer fronts and the profiles of a man and a woman facing one another on the cabinet doors. The desk was fit for a busy, cultivated man. Fra Pietro could imagine taking it with him to Rome. Of course, he would not tell anyone that such a beautiful piece once belonged to a heretic. It wasn't the desk's fault, after all.

Knowing nothing of what was going on in her priest's mind, Marietta smiled smugly at his flattery, hearing only what she thought was his recognition of her skill in displaying the rules of polite behavior. Then, in triumph at the confirmation of her own opinion of herself, she looked to where her husband and son stood by the fireplace. She wanted Aonio to hear those words of praise. But her smile immediately froze. Aonio had not heard. Instead, he was talking quietly with his servant, Pterigi Gallo. She had never liked Pterigi although he had more than once proved his value in managing the estate. She did not trust someone who seldom spoke but seemed to observe a lot.

If her sense of dignity had been affronted, it quickly became worse. Without looking at her or offering any explanation, both master and servant left the room. Marietta's eyes followed them angrily, and the lines set at her mouth as she watched the door close behind them. Her husband should have excused himself and given her a reason for leaving the room. She looked inquiringly at her son, Fedro, whom she expected to protect her position, but Fedro had retreated into sullen silence and had no intention of venturing further opinions about his father. Marietta saw she would have to defend her authority herself. Purposefully she handed the string handwork to Caterina.

Aonio had gone down a hallway and into a small side room dominated by a rectory table along one wall and Fra Pietro's coveted desk against the other. The tabletop was covered with rhetoric texts, religious tracts, and sheets of loose manuscript. The desk was open and balanced on its carved wooden base, waiting for its owner. Along the top of the desk, a couple of books were held in place by a pair of heavy bookends in the shape of lions' heads. The light in the room came from a single candle along with low flames in a simple, undecorated hearth. The dim light emphasized the desk's etched curves and made the letters burned into the books' leather casing turn to gold. In the flicker, the books looked on fire.

Aonio's eyes took in the room and quickly spotted the rain-drenched visitor huddled by the fire. He recognized the broad face and well-formed body of one of his students, Marco de Valterra, the nephew of his old friend, the Bishop of Anagni.

"Marco, for the love of heaven what brings you out in weather like this?" Aonio closed the door behind him and walked quickly over the room's stone flagstones toward the fireplace.

Marco rubbed his hands together against the chill of the room and spoke quickly and to the point. "Professor, my uncle told me to ride all night if I had to. You are in serious danger. You are to be charged with heresy and this time the Vatican intends the charges to stick."

"Does he know why?" This was the news that Aonio had been dreading, but he had hoped to finish out the school year before any move was made against him. His old enemies were mounting yet another attack. He had known it was only a matter of time.

"He doesn't know the details." Marco shook his head emphatically, as if to emphasize that his uncle knew nothing more. Marco was no fool. The Inquisition threw a wide net and charged people just for the company they kept.

Aonio shook his head sadly. He knew the dangers as well. "I've seen colleagues, good men at the university, destroyed by accusations. No one's safe since Caraffa restarted the Inquisition."

"Professor," Marco whispered urgently, "I also have to tell you the Church has a spy in your household."

"I'm not surprised. Caraffa is a devious and dangerous man who sows seeds of hatred that will long outlive him. But I hate to think any of my friends may be involved."

"All I know is it's closer than friends." Marco hoped that his professor would not be distracted by loyalty to his friends. The times were too dangerous.

A distant door closed sharply, and footsteps echoed in the passage.

Aonio held up his hand in caution. "Marco, if this is my wife, please say nothing. It will come out soon enough."

Marco nodded and bent back toward the fire. He had not wanted to carry such news, but his uncle had insisted, and he owed a great deal to his uncle. The old bishop had made Marco his heir and took a direct interest in his future.

A sharp rap and Marietta entered without being invited. She recognized her husband's student immediately and just as quickly dismissed him. To her, he was a trifling reason for her husband's insult to her position as mistress of the house even if Marco's father was a wealthy merchant. "Marco, what brings you here tonight?" She spoke coldly, her face mirroring her displeasure at the unexpected intrusion, and she did not wait for a reply. "Both of you, come and join us." She stood waiting in the doorway, a commanding figure.

"I am honored to be in your house." Marco bowed.

Marietta gave a curt nod and said nothing more. The candles' dim light melted her face into an echo of the younger beauty that attracted Aonio after he decided that he did not want the celibate life of the priesthood. The effect, however, was spoiled by her tightly pressed lips and the stony expression that Aonio recognized as a storm warning.

"Thank you, Wife, for your concern. You take good care of me as always." Aonio moved reluctantly toward her but hesitated at the door, where he turned back. "Marco, please join us. We're celebrating our youngest daughter's fifteenth birthday. Beatrice. You remember her from Milan? Do you have something else you can wear since you are so wet?"

Marco eyes traveled to the sodden pack on the floor by the fireplace. "I do, if they have stayed dry."

"Then come and have food with us." Aonio smiled encouragingly but also in warning at Marco before he followed the silent Marietta back down the hallway.

"Beatrice," Marietta called coldly when Marco entered the room a little later. "Come here. We have another guest for you to greet."

Beatrice smiled in surprise at Marco. She dared for a moment to think she might be the reason for his presence and she forgot the things her mother had said about childbirth. She thought it all might be worth it for Marco.

Marco smiled back at her. She was a pretty girl with an intelligent high forehead, the kind of subject that painters flirted with as they painted a portrait. Her large brown eyes resembled her father's, although without the hazel depths. Marietta gestured around the room and made introductions, mostly for Fra Pietro's benefit since Marco had visited the family the last time they had visited Aonio in Milan. "This is Marco, a student from the university."

After her dismissive introduction, she introduced those present to Marco: "Most of us you have met in Milan. But this is our son, Fedro. He is a very successful lawyer in Siena. His wife is Julietta de Portia. Her father is the senior magistrate in Florence. Perhaps you have heard of him? This is our oldest daughter Caterina and her children. Caterina's husband is the son of Filippi Renzo, who owns the largest estate in the district of Viterbo. He is not here this evening as he was called out on business. This is our priest, Fra Pietro."

Marco nodded to each in turn. They eyed him curiously since he made an attractive figure. He was in his early twenties with shoulder length brown hair and an engaging smile. His clothes were well-cut if crumpled. The knife at his side was of good quality and his manners showed breeding. He appeared consequential and, therefore, interesting, particularly to Fra Pietro. This meant the priest was inclined to listen to what he had to say.

"You're at the university? This is a stormy day to be outdoors and you've come a long way. What brings you here?" The priest still occupied the fireplace.

"Why, to honor Beatrice on her birthday." Marco smiled and bowed to the girl as if to say this should have been obvious.

The priest glanced quickly at Aonio's younger daughter in time to catch a little smile and a flicker in her eyes. He found this interesting. He wondered if the student's family had any idea of what lay ahead for the Palearios. "And who is your patron at the university?" The priest now had a new audience to whom he might display his knowledge of such things as universities and the way of the world.

"My father. He wants a lawyer in the family and has to pay for it." Marco gave a generous, rueful shrug as if to say "I'm being bought, but isn't corruption the way of the world these days?"

"And your father?"

"My father is Giovanni de Valterra. He provides Genoa and much of Tuscany with pepper and nutmeg, sea salt, and silks."

Fra Pietro frowned for a moment. "De Valterra? Are you related to the Bishop of Anagni?"

"Retired bishop. Yes, he is my uncle."

Aonio stiffened. He feared Fra Pietro's suspicions. But the news had the opposite effect on Fra Pietro. The priest relaxed and gave a little giggle.

"I know him. A genial and pleasant man. If he had been placed in a more public position at Rome, he might have been named a cardinal. So your father is a trader, eh? Successful too from the sound of it."

"My father says his business washes in and out with the tides." Marco's face creased into folds of amusement. His father's moods depended on where his ships were at any given time. The only time to ask for any needed funds was when a ship was safely in port and being unloaded.

"You're studying law? What is your connection with the Paleario family?"

A nerve tightened in Aonio's jaw.

"A lawyer needs to argue well. The professor is the most eloquent speaker in Italy. I should have wasted my father's money had I not attended his lectures. I also met some of the family when they came to Milan."

"What kind of law are you studying?" The priest thrust out his chest and pulled his vestment tightly around his buttocks to enjoy the warmth collected in the fabric. The Bishop of Anani, retired or not, was the kind of company he liked to keep.

"The exchange of goods and money between city states and borders," Marco replied without hesitation.

Marietta glared at Aonio. She ran a cultured household and did not like talk of business when she was present. Aonio did not meet her gaze, so she looked at her son. Fedro, however, pretended not to notice. She seethed while she lost control of the evening to a student who had not even been invited.

"You're studying banking laws?" the priest continued.

"No. We have well-established banks and financiers in Genoa. My father is more concerned with the shifting laws regarding insurance, import and export, and taxation. He wants me to be able to defend the family's interests when they are challenged."

"Challenged?" The priest assumed an approximation of authority and jurisprudence. He liked pretending for a moment he was a lawyer like Aonio deposing a young man of education and breeding.

"Sir, every time our goods move in and out of ports, we must pay duty to the city and perhaps to the Emperor or the Papal States. Sometimes there is no agreement about whom we should be paying in the first place. Sometimes we pay the duty only to find by the time we unload our ships everything has changed. Port fees, disembarkation fees, warehouse fees— it's a maze. My father feels a lawyer is needed to make our case before . . ."

Fra Pietro had reached the limits of his interest. "I see you are already practicing your arguments to lay before the magistrates." He smiled slightly and turned away. Any further questioning on his part would only reveal the limits of his knowledge. Still, he had learned something that might be useful later.

"You must be hungry after your ride, Marco," Beatrice said with a small conspiratorial laugh that sounded like soft bells. Her voice was low, not childlike but not yet adult.

"Let us at least offer you food." She glanced at the table to see what was left.

"I appreciate your kindness and hospitality," Marco replied.

Marietta did not look pleased. As hostess, she should have been the one to offer food to Marco. Still, if the girl was willing to assume the responsibility, it might be used to argue that she was ready enough for marriage and a home of her own. If Aonio had been willing to let Caterina become a wife at fifteen, why was he so opposed when she had mentioned Beatrice earlier that day? Didn't he recall that she had not been much older when she married him? Despite her pointing out that in a few more years, Beatrice would be considered too old, her husband had replied that she was still too young.

"Yes, sit down here by the fire," Aonio added as he drew out a stool for Marco next to the hearth.

The young man took a seat by Marietta and Caterina. Fra Pietro even moved over a bit to let the warmth spread more generally into the room. This was a bishop's nephew.

"I've filled a plate for you," Beatrice said as she handed it to Marco along with a glass of red wine from a bottle on the table. She stood as near to him as she could with her mother and sister in the way." How are your studies progressing? I hear that the Whitsunday debate competition will focus on the characteristics of good government. I assume that will involve discussions of Plato and Marsilio Ficino and I hear it is to be conducted in Italian. I would have enjoyed being there to hear it."

"I will be very happy to attend on your behalf and bring you a full account of the positions and arguments of both sides, if you like." Marco took a mouthful of food and gave a polite nod toward Beatrice.

"And what use would that be to you?" Caterina said bluntly to her younger sister.

"I'm sure it would have been as useful to me as it would be to Fedro and Marco. There is nothing wrong with hearing new ideas. Such an exchange could be very informative." Beatrice straightened her back in defiance, hating that this sibling rivalry was happening in front of Marco.

"Women should know what is proper to their station in life," Marietta sniffed. "My education was appropriate for my role as a wife in polite society. And I've done very well without Greek philosophers." Marietta disagreed with Aonio's decision to teach Beatrice. He was filling her head with ideas she would never use. She hoped that whoever the girl married would not see it as a disadvantage and demand more for her dowry.

"Let's be happy on a happy occasion," Aonio said, gently admonishing both his daughters, although he knew very well who had started the unpleasantness. He had been away for much of Caterina's childhood, earning a living to pay for the house and farm. Marietta's dowry had been the down payment, but the rest of the purchase price burdened him with a crippling debt. He had left Caterina's education to Marietta. But that didn't mean he cared more for his younger daughter. Caterina was his first born and she would always hold the special place in his heart. Beatrice came at a time when he could educate her himself. He taught her Latin because he needed someone to respond intelligently to his arguments. She seemed to enjoy the challenge. That was really the reason he opposed Marietta's search for a husband for her. He didn't want to lose his assistant.

"Home and family are far better settings for the beauties of the gentler sex who have been well brought up." Fra Pietro's tone dripped with inflated condescension while Marietta looked beatific and Beatrice regarded him with barely concealed scorn.

"The university can be rowdy," Marco said quickly as he moved to stop the priest before he could start a sermon on the place of women. "I've seen students fight in the streets and yell down the professors if they don't like them."

"But what an opportunity to hear different opinions and learn new ideas," Beatrice said breathlessly. "We women can hear such exchanges only when informed people happen to come to the house."

Hearing the potential for trouble if Fra Pietro decided to ask about visitors, Aonio stepped in quickly to divert his attention. "Debate is the way to truth," he said. "But not everyone knows how to do it well anymore. Those who know the least shout the loudest. Perhaps it has always been so, but it is a pity. Everything benefits from careful examination, and that must be done with knowledge and reflection."

"Including the Church's teachings?" asked the priest hopefully. He had wanted to probe Beatrice more on who might have been coming to the house, but this opening avenue seemed even more promising.

"Again, I exempt questions of salvation. These have a different truth." Aonio did not smile as he ushered Fra Pietro away from the fireplace and toward the almond biscuits and fruit creams that Ceciliana had quietly laid out for dessert on the side table. The priest's earlier question about happiness at the end of life had disturbed him; it made him wonder what Fra Pietro thought he knew.

"Your daughter seems to like your student's company," Fra Pietro said as he helped himself to a generous plate of sweets. "It's good to be young, so let me ask you: What advice do you have for young people about their futures these days?"

"Ah, there you ask an old man of nearly seventy who has become quite useless to recall his youth."

"No, Aonio, we'll not allow the evasion," the priest persisted. "You spoke of happiness before. What do you consider the evidence of a good life well lived?"

It was an interesting question. The others in the room stopped their own conversations to listen to what Aonio was willing to say. He had not been known to address this subject before.

"I believe," Aonio said slowly, speaking as much about himself as anyone else, "that mankind is to be judged by what is left behind. There are too many who leave only discourtesy and ignorance. We do not need more arrogance and presumption in this world."

Marietta cheeks flushed as she heard this; she was sure he was referring to her failure of good manners regarding Marco's visit. Caterina drew her arms around her daughter and was sure he was referring to her barb at her sister. Fedro glared at his father and was sure he meant Fedro's disappointing failure with language. Beatrice stood frozen, fearing that her father was agreeing with the pompous, self-important priest and his assumptions about women.

In fact, all four had misinterpreted Aonio's words since he was talking abstractly about Rome and the Vatican. But his family, drawn into private grievances about which he knew nothing, had seen only the possible application to themselves. It was not a misjudgment easily rectified even by someone who understood what had happened. Aonio did not. If Aonio supposed his family was happy for what he saw as his many sacrifices to support it, he merely demonstrated how great wisdom is so often linked with lack of practical understanding. The Paleario family was riven by resentment, and Aonio was unaware of it.

On his pallet, Bruno stirred, stretched his front legs, shifted his body slightly, and went back to sleep, his front paws bent over his head.

. . .

Later that night, the villa became quiet. The family's son and daughters were back in their childhood rooms. Pterigi slept in his room over the stalls in barn; he said he preferred to be there so he could hear if anything went wrong with the animals. Ceciliana had cleared the kitchen, fed Bruno the scraps since she secretly had a soft spot for him, and resumed her role as nanny by sleeping in Beatrice's room with her. Fra Pietro was stretched out on the bench in front of the dying fire; it made a comfortable bed after the sides were released and laid flat. Marco had pulled together three chairs and was lying across them, his cloak wrapped tightly around him; he would be leaving in the morning with the priest, when it was hoped that the sun would come out.

Behind the heavy wooden door protecting the privacy of the house's primary couple, Marietta felt free at last to vent her anger on her husband.

He knew her furies of old and was prepared to be patient until the storm blew over.

"Have I been a good wife to you?" Marietta's voice was shrill and angry. She sat up in their bed, her nightclothes clutched tightly around her and her hair wound into a night cap. The room was cold. The sole light was a flickering candle.

"The best," Aonio replied, resigned to the hail of words that was to follow a particular pattern and be delivered in a particular tone. It was a catechism with prescribed answers. He sat on a chair beside the bed and waited for the worst.

"Have I been a good mother to your children, raising them when you were never home? Didn't I nearly die giving you Fedro?

"No man could ask for a better wife."

"Then I deserve the truth."

"I do my best to be truthful." Aonio waited for the real issue to be raised.

"Tell me what the message was tonight."

"Why do you think there was a message?" He was not surprised. Marietta was shrewd and tenacious. It was always like this. His best response was to lie low and let her anger burn itself out. Sometimes it worked.

"Because the boy did not come here to see Beatrice."

"How do you know?" Aonio took a small, perverse pleasure in making her work for the knowledge she wanted.

"First, he came here uninvited. I don't care if his father is a merchant with pretensions, he knows enough what good manners are or ought to be. He was sent here or he would not have come. Second, you opposed the idea of Beatrice marrying when I asked you this morning, so why would you welcome someone acting like a suitor? Unless you've lied to me and you've already started talking with his father."

"I did not lie. I have neither heard nor said one word about a possible match. But I will tell you this. Marco is an excellent student and a connection with his family would be a good one. The family is solid and stable and they value learning."

"Learning!" Marietta practically spat out the word. "You've given Beatrice ideas far beyond her position as wife and mother. Who wants a wife who can debate Plato and Aristotle if she can't order a kitchen and run a household?"

"I'm sure she has learned those practical things from watching you," Aonio replied.

"He's not good enough. Our family deserves better than a merchant's son. We should consider only someone from a noble family."

"Now, Marietta, your own family are merchants. He's a good boy. The Genoa merchants are famous for their patronage to scholars and artists. Thanks to his father, the boy's been given a good education, and their kinsman is a well-respected Churchman. I should carefully consider a match if it were proposed."

"Well, I wouldn't. But you're diverting my attention from the real issue here. What did he come to tell you?"

"You're perceptive as ever."

"Don't waste your time on flattery. I'm your wife. I have a right to know."

Aonio sighed. If he didn't tell her, neither would sleep tonight. On the other hand, sleep would be elusive if not impossible once she heard. They had been through this business of charges of heresy before and it never got any easier.

"All I know is that my enemies want me to be investigated for heresy." His words were placid in the hope their simplicity would disarm her.

"Heresy! Not again. What heresy? There's no heresy here. All my children have been properly raised. Why has this charge been made?"

"I don't know that it's a charge. Remember, this is not the first time they have tried to cause me trouble."

"What kind of trouble is it this time? What are they going to do?"

"There will be the usual inquiry. Questions will be asked. People will be interviewed. I don't know yet who is behind this."

"It's already happening then?"

"I don't know, Marietta. I haven't had time to look into it."

"What can be done about this? Is there no way to stop it?" Marietta clutched the cross suspended on a chain around her neck. She pulled on it passionately, swinging it so forcefully that the chain looked as if it might snap.

"I don't know all the details, as I said. But once I know, and if it's true, I'll try to get this inquiry handled in Milan where I have more friends. I don't know anyone in Rome. Everything hinges on getting it moved."

"But why is this happening now?"

"As I said, I don't know yet. All my recently published writing was printed before. Some is over thirty years old. They may think I sympathize with the German reformers."

"German reformers?" Marietta's voice rose shrilly again. " Fra Pietro gave a sermon about them. He warned us all to watch for them for they might be among the congregation. Oh, my God, was he talking about you? What have you had to do with them?"

"Calm down, Marietta. Many years ago, when it seemed possible to reconcile the reformers with the Church, I wrote to them and also to the bishops saying if we allowed ourselves to pursue truth, we might find a way to become one community of believers again."

"Did this happen?"

"No." Aonio shook his head. "The pope sent a letter to the council at Trent and forbade them to enter into the discussion. Later there were meetings where reform issues in the Church were discussed. But the major issue—the final authority for faith, whether it is individual or the Church—was never discussed."

"Do you sympathize with the Germans?" Marietta's tone had become inquisitorial and cold.

"I do not sympathize with the French, the Spanish, the Germans or anybody else. But I cannot dismiss all Germans because many of them are fine scholars. I am interested only in truth. I exchanged letters with the best thinkers on theology. It has been my life's passion."

"So you were foolish enough to write letters? Do they have them?"

"I doubt it. But I never discussed significant matters of truth or faith in my letters."

"Don't you understand that just knowing these people can lead to damnation? Have you considered what will happen to this family? My husband the heretic. Do you have any idea what they do to heretics' families? They'll seize our house. Our children will be cast out. Their children will try to forget we ever lived. Our neighbors will revile us. We will not have the right to Christian burial. We have had a serpent in our house."

"Try not to be so upset, Marietta. It will be all right. I'll speak to what friends I have left and see what can be done. This is not the first time this issue has come up, and it has always been resolved. I am an old man and have lived long enough to gather enemies."

Marietta frowned. She clearly did not understand. Aonio tried to explain.

"You've heard me speak of Caraffa before. Before he was made a cardinal, he was the Bishop of Abruzzi. He founded a fundamentalist movement there. Over the years members of this group have become very powerful. They supported him when he asked the pope to restart the Inquisition and to create a list of forbidden books. The pope agreed and named Caraffa Head Inquisitor. Then he personally set up a spy network to rout out and persecute anyone with the appearance of even the most minor offenses. Universities became special targets."

"How does this involve you?"

"Caraffa does not like anyone who wants to think for himself. Because of his persecution, many fine scholars have been forced to leave Italy, fleeing for their lives. I have been a target from time to time, but my friends protected me. Caraffa must have been frustrated not to bring me down, but it was not for lack of trying."

"Then what has brought this upon us now?"

"I think it was the recent reprint of my works. The printer produced a revised version of a book without checking with me first. I was horrified when I saw it. It's a grammatical nightmare and, worse, it did not reprint the Vatican seal on the front page, which was there on the original."

"So let them go after the printer."

"The printer is in Switzerland. Publishing books now is fraught with danger because ignorant people can read things into them that were not intended. I must believe that examining me has much more to do with politics in Rome than with a printer's mistakes."

"But I don't understand how a printer's mistake can be as damaging as you say. Just tell them it's not your fault."

"Marietta, my dear, it doesn't matter whose mistake it is, or even if there has been one. The Inquisition is all powerful and will find its own justification when it wants to charge someone with heresy."

"Oh God almighty, then we are lost. All hope has gone." Marietta burst in uncontrollable sobbing.

Aonio looked away from his wife. He always retreated from her when she reached this stage. He tried to plan his escape.

"I need to talk with Marco and find out more. Why don't you rest and let me go downstairs to my work?"

Marietta clutched his sleeve desperately. "Fra Pietro can testify this is a God-fearing household. We have done nothing wrong." She looked up at him, pleading with him to reassure her. She had done everything right for her family. She didn't deserve this. She wanted him to say that.

"There is no question concerning your faith or the children's."

"We have gone to confession. We have given money. The children have all been confirmed. I have burned candles to the Virgin. Fra Pietro is a regular visitor to this house. We have done nothing to displease God." Her eyes fixed wildly on the crucifix over their bed.

"Yes, Marietta," he said gently, "you have followed all the rules."

"So why has this happened?" Tears coursed down her cheeks. "Our neighbors will betray us. I have seen it happen."

"Marietta! This is enough. You are imagining the worst."

"How can I be imagining it when I have seen it happen? Oh my God, my God. I did everything I was asked to. What have I done to deserve this?"

She buried her head in her arms and sobbed loudly. Aonio sat quietly by her side and let his eyes wander to the wooden, carved screen that stood at the foot of their bed.

The more he studied it, the more the screen's four panels came alive. The first panel showed two young men standing together by a church door. One was pointing to a young girl just emerging from the dark interior, bringing her to the attention of his friend. Aonio knew what that young man was saying. "What about that one?" Ruggiero had said. "Marietta's pretty enough, her family is respectable, and she should have a good dowry. You can buy a villa here. Why not Colle where you have friends who love you?"

The second panel was the interior of a well-to-do house, where the young man who pointed out the girl was now talking to an older man, her father it seemed, and pointing to his friend who hung back, a little embarrassed. Aonio smiled inwardly as he remembered the scene; Ruggiero spoke of Aonio in superlatives—family connection to aristocracy, a wonderful scholar, destined for greatness, an ornament to whatever family he married into.

The third panel showed the girl and the young man talking in a garden, watchfully guarded by an older woman; the wooing had begun as the father apparently had given his permission for the young couple to walk out together.

The fourth and final panel showed the couple emerging from the same church where the young man had first seen the girl. They were married now and the scene looked appropriately festive as a priest bestowed the blessing of the Church and the spectators applauded.

But if the four panels of the screen were his life to this point, he wondered what other panels might show. Would a fifth show the old couple in happy domesticity with their children and grandchildren around them? Would there then be a final panel showing a crowd of people following their coffins to the graveyard under the shadow of the church steeple? Perhaps for Marietta. For him, the two last panels would more likely show a prison where the inquisitors examined his beliefs and the final one where they led him to his death. He hoped he was wrong.

Marietta's sobs subsided after a while. She raised her head to look at him with accusing red eyes. "Why did you have a family if you planned to betray them?"

"I would not willingly betray any of you. These are the times we live in." Aonio heard his own defensiveness, but there was nothing he could do about it.

Marietta sensed the implacable self-interest behind her husband's words. "When do you leave for Rome? How long before the heavens open up on us?" She asked this sarcastically before she sank back into despair. "Oh my God, my God, how could you do this to us? You thought only of yourself. I shall go to my grave cursing you."

Aonio reached out to take her hand. But even as he sat beside her, he knew his concern was pragmatic rather than sympathetic. He was merely hoping that her sobbing would not wake the household. He was not prepared to deal with Fedro as well as Marietta. Fedro would take his mother's side as he always did. Aonio was sure that Fedro had not come to the villa to celebrate Beatrice's birthday because Fedro was not motivated by sentiment. He must have come because his mother wanted to ask him something about her estate. Fedro would look at the situation in the same way as Marietta, cursing Aonio for exposing the family to loss.

"I may not go to Rome. If the Vatican won't move the proceedings to Milan, the city elders must give permission before I can be released. The city will demand fulfillment of my contract to teach next school year since they have paid for it. I am old and my health may well be a factor. If there is anything to this matter, I doubt much can happen for at least a year." Aonio used the same arguments with Marietta that he had used with himself.

"Once you've gone, you'll never come back," she wailed. "There will be endless talk. There will be only Fedro to care for me. How can you have exposed your family like this? Have you no thought of what will become of us? Who will want to be allianced with this family and marry Beatrice? She'll be called the heretic's daughter."

Aonio had no answer. He sat on the bed, put his arm around her shoulder and tried to pull her close. "Fedro is a lawyer. You will be in his capable hands."

She pulled away from his embrace. They sat side by side on the bed, the candle on the small table alternately sputtering and bending low in a draft and wicking itself upright. The rain had not stopped. It dripped from the tree branches outside onto the courtyard below. For the moment, the sound filled the room until Marietta finally allowed Aonio to put his arm around her while she rested her tear-streaked cheek on her husband's chest.

"My heart is broken," she said. "There will be no one to speak for us."

"We can't worry about what other people think or do," Aonio replied. "We will be all right as long as we believe in one another."

"We should be enjoying our grandchildren. You should be retiring from the university." Her tone was softer but still accusing.

"I know." He stroked her hair. "It is the times. There is no room for people to think or breathe. Sometimes I think the Church will not rest until truth is snuffed out."

"Can't you keep your truth to yourself? Are you so obstinate you can't do what they want and be still about the rest?" Marietta's eyes brightened with hope.

"No," he said definitively. "Others tried. They were been hunted down and not allowed to keep their conscience. Please give me your support and understanding."

Marietta shook her head. "Can't you not go?"

"If I am called and do not go, they will send soldiers to fetch me."

She said nothing but buried her head in her hands.

"Will you be all right if I go downstairs now?" he asked "This is the trouble with long life. One by one my friends have gone. I'll need to take the candle."

He rose tentatively and waited for any further objections. She looked up. Her face was drawn and her lips tight. Aonio knew she would probably pray and weep herself to sleep. He had no comfort to offer her. She believed he was wrong. She always would.

Marietta nodded to let him go. He tucked the woolen blanket around her in a gesture he hoped would suggest tenderness. In the candle's flicker, the undried tears gleamed on his wife's face and the candle threw large jagged shadows around the walls. He shut the door behind him, leaving his wife in darkness. He could hear her start to sob again.

. . .

Aonio walked quietly down the stairs, avoiding the loose board that he knew would creak, and paused at the bottom to listen to the sounds of the sleepers in the great room. Fra Pietro was a semi-circular mound on the wooden bench directly across from the fireplace. Aonio could hear his snoring interspersed with snorts and occasional gasps. Even in sleep, no one could mistake the priest. But as Aonio hoped, Marco was awake and rose awkwardly off the chairs when Aonio's candle illuminated his portion of the room.

They crossed the hall and entered the study, quietly closing the door behind them. Marco's pack still lay in the corner but Pterigi at some point had put more wood on the small fire in the grate, so the shards of wood still held some glow. Aonio added more wood and watched as the pieces caught and sent a small shower of sparks up the chimney. His candle sputtered in the dark but did not go out. They sat on carved wooden chairs next to the hearth and tried to warm themselves.

"What more can you tell me?" Aonio asked in a voice scarcely more than a whisper.

"Not much. My uncle asked me to come here as soon as he heard that the Vatican had sent a letter to the Father Inquisitor at Pisa asking him to start an investigation into your opinions. Apparently it's usual for inquisitors to inform the district bishop when they investigate prominent local citizens. In this case, the inquisitor told the Bishop of Colle who told my uncle over dinner. My uncle expressed concern that someone of your stature and reputation should be challenged in this way. He asked what type of proof they had against you. According to the bishop, the proof was said to be in your own words, particularly your work on the immortality of the soul."

"But my speeches and the poem on the immortality of the soul were licensed by the Vatican and printed nearly thirty years ago."

"My uncle says that the Vatican has recognized the need to ban ideas, even old ones. The preaching of the German reformers is to blame. The Church can't touch them because they're under the protection of the German princes. The Church is also alarmed about converts in the valleys along the north of Italy. The Vatican is prepared to ban every printed work opposing the Church teachings in any way—doctrinally, morally, politically or spiritually."

"If that's the case, there won't be much left. But is it certain the Vatican is preparing charges against me? Won't they wait for the report from the inquisitor in Pisa?"

"As soon as he heard from the Bishop of Colle, my uncle made other inquiries. The pope is definite. He wants you called to Rome and has taken special interest. Caraffa is a dangerous man."

Aonio nodded impatiently. He knew the danger. "Is there anything more?"

"He says the same people who were your enemies in Siena have arranged for this. Friars are involved as well as citizens."

"I know who they are. The friars stole money from the my friends, the Bellantis, and we exposed them. Of course, they denied everything and swore on Bibles that they were innocent, but we knew better and by their perjury they have endangered their souls."

"These are serious enemies. My uncle believes if you go to Rome there is a good chance you will be executed unless you conform to the Vatican's wishes."

Aonio stared moodily into the flames. At his age, he had little concern for his own life. Other things were more important, such as truth and justice. He could still strike a blow for them. Out of respect for the risk everyone had taken to bring him the news, he did not share his thoughts with his student.

"I want to thank you and your uncle for your kindness, Marco. I know the risk you both have taken to bring me this news."

"My uncle believed I would attract the least notice since I was your student. I had no idea I would arrive in the middle of a family gathering. This has called attention to my presence here, particularly with your priest."

"It can't be helped, and I appreciated how you deflected his questions. He has an infinite capacity to ignore his own ignorance. He is Marietta's confessor so I can do very little about it. She is a woman, and women must have their priests. But, tell me. Is Fra Pietro the spy in my household?"

"Be careful of him. He's ambitious and I understand he'd like to be attached to the papal court. As far as being the spy, my uncle didn't give me names, but I don't think he is. I'm riding back to Siena tomorrow with your priest. He might say something, although I doubt it. Ambitious men fetch and carry information but seldom reveal anything themselves."

"Marco . . . ," Aonio hesitated.

He looked intently at the young man before him. He marveled at his honest and eager face. A fine mind, a promising future, a happy disposition, and until this point untroubled by the burdens of the world. Should he ask?

Aonio drew breath and made his decision. "Marco, may I ask you for a favor."

"Of course, professor, anything within my power."

"It may be unfair to ask you this, but there is no one else I feel I can trust. I have to ask if you will be a friend to my wife and my daughter Beatrice. Fedro is settled. Caterina is married. I fear for Marietta and Beatrice. Will you help them if they need it?"

Aonio knew the burden of what he asked. Once the charges against him were known, Marco's father would try to make sure there was no contact with the family. Dealing with heretics was not good for business. His uncle the bishop would forbid all contact lest the de Valterra family be involved by implication. Aonio knew he had placed Marco in an impossible position. But still he had to ask.

"I will do everything in my power to help. I know the bishop, my uncle, will do all he can as well."

"Thank you, Marco," Aonio said sincerely. "Now go and get some sleep. You have been a good friend."

"Professor . . .

"Yes, Marco."

"My uncle describes the danger as real and your enemies powerful. He urges you to seek safety."

"I understand what he is saying. Please give him my thanks."

"Good night, professor."

"Good night, Marco."

Alone, with the candle flickering and the room chilling as the fire died down, Aonio sat before his desk and opened the drawer where he kept his writing implements. He took out a quill and thoughtfully put on a nib. He looked for a moment at his leather-covered desk set—the inkstand and the half-moon blotter—all stamped with the crest of the prince of Salerno, another gift from Marietta. Then he picked up his pen and dipped it in the ink.

Marietta was right. He should not have to deal with this at his age. But to confess error when he knew the truth was to substitute one imprisonment for another. He might be allowed to live out the rest of his life behind bars but he would have to swear allegiance to the falsehoods perpetrated by the Church; even worse, his example would be used as justification to accuse others.

The bishop had suggested covertly that he leave Italy as others had before him. They had fled to Germany and remained out of the Church's reach. By doing this, he might save his family from trouble, but wouldn't he then be sacrificing his life for earthly things rather than for his Savior?

He had little doubt of Caraffa's intentions. He had met him when he was only Giovanni Pietro Caraffa, nephew and protégé of the Bishop of Naples and the family's best hope for a future pope. The two young men had spoken long enough for Aonio to recognize that Caraffa spurned any learning that went against strict interpretation of Church doctrine. Aonio was dismayed as he watched Caraffa's advance through the Church ranks.

"I'm not the serpent here," Aonio said out loud as he sat before his dying fire. His hands curved in a graceful arch as he printed his small upright, jagged letters, mouthing the Latin alexandrines softly as he placed them on the page:

> Those ancient fields where golden
> nymphs once lightly danced
> Have been made barren by a pitiless pursuit.
> Now truth hides its face and women bitterly weep,
> While evil strikes freely all in the name of faith.
> The world struggles under burdens of ignorance.
> Where the charlatans tear apart the robes of truth,
> Knowledge must quickly flee in her tattered raiments
> And torture is devotion's barbarous reward.

When he was done, he rolled the crescent blotter over his words as if he meant to place the parchment in one of the desk's drawers. But then he changed his mind. He crumpled the poem and threw it into the fireplace. "I hate the human race and its inanity," he said bitterly as the flames shrank his words, flared up briefly, and died into ash.

4:00 p.m.

I'M AWAKE. WELL, *not really. It's more as if I'm experiencing a blurry consciousness of my life. I'm back in my bed and the family I've been watching, the villa, and the sodden landscape have disappeared. While I am wondering what has called me back to the present, I feel the pulse that heralds the return of the big pain, the one that can reduce me to tears. I feel it build within my chest until I let out an anguished groan and bang my arm on something. Then I am lifted up and a cool liquid put under my tongue. Anna and Carole have heard me cry out. The pain recedes and my mind is free to range wherever my thoughts take me.*

I am not attracted by this man's self-justifications, but I suppose it's his business what he chooses to believe. I know only that I've heard about this Aonio Paleario before. I am certain of it. The charge of heresy and the family—I know about them too. In fact, I know all these people in one way or another. I can see that my mother and Marietta could be sisters. Caterina is the truth teller. She reminds me of Carole. I recognize the prying priest but I can't place him yet. I know he's someone from my past. I am too confused to work things out further. Marco looks like Michael, except more serious. Are these hallucinations or dreams?

Am I still in the cavern? I don't know. Scenes flick through my mind in no order that I can discern. I can't remember calling for these pictures, but they are coming anyway. I see events from my childhood, my first bicycle, my marriage to Anna in a judge's office, my first job, the time I served on a Navy ship, the day I was told that my cancer had returned, my mother cooking pasta, my father coming back from the war. If anything the scenes look like a giant collage. I feel I am being bombarded by my life. Then another thought hits me: Is this even real? In my state, Anna could be showing me a slide show and I wouldn't know the difference. But then, where would she have got the pictures of my life before I knew her?

Resigned to my helplessness, I realize that all I can do is keep on watching. Then I start to notice that one scene repeats. It's the day last spring when Anna drove us into the mountains. We're going through the cut in the hillside where the highway rises above the Denver plains. I can see her hand steady on the wheel as the different layers of geologic formations flash past the car's windows. I watch her reach up to bring down the sunshield on the driver's side. I force myself to think. Why this day? Then it comes to me in a shock of recognition. She was the one who talked about an Aonio Paleario. She also mentioned a Caraffa. She was writing about them. As I remember, it was one of the few times she explained what she was trying to do in her work—and one of the even fewer times that I listened.

Now I'm curious. Is it possible that this day holds the key to why I am watching this family and hearing this man, Paleario, justify himself? I feel a glimmer of hope that I may be able to find the meaning if only I can focus.

Chapter 3

Denver, April

Aᴺᴺᴬ ᴬᴺᴰ Bɪʟʟ drove down Ward Road and made the twisted left turn onto westbound I-70. The morning traffic congestion had lessened, leaving the road open for trucks gearing down to climb past Red Rocks amphitheater and on into the mountains. On this day, Anna was driving her Camry. Letting her drive was a great concession as Bill did not like to be driven, but his incision pained him where they had removed his lung.

"There they are," Anna exclaimed suddenly as she braked and jolted the car off the highway to pull along the frontage road just before the Chief Hosa cut-off. The Genesee herd of American buffalo were sunning themselves beside the chain link fence separating the park from the highway. Seeing them there was special because the herd was often out of sight amidst the trees covering the park's rolling hills. When the animals were close to the fence like this, a string of cars quickly gathered and people got out with their cameras. Anna parked behind an SUV with Texas license plates.

"They're the Old West," she said as brightly as she could muster when they got out of the car. The morning had not gone well. She and Bill had quarreled over something silly—what he wanted for dinner—and she had proposed driving into the mountains to ease the tension. By now she was used to Bill's moods and could usually make allowance for his brooding, but this morning her patience just had not been there. It was becoming impossible to talk to him about anything that did not end up being about his illness and his discontent.

"Penning them in is like containing sagebrush and scrub willow inside barbed wire," she said. "We must be glad that any survived."

The animals lay in the grass along the fence, quivering their tails to drive off spring flies and tossing their curly heads indifferently in the direction of their excited observers. They were used to being watched and were bored by the attention.

"We're all prisoners one way or another," Bill said morosely. He was not cheered by being remembering Buffalo Bill Cody, whose gravesite was just up the hill. He couldn't think of anyone more imprisoned than Cody who rested under the tons of concrete Denver poured over his coffin to prevent Cody, Wyoming, from stealing his body. Bill found that thought particularly depressing. If Anna had planned this day as a happy diversion, it wasn't working.

Anna stood beside him in silence. The wind whipped her hair and tugged at her T-shirt and jeans. She slipped her hand hopefully into his. His fingers closed involuntarily around hers but did not engage.

"This isn't the world I grew up in," he said finally. "I don't like it"

Anna took back her hand and rubbed her bare arms, chilled by the breeze blown over late spring snow in the mountains. She waited in silence. If he said he wanted to be taken home, she would turn the car around and head down the winding curves back into Denver.

"I hate the human race and its inanity," he said finally. "I think we're all programmed to behave like shits."

"Well," she laughed hesitantly, "That certainly applies to the drivers on I-70. One tried to run me off the highway not far from here. But it's just overcrowding. Even the ski resorts are getting that way."

"Just like shits," he repeated as if he had not heard her. "Nobody can argue decently anymore. No debate. It's all about yelling. People shout as if they believe things are true if they can say them loudly enough. Look at religion. It's become a propaganda mill about money. Business used to be about serving customers rather than cheating them. Universities now are just big corporations driven by their football teams. Where's the morality in any of this? What happened to news reporting? When I was doing radio work, we had to look at both sides or the FCC came down on us for lack of balance. Now you dial your news to hear it twisted to what you want to hear. What kind of ethics is that? It's the loudest voice and the stupidest listener. We're no better than primal animals fighting over a carcass."

"My God, Bill. Where's this coming from? Don't you think people yell because they are afraid and frustrated?"

"They yell because it's easier than to be responsible for their lives. It's like death. People are afraid to die because they think they'll get what they deserve—and maybe they should. People want to blame someone else for their own bad decisions. According to them, we're all victims of something."

"Hey," she said as they got back in the car. "Let's talk about something other than death and retribution. Bet you can't name the seven dwarfs."

"What's that got to do with anything?" Bill assumed Anna had some waste-of-time literary puzzle in mind, probably in response to his crack about universities.

"Accept the challenge. Bet you can't name all seven." Anna knew him well enough to count on his competitiveness.

Bill still looked disgruntled as they sat in the car for a few minutes, warming themselves in the sunshine streaming through the windshield. In spite of himself, Bill started to picture the dwarfs in the movie. The words "heigh ho" caught in his brain and he struggled to stop from humming the tune. But then he gave in. At least it gave him something else to think about than his invaded body and the disappointing state of the world.

"Sneezy, Dopey, Doc, Bashful, Grumpy." He paused and repeated the names slowly.

"Five, she said "What about the other two?"

"It's as far as I get. Snow White wasn't my generation. Mine was Tom Mix and the Westerns. You could always tell the good guys. They had the white hats and were on the side of justice. You want the name of the dwarfs. So, what's the name of Tom Mix's horse?"

"Tony the Wonder Horse," Anna replied immediately.

Bill stared at her open-mouthed. "How do you know that?"

"English majors know strange things."

"What's strange about Tom Mix? That's my childhood hero you're talking about."

"Nothing's strange. I know he was the first big cowboy star. When I took Michael as a little boy to Grauman's Chinese Theatre, we found Tony's hoof prints along with Tom Mix's hand and shoe prints. Now come on. Name the last two dwarfs."

"I suppose Horny and Farty don't count. What's left?"

She laughed. "Some people say they are different parts of life. Maybe the last two will come to you. Shall we go?"

"Sure," he said.

They drove on toward Georgetown. The sun had splintered the steep hillsides into jagged black crevices. The creek alongside the road was snowmelt-full. The water looked agitated and icy, and spray erupted where the waves slapped against tumbled boulders trapped in the middle of the stream. Bill looked moodily out of the window. He had the same problem with Anna as she did with him. It wasn't easy to find something to talk about with her, given how hard she was trying to make life seem normal for him. But how grateful was he supposed to be? How many times did he have to say thanks? Gratitude was becoming a burden.

"What's happening with the Renaissance fellow you're writing about?" The words came from him suddenly as if he were trying to apologize to her without really doing so. If he asked about her work maybe she could interpret that as interest in her.

"Aonio Paleario?" Anna was as surprised as Bill had been when she knew about the horse.

"Yes. Tell me again who he was." Bill felt pleased to have surprised her. He liked the idea he still could.

"A sixteenth-century Italian university professor and writer," Anna said evasively, unsure how much Bill wanted to know.

"What did he write about?"

"Justice—he was also a lawyer—language and religion. He wrote a Latin treatise on the immortality of the soul. The Church considered his work heretical. He's largely forgotten now."

"You don't need to talk down to me," he said.

"I didn't realize I was," she replied.

"You get this university lecturer tone in your voice."

"I'm sorry," she said."

The car retreated back into silence. He knew he'd have to start again while Anna had the sinking feeling that Aonio Paleario was about to become a power struggle between them. This was how their fights began. She waited for the surly question that usually followed.

"Largely forgotten? Is that how you academics find your research topics? Find someone unknown and hope he's worth the trouble?" Bill's voice had the sarcastic edge she expected, but it sounded more question than accusation. She could deal with cynicism by being studiedly upbeat.

"But think of the glory if you find someone who's been overlooked and you bring them to the world's attention." Anna looked out at the leafing aspens along the roadside. This was a lovely time in the mountains, equal to the blaze of gold when the trees turned in the fall. "But seriously," she added so he didn't think she was discounting him entirely, "there must be some connection with the person because you can spend years in his company. I chose Aonio Paleario because I thought I understood him. I also knew that if I'd lived in his age, I would have been a heretic just like him and for the same reasons. I even have a picture of the view from his villa in Colle di Val D'Elsa on my office wall. One day I'd like to go there and see the rolling hills and the town up on the hillside."

Bill thought for a moment. "Anyone worth knowing then probably was heretical except they wouldn't admit it." He knew something about heresy. It had been a hot topic among the priests at his Catholic high school.

Anna smiled. "I'd love a conversation with Paleario about the Sack of Rome. Forty-five thousand Romans were killed or went missing. They said the blood in the streets ran several inches deep, and rats came out in the daylight to feed on the corpses."

"This attracted you?" Bill raised his eyebrows. "You'd really want to talk with him about that?"

"Why not? Wouldn't you like to have a conversation with your ancestors and ask what they were thinking when they did things? History would have to be rewritten, and I imagine in the end we'd find they were just as muddled about life as we are. But it's really the psychology of disaster that interests me. People were killed in the streets pleading for their lives, or they starved in hiding places afraid to come out. The invading troops stabled horses in the Sistine Chapel. All the people's illusions were gone, yet they had to find a way to go on living. I'm sure it's the same challenge after any disaster."

Bill tried not to look bored. He didn't share Anna's interest in communicating with long-dead people. "Human nature," he said, "doesn't seem to change much over time. They were probably dividing themselves into us and them when they lived in caves."

"Probably. Humans can go along without too much questioning as long as things seem to work. But let them not, like the attack on Rome, then there's panic and loud voices demanding explanation. How could God have let this happen? People always want to believe that someone else is to blame. As a species, we've been blame-shifting for thousands of years. "

"But what does this have to do with your fellow?"

"He was an intellectual and suspected free-thinker. For Rome to be safe again, the Church preached that everyone needed to believe the same things absolutely if God were to be pleased with them again. You could call it a retreat to tradition. The Inquisition was restarted to root out imperfection and intellectuals were a primary target. It's all very logical if you look at it from the Church's point of view. Burn a few people and the people are reassured they are being protected. I don't know how many of them really believed this, but it was certainly safer to do so."

"But you said Paleario was a lawyer. He was no Churchman. Why did they pick on him?"

"Sooner or later someone could get ensnared without meaning to. Unlike what was happening in Spain, the Roman Inquisition was directed to universities and Paleario stood out as an academic and public speaker."

"Didn't Italy always have an Inquisition? I thought it had been active for hundreds of years. How was this anything new?" Bill tried to remember his religious schooling. All he could remember were the priests talking about saints, persecutions, and continual self-examination to avoid falling into heresy. Sometimes it seemed that just asking questions was heretical.

"The Inquisition was started back in the Middle Ages; there was even a manual on how to conduct one written by a Churchman named Gui. Did you know that they still have an Inquisition, except it's called something else now and that the last execution for heresy was in 1834? But it depended on who was pope. After the Sack of Rome, a Cardinal named Giovanni Pietro Caraffa persuaded Clement VII to restore The Holy Office as they called it. When Caraffa died the people of Rome rioted from pure joy, stormed the Inquisition prison, and freed all the prisoners."

"Still, why this Paleario in particular?"

"Paleario wanted to examine the Church's founding documents to see if they had been correctly translated. This was dangerous. The Donation of Constantine had already been exposed as a forgery, and that document had been used to justify the Pope's authority over Western Europe. What if the others were shown to be just as false? Caraffa knew Paleario personally and had wanted to try him for years anyway." Anna glanced sidelong at Bill. "Heard enough?" She was prepared to drop the subject immediately if only to keep the peace. But Bill didn't seem ready to let it go.

"Hearing about this chap is better than just watching cars. So why didn't the Church accept that some rituals needed to be adjusted? I would have thought that they would be grateful for the chance to make them right."

"What happens if UFOs exist and we really are being observed by a race of supposedly more advanced creatures? Suppose they want to make contact with us. How well are we likely to take that?"

Bill considered this for a moment. "Well," he said slowly, "I suppose there might be fear if the little green men seemed threatening. If they were peaceful, the Church would probably try to convert them. But, more largely, there goes any idea of us as God's special creation and even who God is."

"Exactly," Anna replied. "There also go government and social order when both are built on religious ideals. Society could fall apart. It was his academic truth versus what the Church felt it needed to do to keep order. Of course, I side with him, but that's me."

"You sound half in love with this man."

"Do I?" Anna darted a look at Bill. "How could I have feelings for a man who's been dead five hundred years?"

"Don't ask me," Bill said. "You just come across that way. So what do you make of all this?"

"I think the times he lived in were not so fundamentally different from our own. There was a clash of values that revolved around personal salvation. One group didn't want to take even one step away from the promised way to heaven. The other group, mainly intellectuals and academics, wanted freedom to think and find their own ways. Paleario is

an interesting conundrum because he took from both sides. He wanted
to think for himself, but he was just as absolute as the Church when it
came to living according to what he considered to be truth."

"So, what happened to him?"

"I don't read him as having any death wish, but I think he looked
on the charges of heresy as a challenge to his faith. Ironically, it wasn't
his fault in the end. He'd done many provocative things, but what they
charged him with was out of his control. Alarmed by the spread of
Protestant ideas, the Church required all published books to have the
stamp of Vatican approval. A printer in Switzerland, out of the reach
of the Vatican, reprinted a book of Paleario's without this required seal
or even his approval. Even though earlier editions had been given the
seal, its absence on the new version was the excuse Caraffa needed. The
Church reexamined his work and charged him with everything he'd
ever written."

"Didn't you say that the earlier work had already been approved?"

"That didn't stop them. People interpret word meanings differently
over time, become convinced that their meaning is the right one, and get
passionate about it. Words are notorious. I wonder we can communicate
at all given the way people insist on having words mean just what they
want them to. Since the Church reserved the right to "correct" earlier
errors, that included banning books that contained whatever was newly
identified as heretical."

"So what do you do with someone who has been previously approved
and is now out of favor."

"You must convince the authors to go along with the changes and
declare themselves previously misinformed, drive them into exile, or
publicly try them. One of Paleario's conclusions was that there was no
evidence for purgatory, and that's immensely important. The Church
collects money for prayers for the souls of the dead, but what happens
if purgatory doesn't exist? Thousands of people around Christendom
will be suddenly worried about their dead relatives and they will be very

indignant with the Church for taking money under false pretenses. Not everyone is comfortable with the Greek poet Pindar's observation that life is a dream of shadows. That's like Plato's argument about most of us seeing life only as shadows in a cave, but Plato thought that scholars could get outside the cave could see life as it really is. Pindar, on the other hand, said that getting out of the cave took spiritual intervention. Either view means that there's a lot more to life than we understand, and many people will be threatened if someone points that out."

"And if the authors refuse?" Bill was considering his own obstinacy. He could see himself doing it.

"The powers-that-be must try to force them to deny their earlier work. In Paleario's case, they wanted him to confirm Church doctrine and ritual as being true. All of it. He would have to agree that purgatory existed. His position was that he didn't know so he couldn't attest to the truth of it."

Bill studied the road ahead and made no reply. Paleario sounded like a man after his own heart: a stubborn old fool who questioned the priests. Anyone who had the guts to do that was all right. He'd done the same thing in walking away from the religion, which probably meant that he was prime heretic material himself.

"How could Paleario be such a threat to them?" he asked suddenly as they went down the curving hill and through the tunnels into Idaho Springs. "He was my age. Why couldn't they just wait for nature to take care of the problem?"

"They didn't have time. Let's go back to UFOs for a moment. If they show up, they'll have their own form of spirituality and may look on our beliefs as primitive. Since they'll bring new knowledge and new science, there will be a burst of learning and adaptation. People react to change differently. Some will think it's wonderful. Some will feel threatened and do everything in their power to keep things as they know them. In sixteenth-century Italy, the new learning based on the recovered Greek texts had turned everything upside down. The Italian intellectuals were excited, but they were only about twenty-five percent of the population. The rest were rural. That meant that seventy-five percent of the people lived off the land and were probably somewhere back in the Middle Ages. If all of a sudden everything these country folk thought they knew was shown to be wrong, there would be riots."

Bill seemed lost in thought as Anna turned the car off I-70 and drove along the frontage road to Georgetown. They ate at a restaurant created within the walls of a Victorian miner's cottage, where he ordered a Belgian waffle with strawberries and cream.

"Unusual for you," Anna said after he had given the order. "You're a meat and potatoes man."

"Felt like something sweet," he said. "I like this place." He looked around at the small tables crowded together with their fabric tablecloths and little flowerpots. "It doesn't feel like they're slopping the hogs."

"How Western." Anna laughed and dabbed at her mouth with her napkin.

"How so?" he asked. He had not forgotten that she knew Tom Mix's horse. He wondered what she meant by Western although he didn't really want another involved philosophical discussion with her.

"Westerners live close to the land," she said. "Or at least they used to. A horse was once the only way you got anywhere or plowed a field for that matter. You'd better take care of it or you're going to starve. Same thing with hogs. They can mean the difference between making it or starving. Slopping the hogs means that someone's taking care of them."

"Fast-food places," he added with a superior chuckle, "you may as well be animals lined up with your heads through the bars waiting for the swill to pour its way downhill to you."

Anna's laughter echoed in the restaurant. Bill smiled. He liked the sound of her laughter. He wouldn't admit it to her, but he'd missed it lately. They paid the bill and drove slowly back through Georgetown. The car radio played Tchaikovsky's First and Bill relaxed.

In downtown Georgetown, the tourists were out in their anoraks and designer walking shoes, looking in windows, buying ice cream and root beer straws, and inspecting art and antiques in the Victorian shop fronts lined down the main street. The fine old, hotel still dominated the town, although it offered only tours now instead of the finest menu of game and imported wines in the West. They drove past the old railroad station with its sense of waiting for a snowfall to hang icicles along its overhanging roof, and past the ginger-bread houses of long-gone mine managers until they reached the gas station and the modern visitor's center on the edge of town. There they rejoined I-70 eastbound back to Denver.

Halfway back to the city, Anna decided to take a chance. "Bill, would you consider us working with hospice?" She spoke resolutely knowing that his reaction would not be good. She risked the togetherness that had developed over lunch, but perhaps this was the right moment because of that. Her timing was never right with him.

Bill frowned deeply, clenched his fists, and banged his hand hard on the dashboard. His anger startled her. "Goddamit, Anna, if I needed special help, I'd ask for it. What do you want from me?"

She waited silently to let his frustration subside before she replied. Then she kept it simple and succinct. "Appreciation and respect."

"I already give you that," he said angrily.

"If you did, why would I be asking for it?"

"I have no idea what goes on in your mind."

The silence fogged the car. Anna knew she must say something because he would not. "It's not special help for you," she said. "It's for me." The tone of her voice intended to tell him that he should have known this in the first place.

He stared stonily ahead and did not reply. If he understood her reasoning, he was not prepared to say.

"What's wrong, Bill?" Anna asked finally just before they started the winding decent near Evergreen. She wondered whether the pain had returned.

Bill's resentment surged. "You are. You're what's wrong. You never know when to keep your mouth shut." He poured into his words his anger with his disability, his loss of control over his life, and his instant, intense need to blame someone else for what was happening to him.

Anna did not bother to respond. She gripped the steering wheel and looked straight ahead. She had known this could happen. His anger and pain had been threatening all morning, like the dark grey clouds of a Front Range summer thunderstorm lingering over the foothills without clear indication of when it will move over the city. She also knew the moment would pass if she let it take its course. They rode silently back down the long winding grade with the warnings to truckers to remain geared down until they reach Arvada. When they reached home, he slammed the car door and disappeared into the house.

She followed him. If she had already taken the punishment for raising the subject, she saw little to lose. "I'm going to talk with them." Her voice rose slightly into the feminine question mark that made her statement seem more like a question than she intended.

"Yes, goddamit, anything. You don't let go, do you?"

Bill stomped off into the bedroom to lie down, leaving Anna to the quiet house. She sat on the sofa knowing she had won but wondering when or if she would have the courage to follow up on it. She looked up in relief when she heard a car come crunching over the gravel in the driveway.

"Where's Bill?" Carole let herself in and looked around the room for him. She seemed surprised that he had not come out to meet her.

"In the bedroom," Anna replied unenthusiastically.

"Come on slugabed," Carole called through the bedroom door, "I've got a goody for you."

Bill emerged, smiling to see her. His earlier mood had passed. He knew he had lost some sort of existential battle with Anna and wanted to move on. In this, he expected Carole to be his ally. Carole would take his side against Anna if the subject of hospice came up again. He was sure of that.

"Is Anna taking good care of you?" Carole spoke playfully, expecting he would respond to her warmth as he always had before.

"Yes, she is." Bill's reply was a little too fast. He didn't look at Anna. He knew she would see through him immediately. His comment was intended to be polite for Carole's benefit, and not applause for his wife.

"I should certainly hope so." Carole handed him a latte and winked at Anna.

"How's Richard?" Bill asked as he took the lid off the coffee and sat down. "You're getting to be old married folks now, aren't you? How long's it been? Six months?"

"Six months next week. He's fine and sends his regards. We finished the wedding pictures. You look great in the tuxedo." Carole sat down on the chair across from Bill.

"Say hello to him for me." Bill sipped the hot sweet drink. Three sugars in a medium. Carole always remembered. "Hope you don't mind if I drink this in the bedroom. I'd like to stretch out."

"You go right ahead," Carole replied.

Bill left the bedroom door slightly open and they could hear him groan as he stretched out on the bed.

"How's he really been?" Carole asked softly, keeping her voice low so Bill could not hear them.

"Difficult. When he's in pain he takes it out on me. I know it's the cancer talking when he lashes out, but it's still unpleasant. Today he told me to keep my mouth shut when I asked about contacting hospice. The bad part is he's smoking again."

"What makes you think so?" Carole looked aghast at the idea of a man with lung cancer still choosing to buy cigarettes.

"I found tobacco grains in his jacket pocket, and I think I smelled smoke when I came back from the market the other day. Rationally, I know I'm not responsible for his choices and yet emotionally I feel I am." Anna did not like how vulnerable she must sound to Carole. She knew she was not. She ran the acreage now and handled everything more and more as Bill's strength failed.

"How could you be responsible? You didn't make him smoke. I don't understand why you are being hard on yourself."

"I've always felt something karmic with Bill. I don't know what it is or what I may or may not have done, but I can't get away from the feeling." Anna bent down to pick up a gauzy dust ball blown in from outside. She wasn't living up to her own image of the rational academic when she talked about such things.

"Blaming yourself isn't very helpful at this point." Carole looked at her impassively, recognizing Anna's balancing act as she dealt with Bill's illness and the increasing responsibility of the land that Bill had wanted, but still wishing Anna to shrug it off and not retreat into self-reflection. "You academics do mental masturbation. Bill agrees with me—you all think too much."

Anna pulled back in surprise. "Bill's just as much an academic. He thinks a lot more than he lets on. If he says anything about intellectuals, he's talking about himself as well."

"You look tired," Carole said abruptly. "It's too easy to slip into heroic caregiving and martyr yourself. Then nobody's helped except maybe a caregiver who wants sainthood. You need to ask yourself what you're getting out of letting him take his frustration out on you. When was the last time you took a break?"

"A break? This doesn't seem the time when so much is needed here with the animals. I'm not a martyr. I'm just trying to get through the day as peacefully as possible. You can't go out when animals have to be fed and cared for. I thought the day trip into the mountains would be a nice diversion. But that didn't work out so well and I'm not going to try that again."

"No," Carole interrupted. "I'm talking about time for yourself. You're not going to be much use if you run yourself into the ground. You're behaving as if being a caregiver to Bill is who you are. Caregiving is not an identity. You don't get up in the morning saying 'Look at me. I'm a caregiver. That's all I am.' No you're not. It's what you're doing right now.

You need to keep that straight. You are a college professor who is taking a break from it. You are not a servant to Bill's moods. Yes, it's tough what's happened to him. But it was his decision to smoke, just as it's his decision right now whether to behave like a regular human being. You need to demand his respect, and if he won't give it, then give it to yourself."

"I haven't thought about it," Anna admitted. It hadn't occurred to her that she should. She had also not recognized before how clearly and firmly Carole saw the world.

"Well, it's time you did. You're not a professional nurse or housekeeper and you can't be expected to keep the land and animals and cater to Bill's needs all at once. You're not superwoman so don't try to be. Pace yourself. Bill's going to have to understand that you have needs too. I think you both should be part of a hospice. He'd get the care and you'd have the support." Carole presented her solution with the confidence of having thought things through in her own mind, made the only sensible decision on their behalf, and expecting them to pose no possible opposition to what she saw as common sense.

"I told you. I tried to talk to him about hospice today. He nearly took my head off. It's not as easy as you think."

"If it's to get you help, he might be more willing. Why don't you at least get someone to help with the house and the animals?"

"I tried that. It didn't work. He finally said something like go ahead if you must, but he wasn't anywhere on board. In the past, Bill wouldn't even let me have a cleaning woman. He said he didn't want strangers in the house."

"What strangers are you talking about?" Bill came into the kitchen with his empty paper cup.

"About getting someone to help Anna," Carole said brightly. "Look," she continued before he could reply, "It's hailing."

The hail fell like mothballs, bouncing off the back porch and rattling down the gutters and downspouts. The house felt under siege as the sound increased with the cloud's approach. A few hailstones were large enough to sound like someone hitting the roof with a hammer.

"Better get your car under a tree," Bill said, "unless you want a cracked windshield."

Carole threw her jacket over her head and ran outside. Bill and Anna stood together at the window watching swirling clouds disgorge their contents and sweep in tattered layers down toward the distant high-rise buildings far below in the Denver downtown. These dramatic but brief storms were expected for the Rocky Mountain spring.

"What is it you want? A cleaning woman? Is that it?" Bill's voice was challenging, a continuation of his previous ill humor.

"No. Carole was just talking." Anna refused to rise to the moment and engage Bill.

"You feel overworked? You want to spend more time writing?" His tone was withering.

Carole came back from moving her car, wet and laughing. "Those hailstones smarted!" She draped her wet jacket back over a chair and shook out her hair.

"Did you hear?" Bill said impatiently to her. "Anna thinks she's overworked and wants household help so she can write."

"Why not?" Carole met his opposition head on. "If you were my father and I'd had anything to do with it, you'd have been having hospice help long ago."

"What do you mean why not? And why do we need hospice?" Bill glared at Carole. He hadn't expected her to disagree with him. Anna opposed him and that was enough. "She has me to help. Why does she need anyone else?"

"You're not well, Bill. You have to accept your health. You both could use some time for other things."

"I don't want a strange person in this house, examining my things, putting them where I can't find them. It was bad enough with the home nurse here after my surgery."

"Bill, you're being obstinate," Carole said flatly.

"No I'm not. I've a right to say who comes into this house."

Carole shrugged.

"I don't want hospice. I'm not dying." Bill's eyes blazed with anger.

"Of course you are, Bill. We all are. We've been dying since we were born."

"Then I'm not dead yet."

"We're all right," Anna said. "I can manage all right." Even she could hear the bleat of the heroic caregiver in her words.

"And why should you have to? Bill, admit that your illness is going to progress, get Anna some help, and have someone come in who knows what to expect. Either that or I will come over here every day and play loud rock music. Just see if I don't."

Bill tried to look angry but couldn't. He laughed and the tension eased.

"Bill, if it gets to be too much—and you know what I mean—get Anna help. Don't let me have to worry about you." Carole spoke slowly and definitely, then she folded her arms and looked at him significantly.

"It's not going to get to be too much," he replied obstinately.

5:00 p.m.

I SMILE GRIMLY *as I hear myself protest. I blustered because I wanted my life back. I didn't want Anna's sacrifice. She said she was taking a break from teaching to make time for writing, but I knew different. It was because of me. Was I being stubborn? I thought I was being perfectly reasonable. I didn't like the fuss around me. But Carole said I was being obstinate, and people have to think you're wrong to call you obstinate. So Carole was telling me I was wrong. I don't like being wrong; I especially don't like people telling me I am. But things look different as I watch them now. It seems an eternity ago as I watch myself through the eyes of a man who is rapidly circling the drain.*

Death is no picnic. I try to stretch, but my arms don't move when I tell them to. Nothing works anymore. I don't know why I thought dying would be over quickly. I suppose I've seen too many movies that show people giving some last final words before closing their eyes, taking a deep sigh, and dropping off to what looks like sleep. That's not what death is: it's sweat-soaked sheets, alternating hot and cold, and struggle. To make matters worse, I think the morphine is upsetting my stomach. I can't imagine why Paleario would so placidly have sought out death. He must never have seen someone die.

All right, so I was wrong to leave Michael and Anna to tell my mother about the cancer. I suppose I felt it was my right whom and when to tell without having to worry about anyone else. A man's death is his own because it's the one thing he does by himself. I never was allowed to grow up alone. My mother suffocated everything around her. She didn't feel secure unless she—and everyone else—followed all the Church's rules even if they made no sense. It was community, she said, and we must all believe together. She was passionate about everything including blame, recrimination, and guilt. If I wanted to please her, I was slave to her impulses and needs. If I disobeyed her, she'd rattle the crucifix at me and say I was going to burn in hell. You'd think it was she on the cross and I who'd put her there. The best way to deal with her was to stay away, which I did.

But what do I have to show for it? I've been watching a man my wife has studied as some sort of historical relic. She says she understands him. But what is she understanding? Isn't he just another stubborn, obstinate old man like me? He's been dead for five hundred years; that means his life is over, sealed, and settled. So why am I not only reviewing my own life but also watching his? Surely this isn't purgatory and it can't be limbo. That leaves only hell, which I don't believe in. But be raised in a religious household and there's always that doubt. Still, I can't believe my mother and her church were right about anything.

In any case, who is this Paleario? Well in a way maybe I do understand him. He says he hates the inanity of human life. I know what he means: cruelty and the lack of freedom. I hate the inanity too, although I mean hypocrisy and selfishness, even including my own. Both of us want integrity and truth. But I'm not sure what he means when he talks of truth. He thinks truth is individual, because he wants the freedom to find it on his own terms. In this, he is opposed to the Church because of its insistence on collective truth—truth is what they say it is. But how does one prove spiritual truth? That's what faith is for, and it means you choose to believe something that can't be proved. That means that for hundreds of years, the Inquisition has tortured people over unprovable things. I wonder what Anna's UFOs would think of us. Clearly, I don't know what truth is any more than Pontius Pilate did.

So how do I explain myself? I was born a rebel to the tyranny of family and religion and I never found a way to reconcile myself to them. The trouble with them is that, over time, the patterns they set become customary, almost self-evident, and people think of them as natural. I and others who have broken away will always have a sense of isolation because we have left behind everything we were raised to know. I would argue that this is good thing, that we should create our own spirituality, and that we ought to be done with organized religion, except that I am also pragmatic. Religion serves its purpose. It creates communities, even if those communities are inspired to inflict harm on others in its name, and it's unclear what will take their place if we shutter the churches and close the temples. Religion is all-pervasive, and even now, to my disgust, my thoughts revolve around the festivals and holy days.

Never really finding any answers, I tried to forget both religion and family. I thought I'd succeeded, but I'm starting to see that my evasions have been only temporary. Someone once told me that all we are and ever will be is the total of our experiences and memories. If that's true, then by choosing to forget, I have denied part of who I am. Adults integrate their lives. I haven't. That means I am still waiting to grow up. "I don't feel old,"

I want to yell. "That reflection in the mirror isn't me. I still have time."
But even if I had all the time in the world, no one ever said that gaining
years would mean gaining wisdom. If maturity means having a clear idea
of life's purpose, I am a seventy-year-old child who is afraid he will die
without ever knowing.

Now I feel impatient. If this is the end, let's not drag it out. Let's get
this over with. I close my eyes as an expression of will for things to happen
and wait for the blackness of oblivion or whatever is waiting for me. When
I open my eyes, however, I am in the backyard of our house, in the town
where I attended high school. It is not where I wanted to be.

I know the day. My father is not yet home from the submarine base
where he works as an engineer. My mother has dyed her hair dark brown
because my father is jealous of the attention her blonde hair attracts. It's
an old argument between them and it sometimes gets vicious when my
father's drinking. He questions whether I'm his son then. She says she had
a period after she arrived in Panama to join him in military housing.
He says that she came down there pregnant and I'm not his. This always
bemuses me because everyone says I am the image of him. I can see it
myself. I think he just doesn't want to.

At that point, I've applied for early enlistment into the Navy because
I want to get out of the house. Signing up was a problem because I was
born outside the US and the Navy recruiters raised questions about my
citizenship. I think I've given them the information they need but it's been
difficult to do it without alerting my mother. I'd had to go through my
mother's papers to find my birth certificate but that and my school records
seem to have done it. At least, the recruiter says that I have been accepted.
I still have to tell my parents that I'm going right after graduation. My
father isn't going to care. He'll be glad to see me go. My mother will be
another story.

This day I am revisiting is the day I planned to tell them. It's also the
day that I lost any illusion that we were or ever could be a family.

Chapter 4

Boston, Massachusetts April 1951

BILL STOOD IN his mother's vegetable garden, a lanky seventeen-year-old with a hank of dark hair swept up into a wave over the front of his head. He was unenthusiastically hoeing the budding mint in the vegetable garden his mother planted after they moved in to the small, clapboard house when his father got his sea orders. Everyone was going to war then. His parents decided she would wait for her husband here since the rents were cheap. She began by growing the basilico and oregano she needed for her cooking and then expanded from there. He helped more or less willingly as his enthusiasm for gardening ebbed or waned. At its peak, they had a generous area of beets, onions, lettuce, tomatoes, and squash. But when his father came home, reassigned to a desk job at the Navy shipyard, his mother had less time for the garden. That meant he had to do it.

His friend, Skipper, was looking over the garden fence. Skipper had always been a small kid with a freckled face and dark hair that hung over his collar, and even his adolescent growth spurt hadn't produced much in the way of height. He barely came up to Bill's shoulder. Skipper was wearing his prized Red Sox baseball cap, which he wore on the back of his head with the bill sticking up vertically. He'd worn it that way ever since Bill first met him. Skipper's little brown and white dog sniffed at bushes, lifting his back paw when he felt the need to warn off some competitor. Bill opened the gate to let them in and bent down to pat the dog while it sniffed at his shoes.

"How's things?" Skipper asked.

"Fine," Bill said too quickly, giving out the message that whatever it was, he didn't want to talk about it.

"You sure?" Skipper looked at him quizzically, hearing the brittle snap in the way Bill said the word.

Bill did not reply.

"I was going to the store to get some pop," Skipper said. "You wanna come along?"

"Let me check with my ma."

"OK." Skipper looked quizzical. The store was at the end of the road and if Bill's mother wanted to yell for him, they could have heard her.

"My dad's bringing over friends tonight. You know how that goes." Bill wanted to explain his abruptness. Skipper was one of the good guys.

"Yeah." Skipper understood all right. His stepdad was a fitter at the shipyard and famous for the quick hand across the face. Skipper pushed his hat bill even higher on his head and waited.

Bill headed into the house. His mother, Carolina, was in the kitchen rolling pizza dough at the kitchen table. She was wearing a flower-print housedress with a ruffled apron.

"Ma, I'm going down to the corner store with Skipper."

"What for? We got all the food we need here." She spoke with a slight Italian accent.

"We're not going to eat. Just meet up and have a soda."

How long you gonna be?"

"Not too long." Bill didn't give an exact time. Last time he'd given one, he'd been half an hour late and she'd gone up and down the road asking the neighbors if they'd seen him. She convinced herself he had been hit by a streetcar. When he came home she was hysterical and the neighbors told him he should be more considerate because he had a good mother who worried about him.

"You gonna be long? Your father's invited people. You don't want me to be all by myself, do you?" Carolina looked meaningfully at her son. It was going to be one of those nights.

"You won't be alone." Bill said this with adolescent bravado as he combed his hair and checked his wave. He'd used pomade to make his hair stand up, and he was proud of it. He made a face at himself in the mirror and did his best to act as if his going out of the house wasn't a big deal.

"They're your father's friends, not mine. They'll get drunk on my wine and talk loud. He's not the same since he got back." She wiped her hands on her apron and pushed back her dyed dark hair; it was already showing the blonde roots at the base.

"Skipper's waiting," Bill said impatiently.

"Yes, you go ahead," she replied resentfully. She bent her head to her job and allowed her voice to sound hurt. "I'll be just fine."

Bill took her at her word. "I'll be back soon." He kept his voice deliberately upbeat.

"You're not meeting no girls, are you?"

"Ma, it's just Skipper."

"I don't want you with no girls. We'll find decent, Catholic girls for you to meet. I don't want you talking with those girls round the store." Carolina's voice hardened. She didn't want those Protestant girls getting her son. She dreamed of him becoming a priest. Everyone knew that Carolina's father had left the seminary because he wanted to marry her mother. It was a big scandal. Her mother said she couldn't go to her church after the word got out because the women stared at her and stopped talking when she walked in. The young couple moved because of it. But it must have been worth it. Carolina's mother had little good to say about anyone, but after he died young, she never said one bad thing about her dead husband. Carolina hoped Bill would restore the family honor but she knew he needed the calling. In the meantime, she watched out for girls in case he didn't hear it.

"What if I don't like a good Catholic girl?" Bill grimaced at the memory of the last good Catholic girl he'd taken out. Carolina set it up with the girl's mother and gave Bill the money to take the girl bowling, which seemed safe enough. The girl, Margarita, was the daughter of one of the hairdressers down at the salon, the one who dyed his mother's hair. He didn't even try to like the girl. They bowled and hardly spoke to each other during the evening. When he got home, he sensed that Carolina had already been thinking about where to order orange blossoms for the wedding. "How did you like her?" Carolina demanded. He shrugged. "OK, I guess." His mother looked angry. "She's a good girl. You treat her with respect. I gotta answer to her mother. You gonna see her again?" "Nope," Bill said with finality.

Carolina remembered too. "What's the matter with you? You should thank God right now that people are looking for nice Catholic girls for you."

"If He knows everything, then God knows I can find my own dates."

"Don't you blaspheme God. I'll slap your face hard, you hear?"

"So I won't tell you."

"Whatta you mean?" Carolina rounded on him with the rolling pin still in her hand, but Bill was gone, slamming the screen door behind him.

She yelled after him. "Don't you forget afternoon Mass, you hear. You're helping at the altar."

Bill and Skipper ran down the middle of the street with the dog snapping at their heels. There was little traffic. Factories were producing civilian automobiles again, but they were expensive and many of those on the road were still the long-nurtured older cars that had been impossible to replace during the war. In the gardens, the women waved at them and seemed always to be putting up or taking down laundry.

"Hey guys, wanna play stickball?" It was Brick, another kid from the neighborhood except he was younger and two years behind them in school.

"Can't," said Bill. "Gotta do Mass this afternoon. We're going to the store for some sodas. Wanna come."

"Nah," said Brick.

"My treat," Bill said. He had a few bucks from mowing the lawn of the neighbor across the street.

"Nah," Brick said. "Thanks anyway." His shock of red hair shone vividly in the sun. It was where he got his name. Brick's family was Irish and poorer than most. Two adults, four boys, and two girls were crammed into two bedrooms, a kitchen, one front room, and a bathroom. His house had overlapping roof tiles nailed on all the outside walls. From a distance it was hard to tell where the roof ended and the walls began. Bill's mother regularly delivered clothing bundles from the church thrift store where she volunteered. Brick and others like him didn't have much future except to go join the military and use the GI Bill to get some training later, if they survived.

"The guys are meeting in the lot for a game. Come on over if you change your mind." Brick gave a small wave and went on his way. Bill recognized Brick's sweater and pants. They were things Bill finally outgrew last year. They hung very loosely on the smaller boy. His mother must have put them in one of the bundles for the family.

The lot was what the kids called the only place they could play. It didn't have much grass, more like tufts poking up through hard baked clay, what was left after a house got pulled down and wasn't replaced. Bill and Skipper had played there, using the old Louisville Slugger bat that one of the other kids had scrounged from his dad, who had once played on a team that was state champion one year. A picture of the team hung on the wall by their front door. The bat must have been thirty years old and the lettering was fading, but it still worked and no one hit it hard enough to break it. There was a more formal diamond down at the

Catholic high school where Bill and Skipper attended, but that was used by the school team and the kids didn't feel comfortable there without uniforms and proper equipment. Bill and Skipper had played on their school team, but not for long. Skipper said he preferred to watch the Sox, and Bill found he wasn't really into sports even though he once tried out for the football team. Anyway, since they're seniors now, they're supposed to be thinking about their futures instead of baseball.

Next to the lot was the store where the kids congregated. It looked as if it had been there since the Revolutionary War. The darkened, planked walls stretched up to a tile roof undulating in rhythm with the rafters. The two steps up to the front door had scooped out hollows in the center. The floor inside had a noticeable slant and creaked when they walked across it; it was black from generations of spilled pop and coffee and God knows what else. The building had kept accumulating layers of the past. The windows were grimed from relentless seasons of East Coast weather, so etched into the glass they could not have been cleaned if anyone had wanted to. The screen door marked the passing seasons. In winter, the wood swelled and the door had to be forced open. In summer it closed with a bang, dislodging flies too stupid to find their way in to sticky counters. Pigeons nested and cooed somewhere between the stained ceiling and the roof.

The proprietor, a wizened dwarf of a man who looked as old as the shop, sat by the front door in front of a cash register almost as large as he was, with shelves of candy behind him. He'd count up their purchases, tapping the heavy keys and pushing the total button, dropping their coins into the cash drawer that that shut like an alligator's jaws. If asked, he'd come from behind the register with a grunt, and walk down the counter to make a shake, put a hot dog on a bun, or throw a frozen hamburger patty onto a greasy griddle. That was the extent of his menu, along with soft drinks, malts, and coffee that looked like sludge.

Bill and Skipper banged the screen door as they entered and Skipper took off in search of their sodas.

"Hey, Billy," a girl's voice called.

Bill looked into the gloom and made out Vera sitting at one of two stools at the counter drinking a bottle of Coke. The Catholic boys liked to talk about Vera in the locker room. She was the prettiest girl in the neighborhood; everyone said she would be prom queen at the public school she attended. She wasn't Catholic and so was safe to think about and, for the most daring, to dream about.

"Hi yourself, Vera." Bill nodded toward her.

"What are you doing?"

"Not much. We're here for some sodas." Bill shrugged in the way of adolescent boys who have begun to think about sex.

"Who's we?"

"Just Skipper and me." He looked at the crease knifed up the middle of her sweater. It bisected her chest, calling attention to her breasts before drawing his eye up to a lace false collar and her pale, oval face. Her eyes were a curious shade of dark blue and she had tied her chestnut hair back in a long ponytail. He was glad when Skipper arrived and put two bottles of soda on the counter with a bang. The soda fizzed inside and would probably overflow when the bottles were opened. That was all right. A bit of foam was part of it.

"We thought we'd walk down to the docks and see what's happening." This was a new thought. Bill glanced at Skipper to see if it was all right.

"I'd like that too," Vera said. "Can I come? Is that all right with you, Skipper?"

Skipper looked overcome to be noticed by her and asked for his opinion. He had a crush on Vera and was tongue-tied. He didn't know whether Bill and Vera were just friends and was too afraid to ask, but to be included by them meant that he could enjoy some time with her. He nodded convulsively.

"Sure," Bill said casually. "It's all right with me."

"Me too," Skipper added quickly.

They paid for the sodas, banged the screen door behind them as they left, briefly dislodging the flies, and walked down the dusty street toward the docks. Skipper's little dog ran along beside them, darting off to sniff the lampposts and bushes as they passed them.

From time to time, Bill glanced at Vera, as if seeing her as a woman for the first time. They had met on the lot when it turned out that Vera was efficient with the Louisville Slugger. Once the kids saw she was good for hitting them home from third base, they all wanted her on their teams. She was always good-natured and played well for whichever team she ended up on. Her father had been killed long before, leaving her widowed mother to move back in with her sister. They all lived in a large house two streets over with white pillars and a porch that had been built at the turn of the century for the local doctor. Inside it had elegantly molded wood bannisters, rose squares carved into the doorframes, gleaming crystal chandeliers, and heavy brocade furnishings. It even had a large greenhouse behind the house, where a gnarled grape vine stretched up to the ceiling glass and was said to have been planted during the Civil War.

Bill had grown into adolescence knowing that nothing more than friendship was possible with Vera given the differences between their families, but appreciating their shared love of art and ideas. They met at the library after school sometimes and just talked. They treated Skipper as their younger brother, though his birthday was only a few months after theirs.

"So school's nearly over." Vera juggled her hair back behind her barrette. "What's next for you both?"

"The draft and being sent wherever," Bill replied. "Not much choice."

"Draft or not, at least I'll get the hell out of this town," Skipper said bitterly. "My stepfather can find someone else to beat up. Bet you feel the same way, Bill."

"My old man's OK." Bill's face set in a hard, defensive glare.

"Whatever you say." Skipper looked away and bent to pet his dog.

"So where do you think you'll go, Skipper?" Vera asked. Skipper straightened up and glowed.

"Korea probably." Skipper tried to sound mature and casual. He kicked a stone along the roadway, sending the little dog running after it.

"What about you, Bill?" Vera turned thoughtful eyes on him.

"I've been talking to the Navy recruiter. Have to wait to be eighteen and get the diploma, but that's coming up."

"You signed up early?" Skipper gasped. Bill had been holding out on him.

"No. You have to be eighteen unless you have your parents' sayso. I didn't want to ask. But I talked with the recruiter and set it up. First my birthday, then graduation, and I'm gone."

Skipper looked impressed. "What's your ma going to say?"

"She'll cry and carry on. That's what she does. She wants me to go to college—Catholic of course. She's hoping I'll become a priest. Not gonna happen." Bill set his shoulders as if he were already preparing to face her. It wasn't going to be pretty and he knew it. His father would be all for the Navy. He told Bill on his seventeenth birthday that it was all right to start smoking. Bill guessed that was his birthday present.

When they reached the waterfront, Vera sat down on the wharf and swung her black and white shoes above the water. The pleats of her tartan skirt spread out around her like a full head of hair. Bill and Skipper sat on either side of her. No one said anything for the moment, so Bill looked at her sideways, noticing the way that the sea wind lifted the curls at the nape of her neck and how her blue eyes changed color when clouds hid the sun.

They looked across the bay to where the shipyard's loading cranes bobbed up and down and people came and went from Quonset huts nestled against non-descript, sand-colored stone buildings where the submarines were built.

"I could go into the Navy with you, couldn't I?" Skipper asked suddenly. "My birthday's only a few weeks after yours. The Navy's better than Korea."

"Guess so," said Bill laconically. He liked the idea of someone from home in the Navy with him, but he didn't want to appear weak by admitting it.

"Maybe I'll go down and talk with them." Skipper brightened up.

"What are you going to do, Vera?" Bill asked.

"I wish I could go with you. Everyone expects me to marry Bob. My mother's been planning the wedding ever since Bob asked me. I told him I needed to think, but she won't let it go and you'd think it was her getting married. She's chosen the pattern for the dress and reserved the church hall. She and my aunt are speaking to one another again because of this wedding, so I suppose that's a plus. But I don't really want to, especially not when Bob's going to be drafted along with everyone else. I'd like to get a job and be independent for a while."

"Couldn't you wait until he gets back?" Skipper asked. "If you love him, of course. And if he loves you."

"I don't know what I feel," Vera said. "It's all confusing. I can't talk with my girlfriends about this because all they can think about is getting married themselves or being bridesmaids. They think he's such a catch."

"Well, he probably is," said Bill. Bob was athletic and good at everything he tried. The local newspaper was full of him and even the state paper was taking note. His family owned the local bank. He was the type of son-in-law that Vera's family would want. Vera's uncle had been a successful lawyer, his wife had been a school principal, and her widowed sister, Vera's mother, had just finished college when she was swept off her feet by an engineering major who was killed in a mine cave-in somewhere out West when Vera was five. The two sisters, both bereft of husbands by the time Vera was twelve, decided to live together in the large, empty house but fought over everything from finances to the cleaning lady. Voices were raised and doors banged until one or the other subsided into silence that could last for days with Vera being asked to carry messages between them. As the only child produced by either of their marriages, Vera had to deal with two ladies united only in their desire to run her life.

"Billy, would you do something because everyone expects you to?" Vera's voice was tremulous and her face clouded. "I've thought about this a lot and I don't know what to do. Bob's a nice guy and I know he's fond of me. But he's very young too. Suppose this is all a huge mistake?"

"I don't know what to tell you," Bill said sincerely. Bad as his situation was at home, he wasn't facing anything like the pressure on Vera. "I'd like to think that I wouldn't do something I didn't want to. But I don't know what I'd do in your place. Like I said, my ma wants me to be a priest. I'm not going to. But I'm not sure that helps you any."

"But you still serve at the altar," she said. "Everyone thinks you're going to a seminary when you graduate."

"I go along with it only so she doesn't get on me. I'll do what I want when the time comes." Bill wished he was as confident as he made himself out to be. Still, on the subject of the priesthood, there was no way he would back down.

Vera did not reply. She swung her feet and stared out across the bay as if trying to peer into the deepest recesses of the world in front of her. Bill felt awkward as if there was something he should be saying to her. By now their soda bottles were empty and he could see little reason to remain where they were, but he didn't want to spoil the moment for her by saying something stupid.

When Vera looked up, her eyes were red. "Thanks for listening, Billy. You too, Skipper."

"What will you do?" Skipper asked.

"I don't know yet. But I'm going to think really hard about it."

A clock struck somewhere in the shipyard and Bill clambered quickly to his feet. He felt glad to be rescued from the feeling of being responsible. He found it hard to deal with emotions. "I'm due at Mass. I'll see you guys later."

He ran the three blocks to the church, passing narrow, gabled houses with identical front yards and entered the sacristy breathless. The other altar boys, already in their lace shawls, had taken up the candlesticks.

Bill quickly slipped on a smock and picked up the crucifix.

"Who's doing service?"

"Father Vincente," one of the boys told him.

Bill felt relieved. He knew the service would not drag on. Father Vincente conducted business with an eye on his watch. He recited the Latin quickly and ended with a gesture of dismissal implying "It's done. Show's over." He also had a curious habit of sighing deeply while his eyes raked the ceiling and his mouth opened in a quick movement that reminded Bill of a parrot stretching its neck. Bill liked him as far as his being a priest went because he was down to earth, took a practical approach to human nature, and seemed genuinely to care. He once told Bill that he felt powerless in the face of so much evil in the world and tried never to inflict more harm on those already suffering. That made him infinitely preferable to Father Onorario who trained his eyes on the fluted stonework of the ceiling like a crucified Christ looking down with disdain on the people who came to the communion rail, and who dispensed judgments that went absolutely by the book. Onorario's incongruous booming voice and manner reminded Bill of a used car salesman.

It was dusk when the service was over, and Bill walked home through streets smelling of family dinners. Once the shipyard day was over, everyone ate at six o'clock and much the same food. One might have pasta fagiole, another spaghetti and meat sauce, another pork chops, all with the same savory smell of garlic, fish on Friday and a roast on Sunday. Life was punctuated by food and church.

His mother took a plate of spaghetti from the oven for him when he sat down at the table.

"Service good?" she asked casually, wanting to hear that Bill was taking the ritual seriously.

"Same as usual," he said dismissively.

Loud voices and laughter came in intermittent bursts from the front room. His mother looked up contemptuously.

"They're eating my pizza and getting drunk," she said. "I don't have alcohol in the house for people to get drunk. Sicilians, they're pigs."

Bill wondered why his mother married his father if she despised his background. But he remembered the pressures on Vera and wondered whether Vera would be happy if she married Bob.

"You had enough?"

Bill nodded and Carolina took the plate away, washing it and putting it back in the ordered cupboard. Her gleaming kitchen floor looked clean enough to eat off.

"You better go to your room. They'll be drinking all evening."

Bill headed up the stairs. He threw himself down on his bed to read. From time to time he could hear laughter and doors slamming. Later on, there was silence and he imagined the guests had left until he heard wailing and yelling and realized that his parents were arguing. Cautiously, he opened the door.

"You clean it up," he heard his father yell belligerently.

"I'm not going to clean up puke from your friends. You do it yourself." Carolina's voice was high pitched and angry. It was starting to be to one of those nights where there would be screams and things broken.

"You're no wife," his father slurred. "The Church this, the Church that, you've started the kid thinkin' he wants to be a fuckin' priest."

"Don't you blaspheme in this house. God's gonna get you."

"Dumb bitch." It seemed to be the worst insult his father's addled mind could conjure at that moment. He spat it out with particular venom.

"Look who's talking. How did I get stuck with you? Sicilians, you're all pigs."

Bill heard the sharp slap of a hand across the face followed by his mother's scream. He didn't know at that moment who had hit whom. He went out onto the landing and looked down. His father had his mother down on the floor and was about to kick her.

"Don't!" Bill screamed

His father swayed and he looked up at Bill. "You keep your nose outta this, you little punk. I don't even think you're mine. Your mother went out catting and there you are."

"That's a lie and you know it," his mother screamed back. She got up and ran outside through the front door. The screen door slammed behind her and knocked a plaster cast of praying hands off the wall. The hands shattered and lay in shards across the floor.

"Come on out, you coward," she screamed from the porch. "Come on out and show the neighbors how you beat your wife."

His father stumbled to the front door and looked stupidly out at his wife. The broken hands crunched under his feet and he kicked a larger piece somewhere into the darkened kitchen.

"Who's gonna clean this up? I can't use the crapper," he said nastily.

"I'm not gonna go in there with you. Get outta my house." Carolina's voice was high and shrill and she became louder as screen doors opened and people came out onto their porches.

"You OK, Carolina?" someone called.

"Yeah, sure," his mother said dramatically. "He hits a woman and won't come out. He's so brave when nobody's watching."

His father backed away from the neighbors' peering eyes. Many were Navy families and he didn't want to be reported. He glanced up to where Bill was standing on the landing.

"What yer looking at, Boy?"

"Nothing," Bill said and backed away to his bedroom.

"Nothing, sir," his father said with narrowed eyes as he started heavily up the stairs. "I've been raising someone else's bastard and it can't even call me sir."

Bill's father was a stocky man, more truck driver than navy officer, the legacy of a youth spent fighting in the Boston streets. It was a tough neighborhood and it produced a tough, angry man. He staggered to the top of the stairs, occasionally banging against the rail, threatening to break through it and fall headlong to the floor. Carolina's shrill voice taunted her husband from outside. She had taken up position on the sidewalk where neighbors gathered in a knot around her.

Bill locked the door to his room, but his father outweighed him by forty pounds and shoved the door out of its frame. It hung uselessly by one hinge.

"Momma's boy," the man sneered as he grabbed Bill by the shirt front and threw him onto his bed. "You're no son of mine."

Bill bounced off the bed onto the floor and tried to crawl away, but his father grabbed him by the collar. "You listen when I'm talking to you. You stupid too?" He then twisted Bill's collar and threw him out on to the landing. Bill landed heavily, stunned for a moment. When he looked up his father was standing over him. A vein throbbed in the temple of his father's flushed face and his eyes had become deep pools of unreflecting black. Bill put up his arms to defend himself. Infuriated, his father grabbed Bill by one arm and threw him hard against the stairwell wall. The house walls shook as Bill tumbled down the stairs and fell in a heap at the bottom.

It was only a few feet to the front door from where Bill had fallen, but it looked unreachable. Out on the sidewalk, he could hear his mother screaming. She sounded like banshees howling in a gale. Off to his side, the kitchen clock hammered out the seconds, click, click, click. As he tried to crawl toward the door, broken pieces of the praying hands scratched under him like sand on a hollow drum. The house smelled of vomit, stale wine, and dirty dishes in the sink. Finally at the front door, Bill looked back up the stairs, but his father had not tried to follow. Then he pushed against the screen door and fell forward out in the open. His mother was the first to spot him. She and the neighbors raced up the cracked sidewalk, but by the time they reached him, he had managed to pull himself to the top of the porch stairs despite a throbbing ankle.

Carolina's face was flushed red and purple with the outline of her husband's hand and she was sobbing uncontrollably. She went to the screen door and screamed at the man she could not see inside.

"You sonofabitch!" she raged through the door. "You hit women, now you beat up your own son. What kinda animal, you?"

Two neighbors pulled Carolina back down the porch stairs and then stood behind Bill separating him from the house and open front door. One put his arm around Bill's shoulders while the other took his arm firmly, between them helping to half-carry him down the stairs to safety. They set Bill down on the grass.

"My baby, my baby. What did he do to you?" Carolina wailed as she sat on the grass beside him and tried to cradle him in her arms.

Bill felt embarrassed and pushed her away. "I'm OK, Ma. Don't make a fuss. I'm OK."

"I think maybe it's a busted ankle," the neighbor from across the road said. This was the man who paid Bill to cut his lawn.

"His ear's cut, but it don't seem too bad," another one said. Bill didn't recognize who he was, but the man sounded kind and concerned.

"Where else you hurt?" the first man asked.

"I said I was all right," Bill said. "My shoulder's just a bruised." He tried to stand up but fell back in pain.

"You betta stay off that ankle. You need someone to look at it."

His mother sobbed helplessly. "All this because his friends threw up all over the bathroom and he won't clean up the mess himself. Sonofabitch. Lazy bastard. Wife beater." She screamed the names to the silent house.

"I'll get my car and we'll drive Bill to the hospital," said the neighbor from across the street.

"I'm fine," Bill said desperately. "It's a sprain. I'm fine."

"Look, kid," said the neighbor. "Your ankle isn't sitting straight. No more nonsense, OK? I'll get something to stabilize it."

"I tripped down the stairs, all right?" Bill said stubbornly as they lifted him onto his good foot and helped him hop out to the street.

"The sonofabitch, he did it," said his mother as she followed them.

"No, Ma, he didn't do nothing. I tell you, I tripped down the stairs."

"You expect me to believe you?" Carolina's voice was accusing and aggrieved.

"It's true, Ma, I fell down the stairs."

The house was quiet behind them. No one could tell whether his father was passed out or was watching from the windows.

Carolina screamed one last insult "Sicilian pig. Then she got in beside Bill in the neighbor's car. Bill was glad when the car drove out of the road and left the silent house behind. His ankle, carefully tied between two pieces of wood to immobilize it, was starting to swell.

"It's a clean break. Should heal well," the doctor said when they got to the dispensary. "You'll need to wear a cast for six weeks or so. You're young. It should heal quickly."

"I'm joining the Navy as soon as school is out. Will that be a problem?"

Bill heard his mother draw in her breath sharply.

"Shouldn't be. If the military turned down everyone who had ever broken a bone, they'd have no one left to serve. We'll take you down in a few minutes to set the bone and put on the cast. Just relax for now. OK?"

Bills nodded as the doctor drew aside the curtains and left him with his mother.

"Well, Mister Sailor, when did you come to this great decision?" Carolina was working herself up into an outburst and Bill tried not to look at her.

"I've been talking with a recruiter since last year."

"Why didn't you tell me about this?"

"I thought it would be soon enough when I was ready to go."

"What about college?"

"I know what you're thinking but I've got no calling to be a priest. You said yourself you need a calling."

"It's that girl, isn't it? She's put ideas in your head. I told you to stay away from her."

"What girl?" Bill was genuinely perplexed.

"That Vera you sneak out to see. I saw you walk out of the store with her today. You told me you were with Skipper. You never said nothing about her. I thought no son of mine would lie to his mother. I told you not to talk to her. She's not right for you. I pray you find the right woman if that's what you want. Not this one. Find someone your own kind."

"I didn't sneak out to see her. She was just in the store and all three of us just talked. I don't know what you're going on about."

"She's the one told you not to be a priest. She's said to go in the Navy. Swear on the Holy Mother you won't talk to her again."

"She's my friend like Skipper. I'm not going to promise that I won't talk with her."

"You're breaking my heart. You go talk to Father Vincente and confess what you've done. You're not a good son. You don't honor your mother."

"I already talked to him. He agreed that I don't have the calling to be a priest and he wished me luck in the Navy."

Carolina sat down heavily in the chair beside the bed. Her hand clutched convulsively at her chest.

"Why don't people tell me things? My own son. My priest says nothing."

"I told him not to."

"You got no right, and he should know better. Now you leave me alone with this animal."

"He'll be all right when he gets sober. He always is."

"He's a pig."

"So leave him."

"Where do I go? You tell me. I married him when I was seventeen. I got no real skills for a job. Who's going to take care of me? My heart is broken."

Bill sighed and looked at the ceiling. He wondered what his mother's heart might look like. It couldn't be good because it had been broken so many times. Would it be shattered like the praying hands on the floor or would it be pierced by arrows like the painting hung on the wall inside the church door? He couldn't deal with his parents' troubles. He knew only his mother's side. His father kept silent until he drank too much and released in one violent outburst all the angers and irritations built up since the last explosion. Bill had only a small child's memories of his father before he went to war. He suspected that war must have changed him, but he didn't know how.

"Don't you sigh at me, Mister," his mother said angrily. "I deserve some respect here. You may be taller than me, but I can get on a chair and discipline you."

"If I wait until I get drafted, it's the army. I'm going either way. I prefer to choose."

"It's not fair. We just get done with one war and only a few years later, here's another. It was bad enough what it's done to your father. I wanted to protect you, see you safe in college. They don't draft if you're in seminary."

"We're all going, Ma. No one's safe anywhere. It's what's going on in the world."

Carolina held her hand to her chest, finally admitting defeat. "I'll pray to the Good Lord for you every day." The tears coursed down her cheeks. "I hate the war. I hate your father for doing this to you."

"I told you, Ma, I tripped going down the stairs."

7:00 p.m.

I WASN'T GOING *to give my mother more ammunition against my father even I if couldn't love someone who said I wasn't his son whenever he was angry with my mother. I'm not sure what I felt about him, but I don't remember feeling any sadness when I heard he'd died, just about the time Anna was about to give birth to Michael. By then, my parents had been long divorced and he was living with some girlfriend. Someone sent me his watch later, but it got stolen and that was the last I ever had of his or even heard of him. Anna ordered his birth certificate once when she was on a family-tracing kick and even that was a surprise. His father was a barber who emigrated from Salerno and was processed through Ellis Island. I hadn't known that.*

But then I never knew my father. When he stood over me on the stairs, I looked up into uncomprehending, almost manic eyes, black as the clouds before a summer-heat storm. I had never felt pure terror before. I knew that he meant to hurt me. He was not my father, but some force out of nature, something before life itself, and something malevolent. Perhaps he also realized that he had crossed some line because after that night he and I never spoke and never looked one another in the eyes. On the day I left to be inducted, only my mother came to the train station. Neither of us mentioned him.

God knows what my father saw when he was away in the Pacific. Sometimes when he was in a good mood, he let me look at his service book, perkily called "My Days in the Service," as if it were a Boy Scout book. In it were pictures of the men he had served with but there was also one of a grinning Fijian holding the severed head of a Japanese soldier. I can't forget the dead man's sunken eyes and his gaping mouth. These are not the sort of things that a man forgets. I was eight when he shipped out and thirteen when he came back for good—a lot of time to lose. He'd been in heavy fighting. I knew that but not much more because he never talked about it. Perhaps if he had been able to, maybe if an anguish could have been released, he might have been different. But there was no one to listen to him who could understand. I think of him as a broken man who could not reclaim the pieces of his life. I prefer to think that to remembering him as violent and mean.

Strangely enough, I envied him in some ways. My mother never insisted that he go to services and confession. I think she liked the idea he might go to hell, so she never argued with him. Not like she did with me if I missed a service. All I know is that I joined the Navy to get as far away as I could from both of them.

As I grew up, the Church defined everything. It said what was bad and gave out the punishments. It made the rules and could enforce them. It even defined what was on the dinner table. It reminded me of a terrarium I had once. The only way for things inside to escape was to smash the glass. I'm not sure I really broke that glass where the Church was concerned, although marrying Anna was certainly the most visible rebellion I ever made. Anna, in fact, was the Vera of my adult years; she even reminded me of her with her wistful questing into life. But through it all, I maintained my detachment. I never directly confronted my mother with the fact of my hostility to her religious preoccupations and I never told Anna about Vera. How selfish and hypocritical it seems now.

Here comes a new confusion in my thinking. I have always said that I despise hypocrisy, but was that only because I saw it in myself? Why couldn't I be honest enough to say what I really thought and why did I let my mother continue to believe that I had drifted away from the Church because of Anna? It's an uncomfortable feeling, this looking in the mirror and not liking the person who looks back.

I stretch and groan in disgust. This revisiting the past is not working for me. I don't want to confront the question of my own passivity. I don't want to think, and I certainly don't want to analyze anything. That's Anna's show. I just want to be left alone. That's all I have ever asked. Just leave me alone. Let the past be the past and not make too much of it. I don't have the intellect and generosity of soul to deal with these issues. "Make this all stop," I say and close my eyes tightly. But my feelings don't seem to matter. When I open my eyes again, I am in a sun-lit garden.

Chapter 5

Bishop of Anagni's Villa, near Siena, June 1568

Two old men walked within the walls of an enclosed private garden. One was Aonio Paleario. The other was the Bishop of Anagni, Marco's uncle, the man who sent the warning to Aonio through his nephew.

Despite being officially retired, the bishop still wore his dark ecclesiastical robes out of long habit and perhaps out of pride. His bearing was erect, but his age showed in the few strands of dark hair left at the back of his head. the thinning grey everywhere else, and the pink where his scalp showed through. His dark eyes made him look of southern descent, perhaps with the Spanish blood of the rulers of Naples. In his dark complexion and the dark color of his robes, he looked as if he had stepped out of a Titian painting: the same Titian deep-set eyes, the narrow pointed beard, and the shrewdness of someone who has learned to manage politics and human nature. He was not a zealot and he was not a fool—he could not afford to be in dangerous times.

The bishop's small villa loomed behind them. It was two solid stories built of local stone, with two symmetrical rows of windows deeply set along its length. It was a dignified house, very Palladian, ordered and balanced in keeping with the ethic of its day, with a simple set of scrubbed semi-circular steps at the back leading down to the garden. Alongside the main building were outlying buildings serving as greenhouses and storage sheds. Nothing seemed out of place and everything looked manicured. It was the home of someone enjoying comfort and establishment, not ostentatious but well appointed and complacent.

The two men walked together through the villa's vegetable plots set alongside a gravel causeway that ended at the bishop's private garden, where confidential conversations could be held. The bishop stopped at the entrance gate of his garden to look at the grapevines growing around the entrance. He was the creator, he had ordered this place, and he was pleased with what he saw. Then he led his old friend down a set of stairs into the secret pleasures of the things that he kept for himself.

"I asked Marco to bring you my message." The bishop pushed away a tendril of ivy, carefully tucking it behind a trellis as they entered.

"I was grateful." Paleario spoke with restraint and proper politeness.

"I had thought you might use the time . . . usefully." The bishop spoke with a slight distaste and even a touch of reproof. He had expected Paleario to take the hint and be safe in Germany by now, not forcing him to have this conversation.

"You thought I might leave my home and country?" Aonio asked rather too bluntly.

The bishop recoiled at the indelicate response. He did not like bringing matters so clearly out in the open. "You're a lawyer, Aonio, " he said. "You know what the Church does to the family and property of anyone it convicts of heresy."

"I know." Aonio clasped his hands behind his back. He looked down studiedly at the pathway as they walked along it.

"Yet you have decided to go to Rome?" The bishop raised his voice slightly to let the accusation hang in the air. There was no need for this nonsense. The Vatican had expected Paleario to flee rather than force this confrontation. Why was this man making it difficult for everyone?

"They are wrong."

"Who is wrong?" the bishop asked.

"The Vatican. The pope. Most particularly the ignorant priests and monks that they set loose on the people."

"I see," the bishop said.

The men walked along a path amidst the scent of roses wet with early morning moisture clinging to the petals in shimmering globules. The flowerbeds were emptying of early pansies and anemones but buds had formed amidst light and dark green shoots promising carnations and phlox. The bishop stopped in a small grotto to admire a statue of Hercules entwined with a serpent. Hercules strained in agony as he twisted the serpent's neck. The serpent's sinuous coils wound tightly around him, pressing deeply into his flesh.

"I have never known the Church to consider the possibility of being wrong," the bishop said slowly. "Did not Christ promise Peter that the Church would be perfect and removed from the possibility of error?"

"Yet highly placed men in the Church, among them former popes, have been excommunicated by their successors because of perceived errors."

"Is this what you want to present in Rome?" the bishop asked. "You strike to the heart of Church doctrine and I can promise you that you will not get far with it."

"But it's self-evident that there are Church doctrines without any justification in the Bible."

"Self-evident?" The bishop spoke distastefully. "Many will disagree with you. This is a matter for Church fathers to settle. Synods have been called where this was discussed." The bishop abruptly changed the subject before Aonio could object that there had been no freedom of discussion at these meetings. "When do you report to Rome?"

Aonio did not try to argue. He realized that the bishop wished for the conversation to be over but was too polite to say so.

They walked on past an apple tree espaliered against the wall. The blossoms would soon drop and the fruit form in their place.

"I have been permitted to complete the school year at the university. The City of Milan insisted on receiving its money's worth for my salary." Aonio offered this by way of explanation for his lack of departure, but they both knew it was not the reason.

"Over the years since the Inquisition was restarted," the bishop said thoughtfully, "I have watched men and women undergo its examination. Most were frightened and recanted freely, returning gratefully to the arms of the Church. Some have been more reluctant but have been persuaded. You are the only one I know who embraces this. Have you reached the point where your faith has become obstinacy? Are you determined to become a martyr, and if so to what end?"

"I believe excellent scholarship and the discovery of truth are worthy ends in themselves."

"Among generous, scholarly minds perhaps. But the Church has different interests, don't you think? I fear you have mistaken your own ideas and preoccupations for ideals that you expect everyone else to adopt."

They resumed their walk between the heady fragrance of two rows of rose beds. The bishop stopped before one particular rose with the velvet color of aged, orange silk. When he lightly touched a petal, it set off a wine-like fragrance.

"You are so determined to become a martyr that you cannot be dissuaded?" the bishop asked.

"Dissuade me from arguing my case before the Church? I am nearly seventy. My father died in his fifties. My children are grown. What would I do in a foreign country when every part of me would wish to be back here?"

"You could write and teach. You could explore new forms of beauty and art. You could focus on law and jurisprudence and leave theology alone. Others have done so. I hoped you would choose this path."

"What would I find in Germany beyond a demeaning survival?

People would say I fled because I lacked the courage of my convictions. And what joy is it to be among the Protestants? They have broken with the orthodoxy of the Catholic Church only to establish one of their own. I have been gravely disappointed. They have no interest in truth and scholarship. I've heard what happened to Michael Servetus at the hand of his former friend John Calvin. They strapped his books to him, piled green wood up to his neck, and set fire to it. All because he wanted the freedom to study the Bible on his own. Protestants burn truth as readily as Catholics when they have the power. It is the nature of absolute belief. No, I have little interest in fleeing from the truth. There is nowhere I can run."

"Don't you also have absolute belief, Aonio?" the bishop asked. "Do you think offering yourself to be tried by the Inquisition will make any difference in the long run?"

"I have no wish to limit what others believe. I wish to be free to examine my own beliefs. The word of God is the one absolute source of truth. The Church not only wants to prescribe what we should think but how we should think it."

The bishop straightened up from his rose bushes. His robes rustled slightly with his movement.

"What is your alternative, Aonio? Do you wish to destroy belief when you have nothing to replace it?"

"Human beings are responsible for their own souls. People can build their faith much better when they build on the authentic words of God." Aonio looked up at the cumulous clouds promising evening rain. He wondered when people abdicated their responsibility to find truth for themselves in spiritual matters.

"But who determines whether the words of God are authentic if not the Church Fathers?" the bishop countered. "Or do you believe everyone should be free to create faith based on whatever interpretation they place on the words in the Bible? Are you proposing everyone build a private religion? We should have thousands."

"Precisely why we need to be free to evaluate the original languages. Any translation must be true to the sources," Aonio said eagerly. "People can freely agree on a true religion once they know the truth."

"Then salvation is to be based on the agreements formed by scholars such as you who believe that they know what words mean?" The bishop sounded unimpressed. "You know that individual conscience is the goal of the German reformers."

Aonio stroked his hand nervously across his beard. In a formal debate on a university campus, he would have been forced to concede a major point to the bishop.

"When there is truth—an accurate translation of the works, without the intervention of human hands on the words of God—we will have true piety," Aonio replied carefully. "I am not subverting the Catholic Church. I am a deeply religious man. I ask to live free to glorify God in His universe and by the words He gave us. My quarrel is with what the Church has chosen to interject between us and God. Surely the Church is stronger for the truth. I can't help it if people choose to see a tendency to reform in what I think."

"These are dangerous ideas, Aonio. The Catholic Church does not deal in tendencies. Only in absolutes. You question the Holy Fathers who have provided us with authoritative interpretations of the Bible. They have shown us how to please God. You must yourself understand that when men's eyes fix on the world instead of on the Church, mankind will return to chaos and danger. You were there when Rome was destroyed. It could happen again. It is the responsibility of the Church to stop this happening."

"The Church has taken this role upon itself," Aonio said indignantly. "No one I know of has agreed to such a bargain. The Church imposes peace by suppressing all disagreement. Tyrants impose such solutions."

The bishop sat on a bench in front of a large, circular grotto where water trickled over mossy stones. There was a statue of David there, bent double as he put a stone into his slingshot. If the garden were a maze, this grotto was the sanctuary from which all pathways radiated.

"The Church," said the bishop gravely, "wants to remove doubt. It builds its rituals and doctrines on what has gone before to create goodness and happiness among mankind. If the Church does not uphold the law, there is no civil government strong enough to hold the people together."

"Then," said Aonio. "if the Church represents such certainty in pleasing God, how does one explain the destruction of Rome and the desecration of the Vatican?"

"That involves the nature of evil in the world," the bishop said. "Surely you cannot blame God for what man does. There is the matter of free choice. Men choose to be evil."

"But how can there be free will if the Church decides what men should believe?"

"The Church guides men to what is good. Then they must decide whether to accept what they have been given. You have children, Aonio. Did you not guide them to see the right choices and did you not show them when they were approaching error? The Church acts as a loving parent who hopes that those who stray will recover their souls by finding their salvation in belief and turn away from their former ways."

"Then what happens when the Church itself is evil?"

"The Church cannot be evil. If there is any harm, and I dispute that, it is caused by the people who misunderstand and do harm in its name. These matters are well established."

"So the destruction of Rome was God cleaning out those who erred in his name?"

"No," the bishop said firmly. "It was the princes of Europe misunderstanding God's intention. The Church suffered from their errors. And need I remind you it was not long after the troops had been withdrawn and the pope returned to his see that these same princes came on bended knee begging for forgiveness. That is the work of God in the world. As God's representative on earth, the Church wishes to avoid strife and contention and offer the way to personal salvation."

Aonio sat beside him. "By selling indulgences and extracting payment for penances?"

"I do not find offerings to the Church as repugnant as you imply," the bishop replied levelly. "Even the Church must feed itself. But if those salving their consciences by sharing their God-given wealth find comfort and greater faith, a positive end has been served by it."

Aonio stared moodily at the water trickling over the stones. It was as if the statue of David were bleeding into the little pool at his feet. He wondered for a moment whether the gulf between him and the bishop had always been this wide. Did he not see it earlier because he wanted to believe that his arguments had won over a Churchman? How could he have been so vain?

"I would say the Church does not serve your need to find the truth you want," the bishop continued. "There are other truths and you must respect them. The Inquisition will find the truth it wants within the walls of the Vatican prison. There will be no dark corners to hide you. There will be little light and a great deal of unhappiness."

The bishop smoothed his robes, running his fingers down the black beads of his rosary.

"Do you believe in confessions gained by torture?" Aonio asked.

The bishop looked down at violets growing wild in the edges of the beds and sighed. "The rules about this date back to Gui's time several hundred years ago. Confessions under torture are not valid. They must be voluntarily repeated the next day."

"Under the threat of pain, someone may be desperate enough to confess to anything. What happens the next day if the prisoner cannot remember what was confessed to?"

Aonio knew the answer. He wanted the bishop to admit it.

"Are you trying to persuade me to contradict myself? Show myself to be illogical? You are not Socrates talking with his students. A dialog works only with people willing to accept its conclusions. Even if you have the chance to speak to anyone in Rome, which I doubt, the Vatican will deny your points of logic no matter how eloquently you present them, and then where will you be? What may seem so glaringly obvious to you will just be brushed aside. But, yes, you are right. There have been such cases where the prisoner could not remember, and the first confession has always been ruled not genuine. I was never involved with the Holy Office of the Inquisition and I am very glad of it."

"So the torture would resume?"

"What is your point, Aonio? You are not hearing me. The Inquisition was set up to assure certainty about life and death. Because we cannot find that on earth, as individuals, we must turn to spiritual community. There have been many assaults upon the Church; you know that as well as I do. The only thing we have ever been able to count on is our faith. It is our community and our salvation. As long as we obey the laws we have been given, we can maintain our faith intact and endure as human beings. This is mankind's hope you are bent on destroying."

"Yet you encouraged me to leave this community and flee to Germany, the site of the greatest threat to this security you describe?"

"Aonio, I have respected you as a man of integrity. I have felt for you all the love of a friend. I do not see in you someone who wishes to destroy the faith upon which others build their lives. I also do not want to see you imprisoned in Rome as an enemy of the Church. But you must ask yourself whether the Church has any choice. Should one individual be allowed to threaten the communal security of faith? You wish the right to individual conscience, and this makes you dangerous. I myself have stepped a careful path. It was my duty to uphold the Catholic Church, and I took Jesuits and Dominicans among my closest advisors. It is the times we live in."

"So you want me to outwardly conform? I could not live with the personal consequences of that decision. It is not a way open to me."

"I cannot urge you to hypocrisy in the name of friendship. If you were to conform, it must be to uphold the community of faith. If you were a lesser man and you kept the secrets of your heart, you might not be such a threat. But you have openly challenged preachers in the streets."

"Once. I exposed a wandering monk who was preaching nonsense." Aonio remembered the man well. He was grossly misrepresenting the Scriptures and denouncing Aonio by name, an insult that could not be ignored. Aonio proved the man's ignorance in a public lecture, leaving the monk to slink back to his monastery amid general scorn. Aonio had savored a sweet moment of vindication. But he had thought that the matter had been settled by a mutual apology. Apparently not.

"He was a Dominican and I believe you publicly called him a wild swine. They have long memories and are prepared to wait their turn to take revenge. When you expose one of them, you incur the enmity of them all." The bishop shook his head at the folly.

Aonio did not reply. The man's slander was not to be tolerated. But even beyond the monk's personal attack on him, there was the matter of truth. The man was spreading his ignorance among people who might believe him.

The two men stood and silently walked along a wall lined with tall cypress. Aonio felt the total breach between them. Since there was nothing now to lose, Aonio devised an abstraction about the nature of the world and, by long habit, formulated it into a proposition. He hoped that he might still be able to explain his motives to the bishop even if he could not persuade his friend to see the logic of his position.

"In times of political and economic struggle," Aonio asked, "is there is no room for individual integrity and truth?"

"But whose truth, Aonio? I have enjoyed debating with you through the years. But there are real consequences now. Since you are determined to go to Rome, once you get there, there will be no debate. You will have no control over the process. Your inquisitors will be handpicked by the pope. These inquisitors will be ambitious men early in their careers. They will use you as a steppingstone to their advancement in the Church and will do whatever the Vatican asks. For the most part they will be sincere. They will truly believe your confession and penitence will save your soul. Any pain they inflict will be justified as the price of the cure.

Your soul is more important to them than your body."

"This is where I stand against the pope and the Inquisition. We alone are the guardians of our souls, not the cardinals, not the pope, not greedy, ambitious inquisitors. Our souls are a precious gift for which we must answer later to our maker."

"I have known His Holiness from the days when he first came to the Vatican," the bishop said thoughtfully. "He is as committed to truth as you. He was like a wise prophet when we were both young priests. He loved to debate as you do. But he chose a different path and has accepted responsibility for the collective good of the faithful. He became bitter after the destruction of Rome, but he is still a worthy man committed to the service of God and to restoring the Holy Church to those days before there was schism."

"Then isn't talking with me dangerous for you?"

"You are merely being investigated. I may well be trying to dissuade you from your errors."

"And have you been asked to?" Aonio looked into the bishop's eyes as if trying to see into his soul.

"Yes, Aonio, I was asked to talk with you to see if you could be persuaded back into the arms of the Church. No one wants to see you tried and executed. Rome prefers to see you renounce the teachings of your book on the benefits of Christ's death. You argued there that salvation comes from divine grace and not through Church teaching. But I am not the only one. The Bishop of Colle from your own district has also been asked. He mentioned it to me immediately because he knows you and I to be old friends."

"And are you going to report our conversation to Rome?"

"Yes. I must report it. But I will attest to your piety and earnest feeling for all things holy. It will also be a marvel of polite assurance. I cannot be your defender, but I will not be your enemy."

"What about Fra Pietro?" Aonio was starting to view everyone around him as a potential spy for Rome.

The bishop frowned. "Fra Pietro? What of him?"

"He's one of the priests attached to Colle. Don't you know him?"

"Yes, I know him. But Fra Pietro keeps his thoughts private." A long silence. "He is an ambitious man. I would not make my confession to him."

"I never have. But my wife has relied on him to provide instruction to our children."

"Are you worried about them?"

"If you are asking if I have I shared my work with my family, the answer is no. Marietta knows nothing. My son is a lawyer and knows the value of silence. My daughter Caterina is married. I worry more about the youngest, Beatrice."

"You think she might have repeated things she has heard in the household?"

Aonio looked pained. "Beatrice has delighted me with her eagerness to learn, and I have taught her many things. If she had been a boy, she would have made a fine scholar. She understands the dangers of the world and she has a firm grasp of how human beings treat one another. Of all my children, I think her the most talented of my children, and I should have liked her to pursue her studies more thoroughly. But she is a woman, and a young one at that. There are limits to what she can do, and her future is unclear. At one point I had hoped that Marco might have feelings for her. But it would be most unwise for him now to jeopardize his future by association with my family."

The bishop nodded. "Marco has a good heart, but he is young and dependent on my brother. By nature Marco is compliant, and he is also powerless to step outside the pathway the family has chosen for him. If he is ordered to have no contact with your family, he must obey. So your doubts are well founded."

The two men stopped at the foot of the mossy stairs leading out of the garden. The only sounds were birdcalls, the hum of insects, and the grate of their shoes on the pathway.

"Do you think Fra Pietro has used his position with your daughter to learn things about you?" The bishop looked at his friend with sad eyes. He was glad that he had his garden to cultivate, far away from Rome and its intrigues.

"He may have tried. I doubt he learned much. But if he chooses to claim otherwise, we have little with which to challenge him. I cannot believe that Beatrice told him anything damaging, but if there was anything said it was only because she did not understand the implications. As I said, she is intelligent, and I have seen that she had a good rudimentary education, but life is complicated and words can be misconstrued. I accept the responsibility if she did tell him something that can be used against me."

"Heavy concerns, Aonio. But with whatever limited opportunity I have, I'll speak with the bishops of Colle and Siena and do my best to see your family is not troubled."

"I shall bless you a hundred times. Things were much easier in the old days when the Church was content to let matters be and people did not betray one another."

"I must warn you," the bishop said as they slowly climbed the stairs from the private garden and stopped at the gate, "that it is customary for the local priest to be involved in the investigation. Fra Pietro will certainly be asked to Rome. Everything will be secret. You will have no chance to question him yourself. In fact, you will not know who testifies for or against you or who issued the complaint against you."

"I'm sure I know already. My enemies in Siena have long tried to attack me because I defended the Bellanti family and proved the charges made against them were based on envy and greed. Siena is rife with factions and while I am proud that I helped my friends, it has long been my regret that I became involved with that city's politics."

"I wouldn't make assumptions. If you have guessed incorrectly, you may go astray in preparing your defense. But you should know whenever the Church inquires into heresy, there is always someone in the household who reports to Rome."

"A spy?" Aonio remembered Marco's warning at the villa. He had still not settled on whom he thought it might be.

"If you wish to call it such." The bishop closed the gate and they started to walk toward the villa.

"I find it painful to believe someone has betrayed me." Aonio tried to speak levelly without revealing the depth of his feelings.

"It's the way of the world, Aonio. This person may believe the path to heaven must be littered with the bones of those who betray the certainty of belief. Sometimes the mere exchange of money is enough. But there is always one who can be convinced. You might look into this yourself when you go home on the way to Rome."

"I plan to go directly to Rome."

The bishop stopped and raised his eyebrows in surprise. "Your family will not be able to visit you in Rome. Your wife may come if she will but not your children."

"I doubt she will want to." Aonio did not look at the bishop. He did not want to go into the relations between members of his family.

"Well, you know best about such things. But may I ask why?"

Aonio looked at the gentle green hills in the distance. Not far away, he saw a donkey cart stopped in a lane while the driver talked lightly with a young girl whose hair was tied up in a bright red scarf. That scene of country life seemed remarkable to him. The young people were not concerned with ideas and beliefs. Their life was going on even if he was about to be tried for heresy. He supposed that life would always go on, but perhaps those living hundreds of years after him might be more committed to finding truth.

"When I began my scholarly work," Aonio said, "I believed I could be a scholar and also have a family. But it proved much more difficult. My wife came from a wealthy family and had expensive tastes. I was forced to provide her with a suitable house that brought heavy debt. My son needed an education and my daughters their dowries. I had to move from place to place wherever I was offered work. Marietta and I agreed that she and the children would stay at our villa in Colle, and I would come when I could. The years passed. I sent my earnings and came home in the summers. When I could afford it, Marietta and the children came to stay with me. But I was not there when Marietta nearly died giving birth to Fedro and I missed many things, particularly with my daughters. Caterina married and slipped away to her husband. I had more time with Beatrice because the family was with me in Milan for a time, but she too is grown. They are busy with their lives and I am the absent father who abandoned them. I expect no support from them, nor would I ask it."

"You do not think your son would want to say farewell to you?"

"No. He is a lawyer. His thoughts will be with securing his mother's property. I have trained him well, and in his place I should do the same."

"I must believe you are far too harsh both on yourself and on your family."

"I'd like to believe so, for I love my wife and children. But I do not want to test their affection or cause them more pain than I already have. I believe this is the easiest way."

"Easiest for them or for you, Aonio?"

"I believe for both."

"You do know that your family will not love you for your decision."

"I believe I have their respect for the things to which I have devoted my life." Aonio's voice rose in the passion of his certainty.

"But is respect the same as affection? Do they share your love of these things that are so important to you? Will they willingly share in your separation from the Church?"

"They must understand the importance of what I do is for the benefit of all mankind."

"And if they don't?"

"Then I have not taught them well."

"Aonio, I weep for you then and will remember you in my prayers."

"I thank you for your friendship" Aonio replied quietly. There was nothing more to say. He knew he would never see the bishop or his garden ever again.

8:00 p.m.

*T*HE NAUSEA HAS *gone. Perhaps they aren't giving me as much morphine because I'm not waking so often. I feel numb but also restless and agitated. I am saddened but not surprised by the bishop's accommodation and outward conformity. He probably fancied himself quite the rebel by discussing spiritual matters with Aonio, but those were different times and now such discussions have become dangerous. Conforming is the only prudent thing he can do in a world gone mad. There's nothing he can do about ultimate power being in the hands of self-serving people willing to manipulate fear. All he feels he can do is keep a low profile, cultivate his own garden, be wary of anyone who might expose him, and be damned to the rest. It's the times we live in, the bishop says. How much should corruption matter as long as one has a garden of one's own? I admit it, I've lived in my own garden too. I've been rocked to sleep in Plato's cave while my life passed by outside. Why is it that we think only of purpose and death at the very last hours of our lives, when we should be thinking about them all the way through, marveling at the gift of the present that we have been given?*

So what right do I have to judge the bishop? Simple answer, I don't have any. I still don't like what he stands for. He doesn't like torture much. It's distasteful. But he's part of the Church that's doing it. He believes he must accommodate to whomever's in power. If he sees injustice, it's just the times we live in. This delicate intellectual dance absolves him of responsibility for anything that happens to him or around him. He is the premier solipsist of the way we live our lives: if he doesn't see it, it doesn't exist.

Still, I'm not sure I like Aonio much better. Am I supposed to care about him? What does he think he'll prove by going to Rome? He's been warned enough that it's futile. The bishop's right. His family is not going to love him for this, particularly if it costs them their security. I'm willing to bet his family would tell him the same thing as the bishop has: Accommodate. Except he hasn't given them the choice. It sounds as if they have their own gardens too. But are they wrong? If they have conformed, worked hard, and prospered, haven't they earned their reward however they define it? Why should he be able to destroy their lives in the name of ideas they don't share?

A man could go crazy trying to figure this all out.

What a pair we are. Aonio who wants to sacrifice himself to truth. Me who deliberately detached from it. Why was I so repelled by intellect? Was there something fearful in my soul? Did I think seeking truth would box me into some corner where I would become responsible for other people? All I know is that I didn't want to be responsible for anything beyond myself. Anna never asked much of me, and I took what she offered without asking why she gave it. But I'm starting to think there were a lot more strings than I ever realized.

And as for this business with intellect, much as I denied it, it crept up on me. "Write," it demanded. And so I did in the later stages of my illness, where no one could question what I thought and meant. I wrote, and I did it in secret. I was not the public man seeking truth in public place like Aonio, but the damaged man hiding from the consequences of thinking. Was I wrong? Or is there no such thing as right or wrong, and are we to be judged by the results of our actions without concern for the reasons we do them? Anna will be dismayed when she learns that I wrote in private and never discussed my ideas with her. She will learn about it the worst possible way—by finding the writing that I kept secret from her. She will assume that I never trusted her. She will not understand that I had to do it that way. I do not understand yet myself why it had to be so.

I have no answers and no explanations. All this forced thinking is difficult for me. I need to sleep. I need not to think so much. If I must revisit my past in these final hours of life, why can't I see something happier? I want to be back in my own time, where things seem more clear and easier to deal with. I close my eyes and wish myself away.

Chapter 6

Pusan Harbor, April 1953

M AYBE THE PEACE talks will work this time." Skipper pushed back his white Dixie-cup hat and rubbed his hairline. They were off duty, lounging at the back of the troop transport they'd been assigned to, watching cranes deposit cargo crates on the crowded docks below, to be tallied before Korean longshoremen loaded then onto waiting trains destined for the front up north. Two ships had docked at once, creating a frenzy of unloading.

"They've been talking ever since we first got over here," Bill replied. "Then they keep on fighting. Pusan's full of refugees sleeping under bridges or in the cartons our equipment came in. I don't know how they survive." He was troubled by the misery he had seen and by the helpless feeling that there was nothing he or anyone else could do about it.

"It's worse up north," Skipper said. "One of the infantry guys on rotation told me that Seoul's in ruins. On the train coming down here, he gave his rations to the orphans lined up along the tracks wherever the train stopped. Everyone gave away their food. It's heartbreak, he said. Another one cried when he told me he'd seen a Korean mother and two babies lying frozen in a ditch."

"Those are the guys who deserve medals," Bill says. "I don't know why they're giving us swabbies anything. They should save them for the Marines who were at Inchon and Chosin and the infantry up by the Yalu River. They did the fighting, not us on this tub. All we did was ferry troops and supplies from San Francisco and Seattle to Sasebo and Pusan."

Bill shook his head. All the killing and the suffering seemed pointless. He had no wish to know about international politics. No one ever explained to him why he was in Korea. He came because he had to. He also came to get away from the drama of his parents. He patted the pack of Camels in the pocket of his blue fatigue shirt, ten cents a pack in the ship's store. He was impatient for the loudspeaker to announce that the smoking light was on. Smoking helped to ease the boredom and had become part of his life since his father said he was old enough to smoke.

"If they sign the peace papers, we'll probably get discharged pretty quick." Skipper sounded hopeful, as if he had much to go back to. He'd been thinking about what to do once he heard it might be over soon. So far he hadn't seen much on the horizon, but then he was always the optimist and believed that something would show up. It had to. He couldn't go back to the family crowded into two rooms lorded over by his mother's second husband. Once a child was out of that house, he wasn't welcomed back.

"Maybe. Our enlistments are up soon anyway." Bill never let enthusiasm get in the way of doubt. He had plenty of doubt about wanting to be in the same town as his father. The old man nearly killed him last time. Bill might not be so lucky as to get away with just a broken ankle if there were a next time. He couldn't forget that terrible blackness in his father's eyes. They were the eyes of a circling shark.

Skipper looked enquiringly at Bill. "Have you thought about what happens after we get out?"

"Only that I'm going to use the GI Bill to go to school. I'm thinking about art," Bill said.

"Art? But you're an electrician's mate—technical stuff."

"You mean I should be looking at more practical things?" Bill was amused at the assumptions Skipper was making.

"Maybe. I dunno. Who the hell am I to know?" Skipper backed away. He hadn't wanted to offend Bill, merely to see whether he could borrow ideas from him. Skipper tried not to offend anyone.

"I like math and science. But I like art as well, better I think. I've been doing sketches over here. Maybe I'll show you some. So are you going to be an engineer since you've worked down there?"

"Not after seeing what being in the engine room does to you. The chief checks the gauges wearing his pajamas. Which is OK, except they have large red lips printed on them. I figure it must be boredom, or else the smell of diesel has driven him loony. Sometimes I think I'm going to miss the Navy. Remember the pictures we took in San Francisco? The one where we dressed like gangsters and made out we were drinking whisky? I'm going to miss having someone to do crazy things with. These guys have been like family."

"Well, you've got a choice where you get discharged. You can go with them," Bill said. "Most of them came from the East Coast so they'll be heading home."

"All I know right now is that I'm gonna stay as far away from home as I can. I don't care if I starve. I'll find a job, open a shop, and fix cars one day," Skipper said.

"Cars?" Bill raised his eyebrows quizzically. This was the first he had heard Skipper talk about it.

"I've learned a lot in the engine room. I figure to get trained as an apprentice mechanic with the GI bill and save up for my own shop. Doesn't matter where I am. I hear the guys talking about their girls and about how their families are planning parties and welcome banners when they get back. There's nothing for me at home."

"I hope it turns out OK for you," Bill said sincerely but a trifle doubtfully. Setting up a shop took money.

"Say did you ever hear what happened to Vera?" Skipper asked.

Skipper had heard the hesitation in Bill's voice about his dreams of his own shop and didn't want him to go there. He had his own doubts.

"What made you think of her?" Bill looked at Skipper with a sudden pang of guilt. He hadn't written to Vera or even thought much about here since he and Skipper finished basic training.

"Must have been the talk about going back." Skipper tried to sound as if he had not thought about her every day since they had shipped out.

"My mother said she married Bob."

"Oh, she did?" Skipper tried to hide his disappointment.

"I heard later he was killed somewhere up north along the Yalu." Bill said this casually, unaware that his words were having any impact on Skipper. Truth to tell, Bill hadn't thought much about home except briefly when his mother's letters arrived. Sometimes he didn't bother to read them as they all seemed the same, full of information about her work with the Church and lists of the prayers for his safety. She'd been eager to tell him about Vera's wedding, maybe so he could get her out of his mind.

"Vera was afraid she'd be a widow," Skipper said. "How come your mother told you?" He left unasked the question of why Bill had not shared this news.

"She didn't. My mother told me Vera was married. Father Vincente told me about Bob's being killed. I think he said that she was expecting a child, but that was some time ago so she's probably had it by now."

"Strange world, isn't it?" Skipper looked perplexed. "Nobody ever tells me anything."

"Sorry, Skipper," Bill said. "I forgot that Father Vincente just wrote to the altar boys in service. I thought you knew."

"I always thought Vera was great. She liked you a lot."

"You too, Skipper. You were part of everything."

"You weren't interested in Vera?"

Bill shook his head. "I liked Vera, sure, but not enough to deal with all the rest of it."

"You mean your ma?"

"Everything. The whole Church bit, the family, the endless yelling, the you've-broken-my-heart crap. It wouldn't have made for much of a relationship."

"Couldn't she have become Catholic?"

"And have all the same problems with her family?" Bill rumpled his forehead at the thought of the trouble that a relationship with Vera would have brought them both. You had to really be committed to cross the religion divide. It wasn't something he wanted to be bothered with.

Skipper smiled mischievously. "So you're gonna let your mother pick your girls?"

"No way," Bill said heatedly. "I won't be marrying any good Catholic girl my mother chooses. I'm going to live my life the way I want to. "

"So you have someone in mind?" Skipper asked innocently.

"I'm never getting married. I've seen what it does to people." Bill's tone spoke of both determination and disgust. He lounged in silence, feeling the steel seams of the gun mount hot beneath him. Talk of home always made him bitter. He let his thoughts range for a few moments and then focused back on the present. "I want to thank you, Skipper," he said finally.

"For what?" Skipper looked at him with wide eyes. Bill was not much into being grateful.

"For never asking. I liked how Vera never asked as well."

"If you mean about your family, mine was enough." Skipper shrugged.

"Still, of everyone, you seemed to know without my saying anything. I always knew I could ask you if I needed something, and you'd be there." Bill smiled ruefully and ran his fingers through his short hair. The wave was long gone, a victim of Navy barbers.

"It's the way things were," Skipper said. "You get put in a situation and you live it. Not much good complaining if things can't change. That's how I figured Vera looked on things."

"Vera's the kind of girl who gets a lot of pleasure from pleasing people. I couldn't see her standing up to her mother." Bill scratched his head thoughtfully. "She seemed to understand about my art. I made things for her. Sketches, carvings, little stuff. She'd talk about school and what we did. I'd talk about football and music. I thought of her as a sister. I wonder whether she's changed. She must have. She's got a child now."

"Well," said Skipper, "if I've learned one thing out of this war it's this: nobody's going to stop me from living once I get back. If I find someone who isn't Catholic, so be it. Nothing's going to stop me. Not even the priests saying I am committing a mortal sin if I don't insist that my wife converts and raises the kids as Catholic." Skipper crossed his arms in determination. "I'm gonna go the way I need to."

"Skipper, do you think we get what we deserve in life?" Bill looked curiously at him, wondering whether Skipper had been thinking about the same things he had. It sounded as if Skipper might have been questioning things too.

"Now that's a crazy question, even from you. Why do you ask?"

"When we bring troops over here, they're all saying things like, 'Now we're here, we're going to win the war.' They go up north to fight and when we take them home on rotation, they just sit staring at the ocean until they see the Golden Gate. They don't play cards, they don't talk— they just look right through you. It's like they feel guilty for surviving. What did they ever do to anyone?"

"Born at the wrong time, I guess."

"But there's never a right time. There's always a war going on somewhere. My dad had the Second World War. There were others before. There'll be more after this one."

"Maybe that's life," Skipper said. "There'll always be someone who thinks he's bigger than everyone else."

"I remember something Father Vincente said when we talked about why I didn't want to be a priest," Bill said. "He said my destiny wasn't to go to the seminary. I asked him whether he thought our lives were foreordained since he had used the word *destiny*. He went on about free will and told me to have faith."

"That was what he always said," Skipper laughed. "I asked about what happens after death. He said 'have faith,' except I didn't know in what."

"Did you ever find an answer?" Bill was impressed by Skipper's daring. To ask a priest anything could invite a lecture on heresy. But Father Vincente was more approachable. No one liked Father Onarario because he was doctrinaire and unapproachable. It was amazing how different priests could be.

"Not really. I don't think it ends with death. But I don't believe in purgatory either. I don't know what I think. Maybe we come back with the same people, getting together again to try to work things out. I like that idea. People who don't do right by someone have to come back and straighten things out. That would serve my stepfather right. With my luck, though, he'd come back and be a bigger asshole." Skipper gave a small half-chuckle.

Bill found Skipper's idea intriguing. "What happens if someone does comes back to make things worse? Sort of unfinished business? People assume you'd want to come back to be a better person. What happens if someone comes back for, say, revenge?"

Skipper shrugged dramatically. "Anything's possible, I suppose. It's not what I'd like, but it takes all kinds."

"Now hear this," the ship's loudspeaker blared. Bill expected to hear that he could smoke. But he was to be disappointed. It was mail call. Bill shoved his Camels back into his shirt pocket and they scrambled down the narrow gangway to the mail window.

"Here's your mail," the mail clerk said. He handed Bill a couple of letters. As usual, there were was nothing for Skipper. "Mystery-meat casserole again, tonight," the clerk added with a giggle, knowing he was delivering unwelcome news. He didn't much like the double duty of mail clerking. He was also responsible for the daily news bulletins he took from the radio and broadcast over the ship's loudspeaker.

"Casserole again, Sparks?" groaned Skipper.

The mail clerk smirked. "Better talk to the cook. What are you complaining about? The guys in the MASH units say that when Cheerful Charlie comes by with the honey buckets, he says that American latrines have *takusan* paper and *sukoshi* shit. Too much paper and too little of the good stuff. The Koreans want plenty to put on the fields. That's why all the local eateries are off limits here. Not that we ever get off the ship."

"Thanks," Skipper said. "I needed to hear that."

"All the news at your service," Sparks sniggered.

Bill had two letters. One from his mother and one from Vera, the first he had received from her. Surprised, he opened her letter while he was still in the corridor outside the mail room. He tore it open along the narrow end to keep the seal on the back intact.

> Dear Billy:
> You may have heard that Bob was killed. I received a telegram telling me, all official and final. I thought about what you said when we were on the dock. I knew I wasn't ready to marry. But he was sure and I wasn't strong enough to say no. I wanted to take your advice and do what I wanted but the expectations kept on coming. Then I was married and a baby on the way. I think it was important to Bob to think if he didn't come back there was someone to miss him. He was killed a couple of months before the baby was born.
>
> I used to ask your mother about you from time to time. She never told me much except to say you were OK. But she moved away suddenly. Nothing's changed here, except some of the boys are not coming home. It seems senseless to die when peace talks are supposed to be going on. Otherwise things are quiet. The shipyard is busy. I've been working there while my mother watches the baby. I've fixed up the basement of the house into an apartment and it's quite nice although the ceilings are a little low.

How are you and Skipper doing? I saw Father
Vincente the other day. He was in a hurry as
usual but said he'd heard from someone who
mentioned you. He said I should say hello if I
wrote. That's what gave me the idea to write to you.
I hope it was OK. He gave me your address.

Take care of yourself. We think about you lots back
here. Please tell Skipper I have Buddy. His mother
said she was going to take him to the pound. I said
I'd keep him. He's doing fine but I know he misses
Skipper. He sometimes sits at the front door watching
the street. But he's real good with Robert junior.

Love to you both,
Vera

Bill folded the letter back in its envelope and handed it to Skipper.
"Looks like you have strong intuition," he said. "It's from Vera." Skipper
took the letter and read it eagerly.

Bill opened his mother's letter after they had gone back up on deck.
He figured he should read this one as he had blown off the others. He
hadn't known she'd moved, but there were two unopened letters still in
his locker. She must have told him about it in one of those.

Mio Caro Bill:
Hope you are well and safe, carissimo. I haven't heard
from you in some time and hope you are safe. Please
write to put my poor heart at rest. We are good here,
except I have bad news. Your father has decided to
leave us. He's done his twenty years in the Navy and
is getting out. He says you're old enough and doesn't
have to support you no more, so he can go find a better
life. He's chosen a bad time to do this because here
I am in California, not knowing many people and I
came down here only because he said he wanted to.
Maybe I'll be all right. I'm going to see a lawyer about
what is due to me. I wish I hadn't come down here

with him. I had good friends back on the East Coast.

But I must ask when you get out, and the papers say it may be soon, you plan on coming here and living with me. I'm sure you can find work, and I need you to pay rent and help with the other expenses until things become clear. You've got money coming from the Navy. I've always tried to help you and I don't think this is too much to ask of you. Many young men coming back from the war would appreciate having a good cooked dinner waiting for them every night.

I have a job cleaning houses. I know a few people through the Church. I sewed the curtains for the altar and I sometimes go with the priest to visit the sick. He includes you every day in the prayers of the faithful and we all hope to see you home soon well and happy. I have sent money to the sisters for them to say novenas for you. I thank God every day he sent me such a fine son who has never given me a day of trouble.

All my love to you always
Mom

Bill folded the letter back into its envelope. Skipper looked up from his multiple rereadings of Vera's letter. "Anything interesting?"

"Nah," replied Bill. "Same old stuff."

"Sounds as if Vera would like to see you." Skipper offered his thoughts hesitantly as if afraid of hearing the reply.

"I'm going to the West Coast when it's over," Bill said. "So I won't be able to."

"Something to do with your family?" Skipper tried to control the relief that obviously spread across his face.

"Something like."

Skipper thought for a minute. "I always thought she's a hell of a girl. Kind too to take in my dog. Think she'd look at someone like me?" The words came tumbling out as a hope that was prepared to be extinguished.

"Skipper. If you can make this work, she'd be lucky to get you. You go find her with my blessing. Like you said, if it works don't let anything stop you."

"Thanks, Pal." Skipper folded Vera's letter and put it in his shirt pocket. He didn't offer to return it. "You asked me before if I believed we get what we deserve in life," he said. "I don't know about the deserve part. Sometimes we get better. But I think there's a reason for everything, and I think things work out."

"That's deep and meaningful," Bill said. He meant to sound ironic, but his words sounded more serious then he intended. There was a part of him that hoped Skipper was right.

Later, after chow, Bill climbed the steep gangway to the shadowy deck to stand his turn at watch. The unloading had paused until the morning. He knew as soon as the job was done, they'd be heading out to sea again. He leaned against a gun emplacement and absorbed everything around him.

The Pusan waterfront filled his senses. He heard someone come up from below, throw a pail of something overboard and then slam the hatch back down to the galley. The smell of diesel came wafting up through the ventilators, and deck smelled from the oil used to keep the gun covers supple. He saw the occasional flare of a match down on the pier where guards watched the supplies and medical equipment unloaded today, destined tomorrow to be loaded onto a train bound for the railhead and the front. He could just make out the stirring of the vendors and beggars outside the gates and the sweet-sour smell of the braziers that both cooked the food and heated the houses outside the waterfront's perimeter. On either side of the city, he could see the dark, towering hills where the military had installed antiaircraft batteries. Finally, he looked up into a woodblock moon bone-white against the darkness of the sky. Only small clouds blew quickly across the multitude of stars.

He stood for some time staring deeply out into the galaxy. He felt insignificant before the tangled sheet of stars above him. Skipper believed there had to be a reason for all this. Bill hoped he was right.

Then he pulled out his mother's letter from his dark blue trousers, tore it into little pieces and dropped them over the side of the ship into the luminescent, oily water of the harbor.

9:00 p.m.

*I*GROAN AND *try to run my hand across my forehead. I was happy on board that ship, perhaps for the first time. But even that feeling is tinged with regret. I feel ashamed seeing Skipper again. He was my best friend. He had joined up to be with me. He wrote to Vera, heard back from her, went home to the East Coast, and found her and his dog. They kept in touch with me, writing to let me know as things progressed. Skipper went to school as he said he would and in time they were married. It was if Vera had been waiting for him, his reward for finding the courage to believe he deserved her.*

Over the years, I'd hear from Skipper and Vera, particularly when a new baby arrived, until they tired of sending Christmas cards to someone who never replied. They had four children by the time they gave up on me, including Bob junior. Skipper bought his automobile repair shop and did well by going to people's homes to do the repairs. He became respected enough to win a seat on the local council. When Vera's mother and aunt died and left the house to Vera, Skipper became proprietor of the old grapevine. In a way he entered history because of that vine. Local school children were required to write about it and imagine what changes it must have seen in its lifetime. Once a year, a straggling line of twelve-year olds from the local American civics class made their dutiful way to the greenhouse to see it.

Skipper's was an American success story: Irish kid raised in a two-room shack who started his own business, married the woman he loved, and merged his blood into the line of New World emigrants who landed at Plymouth Rock. Skipper and Vera raised their kids Protestant as part of that tradition, which soothed Vera's family. There was no one on Skipper's side to object, not even Father Vincente who did not marry them but kept polite silence about Skipper's choices. Losing so many young men to war had changed a lot of things. Raising the kids Protestant was all right with him, Skipper said, because it was the same God after all. My hat's off to Skipper. He developed character in the best sense of that word, and he did it not by following rules but by pursuing the good that he saw in the world. I wish I could have developed that sane, simple recognition of what is right and just.

And while Skipper sought his future, what did I do? The great artist who never was went running home to mother. I took a job with the telephone company on the West Coast to help support her. The only art I did was little dabbles in commercial art. Advertisers didn't much care whether a wallet in a sale catalog was done in any particular style as long as it looked somewhat recognizable. Looking back, I know I un-decided to go home and support my mother. I didn't do it out of any sense of love or duty for her. I didn't do it because I was wildly excited about living in California. I did it because it was the easiest thing to do at the time and because I didn't care. I was acting not out of courage, as Skipper was, but in a strange way out of fear. Yet, what was I afraid of?

Skipper deserved better from me. He wanted to keep alive the contact. I was the one who let it lapse and for the most vapid of reasons. Skipper's friendship was a burden at a time when I wanted no attachments or responsibility. I had detached to the point where all I thought about was convenience. I had no spiritual foundation to give meaning to my life, and I had no respect or affection for anyone, not even for myself. When you live your life detached, you cannot say the normal words of endearment because they give power away. Someone knows something that can be used against you. To someone detached, the words. "I love you" are the most dangerous in the English language.

"Your family will not love you for your decision," the bishop told Aonio as they discussed his intention to go to Rome and allow the Vatican to try him. Not understanding, or perhaps not wanting to, Aonio replied that his family would respect his choice. Only the most self-absorbed could have believed that. How could they respect a decision in which they played no part and for which the consequences would be so damaging? He said he loved his family. But what did he understand by that? Can there be love without respect? People talk about these terms glibly, as if anyone can understand the nuances of language or the slippery way that words shift their meaning. Love can be destructive and unhealthy, and respect can devolve into fear. What did the bishop mean to tell Aonio? Perhaps he meant merely that his family would curse Aonio because he had brought ruin on them. Or was he saying something much more pointed—that Aonio's love was only for himself?

I feel water dripping on my face. Is it Anna? I open my eyes expecting to see her, but it is not. The moist coolness I am feeling is rain spattering down in a grey blur. I am watching Aonio on his way to his trial at Rome on a wet September day.

Chapter 7

Outside Rome September 1568

AONIO AND PTERIGI picked their way around water-filled ruts, past low squat farm buildings and suspicious peasants who stared at them sullenly from under lean-to barns where chickens huddled with matted feathers and pigs routed in the mud. Occasionally they stopped to buy cheese and milk, the transactions conducted mostly in grunts. The rain was more a September drizzle than a downpour, but it had soaked both man and beast. Cows stood motionless in the fields, so caked with mud it was hard to tell their color. The flies that had pestered Aonio on the first part of the trip from Milan had gone. The world was on hold, waiting for the mist and damp to end.

In the distance, they saw a group of riders coming as slowly from the opposite direction, and they pulled off the path to let them pass. Pterigi stiffened and half drew his servant's dagger at his waist as the fellow travelers came close. In this rain, when everyone was hunched under sodden clothing, it was hard to know who else was on the pathway. If Aonio was uneasy, he did not show it. In fact, he became talkative while they waited for them.

"This rain reminds me of the time I went to Pisa to retrieve Marietta's belongings. You remember, don't you? It was when she and the children came to live with me in Lucca. The Pisa customs agents wouldn't pass her boxes. They said somebody must be present when they inspected them. It took me three days to go the fifteen miles there and back. It was raining just like this. Those were the worst roads I'd ever been on. My friends in Pisa didn't recognize me ride by their houses because I was so caked in mud."

"You're not much better now." Pterigi smiled slightly while still keeping his eyes trained on the riders now just up ahead. "We had some adventures in the rain with that big desk of yours—getting it into and out of the cart was a major task. Then we had to keep it covered so the rain didn't damage it. Every rut we went over was an enemy, and I was always afraid we would get stuck somewhere."

"That desk has been a good friend. I am sorry that I shall not have in Rome." Aonio glanced down at his clothes. His boots were caked with clay, and his cloak had splatters as high as his waist. Pterigi was right. He was not fit for polite company. Both he and his horse would need a good scrubbing wherever they stopped for the night.

The riders approached and hallooed politely. Aonio responded in kind and raised his hand in the traditional gesture of welcome and good intention as the two groups approached one another. There were five of them and Pterigi quietly pushed his knife back down into its sheath. The crosses blazoned on their clothing and bundles indicated that they were Churchmen. The riders came parallel to one another, exchanged greetings, talked for a moment about the road ahead, and plodded on. Aonio and Pterigi then picked their way around the new hoof prints slowly filling up with water. Aonio pulled his muddy cloak even more tightly around him. It had kept the wet and dirt away from his body, but in the rain it smelled of sheep.

Overhead, the clouds turned dark again and the rain turned from a misty drizzle into a steady downpour. Aonio brushed the raindrops away from his eyebrows and smiled slightly. "The angels' tears, the women call these rains," he said. "When I was a child, they used to tell me the angels cried because human beings had given them so much to grieve. I was never sure if I had caused the rain."

Pterigi tipped his hat to let the water pour off the brim. "Well, if you're the one responsible, I wish you'd tell the rain to end."

"You're right. The rain is making the going hard. I think we should stop early today and stay at the Benedictine monastery a few miles ahead. I understand that the monks are very hospitable."

"Anything's better than the snoring at the inn last night. Those farmers smelled of garlic at both ends."

"They were definitely earthy, weren't they?"

"They stank," Pterigi corrected him. "They were full of fleas, or maybe worse. I've been scratching since we left. I'll have to groom Bacci carefully with all this mud. He's a good horse and I'm glad that he's going to spend the rest of his life with me."

"I hope my wife gave him to you for your good service to us all."

"Fedro came up with the idea. Your wife said I should buy him from my wages, but Fedro said it was good reckoning for my years of service. I think he was afraid I might ask for more. I think your wife became convinced that an old man and an old horse were good riddance. Two fewer things to feed."

"Your loyalty deserves more than that. I am grateful for your willingness to ride with me to Rome. I fear it was a great imposition."

"No imposition. I was glad to accompany you. I've been with you for well over forty years. A lifetime. You took me into your house and never complained when I was unable to do things for you."

"Whatever would I have complained about? I would trust my life to you."

"I would give mine for you," Pterigi replied. His eyes filled with the force of his emotion.

"You have been the finest friend a man could ask for," Aonio said firmly. "You have been part of my family. I have trusted you with things

I would never give to another living soul. Complaints? If there were any, you would be far more justified in making them of me."

"Serving you has been an honor. I will admit, though, there have been others in the house who were more difficult."

"They are good people in their own ways," Aonio said.

Pterigi glanced away. He face disclosed his discomfort in talking about the family he had always served. In his mind, he was still a servant. They rode in silence for a while.

"Fedro will take care of them," Pterigi said finally. "He's the wild one, always was. He belongs to himself but he's strong. Caterina, she can calm her mother down when she's upset. She'll keep order. Beatrice, well she's young yet, lots of energy and intelligence but impulsive."

"You never chose to start a family of your own?" Aonio smiled at the acute observations.

"There was a woman once, but I didn't speak, and she married someone else. There was never any other."

"I didn't know," Aonio said quietly.

"I didn't have the courage to ask," Pterigi replied. "I could not have lived if she had looked at me with pity and thought me a cripple. I would like to think, though, that if I ever had the chance again, I wouldn't let it slip away."

"Didn't you miss having a wife?" Aonio remembered his own decision against the priesthood in favor of a physical life and family.

"If you mean my pleasures, I've had my share. It's not hard to find if you know which doors to knock on. Such women are not choosy." Pterigi glanced furtively at Aonio and spoke deliberately. "It wasn't Ceciliana."

"It never occurred to me," Aonio said in surprise. "But since you mention it, it would be logical since she was widowed and in the same household."

"Logical," Pterigi growled, "but not likely. Who wants to sleep with someone who sounds like a duck? Let her open her mouth, which she does far too often, and you can't mistake her. I said to her once, 'Do you know they can hear you down in the valley?' She was so angry she overturned a table and spilled a water bucket over my feet."

"Well, I admit I said once that if her husband had broken her jaw, he would have done everyone a favor." Aonio laughed as the horses plodded along, stumbling and slipping from time to time. "But I am sure Ceciliana has been a big help to my wife—with me traveling as often as I did."

"My most vivid memory of Ceciliana," Pterigi replied, "is her standing with her hands on her hips, her chest thrust out like a rooster's, and a surly smirk on her face because someone else was in trouble."

"Yes," smiled Aonio. "Ceciliana is Bolognese. They say the women there fight on the walls alongside their men when there's trouble, and make their husbands' lives hell from boredom when there's not."

Aonio's horse stumbled then and jolted him. He grimaced and involuntarily put his hand up to his cheek. He pressed deep into the bone above his left cheek as if he were trying to push something through his jawbone.

"Are you in pain?" Pterigi urged Bacca alongside Aonio's horse.

"I've had a toothache on and off for the past several days," Aonio replied. "The horse's stumble jolted it. Unfortunately it's getting worse."

"My old mother used to swear by a garlic poultice. She said once the gum opened and the blood ran out, the pain went away. I've few teeth left myself. The devil can take them as far as I'm concerned."

Aonio nodded. It was a sentiment he could agree with. Very few people escaped the tyranny of teeth and the kindest thing was to wake one morning to find a tooth lying on the pillow that had extracted itself during the night.

The sun was setting among scudding clouds, and a tapering rain had turned back to occasional drizzle as they rode past ramshackle houses perched precariously on a hillside and on through the monastery's heavy gate. The main building crested a ridge with a steep approach from the village it towered over. The outside walls were several feet thick, made from local stone carved into rough blocks divided by high, narrow windows. The walls seemed designed as much to withstand assault as to enclose a place of meditation. The out-buildings needed to cultivate land, raise livestock, stable horses, make wine, store food, and maintain community life clustered along the inside walls. The various shops were shut down for the day, but the smell of coals from the blacksmith's shop lingered in the air. A cloister linked the chapel and library to the long rectangular building housing the monks and their common areas.

Once inside the courtyard, Aonio and Pterigi were met by a brother who offered to take their horses. Pterigi went to the stable with him while Aonio followed the soft slap of sandals and the chink of rosary beads as another brother led him up stone stairs and along chilled passageways. The room he was taken to was plain and the door without a lock. It was small, with only enough room for a cot, a chest with a bowl of water and jug, and a chair. A large crucifix hung over the bed. Aonio cleaned himself as best he could and quickly drifted off to sleep once he lay down.

Aonio did not hear Pterigi come to the room next to his and did not wake until a monk knocked on the doors and offered to guide them to the refectory for supper. The room they were guided to was narrow and high-ceilinged, furnished with a plain sideboard on one wall and two long trestle tables down the center with a row of benches on each side. About twenty brown-robed men sat silently while Aonio and Pterigi were invited to sit beside the prior. The silence was according to the monastery's custom and the room echoed only with the sound of utensils scraping as the food was served. Placed before each man was a plate of bread, vegetables, salt-fish, and herbs, and a small glass of wine.

Once the meal was over and the brothers departed to their designated areas, the monastery's prior was in a mood to talk. He turned out to be a congenial and well-educated man, obviously curious about life beyond the cloisters. "Have you come far?" the prior asked as he offered them more wine.

"From Milan," Aonio answered.

"How were the roads on your travels?"

"From Milan to Empoli they were bearable until the rains came. The going has been hard ever since."

"Such weather is most difficult for travelers. Were there many others ventured out?"

"We saw some," Aonio replied. "Surprising given the weather. They must have had good reason to be out in rain like this."

The prior nodded. "We had five Churchmen from Spain staying here yesterday. They were on their way home from visiting the Vatican to plead a special dispensation. They had to wait for weeks and never did deliver their petition to His Holiness. They were quite upset because the weather turned bad as they were leaving and had been good before. You too are going to Rome?"

Aonio nodded with a slight smile and offered no further explanation. The prior gracefully changed the subject.

"Milan. Ah, a beautiful city. I am from Mantua, myself. My father was an overseer for the Gonzaga family. He brought me to the palazzo with him when he came to report on the estate. While he was busy, I was allowed to wander the great hall, looking up at the painted ceilings and wondering how the artist managed to get up there to do his work. But more than the grand battles and gods painted on the ceiling, I loved the tapestries. I'd walk around staring at the beauty woven into the threads, trying to recognize the stories they depicted. Most of them represented the history of the noble Gonzagas and the city of Mantua but there were others that illustrated virtues, good moral instruction for the young person I was. The weavers must have been touched by the divine to be able to create such pure depictions of human life. Their beauty lay in the perfect blending of color, subject, and form. I felt elevated by being in their presence. Once we were there when Duke Ercole was hosting a wedding banquet. The long tables were set with golden dishes and silver candle holders. In that gentle light, those tapestries came alive and glowed."

"Which were your favorites?" Aonio asked. His tone implied he was familiar with them and had his own preferences.

"Have you seen them? Do you know them?" The prior leaned forward eagerly.

"Yes, I've seen the Gonzaga tapestries, but I have not studied them closely. Everyone visiting Mantua is encouraged to visit the hall you describe. It's one of the attractions of the city. But truth to tell, I am more familiar with those owned by other family members. Ferrante, Duke Federico's brother, for example, built the Villa Simonetta outside the city and also commissioned fine tapestries from the Belgians while he was in the Low Countries. One of my friends tutored the Duke's son and we were all invited in one day to see them. It was just after he had them moved to the villa. I remember seeing the *fructus belli* panels there.

"I'm not familiar with those. What are they like?" The prior's eyes shone with delight. "Having you here is more than I could have hoped for—to talk with someone who has seen Mantua's tapestries. The Spaniards were polite enough but so angry with Rome there was little else they talked about. I couldn't blame them. Rome's bureaucracy can crush the unprepared. But you have brought good conversation indeed."

"The first *fructus belli* panels showed Ferrante as a conquering military leader with a wreath of laurels being held over his head. But the other panels showed the costs and consequences of his success. Men had to be paid and equipment provided, the countryside was ransacked to feed the army, and the aftermath was terrible carnage, dead soldiers and animals piled on one another, people driven from their homes, and vengeance taken on the losers. It was sobering experience to see these illustrations of warfare. Ferrante must have had his fill of war when he commissioned them. I regret my lack of knowledge to describe them more vividly. The tapestries were of impressive size, and it seemed as if I could see for miles into the landscape they depicted. As you said, the colors shimmered, and I could swear the scenes came to life as I looked at them."

The prior nodded in pleasure at even a partial description. "This is the purpose of art," he said. "The message of peace is a worthy topic, and I believe it is the role of beauty to present the world in ways that allow us to see what is possible. Without beauty, people might not study the tapestries as you have; they might not see what the artist intended. From your description, I believe he wishes us to see that people are as grass, trampled beneath elephants who fight for power. Using beauty to instruct in the ugliness of war also makes the message one we will remember. One day I hope to see the tapestries at Mantua again," he sighed. "Sometimes I am not sure following my career in the Church and leaving home was such a good bargain. I have always felt that tapestries are like our lives. They are interwoven and one thread can play a role in many different parts of the picture. Have you noticed how tapestries can change if you look at them from different places?"

"Perhaps it would be as interesting to see these tapestries also as a *fuga*, a fugue of life," Aonio said.

"What a delightful idea," the prior replied. "How would you compose such a fugue to include this message of the horrors of war?"

"There would be five voices. A young General Ferrante would be the obvious first voice, setting the theme of war. His would be a manly voice of someone seeking glory through the force of arms. The second voice, perhaps a soldier's, would answer him, singing of the hardships that constant wars brings to the men who must go out and fight them. This would invite the third voice, perhaps that of a grieving father, singing of the losses that any parent feels when sons go off to war. The next voice, soaring above the others, a woman's or a boy's voice, could sing the anguish of famine, siege, and the death of children. The fifth voice, that of the victorious General Ferrante, would sing of war but in the tones of an older man who now questions what he gained: he knows there will be only other wars and other deaths, and it all seems pointless. The fugue could end by reprising the warlike song of the young Ferrante, but in a melancholy trope that is really a lament for the fallen, which leads to all the voices combining to sing the glories of peace."

For a moment Aonio forgot the Church and the difficulties of what lay head. He played with ideas as he had not in a long time. This freedom to think what he had most loved about the university life. All it had taken was a brief moment to remind him of what it felt like to be liberated into the pure joy of creativity.

The prior seemed to have been transported with him. He clapped his hands in delight. "My dear sir," he said enthusiastically, "you are a philosopher and a scholar. Are you also a composer who could give the world the fruits of this creativity?"

"I fear not," Aonio replied. "Art and music are delightful pastimes, but they would require another lifetime of learning to really do them justice."

"I cannot tell you the pleasure you have brought me. To share the tapestries with me and then to offer me the glimpse of such a fine performance. I shall dream of it." The prior offered to refill their wine glasses.

"The wine is excellent," Aonio said as he politely demurred. "But I am already sleepy."

"This is our own wine, made on our grounds," the prior said proudly. "Everything you ate tonight was grown here as well."

"It was all excellent," Aonio said.

Pterigi did not refuse the prior's offer. The monastery's wine was golden in the candlelight, and it creamed as it poured into the glass

"Are you looking forward to your visit to Rome?" the prior asked Pterigi.

"I am on my way to join my sister who lives in Citavecchia. A few months ago she was widowed, and I'm going there to live with her." Pterigi felt the wine's warmth. He was glad to be included in the conversation even though he knew he had little to offer in comparison to the brilliance of the man he worked for. He could read Italian and basic Latin, but he had not learned the scholarly vocabulary of the latter language. This meant he could quietly read Aonio's manuscripts when he might, but he would be the first to admit that he had not understood them. True, he had overheard spirited discussions when Aonio invited fellow university scholars to his rooms in Milan, but these discussions were also elevated and he had never asked Aonio to explain them to him. It was probably better not to know just in case he was ever asked. His father told him to keep his mouth shut: say nothing, the old man stressed, and nothing will be all you have to regret. It was good advice. But tonight he was tired and the wine loosened his tongue.

"She's also from Milan? A long way." The prior remembered taking weeks to cover the distance between the northern cities and Rome. Horses could travel only so many miles before they needed rest, their riders too, and when bad weather turned the tracks to mud, it was sometimes better to turn around and just go home.

"Our family is from Genoa originally." Pterigi spoke with pride. "We've always built ships. My father was a master carpenter who built the oak framework for the hulls, stem, and sternposts. Through my father's work, my sister met a sailing man who ordered several smaller fishing ships from us. He took her away with him to Citavecchia. We missed her very much because there had been just us two children since our mother died."

"You didn't wish to follow your father's trade?"

"I did for a while. I attended school at the monastery and was an apprentice in the shipyard. But my father was killed and I was injured. I couldn't lift heavy loads let alone lift my arm to direct workmen where to place the wood, so I had to leave my father's profession."

"How did your accident happen?" the prior asked kindly.

"We were building a merchantman, 500 tons, a magnificent carrack with main mast and multiple sails. Everyone was proud and the new owner, Pietro de Valterra came daily to the dock to see her grow. My father said it would be his masterpiece, and he scoured the wood we acquired to be sure each piece was perfect. The shipyard in Genoa was devoted to building many different ships. We were in the part where the merchantmen were built, but there was another place set aside for the state warships ordered by the city fathers. Powder and cannon were stored there. One day a workman's hammer struck a spark and ignited the powder. We were inside the frame of the carrack, below what would be the water line and looking at the ribs where the planking was to be attached when we heard a tremendous explosion. The ground shook and earth and stones started to rain down on us. For a moment all I could hear were things breaking and rocks falling. We put our arms over our heads and shrank against the ribs, but there was no cover and it was over quickly. One stone the size of a man's head struck my father and I could see he was dead right away. Another, smaller rock struck me on the shoulder and knocked me down. I could not move my arm. Over fifty men lost their lives, many master craftsmen like my father. Houses all around the shipyard were also damaged or destroyed. Many died who were not working. They carried out bodies for days from the rubble, some impossible to identify. The city ordered a mass grave for the victims and placed a memorial tablet with the names of the missing. My father was given a special stone with a caliper on it. Afterwards, there was precious little work while they rebuilt the shipyard."

"How did you come to be in Milan and, I assume, enter upon service?" the prior inquired.

"I was fortunate. The de Valterra family ordered their ships from us. Pietro de Valterra knew my father well. When he heard about my father's death, he sought me out and insisted that I stay in his house while I healed. I played with their sons, Giovanni and Joannino. Giovanni, the eldest, was thirteen and being prepared to carry on the family business. His brother Joannino was being educated to enter the priesthood, and he later became a bishop. Giovanni was endlessly curious about building ships and about how they were sailed. The time passed as pleasantly as it could under the circumstances. The family physician saw to my shoulder. I was eighteen and had no family left. I could not pursue my profession, so an appeal was made to friends and relatives to help me. They learned the Paleario family in Colle needed a manservant free to travel. It seemed a good choice for a cripple since the duties were light. I have been with the family ever since."

"Pterigi is far more than a servant," Aonio interrupted. "He has been my friend all these years. Although he is younger than us old men, he is himself now retiring to a well-deserved rest."

The prior smiled at Pterigi. "You plan to live with your sister. Have you seen her in the intervening years?"

"Whenever I was in Rome, I would slip away to visit her. It's not far. My sister has several children, and there are grandchildren who are having their own children. I look forward to noise and squabbling, all the things part of family life."

"Your sister is fortunate you wish to share your life with her."

"Oh no, Sir, it is I who's fortunate someone wants me. I should hate to die alone."

"Will you not miss your old friend and retainer?" the prior asked Aonio.

"I have reached old age and my needs have lessened," Aonio replied. "My children have grown. My former students have become professors and lawyers and recognized in their own right. It's time to wind down my affairs."

"You are a professor? I thought you had the bearing of a scholar."

"I have been fortunate to teach eloquence and debate at several universities although I have attributed these positions to influential friends who worked hard on my behalf rather than to my own merit."

The prior smiled. "I'm sure you are far too modest. We are honored to have you here. As an order we are devoted to education and learning as well as to self-sufficiency and serving our neighbors. We cultivate our lands, provide alms, and educate the local children if they have the urge to learn. I myself was educated by Benedictines and became a novice. Of course, our abbey is nothing in comparison to wonderful Monte Cassino, but we pride ourselves on our library nonetheless and on providing hospitality for wayfarers. But our greatest honor—ah—did you notice the papal tiara over our front gate?"

Aonio shook his head. He and Pterigi were too tired to notice anything when they came through.

"You may not believe this, but once we provided shelter to two popes at once. They were not popes at the time, of course, but they were to become so over their lifetimes."

The prior smiled in pleasure and waited for his guests to appreciate the enormous honor he was describing. Aonio nodded his head to satisfy him.

"It was many years ago. I was still a novice. We had heard about the terrible events in Rome, how the pope and many others were trapped in the Castel Sant'Angelo while mercenaries ransacked the city, but we ourselves had not been much affected by it since—as you saw—we sit on a steep hill with a narrow approach to our gate. Luckily for us, we look too formidable to be worth the effort. Early one day, a rider dashes up to our gates and demands to be let in. He says he has an urgent message from Cardinal Colonna. 'Expect visitors early tomorrow,' he tells us. 'Some may be unwell but all will be tired and need care.' I ask who these people are. He says he can't tell us anything more than they are Churchmen from Rome. We, of course, are surprised for it was our understanding all the Churchmen in Rome had fled or were being held for ransom.

"Naturally we want to help and make every preparation we can without knowing exactly what is needed. One brother thinks His Holiness Pope Clement might be among them, but nobody can believe it. From dawn on, we take turns watching the road. The morning passes with no one in sight. In the mid afternoon, we see a farm cart laden with dirty straw approach our gate. Surely this can't be our guests, we say. Nevertheless, we go into the courtyard and stand ready. When the cart enters our gates, we see the straw move as men emerge from their hiding places. One by one we assist five of them down. Our prior is openly crying since he recognizes them. One is an archbishop, an elderly man, who looks as if he is about to die on the spot. The others are disheveled but do not appear to be in such a bad way. They need hot water and clean clothes, which we provide, although all we have is the clothing worn by the brothers. They tell us about their miraculous escape through the city's sewers and give us the first real account of Rome's destruction. They tell us terrible things. Rome's streets were deep in blood, rats desecrated bodies in daylight, and no one—man, woman, or child—had been spared. They told us how the Holy Father and others were trapped, starving in the Castel Sant'Angelo, and how the Vatican had been taken. It broke our hearts. We sheltered them in safety for several weeks, particularly as a number fell ill from exposure to the filth of the sewers. Thanks be to God we were able to save them all. Amazingly, two were later elected to the papacy. They never forgot us, and each one in turn gave us generous gifts. Marcello Cervini became Pope Marcellus although only for a short while before a fever took him from us. Our sadness over his death was lifted only by the election of Cardinal Caraffa. When he became Paul IV, he gave us a license to display the papal tiara over our gate. So you see, the world finds us."

"Sometimes it's a blessing, though, not to be involved in the winds of change," Aonio replied politely.

"We are not cloistered here," the prior gently corrected him. "We teach those who wish to learn. We support the poor among us, and we do our best to remain apart from the politics of Rome. The snares of the world lie in wait, and we do what we can to lift the burdens of those who get caught in them." The prior's remark was kind but pointed. He was letting Aonio know not only that he understood what Aonio might be facing in Rome but also that he sympathized and would be ready to help him if he could.

"We appreciate your hospitality," Aonio replied, carefully avoiding any reaction to the prior's offer. "We shall be glad to provide our offering for your hospitality."

"Tomorrow will be soon enough. We retire early here. You will find your rooms clean but the candlewicks short."

"We have no desire to stay awake, I can assure you," Aonio said. "After a full day's travel, we want only to sleep."

"Then I shall bid you both good night and must tell you not to be alarmed if you should see our resident spirit."

"A ghost?" Pterigi's eyes grew wide and he quickly made the sign of the cross.

"There's no need for fear," the prior said quickly. "There is no necromancy here. We believe he is one of our brothers who took as his special mission the care of troubled souls. After his death, he was said to come when there was sadness and struggle within our walls. I glimpsed him myself when we welcomed our Vatican guests after the fall of Rome. Those who have seen him say he offers comfort. So if you should be lucky enough to see him, accept his message of love."

The prior smiled warmly as he called for a brother to lead them to their rooms. It was a good thing that they had been provided with a guide, because they would never have been able to find their rooms again. As the prior promised, the candles provided in the rooms lasted just long enough to prepare for sleep.

With his candle burned down, Aonio stood looking out of the window of his room. It overlooked a small courtyard outside the chapel. Despite his fatigue, he stood for some time, mesmerized by the night. Inside the chapel, a solitary candle flickered through the narrow windows. Above him, he saw a multitude of stars that made him feel the insignificance of human life against the background of God's heavens. He watched a pale emerging moon rise up and turn the lingering clouds to grey gauze. The countryside around was silent except for the occasional sound of horses and a barking dog. Finally overcome by fatigue, he lay down on the narrow bed and pulled his still damp cloak over the blanket, as much to dry it out as to provide more warmth. His tooth was constantly bothering him now.

When Aonio finally fell into slumber it was to the rise and fall of the

Latin verses of evening devotions and praise to God. Then, as the hours of night turned toward dawn, he was not awake to see the shadowy, wispy form of a figure in monks' habit lingering at the foot of his bed, reaching out with a hooded hand to make the sign of the cross over the sleeping man, conveying in that simple gesture the wish for comfort and blessing.

Next day, Aonio and Pterigi made their offering and rode on. A blustery wind had blown the heavy rain clouds to the east. From time to time the sun broke through the racing clouds overhead. The pace was still slow, but by late afternoon they entered into the mass of old and newer buildings piled one upon the other on the crowded Roman hills. They rode through noisy, cobbled streets filled by the mingled smells of cooking food and raw sewage. The city appeared both lively and depressing. Aonio remembered how differently he felt when he first came to Rome, fresh from his parents' home in Veroli to continue his studies in Latin and Greek. He had friends then waiting to welcome him.

They stopped along the way to sell Aonio's horse at a livery stable. The man bargained hard but the price was fair. Aonio carefully wrapped the money in a pouch next to his body. He would need this to pay for his meals and bedding in the prison.

"It's time for you to go on, Pterigi," he said as they emerged from the stable. "I will go the rest of the way alone."

"We could both ride Bacci." Pterigi looked at his friend and former employer with sad eyes. He knew he would never see him again. He wanted to hold back the final moment.

"No, thank you, Pterigi. You've done enough keeping me company to here. This is something I must do myself."

Pterigi's grizzled beard scraped against Aonio's cheek, as the two old men embraced.

"God bless you." Pterigi said. "I don't know what to say. My life has been spent with you. It does not seem right."

"You have been my friend all these years, Pterigi. There's nothing to be said. Whenever I was in need, you were there. Please go on your way to your sister and give her my regards. Tell her for me that her brother is a loyal and decent man who deserves to live life for himself."

Aonio watched as Pterigi stiffly mounted and rode down through the crowd along the street. Pterigi kept turning back to look until he had to turn a corner. He gave one last wave. Aonio lifted his hand in return and waited until Pterigi was out of sight. Then he swung his pack onto his shoulder and started his walk toward St. Peter's. All around him, people carried on with their daily lives, but despite the bustle, he felt completely alone. He threw his head back and allowed himself to focus on the moment's importance. He saw his life as leading inevitably to this moment. There could have been no other outcome. He was about to do something monumental that would turn his incarceration into a vindication.

He walked on for half an hour until he entered the vast square before St. Peter's and the Vatican. Black-robed men crisscrossed the area; their crucifixes swinging on rosary beads and their sandaled feet slapping the stones. The pope's special guard, the Switzers provided a colorful splash against the vibrant white columns. People milled about, some crossing the vast square on their knees. He stopped for a moment to take in the pageant of the Catholic Church before turning down the side road to the Torre de Nona, the Inquisition prison.

10:00 p.m.

*M*Y BODY IS *numb but my mind is agitated and almost out of control. I feel no longer tethered to life, and as if I have become pure thought. I envy Aonio the loyalty of the servant who would give his life for him. I wonder how many other people like this Aonio has nodded at politely before moving on to what he thought were more important things. I find myself questioning him and his assumptions in new ways. I want to ask him if thought and freedom were so important, why didn't he retire from* the world as this prior has and still lead an active life? Even I can see that he could have left Italy and helped to build the climate for freedom of thought from outside the country. Others did. I would have left—or I'd like to think I would have—to save my family.

My mind continues its dance and my thoughts course erratically through my flooded brain. Why can't Aonio recognize what this prior represents? The prior talks of education, libraries, music, and tapestries, not of conformity and Vatican politics. He is the human face of a vast bureaucracy. He hasn't withdrawn like the bishop to tend a garden and ignore the evils of the Church he serves. He is not seeking people to denounce to the Inquisition. He may have his suspicions about Aonio's journey to Rome, but he is too subtle even to ask his guest's name. This is a man who cares about people. Aonio is too wrapped up in himself to see it. But it's not just Aonio whose self-regard is a curtain between him and the world. Sadly, I realize I had my Pterigi in Skipper and couldn't see it either.

All this talk of art makes me think about my own stillborn art career. I said I wanted it. But was I ever as committed to art as the prior is? For him, art is history, family, and civic pride. If I had been as dedicated, I could not have walked away from my urge to create. I was a dilettante, merely playing with the idea of being an artist. Ferrante's Belgian tapestries may express his disenchantment with the realities of war, but it took the weavers in Brussels to bring his feelings to life. All I can claim is my interest in music. That at least endured. But art wasn't the only thing I didn't see. There were so many other things--my son among them.

Poor Michael. I didn't know how to be a father to a son. When Michael was born, I regretted he was not a girl. I don't know why I wanted a daughter. Maybe I thought it might be easier to raise her. My mother's needs were paramount in the family so I never learned how to be a parent. She felt powerful when she had people's sympathy: "Poor Carolina. Such a saint." Friendship between my father and me would have diminished her, *so she needed to keep us apart to maintain her own illusions. I wonder if Michael feels that he never knew me either. I never encouraged his interest in flying any more than my parents were interested in my art. The sins of the fathers are indeed visited on the children, but carelessly, each generation handing down the mistakes and ugliness of the one before until someone can see the truth and put a stop to it.*

My head is spinning. My ideas are overflowing the limits of my memory. Why do I see these things only now? Why can I see the things I've lost when it's too late to do anything about them?

So this is death? It's not what I thought it would be. If I expected judgment and brimstone, I was very wrong. It's certainly not the final ringing down of an immense black curtain. Instead, I am learning things that every relationship in my life has had meaning, and I am the one who must do the work of finding it out.

I wonder if Anna would understand if I said I see now how she rescued me from loneliness and bitterness? Anna might—she always made her own way when it came to spiritual matters. She was a surprise when she came into my life. I didn't want to marry. I didn't want anyone making claims on me. But one day, she was there. I should have known immediately how special she was even if our meeting was a comedy of errors that nearly ended us. I have to laugh as I think of it.

"Is he crying?" Carole asked as they slipped more morphine under his tongue. He had been restless and it seemed he might be in pain. He couldn't tell them, so they had to guess when he needed more. He had taken hold of the sheet covering him and was tugging intensely on the two edges, alternating one arm after the other as if he were hitting a punching bag. Something was agitating him and they hoped the morphine would calm him.

"Don't think so," Anna said as she wiped Bill's forehead and watched as his convulsive arm movements slowed and then stopped as he drifted into sleep. "He hiccups like that when he's laughing. I hope he's found something to laugh at."

"I feel like we're intruding on something," Carole said. She looked worried as she put the little bottle back on the nightstand before looking inquiringly at Anna. When Anna did not respond, she retreated to the front room and left Anna and Bill alone.

Anna gently touched Bill's cheek. It was grey and cool. "Wherever you are, be happy," she said as she bent to whisper in his ear. "I loved you from the moment that I saw you."

Chapter 8

Los Angeles, 1965

H E BEGAN TO recognize her voice when she phoned his radio station with requests. She sounded young, but she also seemed to know what she was asking for. They had their first argument before they met.

"You didn't play the first cut of the Verdi Fountains of Rome," she phoned up one day to tell him. She had been listening and missed her favorite part of the music. She hummed a few bars to let him know what it sounded like.

"I did," he replied. "Are you thinking of the first cut of the Pines?"

"I don't think so," she said.

"Let me cue up the pines," Bill said, knowing that he was right. He didn't want to come right out and tell her. He wanted her to listen to the music and hear it for herself.

"You're right," Anna said when the record scratched to life. "Sorry to disturb you."

"Hold on a minute," he said quickly. "You called me a while back about Rossini's overture, *The Thieving Magpie*, right? La Gazza ladra?"

"Yeah, apparently I don't have a great track record with remembering music." She sounded disgusted.

"Well, actually, you were right. As soon as you hung up I looked at the record jacket and there was a picture of a magpie on the cover. It had a ring in its beak, so I assume it was the thief. My Italian isn't good, in fact it's non-existent even though my mother was raised in Italy. If I knew anything, I'd have known that *gazza ladra* means thieving magpie. Easy if you know."

"I'm glad to hear I'm not completely off course." Her laugh sounded to Bill like low-pitched wind chimes. It suggested seriousness and levity at the same moment, and it sounded familiar even though he knew he could never have heard it before. He would have remembered that laugh. He was sure of it.

"I take it you enjoy classical music." It wasn't much of an opening line, but all he could think of to keep her talking.

"I'm taking a class in music appreciation on campus, but it was always played in my home." She sounded cautious as if wondering why he wanted to know.

"You're a student at the university? How do you like it?" Bill jumped to the immediate conclusion that she was attending UCLA, where he went with the GI Bill. He'd had to go part time because of his day job with the telephone company, but he'd made it through finally. He hadn't distinguished himself academically mostly because he only took seriously the courses that interested him, but he stuck it out and graduated.

"It's OK." He imagined she shrugged as she said this. She sounded non-committal, not ready to share much information with a stranger.

"I went there a few years back," Bill explained. "After I was discharged from the Navy." He didn't know how old she was. He hoped he didn't sound ancient.

"What did you major in?"

He thought he detected a faint glimmer of interest. Or was she merely being polite while she looked at her watch and wondered how soon she could end this call? But he'd take it. Something told him to persist, and any interest for whatever reason was good. "Art history," he replied.

"So you're an artist?"

"Only commercial art," Bill said, wondering if she was going to be disappointed. "I do advertising, sometimes illustrate short story stories—things along those lines."

"Most artists are interested in selling their work. Doesn't that make all art commercial?"

"Not in everyone's mind. One of my professors sneered at what he called the art marketplace, the bazaar where artists prostitute themselves."

"Hmm," she said. "Sounds rather fashionable, doesn't it? Like this is what they tell themselves either because they are academic snobs or else their work didn't sell. What about all those artists who painted portraits and competed for commissions? Was Michelangelo "just" being commercial when he painted the Sistine Chapel? Self-expression is all very well, but artists have to live like anyone else."

"Stand by a minute," he said, "I need to change records." He was liking her more and more, and he didn't even know her name.

"OK, but I can't talk for long. I'm due at the library." Now she sounded impatient.

"Just a sec," he said. He cued up the next record and announced it on the air before he set it spinning. He did it as fast as he could, worried that she might not be there when he picked up the phone again.

"I have to go now," she said definitely when he came back to the phone. He knew if she hung up, it might be weeks or never before she called back.

"OK," he blurted out, "but would you like to see the studios? I feel I owe you an apology about the magpie. Since this is a classical music station, it might work as a field trip for your music appreciation class."

There was a pause on her side. He'd been impulsive with his invitation, and he'd have to check it with the manager, but he assumed he could wangle it all right. He knew she was weighing her interest in music with how much she should trust him. He also knew that something important was hanging in the balance and waiting for her to make her decision. "The staff's always here with me," he added.

"Where are the studios?" she asked finally.

"In the bank building by the interstate. Not far from the campus." He was surprised how much he wanted her to agree.

"What's there to see?"

"We have a record library, two recording studios, the main radio room, the offices and the transmitter. As I said, there is always staff here. The recording engineer's here to shut down the transmitter after hours."

"Let me think about it," she said.

"I'm on the air every weekday night, from 6:00 to 10:00 p.m."

She hung up without saying anything more than goodbye.

A week passed and he heard nothing. Bill concluded that she must have decided against it and felt an unaccustomed sense of loss. The next night, when he was playing *Carmina Burana* and hoping no one understood the lyrics, she called back.

"Hello," she said as if there had been no gap in her calls.

"Hello," he replied, unable to find anything original to say.

"I've been thinking about your invitation." Her voice was droll, as if she knew the confusion and anxiety she had caused him.

"And?" He tried to sound uninterested and debonair. He knew he was failing.

"I asked one of the fellows who lives in my rooming house about you. He said you are bald and fat."

Bill's laughter filled the telephone. It was quite a while before he stopped.

"I take it you're not bald and fat?" She sounded amused.

"The opposite. I'm skinny and have thick, dark hair. Who is this genius you asked?"

"He's a disk jockey at a local rock station. I figured he might know you."

"Well, tell him he's full of it."

"He also said he thought you were harmless. Something of a crank."

"He might be right there." Bill laughed so hard again that his eyes teared.

"Maybe I'll accept your invitation." She sounded almost coy as she said this, but he felt only relief, although now he had to worry how to maintain her interest once she met him. Boy, you've got it bad, he said to himself. And he still didn't know who she was.

"When would you like to come here?"

"I could manage next Friday about seven. I'll have a friend drop me off and come to pick me up."

"Sure. Come to the front door and ring the entrance bell. I'll ask Sparks to let you in if I can't. He's the station engineer. But first, what's your name? I need to let the station know you're coming."

"Anna," she said flatly, not offering any further information.

"Hello, Anna," he said. "I'm Bill del Vecchio."

"Del Vecchio," she said musingly. "Of the old ones? Or does it mean of the past?"

"I don't know," Bill said, slightly embarrassed. "I've never thought about it. It's never come up."

"OK." She sounded self-composed. "I'll see you on Friday."

At seven on Friday Anna was dropped off at the side door of the bank building. Her roommate insisted on waiting by the curb while Anna rang the bell. After a few minutes, the door was opened by a man who wore a loose shirt barely concealing a noticeable bulge over his belt. He asked if she was Anna. She nodded and momentarily winced, wondering if this was Bill and whether he was fat and balding after all, but she turned and waved to the car and watched it drive off, feeling that the die had been cast.

The man she feared might be Bill quickly introduced himself as Sparks. He ushered her inside to the bottom of a steep stairwell and shut the entry door behind then. "Up we go," he said with a slight giggle. As they walked up a steep flight of stairs to the studio, he gave her a running account of what she would be seeing. "It's hot up there with all the equipment running at once, but the outside studio's air conditioned because of the LP library. Gotta keep them cool or they'll warp. The broadcast booth is glassed in, so from the library you can watch what's happening on the air. Bill's working in the booth. But don't be surprised when you see him. A lot of people say Bill looks like Abe Lincoln, without the beard of course. No one wears beards these days. Don't get me wrong and don't judge him because of that. He's one of the good guys round here." Sparks gave another giggle, reminding Anna of a large puppy with soulful dark black eyes. He told her that Bill was doing the news and pointed him out to her before giving a jaunty wave and disappearing into a control room which itself was packed with stacked equipment and dials with wavering needles.

Anna looked through the glass to where Bill sat in the sound booth. His polished voice never missed a beat as he nodded to her. He held a headset up to his left ear while he read from yellow pages torn from the teletype machine that was periodically issuing bells and tapping away in the corner behind her. She saw a man with a narrow studious face, craggy features, and prominent nose concealed behind a large microphone. Sparks was right. He looked a bit like President Lincoln. But Bill was right also; he wasn't bald and fat. His shoulders seemed almost too broad for his thin frame and his hair was dark and wavy even if receding a bit at the temples.

Through the booth's window Bill could see a young woman with dark long hair pulled back into a ponytail. She was wearing jeans, a plain blue T-shirt, and a bulky white cardigan with sleeves rolled up to her elbows. There was something about her that unsettled him. She was like a haunting memory from a time he could not quite remember. He watched her look curiously at the floor-to-ceiling shelves jammed with record jackets arranged alphabetically by composer. He could also see his own reflection in the glass of the recording booth. It made him wonder what a young woman like her might see in him. But at the same time, it made him wonder why he cared what she thought. He still hadn't even formally met her.

"Hi," he said as he came out of the sound booth leaving Cesar Franck spinning on the turntable behind him. "Come on in and see the set-up."

The cramped sound booth had three turntables, corresponding banks of dials above each one, and two stacked reel-to-reel tape decks. The microphone hung like a goose-necked lamp over a cluttered counter bearing a logbook. "This is the one on the air," he said, pointing to a dial with a jumping needle. "I can control the sound levels here. I also write down in the log the time of every piece of music we play and all the commercials. FCC requirement. We have to account by the minute. If a program runs short we can't start another early. I have recorded filler music to bring us up to the next minute or else I'll ad lib. You'll often hear music fragments die away as the next program comes on."

She looked impressed at the precision he was describing. It was obviously all new to her. He felt that he had that advantage at least. The lights were hot in the booth, and when she stood next to him, her hair smelled slightly of shampoo. He secretly studied every detail of her, knowing it was important but not knowing why.

"It all sounds complicated," she said.

He felt complimented that he was doing something that impressed her. It was a good start.

"How did you get to be an announcer?" she asked eventually when he said nothing back.

He felt tongue-tied, almost afraid to speak. If he said the wrong thing, would she bolt through the door, walk out through the library, and be gone from his life? A young girl like this, she had to have boyfriends and plenty to choose from. Why him? Why did it matter so much?

"A friend said I had a good voice for it. I recorded a newscast. The station liked it and I applied for a license." That was the best he could do.

"It came easily for you?"

"You might say so. We get many fellows in here who want to do it but don't have the voice. We tell them to try the rock stations where they don't do as much news."

"Have you ever had a woman try out?" She looked at him curiously.

"Once we did, but she didn't sound authoritative enough." He restrained himself from saying that he didn't think anyone wanted to hear the news read by a woman. He knew intuitively that would be unwise.

"Just her or all women?"

He was right. She would have been annoyed if he had said what he was thinking. He changed tactic immediately. "Would you like to try reading the news?"

He sat her at the console and handed her the earphones and the yellow sheets of paper he had been reading from. They contained headline news entries that he had either underlined or edited. "Go ahead and read something," he said. "I'll record you on the tape deck over here. Wait for my count." He cued up a reel and held up his hand. When he had counted three fingers and pointed at her, she read a thirty-second account of a Viet Cong attack on a US base.

"Reading that was much harder than I thought it was going to be," she admitted while he rewound the tape afterwards. "I kept breathing in the wrong places. I didn't think thirty seconds could go by so slowly."

"A lot can happen in thirty seconds," he agreed. "Boxers can tell you that. Three minutes in the ring can be a lifetime. Presenting the news is a skill. You did well for your first time. You had modulation in your voice. Most chaps who try out tend to be monotone. You have to look on broadcasting as public speaking. It's not reading. You put the emphasis on the first statement, because the first one sets the tone for the rest. You use the pauses to indicate where the listener can take a second to digest the information. The other facts rise or fall in tone depending on their importance."

They listened together to her effort.

"My voice sounds very high."

"You'd have to bring it down if you wanted to broadcast. Your voice sounds classy but, you're right, it's pitched too high for easy translation on radio receivers. They tend to lose the highs and lows. Think of broadcasting like a hearing aid. The high sounds squeak and the low sounds growl. You want to aim for the middle."

She laughed her tinkling laugh. "Thank you for the lesson. I learned something."

"Stand by," he said again. "I'm going to cue the next cut. It'll be a while before it's on, but I can relax and talk for a few minutes if I get it ready to go."

She stood behind him as he used a finger to spin the second Rachmaninoff piano concerto forward until he heard a whine and then back until before the cut began.

"Do you choose these pieces yourself?" She looked out through the booth window at the multiple shelves crammed with record jackets. There was a lot to choose from.

"No. There's a program person who does it. Many stations have it all prerecorded, including the announcements. This station allows for breathing human beings to do it."

"So tell me about yourself," he said as he ushered her out of the warm sound booth. "It's much cooler out here in the library. They have to keep the records in air conditioning."

"That's a very broad question," she said. "What do you want to know."

"Well," he said. "Let's start with where you come from. Are you from around here?"

"Arcata. This is my second year here."

She wasn't giving him much to go on. "What brought you down the coast?"

"UCLA gave me a scholarship. That made coming here possible. I work at the library and have a cheap place to live with other students. If I'm careful, it doesn't cost me any more to be here than to go to school up north. Besides, I wanted the adventure."

"Your parents weren't worried?"

"My mother. My father is out of the picture. Of course, if it were up to her, I'd be safe back home. She's the force in the family and the one with the ambitions for me. You must go to college, she insisted. Too many girls don't get the chance."

"Do you mind if I ask you a personal question?" he said "You seem to be sensitive about women not being allowed to do things. Am I right?"

"I was raised by a very determined mother who said she wasn't going to let what happened to her happen to me as well. She wanted to be a pediatrician. In her day, there weren't scholarships for women. She asked her father for help. He told her it was a waste of money to educate a girl because she'd marry and he'd be giving something to another man."

"What did she do?" Bill thought of Vera as he asked the question. How many other women were trapped by society's expectations. He supposed it was a very large number.

"She went into nurse's training, which also had to be paid for, but her mother had inherited money from her family and gave it to her. My grandfather couldn't object since no one told him. When I was born, my mother primed me for college. I've seen enough easy assumptions about who deserves to be educated for me to be wary."

"And your father never participated in your education?"

"As I said, I never knew him. He left shortly after I was born and was never heard from again. It created an interesting situation for me. I never had a childhood. My mother needed a companion and partner, so anything childish was discouraged and I took responsibility from early on."

"An old head on young shoulders?"

"I've always been more comfortable around adults than children. Children my own age seemed very silly. What about you? Where are you from?"

"East Coast mainly. Two years in the Navy and then discharged here in California. I work for the telephone company during the day and do this radio gig several nights a week." He didn't want to say more—certainly not go into his family situation. "So how did you come to know classical music?"

"Maybe I should ask you that." She looked composed and willing to turn his questions back onto him. "I was given piano lessons while I was in school. My mother insisted on them because she could play quite well."

"So, do you play well?" Now he was gently bantering with her.

"It didn't take," she said firmly. "Your turn. How did you get interested in classical music?"

"I can't remember a time when I didn't enjoy it. Italian families tend to play opera recordings. Consider the stereotype of the Italian baker breaking into a Verdi aria as he pulls the bread out of the oven."

"Did yours do this?" She looked amused.

"No, but there were other Italian families in the neighborhood. Rocky Marciano's family were neighbors, and one of my grandfathers was a journalist who was friendly with Caruso. I don't know what the other one did, but I think it's in the blood—Italian music I should say."

"So you like Rossini, Vivaldi, and Cherubino?"

"Ah, you know how to wound a fellow. You have exposed me. I like Brahms and Beethoven, the major rebels. I like to be swept by grand passion like Fingal's Cave."

"Mendelssohn."

"I'm impressed. You do know something about music."

"You mean you invited me up here on false pretenses? You thought I didn't know anything." Her eyes darkened indignantly.

"Hold on there. I didn't know how interested you were. I've only spoken with you a couple of times, remember? Who is your favorite composer?"

"It varies. Mozart, Beethoven, Prokofiev."

"Apparently Respighi as well."

She smiled. "Especially pieces about thieving birds."

"So what's your major?"

"English."

"May I ask why?"

"I love the English language. Carl Sandburg says it's a language that rolls up its sleeves, spits on its hands and gets to work. That means it belong to all of us, not just academics. It's willing to adopt words from all other languages as long as they're useful. The French purified their language to the point that it can't adapt; the French may love it, but no one else finds it workable. Language comes easily to me. On the other hand, I have a mathematics block. I resent it. Why pi, for example? I can work with it and apply it to circles, but I don't understand why it works. I want to know its consequences and origins rather than its utility."

"It just is, so you'll have to talk with whoever's in charge of the world about that." Bill smiled ruefully.

"I belong in the humanities because I can ask those questions."

"Of God?" He furrowed his brows in mock confusion.

"No," she laughed, "of my long-suffering instructors."

"If you have problems with math, I am quite good with it." He looked at her steadily and wondered how she was going to react to such an obvious line on his part. He wanted to see her again.

She looked back at him with the same quizzical expression she had when he talked about women announcers. "Are you offering to tutor me?"

"Up to you. While you're thinking about it, would you like to have dinner after my shift is over? We could talk more about it."

She looked at him blankly. "My friend is picking me up, remember?"

"Would he like to come too?"

Anna shook her head. "It's a she. But I don't think I should go out with someone I don't know. I've appreciated the tour of the studio, don't get me wrong. But I hardly know you and don't know how would I get home if I tell her not come for me."

"It will be very proper. I promise you. I'll invite our engineer, Sparks, to come with us. You met him when you came in. He's harmless enough, in case you didn't notice. If you can change your plans, we can take you home." Before she could answer, Bill opened the door to the control room. "Hey, Sparks," he yelled. "Come help me persuade this young lady to have dinner with us."

"Come out with us," Sparks urged her when he came out from the warm, droning machines that kept the radio station on the air. "I'll tell you all about Mr. Mellow—that's what we call Bill here because he has such a great radio voice. I'll also tell you about how I met him."

"So how did you meet?" Anna asked Bill.

"I'll answer if you let us take you out to dinner."

"Blackmail," Anna laughed.

In the end, they went to a nearby Mexican restaurant where Bill and Sparks were known and greeted when they came in.

"Mr. Mellow?" Anna said quizzically after they had been seated and placed their orders. "How did that come about?"

"We served on the same troop transport in the Navy, and Bill here, would read the news and make announcements over the ship's public address system when we were at liberty. I was in charge of the radio as well as being mail clerk, so I listened to everyone on board to find someone who sounded good since my voice is squeaky. He was a natural. We stayed in touch and when I got the job here at the station, I recommended him for an opening for a part-time announcer. When you serve with a bunch of guys, you get to know who's gold and worth keeping."

Bill smiled. "I started out working days, went to school at night, and did the radio work on the weekends. Kept me busy and out of trouble. Once I'd got my diploma, life became easier because I had just the day job and the radio at night." Bill shrugged but also felt proud that he'd managed to pull it all off. The GI Bill had helped. So had Sparks' keeping an eye out for him.

"Only thing," Sparks said. "He's something of a skeptic about things.

We're working on him though."

"A skeptic?" Anna said musingly. "About what?"

"Bill doesn't believe in anything he can't touch or taste or hear," Sparks replied.

"I'm just a sensory guy." Bill admitted. "I'm a bit boring really. It's all here and now."

"There's no mystery for you?" Anna asked. "Nothing more out there somewhere?"

"Depends on what you mean by *somewhere*. If you mean the paranormal, I think the world is crowded with charlatans and the credulous. If you mean spiritual, I try not to have an opinion. One reason you won't see me in Church. I can't accept things like miracles and resurrections."

"I didn't know you felt like that." Sparks looked at Bill as if he were seeing him for the first time. "I didn't know you thought going to Church was a waste of time."

"I didn't say that. You and I have talked about this before. It's no big secret how I feel. I just don't buy into things. I don't interfere with what others want to believe, but I ask them to respect what I choose not to believe," Bill replied.

"I knew you were skeptical about things like UFOs," Sparks said. "I didn't know it extended to religion."

"Everyone's skeptical about UFOs." Bill tried to laugh it off. He didn't like the crestfallen look on Sparks' face. He could see this conversation leading to something he didn't want to deal with.

"But how can you live without belief? Religion is what gives you purpose." Sparks' cheeks puffed out and he looked vaguely as if he were going to cry.

"Do you think there's purpose to life? Something after the end?" Anna asked Bill this question directly.

"To be honest," replied Bill. "I believe that once it's over, it's over. You go to sleep and there's the void. But that doesn't mean I disrespect people who think differently. In the end, it's whatever gets you through the day."

"That's a bit depressing." Anna's voice was musing, as if she were trying on a new identity and asking herself how it would feel. "I'd like to believe that there are rewards. That may be childish, but it's consoling to think that people who are awful get theirs someday."

"That's a very traditional viewpoint," Bill said. "Marx said that religion lulled entire populations into accepting brutal conditions in the hope that there would be heaven at the end. 'An opiate,' he said."

"I don't think I look on it as an opiate," she said, "but rather as a way for justice to work itself out in the world. When I'm driving and someone races past me, it would be nice to come across the driver stopped somewhere down the road and getting a ticket—an expensive one. He gets to pay and I feel virtuous. Probably very shallow of me and there are much better examples. I always thought of karma as a sort of reckoning, although there seem to be a lot of people who get overlooked."

"Each to his or her own," Bill said. He wanted this conversation over. He got enough about religion at his mother's house. "If I am cynical about religion and purpose, it's only because they don't allow much choice. You either accept or you don't. You're either saved or you're not. It settles matters and some people find it comforting. I prefer to do without an imposed faith." Bill assumed the conversation would now change direction, but he had reckoned without Sparks.

"I don't believe it's possible to live without faith. You seem to think that it is bad to have faith." Sparks looked at Bill with challenge in his eyes.

Bill cursed that the topic had ever been raised. He couldn't see an easy way out. "It depends on what you have faith in, Sparks," Bill said seriously. "But whatever it is, it ought to be consistent and sincere. I respect people who have a set of ethics and follow it. Unfortunately, the biggest hypocrites I've ever met were churchgoers." Bill's heart sank as he said this. He had a good idea what was coming next from the offended look on Sparks' face.

"Churchgoers are not all hypocrites, if that's what you mean. The only time I think there's any decency in the world is when I see the congregation at my church pull together to help someone. Faith may come from God, but people have to allow it to work through them." Sparks' face was tinged with pink and his forehead shone with a light film of sweat.

"I don't disagree with you, Sparks." Bill tried to soften the impact of his words. He had broken his own rule: never discuss politics or religion. He had meant only to impress Anna. Now his cavalier statements had opened up a world he didn't want to enter. It reminded him of the mini-inquisitions his mother conducted on the condition of his childhood soul.

"Are you in a congregation now, Sparks?" Anna asked. Her voice was inviting as if she were trying to soothe him.

"Yes," Sparks replied. "I used to question things, but when I returned home from the war, I realized that for all of us just being alive was a miracle. God must have had to have a purpose or we could have been killed. Plenty of others were. I go to church to meditate and to give thanks, and the people in my church help me. People trying to care for one another is what it's all about."

"I think that's what congregations exist for," Anna said. "It's the best thing about religion. Someone can be there to help you."

Bill chose his words carefully. "Sparks, I'm not talking about you. I meant the Sunday morning gang on this station. Have you listened to them? All those religious programs and preaching. They're the ones I mean. They're spewing venom in the name of Christianity."

"If they're preaching hate, it's a distortion. Those preachers are little people. We have to be better people because we recognize them for what they are. The members of my church are good people." Sparks was working himself up into a frenzy of defensiveness. In such moods, it would be possible for him to defend the Antichrist as long as he belonged to Sparks' church.

"I've often wondered if one can be a good person without joining a church," Anna said.

"I don't want to try," Sparks told her heatedly. "After the war, I wanted to help others. I'm a lay preacher and sometimes I go out with the pastor when he visits the sick. There are lonely people in the world. Many people don't have anyone to call them up and ask 'Are you OK? Did you die in the night?'"

"I'm sure your work is appreciated, Sparks," says Anna. "Your church is lucky to have you." She also appeared to want the conversation over.

"No, I'm the lucky one to have the connection," replied Sparks. "We have to help each other be ready."

"Ready?" Anna furrowed her forehead and studied Sparks. Up to this point she had been conciliatory. Now she too was afraid of what was coming next.

"For the prophecies guiding the world. It's up to us to reach out actively to regain the dream and help others to see it." Sparks looked almost benign as he described the vital role he saw before him.

"You are trying to live by prophecy?" Anna's eyes were wide.

"It's from the *Book of Revelation*," Sparks explained as if its truth should be self-evident.

Something changed in Anna's face. Now she looked grim rather than bemused. "I thought Revelations was not to be read literally."

"No, no. Our pastor says it's prophecy, and that makes it true," Sparks' cheeks glowed rosy with enthusiasm. "Those who have been saved and born again will be taken up to be with Christ. They will disappear one day. They will be saved from daily life and made immortal by their own worthiness."

"I thought Christ was to return at the end of history." Anna rested her knife and fork on the plate beside her half-eaten burrito. She stared at Sparks. "You mean the so-called Rapture, right?"

"It's not so-called. Christ is coming. You must have faith. The signs are around us. Can't you see them? The conflict in the Middle East, the destruction of those who would destroy the world, the coming of angels among men? Armageddon will begin with the saved being taken up into heaven. Israel will make covenant with the Anti-Christ, followed by war, disease, pestilence, earthquakes, and death. There will a terrible battle between Christ and the anti-Christ and a thousand years of peace when Jesus returns to establish a kingdom here on Earth."

"You believe everything is predestined?" Anna folded her hands in her lap and sat back in her chair.

"Not everything. We have to freely accept Christ as our savior and be born again into his love. Unless we accept Jesus, we will not participate in the final redemption."

"Forgive me, Sparks, but wasn't Christ's death meant to redeem all human beings?" Anna asked.

Bill groaned. This was worse than he could have ever anticipated. Sparks was spouting off evangelical preaching and Anna was looking more contemptuous by the moment. He felt stuck in the middle with no way of extricating himself. It could not end well. And all this about religion, his least favorite topic in the world.

Sparks shook his head impatiently. "Only those who accept Him as the way," he argued.

Anna looked grim. "What about people who have other spiritual ways up the mountain?"

"Those are not true ways," Sparks leaned forward eagerly and placed his hands flat on the table.

"How do you know that?" Anna asked.

"Because it's in the Bible."

"Sparks," asked Bill, leaning back from the table, trying to distract Sparks' attention away from Anna, "what happens to the non-Christians in this world?"

"The Bible is clear. They will be ruled by Christ and will convert or they will be destroyed."

"Including Jews and Muslims and Buddhists and Hindus? Why ever would God want to destroy his own creation?" Anna asked.

"Sparks, you've always supported Israel," Bill said. "How can you fight for Israel on the one hand and send all the Jews to damnation on the other?"

"Because the prophecy is clear. Israel will work with the anti-Christ. Jesus will return. The Jews will all convert when they see the truth."

There was silence at the table. Anna seemed frozen in her indecision about what to say next or even if it was worthwhile to try. Bill worried about what she was going to think. Sparks was a damned idiot. What if he'd cost Bill the girl? Bill didn't think it could get worse until it did.

"Are you both born again?" Sparks asked suddenly. His tone was almost accusatory.

Bill gulped and fought the urge to throttle the man across from him. "Once was enough," he managed to choke out.

"Spiritual but not religious," Anna said evasively. She looked angry and uncomfortable.

"You must embrace Christ as your savior. It won't be much longer before He comes." Sparks stared pointedly at Anna.

All Bill could think was that they needed a striped tent overhead and people screaming Hallelujah in the aisles.

"Sparks," Anna said slowly and distinctly. "Forgive me if I am being impertinent, but I want to ask you a serious question."

Sparks nodded eagerly. He thought he had made an impression on this girl. Perhaps she might even want to attend a meeting at his church.

"I was wondering," Anna continued, "how you interpret prophecy?"

"What do you mean?" Sparks frowned. This wasn't the question he was expecting.

"I'm concerned about people going out to make prophecy come true rather than allow things to work themselves out," she said.

"But prophecies are truth," Sparks objected passionately "It's been foretold. It's going to happen."

"Truth?" Anna sounded unimpressed. "I'm not sure what truth is these days. But I wonder if people's actions change because they believe something is going to happen. What if prophecies are possibilities or warnings and people act on them as if they are bound to happen? If we say we are all going up in smoke in a few years, why bother with protecting the Earth or being good to one another? It's all going to be dust anyway."

"That's not the point." Sparks was almost shouting now. "You have to be good to be saved. Don't you have faith in God?"

"There is a big difference between faith and truth."

Sparks looked confused.

"Why don't we call it a night?" Bill said and called for the bill.

"Don't you believe there will be a thousand years of peace when Jesus returns?" Sparks demanded of Anna.

"I believe," Anna said steadily, "that we have power over our own lives and good things happen to us when we reach out for them with open and tolerant hearts. I do not believe anyone faces a destiny imposed by prophecies in the Bible. I also don't believe in being bullied into faith by threats of Armageddon."

Sparks' cheeks turned pink and his eyes grew moist. Abruptly, he stood, looking as if he has been struck in the face. He wavered for a few moments looking distracted and disappointed. He didn't make eye contact with them as he walked quickly away from their table and out of the restaurant. Bill resignedly accepted the bill from the waitress. He would have paid anyway.

"I'm sorry if I embarrassed you, Bill," Anna said.

"It's no problem for me. I agreed with you mostly."

"Mostly?"

"I haven't thought enough about prophecy and destiny to have an opinion. I hope that doesn't disqualify me from something." He gave a small laugh to defuse the charged atmosphere.

After a few moments Anna smiled shakily. "I've turned down the fast way into heaven. I hope you weren't counting on it. I don't think

Sparks will let either of us in his church."

"I live for the present. Remember? I try not to let too many things upset me. I'll take you home now, and I hope you'll let me call you. But I don't think we'll go near the station again while Sparks is there. At least not for a while."

11:00 p.m.

*F*RA PIETRO! *So that's who Sparks was. Poor old bumbling fool, still bumbling, but at least now trying to help someone beyond himself. And that's how I remember Anna: clearheaded about what she thought and willing to admit it. But perhaps that's only how I want to remember her. Poor Sparks. He liked the girl and was trying to impress her just as I was. He was too clumsy to understand that Anna did not want a confessor, nor was she trying to destroy his belief; she was merely asking him to justify it, and he could not. It must have startled him because he couldn't know that if anyone was born to resist traditional religion, it was Anna. And if anyone was born with a mission, it was she. At that point I don't think she knew what it was. But she was not about to accept Spark's easy offer to salvation, no matter how kind he thought he was being.*

But there are differences between Fra Pietro and Sparks. Pietro used his own self-interest to justify his betrayal of Aonio's family. Sparks, at least, was trying to help others in the only way he knew. I suppose if we'd agreed with what he believed, he might have been reassured that he was on the right path, but I don't think that's what motivated him. He seemed genuinely sincere in wanting to save us. That's different from Fra Pietro. But there they both are: performance artists, navigating the labyrinth of life through revelation and ritual.

I can imagine what he prayed for that night: Dear Lord, please send the elevator from Heaven for your true believer. I want to be worthy of Rapture and rise in splendor above the masses of your lower beings. But please, dear Lord, do leave some sinners back there in the basement so I can feel blessed indeed.

And as for me, I was fascinated by Anna. I had never met a woman before with that degree of self-possession. She didn't seem worried that I was older than she was and I soon forgot her youth. I thought of her as the sibyl who saw what was past, or passing, or to come. But that did not stop me from fighting my attraction to her. I had told Skipper on the transport that I would never marry, and I meant it. But when I made that vow, at a time when Anna could not have been out of elementary school, I could not have predicted her. How could I imagine a woman who so closely echoed my own ideas and skepticism yet who could also offer hope? It was as if she had been sent to tell me I was not alone and that I should remove the wall I had built up between myself and life.

Chapter 9

The Inquisition Prison. Rome, September 1568

Giovanni Gubbio sat at a stained wooden table inside a small room not far from a the heavy, studded door to the outside world. The building had been a public prison, one of the worst in the city, before it was taken over by the Inquisition. His office, if one could call it that, was more cave than convenient, but it did its job. He was the head guard of the Inquisition prison, in charge of security. It was a position of respect within the prison's small world because if anyone escaped, it was his head on the line. No one ever had.

Giovanni's fellow workers knew little personal about him, which was how he wanted it. He didn't want them to know that when he lived in Bari, he was Giovanni Bovi until an altercation with a local street tough involving a knife and a woman left him little choice but to accept his family's suggestion to get out of town quickly. He walked four days to reach the anonymity of Rome. Once there, a relative of his mothers who worked for a cardinal helped him find a job at the prison. This was how things worked in the city: most Vatican jobs were filled through patronage. On the spot, Giovanni changed his name.

For a long time he feared that the Bari magistrates might enquire about him, but names were not a high priority in the prison and any inquiry would have been met with a shrug. His supervisor called Giovanni and everyone else by the common name of "guard." Giovanni lay low anyway. Because he never spoke about himself and never asked questions of anyone else, he earned a reputation for discretion. "That Gubbio's a quiet one," the other guards said. "Watch out for him. His eyes are sharp. Nothing gets past him." While other guards came and went, Giovanni sat tight. In time, he worked his way up until he was the logical successor when his most last supervisor drank too much, fell down a flight of stone stairs, and broke his neck.

Ensconced in the office that had been his for the past five years, Giovanni had just laid out his lunch of bread, olive oil with crushed garlic, sausage, and a small mug of beer. He was pleased with his life and untroubled by his duties. He took a detached view of the prisoners, assuming that they must have done something to deserve being brought in by the Inquisition constables. Their innocence or guilt was not his concern. He lived by the proverb that eggs have no business dancing with stones. He processed the prisoners when they came in, supervised the guards, made sure that the prisoners were tended to and never saw one another or received unapproved visitors, and filled out daily logs of comings and goings. There were others to handle the money and do the dark things that happened in the prison's lower levels.

When the prison's entrance bell rang, he put down his bread in annoyance. No new prisoners were expected. He looked at the incoming log on the table beside him to make sure he had not overlooked something. He had not. He heard the duty guard slide open the small eye slit in the door and demand gruffly who it was and on what business. The reply was not distinguishable, but he heard the small door slide shut and footsteps as the guard came into his office for direction.

"Name of Aonio Paleario. Says he's been told to report." The guard, a swarthy uninterested man from the south whose Neapolitan accent made him sound crude even to someone coming from Bari, had also been eating his lunch and was also annoyed at being disturbed.

"Who's with him?" Giovanni asked. "Who's brought him in?"

"Alone as far as I can see."

"Did he say who told him to come here?"

"Cardinal Rebiba."

Giovanni snorted. Another one of the Vatican crowd lacking the basic courtesy to inform the prison before sending someone over. Didn't they know that even prisons had policies and routines? As usual he said nothing that might be reported. "All right," he muttered. "Bring him in. Put him in the admitting room and get the Dispenser. He needs to inventory whatever the prisoner has on him." Giovanni then turned back to his interrupted meal.

The large, paneled door grated heavily on its hinges to admit Aonio into an narrow entrance corridor before it slammed shut behind him with an alarming finality. The sound made Aonio think fleetingly of the many others who must have heard that door before him, but he doubted if any of them could have stood with such resolution as he. He stood straight and imagined how he would be admired and perhaps even envied if someone only knew who he was and the nobility of his intentions.

Once inside, he looked around. There was little to see. The arched passageway extended about thirty feet before it dead-ended into another heavy, studded door that stood ajar, not enough to show what might be beyond but sufficient to provide light into the passage. Aonio assumed there must be some sort of central courtyard behind it. That's the way these old town buildings were constructed. The passage was bare and the ground paved with cobblestones. On each side were two doors with a staircase between them. One staircase led to upper floors, the opposite led down into the depths of the building. Aonio could see into the first of the doors on his right, which appeared to be the duty guards' room. Inside were a table and chair and heavy metal key hooks along the wall. His arrival must have disturbed the guard's lunch, as he could see bread and an earthenware jug on the table.

The guard took Aonio into the first room on the left, a small, bare area lit by a barred window set high on the wall. It contained only a table and a stool. He was told to place everything he had with him on the table. While he did so, the guard leaned back against the wall with his arms crossed. After a few minutes, the table held the contents of Aonio's pack and pockets: money, clothes, personal items, books, and writing instruments. "Shoes and cloak too," the man said. Once these had been added to the pile, Aonio was told to sit on the stool and wait.

"Will I be here long?" Aonio inquired impatiently. His mind was filled with the importance of the challenges he felt he had undertaken.

The guard shrugged and gave no reply. The Inquisition prison was not a travelers' inn. Here, questions flowed to the prisoners, not from them.

The Dispenser arrived after about half an hour and Giovanni was summoned from his office to witness the induction procedure. This mostly involved inventorying the prisoners' possessions and carefully counting the prisoner's funds, which would be used to pay for food and services in the time before the trial and final disposition. If the prisoner wanted decent food, clean clothes, and an occasional bath, he or she had better be prepared to pay for it. Otherwise the prisoner became dependent on whatever the prison was prepared to provide, which was minimal. Since the Dispenser reported directly to the Vatican and was responsible for paying for whatever services the prisoner requested, the accounting was scrupulous. Anyone caught stealing from a prisoner was stealing from the Vatican, and the Holy Office did not tolerate thieves.

In short order, the money from the sale of Aonio's horse was laid out in piles of coins, and the contents of his pack inventoried. The books, writing implements, and knife were all confiscated. The money was tallied in a large book. Aonio was not indigent, so he could be treated with a modicum of respect. It all depended, of course, on how the Inquisition wanted him dealt with and how long it was before his actual trial. If his money ran out before then, he would get nothing more than gruel and maybe a greasy piece of fatty pork for his meals. One never knew in these cases how long he would be there.

No one said anything to Aonio, who sat hunched on the stool, naively unaware of the standards by which they were judging him. Finally, the Dispenser nodded to Giovanni and said he was done. He finished his tally, scooped up the coins and Aonio's possessions, and made ready to leave.

"May I have my books?" Aonio asked plaintively as he saw them about to disappear.

The Dispenser didn't stop what he was doing. "That's up to the inquisitors," he said. He picked up Aonio's pack and was gone. Giovanni nodded to the gate guard. It was time to take the prisoner to the holding cell until they could find something more permanent. If the cardinal had been more considerate, of course, this matter would have already been settled.

Aonio was led back into the corridor and taken to the flight of stairs that led down into the lower part of the prison. The guard walked behind him, urging him on until he told him to stop outside a heavy door that he opened with a massive jangle of keys. When he pointed inside, Aonio had little choice but to enter. The guard then threw a thin blanket on a sagging mattress in one corner and left without saying anything more.

As Aonio's eyes became accustomed to the gloom he studied his surroundings. The room was almost completely dark. Spiders' webs stretched across a narrow window slit far up above, and the walls were stained by mildew. The cell was already chilled. In another few months when the winter rains came, it would be icy. "How poor" he thought, "are the wages of scholarship and the search for truth."

He sat down on the rough mattress, greasy with the pain and sweat of others, and listened to the sounds emanating through the walls. He could hear a woman sobbing down the hall. A man groaned and cursed. He could hear someone yelling gibberish and the clang of metal on stone walls. The outside world was somewhere up above him, muted and indistinct. He could occasionally make out tradesmen's shouts in the street. He had fallen out of time. All he could do was wait.

The sliver of daylight in the window darkened and, after long hours, became grey with the dawn. Aonio had not slept for the toothache and the building's sounds. In the night's stillness he could hear screams and doors opening and shutting. No one had come to see him and he was hungry. A few hours later, he heard shuffling feet and someone shoved coarse bread, cheese, and a water jug into the cell and slammed the door. He did not see who brought the food, but he ate it gratefully, if chewing only on one side of his mouth.

Hours passed until he assumed it was late afternoon before the door to his cell opened. He did not recognize the man who entered. He wore a priest's vestments and fluttered his hands as he peered into the gloom.

"Aonio Paleario? I am sorry you have had to wait. We were not notified concerning your arrival until late this morning. I've been sent to move you to another accommodation. This room is used for new admissions." The man seemed genuinely apologetic as if the whole admissions process had been some mistake.

"May I ask who you are?" Aonio cleared his throat, surprised at how hoarse he sounded.

"I apologize. Please forgive me. I am Sandrino Calla. I am responsible to the Father Inquisitor for the prisoners in the Torre de Nona. Not the physical surroundings, unfortunately, but certainly their mental and spiritual affairs." Calla's hands gestured nervously like a bird's wing and when he sighed deeply, as he tended to do often, his mouth opened as his head went back until his neck stretched out. He turned to the guard. "Have you been told where this man has been assigned?"

"Third floor, sir." The guard sounded somewhat polite, suggesting that Calla had some influence within the prison walls.

"Good," said Calla. He nodded at Aonio approvingly, as if expecting the gratitude of some weary traveler who has just been assigned the best room in the house. "You will sleep better up there and you can make any special arrangements for your food with the guards."

"May I have my books?" Aonio asked. He had brought favorites with him and planned to reread them both for comfort and instruction.

"I'll see what can be done. The Holy Office directs these matters." Calla gave another sighing gesture that hinted it might be possible but that Aonio should not expect miracles. He indicated that Aonio should precede him out of the cell's door and follow the guard.

They crossed the entry passageway and this time climbed stairs that led to the upper floors. The new room had more furniture and was obviously intended for a longer stay. There was a small brazier in a chimney, a table, a chair, a bed with a high headboard and horsehair mattress, a water pitcher with a basin, and a hole in the floor with a wooden seat over it. A small plate of chicken, beans, and bread was waiting on the table. Through a single small window, too high in the wall for any view, he could see the top of St Peter's golden basilica.

"Do you know when the process will begin?" Aonio asked.

"These things take time, I'm afraid." Calla gave again his curious stretched neck gesture which Aonio decided must occur whenever Calla was asked a question he found difficult to answer. "There is always a problem coordinating schedules and determining when the inquisitors will be free to come to Rome. Generally you will have several months to wait until the initial inquiry."

"Have we met somewhere before?" Aonio asked. "You seem familiar to me."

"I should think it unlikely," Calla replied. "My life has been spent with Church missions far away from here. I was recently called back to Rome and I'm told I'll be here only for a short time."

"I would be grateful for my writing equipment, paper, and candles."

"As I said, these requests must be considered elsewhere. But I will mention them." Calla looked uncomfortable and Aonio realized that the man knew more than he was saying.

"To whom?"

"The Father Inquisitor. He will determine all matters." Calla gave one last sigh and neck stretch before he left Aonio alone in the cell. The heavy keys clanked as the guard locked the door.

Aonio sank onto the mattress. The rope grid under the pallet creaked with his weight, and when he leaned against the headboard, it banged against the wall. It was quieter in this part of the prison, but if he concentrated, he thought he could still hear the groans and crying, more distant, softer, but still echoing as if they had permeated the very walls.

That night, even though Aonio's eyes burned, the pain from his toothache would not permit him to sleep. He paced restlessly, now and then looking up through the window to where moonlight glistened off the golden dome of St Peter's. The dome was coldly beautiful, impressively indifferent to the city whose skyline it dominated and the lives snuffed out in the name of its teachings. He watched as dark clouds scudded across the moon, causing alternating light and dark on the dome's gold. His face had swollen around his bad tooth until he could no longer feel his jaw. It was to the point where he knew something had to be done, but without his knife he could see no immediate way to do it.

Driven by pain and desperation, he walked the two paces to the door and ran his fingers around the frame, looking for wood splinters. There were none to pry free. He stumbled back to the table and ran his hand over the top. Again, there was nothing beyond old gouges and scratches. But when he ran his hand underneath the table, he found a promising lift in the wood grain. He tried to start an edge with his fingernail, but the wood was too hard. In desperation, he took the spoon left with his dinner and ran its edge along the stone wall until he had something that might be able to make an impression at the splinter's tip. It took him nearly an hour to free it, but the constant pain in his mouth gave him the motivation and persistence to keep at it. Finally, he had what he wanted—a small, jagged splinter with a sharp tip, fragile, but enough to pierce his gum.

Sitting on the bed, jubilant in the thought of possible relief and without thinking about it, he jammed the tip into the crease between his gum and jaw, right above the rotten tooth. With a loud groan, he forced the wood in as far as it would go. The tissues in his mouth cracked apart with a warm rush of pus or blood, he didn't know which, filling his mouth with a foul taste; he stumbled across the room to spit whatever it was down the hole. Then he stood over the hole, pressing his cheek and spitting until he felt the throbbing lessen. When it seemed to be done, he lay down again on the bed, leaving the tip from the splinter embedded in the gum to keep the incision open and the abscess draining.

After a fitful, exhausted sleep, he realized that the tooth had to be removed or he might run the risk of the rottenness returning. This was a completely different challenge and he thought of Archimedes: he needed a lever to move the tooth. With the abscess gone, the area was anesthetized, and he prodded it as carefully as he could, pushing with the spoon's handle until he felt it catch on one of the roots. When he started to press downwards, he was stopped by a sharp pain that told him he must have scraped the bone. He rested for a few moments to let the throbbing subside before repositioning the spoon against the root. This time he was in the right place. The tooth gave to the pressure and the gum started to release it. The tooth hung for a few seconds before one final pull dropped it onto his tongue and he spat it down the hole. He tore a piece from his shirt then to press up into the cavity before breaking out in a cold sweat after which he lay down on his side, and fell asleep.

In the afternoon, Calla came back to see him with a guard and more food. If they noticed anything different with Aonio's face, they said nothing. Aonio assumed the swelling must have gone down. Whatever the case, he felt the wonderful release of no longer being in pain.

"The Father Inquisitor has agreed to allow you some of your texts. The others will require further review," Calla told him. "You may, however, have your copy of Boethius."

"But all the others were authorized for printing from the Holy Office." Aonio could not see the objection.

Calla smiled apologetically and waved his hands in remorse. "I can only repeat what I am told."

"And my papers and writing utensils?"

"I know nothing of that." Calla gave another of his deep sighs and neck stretches.

"I understand." Aonio did not, but he sat back, seeing perhaps for the first time how much his life was to be controlled by the golden dome of St Peters.

"This afternoon you will be able to make your arrangements with the guard, and he will bring those of your books that have been approved so far. Every detail of your life here is recorded. He must always ask for approval."

"Have you learned anything further about when I will be examined?"

"It will take place once all the necessary arrangements have been made. I can't tell you more." Calla did not sigh this time. He was merely repeating what he had been told.

The next day the Dispenser started the flow of coins from Aonio's account. A prescribed number of coins went out for his food; it was cooked by a local woman and delivered to prisoners who could afford it. The bowls came once a day in the morning. It was acceptable and Aonio did not worry about it being poisoned except to the extent that his death would rob him of his chance in court. Once a week a man came with water to pour down the hole to the street below. Every two weeks another man came whistling down the passageway outside. He offered coals for the fire, clean bedding, and small toiletries if Aonio could afford to buy. If Aonio wanted his linens laundered, it could be arranged. But everything had its price. Aonio calculated he had enough money to last perhaps a year if he were frugal. As the time passed, he was forced to realize that his imprisonment might outlast his funds.

As the days turned into weeks, Aonio found time dragging. He had read and reread the books he had been allowed, but there was only so far he could go with them since he had nothing to write with or on except for the walls of his cell. He marked the days using a piece of charred coal. His other books had not been released to him; he supposed that they must have offended someone. Left to his own devices and boredom, he began to work out the prison's routine. He got to the point when he could tell when someone was late or had forgotten one duty or another. This in turn led to him becoming fixated on little diversions from the day-to-day schedule. He didn't like the guard being late when he walked his round. He waited impatiently for the man who flushed out the hole to the street. Then one day, his meal was delivered late. After he battled mounting hysteria, he realized that he had to find an outlet or lose his sanity.

That was when he started composing orations in his head. He found the days flew if he could think about the type of abstract propositions he used to debate. Not only did it occupy him, but it also reminded him of happier days when half the city would cram into the university auditorium to hear him and his colleagues speak. On those public days, sometimes the elders assigned the topics. Other times it was a challenge from one scholar to another. What is jurisprudence? Eloquence? The Republic? Happiness? Fortitude? Liberty? Popular government? Many times the audience voted him the winner in these contests. Sometimes he had no opponent willing to take up his challenge. If that happened, he would talk from memory as if he were providing a classroom lecture. He took pride in his power to persuade and the respect it earned him.

Within the prison walls, he tried to recreate this world. He pictured himself standing in the speakers' space on the floor of the great lecture hall at the University of Milan, looking up at the tiers of circular galleries above him; they were packed with scholars and students. Anticipation electrified the air because today there had been no announced topic so no one knew what to expect. The debaters would have to speak extemporaneously since they didn't know either. He could hear the hush as the elders entered the hall and took their seats behind the carved wooden rail of the first gallery. He imagined the prime elder, perhaps the rector, rising from his seat to announce the day's proposition, his sonorous voice reaching throughout the hall and echoing off the intricately carved wooden ceiling far above them. "Today," the rector pronounced, "our learned speakers will debate the sources of evil." Aonio could hear the buzz that echoed through the galleries. This was new, something never heard before.

"In particular," the rector continued, "our speakers are to address the nature of evil and then debate from whence it comes. The proposition is whether or not evil comes from human free will."

The topic was a firebrand, and lives could be lost over the outcome. It required the speakers not only to define evil and free will but also to deal with a set of ancient questions: if a perfect God created a perfect universe where did evil come from? Was it caused by humans perversely defying their Creator? Was it caused by rebellious angels taking advantage of weak human beings in order to destroy God's creation? Was evil part of God's plan?

That was a topic that Aonio had always wanted to address but never had the chance. The resident Churchmen had always forbidden it, saying that it was reserved to the Church to discuss. Any secular debate, they thundered, could only be blasphemous. But things were different now. There was no one in this prison to prevent his mind from choosing the topic. In his mind and in this setting, it seemed more than appropriate. He intended to see where the argument took him.

He paced his cell as he composed this oration, changing words as he went, trying out new ideas. He declaimed out loud as he would on stage. He composed and recomposed, following the classical pattern, the one established by the Greek orators. He wished he had his copy of Cicero's orations to help with his delivery, but he had committed much of those to memory and could draw on them as he needed.

His oration started, as all classical speeches were expected to, with an *exordium* or introduction. It was up to him to establish who he was and catch his listeners' attention. He decided to use the Sack of Rome as his prime example of evil. The second part was the narratio or history. Here he could provide an account of what happened and why. What were the causes of the Sack of Rome and did it settle anything? Did it perhaps make the world safer? Aonio doubted it strongly. The mercenaries who plundered Rome dispersed to wherever there was money to pay them, their leaders too well placed politically to be touched. In this part, he cautioned that it could all happen again given the same circumstances. That was the point he wanted to make about evil: through the ages, it had proved itself pointless and as ambiguous as Croesus learning from the Delphic Oracle that if he attacked Persia, a mighty empire would fall. What she did not tell him was that the empire would be his own.

The *propositio* or statement concerning the case came next. This involved presenting his major points as he broke down his topic. Here he could consider whether God used evil for His own purposes. But what kind of purpose might that be?

At some point, he knew he had to define what he meant when he called things evil. In the fourth part, the *partitio*, Aonio intended to provide that definition. There were two types, he decided. One was intellectual and driven mainly by greed for material things or for power. The other was spiritual, which was represented by people moving away from the will of God. Here is where he could perhaps slip in the Inquisition and argue that it was contrary to God's wishes.

In the *conformatio* or presentation of evidence, Aonio was now free to state his own beliefs. He had examined his thoughts carefully and planned to argue that he could not believe the world was inherently evil. People could not legitimately blame the physical world for storms and earthquakes, for example. The sorrows those caused were indiscriminate. Genuine evil, on the other hand, had to be targeted and it had to be intentional. This meant it had to be human because no one in his right mind would call a wild animal evil. But did saying that mean that everyone was evil?

This left Aonio with the *reprehensio*, where he was expected to pare away competing theories of evil and let his own shine through his discourse. Who had others called evil and did he agree with them? Were his jailers evil because they did evil things? No. They just did their jobs as they understood them. They probably wished him no particular harm. Calla and the guards might be misguided in their indifferent acceptance of authority, but they were not evil because they lacked the power to control or benefit from the outcome. Ah, he thought. There was the key. That had to be it. He would argue that the truly evil person knowingly abuses others for his own advantage. Was greed the motivation for this evil? Perhaps. But, Aonio reasoned, many greedy men did not directly harm others. Was it power? Perhaps. It seemed that the more the power, the more evil possible. But, he remembered, there were men in lowly places who had done things that any reasonable person would describe as evil. Position in life seemed only to control the number of people who could be harmed and not the evil intent of the perpetrator.

Aonio thought about the friars he denounced in Siena. They robbed an old lady, the aunt of his friends, the Bellantis, while supposedly providing her with spiritual guidance. He had publicly shamed them for their hypocrisy and greed. But would he call them evil? They were gnats, annoyances, and criminals, but to call them evil was to over credit them. Evil, as it turned out in this stage of his thinking, was a knotty question, one to set aside for the moment.

In the *digressio*, he was free to illustrate what he had been talking about so far, using contemporary examples to put flesh to his ideas. He knew it was safe to talk about the evils besetting Italy and the constant warfare between the pope and the emperor because everyone could agree on that. Whole cities had been destroyed and inhabitants killed or scattered because of these conflicts. People would know this history only too well. He could talk here about the terrible aftermath of the Sack and then quietly make the comparison between being trapped in the city and being trapped in the Inquisition's prison. Personal testimony always went over well as long as it wasn't too inflammatory.

The *peroratio* would be his summation. Here he would present his conclusions in majestic Latin phrases that rolled off his tongue and might be remembered and quoted in future. He would soar as he referred to the best thinking of the world's most respected Latin thinkers. Evil, he would declaim with magisterial tones, is introduced by human beings, it is particular to human beings, and it requires human beings to inflict it on one another. It involves falsity, hypocrisy and violence, all intended to harm others. Its tools are lies, manipulations, and callous self-interest. Vicious people use evil to subvert the human power to do good and to honor God.

As the days passed, Aonio added to this speech. As he repeated it and spoke it out loud, committing it to memory, he also polished the sentences. He bolstered his evidence. He practiced his tone and the cadences of his delivery. It became for him the exempla of who he was as a scholar. It completely occupied his mind until the day he was told to prepare himself for the first stage of his trial. It was also the day when the Dispenser informed Aonio that his funds were starting to run low. Aonio was thus left wondering not only when and where he would deliver his *magnum opus* but also whether he would survive on whatever the prison was willing to provide. All he could do was trust that his Savior would take care of him.

12:00 p.m.

*A*ONIO FASCINATES ME. *Here is a man who has given up his freedom in the name of freedom. He talks about truth without acknowledging there may be other truths equally as valid as his own. He looks at the world through the lens of his own choices, yet does not allow others to choose differently. It is not sufficient for him to protest—after all the Protestants only established another intolerant orthodoxy. He wishes to remove the crushing weight of religious belief, yet he is religious and his belief system is an orthodoxy also. Why can't he see that?*

"Easy, sweetheart," Anna said. "He's very restless."

"He could probably use more," Carole replied. "It's been a while."

Anna curved her arm under his shoulder to lift him up.

"Why don't we put his teeth in at the same time?" Carole pushed his uppers and lowers into place. They give him the morphine and laid him down.

I am not bothered by the thought of dying with my teeth out. It's almost endearing that they think it might make a difference. But I suppose it can't hurt to die with the dignity of a full mouth. But it's not over yet, not even with my teeth in place. There's more to learn. Aonio doesn't see that free inquiry and peer review may not be free of bias either. After death, the soul rejoins its maker. Aonio is clear on this. But what about the cavern? How would he account for it? I wonder what he will learn when he dies. Will all this clamor over academic freedom seem so important? Will he be shown things in a way he can comprehend? I think I am now more interested in his death than in my own.

This speech he is creating also fascinates me. He is composing it for its own sake without any assurance that anyone else will ever hear it. I listen to him walking up and down his cell, committing it to memory and I am struck by how widely he draws for his definition of evil. The Christian concept is clear: evil is whatever goes against God's will. My skeptical self has trouble with this. If God uses evil for His own purposes, then we must all be on some sort of celestial treadmill. If God ordains the evil, then why does He punish we puny humans who do His will? Why do we get to pay the price for it? Is he just making examples of us? I'm having trouble here, and I don't want to be told to have faith. Contradictions pile on themselves and leave me more confused than ever.

Anna rejected Sparks' idea of heaven because it was exclusionary. He told her who would not be admitted unless they made some sort of conversion. Where is the rationality in that? God made man with reason, they say. At least, the human species is said to be the only one with reason, unless one wants to recognize all the experiments that show animals thinking, feeling, and remembering. Now, it even turns out, the Neanderthals had the capacity for speech. How arrogant we are in our assumptions of our own special creation. How arrogant we become when we take for granted the people who come into our lives.

I am not the destroyer of worlds. I am not the alpha and omega of my own existence, even though I have sometimes behaved that way. I am, instead, someone who is starting to see the beauty of human relationships. And, above all, I am starting to feel the gratitude I should have felt for the presence of the others in my life.

Chapter 10

Los Angeles, 1962

"WHAT'S THIS?" ANNA asked. He had taken her to his mother's house to get a change of clothes. He spent most of his time with Anna and went home to his mother's only occasionally to get his things. He still fancied himself as detached even as Anna thought they were becoming closer. He kept private the part of him that thought he could walk away at any time with no real regret and a sense that he had no obligation.

"Don't know. What is it?" He felt slightly invaded that she was looking around as if she had some role in his life other than the one he assigned her.

"It's a letter. Your name is on it."

He picked up the envelope from the kitchen table. It was in his mother's handwriting. She must have written it before she went to work. "Just a note from my mother. She probably needs something." He was prepared to ignore the note—probably a request for more money—as he had on the ship. But he couldn't ignore Anna's inquiring look. He tore open the envelope, read it, and threw the contents on the table impatiently.

"What is it?"

"Just my mother sticking her nose in where it's not wanted. Read it if you want." Bill was scornful and uninterested. The note meant nothing to him, and he assumed it would mean nothing to Anna either. He was wrong. Anna picked it up and her face set as she glanced over the page.

> Carissimo Bill:
>
> I pray night and day for you to find a good woman. I want you to be happy and to have your own family. One day you will want to buy a house and settle down. You need a good, mature wife who can earn a good salary to help you. I would not feel right if I didn't say to you this girl is not for you. She is too young. She will think only of herself. She will expect to stay in school and will be a burden to you. I am asking you as a mother to end this foolishness. Please, carissimo, let her go and end your relationship with her. She is not worthy of you.
>
> Love always,
> Mom

"Well, I know where I stand with her." Anna face was set and offended.

"Ignore it," Bill replied. "I'm going to. She means well."

"I don't think so." Anna looked as if she was about to bring matters to some sort of head and he didn't like that idea at all.

"You're not going to let this upset you, are you? It's not worth it," he said, as much as a comment on his mother as on Anna's apparent intention to make some sort of federal case of the matter. "She's always been like this. If I'd thought it was going to get to you, I wouldn't have let you read it. It means nothing." He tried to make his tone accusatory, both for his mother in creating him trouble and for Anna who was about to allow her do so.

"Bill, we've been together for over a year, now. I think it's time we made a larger commitment. We've talked about it enough." Anna's voice quavered as she struggled with her feelings. She was tired of the issues and of the evasions. She had long ago lost any expectation that Bill would come on bended knee with a proposal. If anything, he would slide backwards into commitment. That was the way he was and she knew she would have to accept it or walk away.

"You know we'll get married one day. You need to finish school. Things are great the way they are, aren't they? Why ruin something good. I've seen too many people ruined by a piece of paper."

"This isn't something I would joke about." Anna looked perturbed.

"Nor would I," he said "I've seen people staying in horrible relationships because they have nowhere else to go. I don't want either one of us to feel that way." He tried to convince himself he was thinking only of her.

"Bill, I do not want to be someone's hell. I want someone who asks me freely. I need assurance and stability if this relationship is to continue."

"Maybe I'm not who you think I am."

"What do you mean?" She was angry now.

"I don't like pressure. I don't like ultimatums. If you're going to pull crap on me, it's over."

"I see," she said in a small voice. "It's all about you, isn't it? Not about us. Maybe your mother's letter is right. Maybe we should stop seeing each other."

"If that's what you want." Bill snatched up the keys from the table and waited coldly at the door. He did not look at her on the drive back to her apartment. He got his things, felt justifiably self-righteous that he had made her no promises, and walked out through her front door congratulating himself on imposing a set of standards and being willing to stick by them. She said nothing further, convincing him that he was right. He drove back to his mother's house and put his clothes back in the chest of drawers. When his mother came home later, she smiled but he said nothing to her and things returned to normal. He started dating a woman he had known before and occasionally spent the night.

"Bill, I can't take no more of this. I deserve better." Carolina sat with him in the kitchen four months later.

"What are you talking about?" He looked at her in surprise. As far as he knew, his life was progressing just as he wanted.

"You never talk. You just come in and eat and say nothing. I fix your meals. I do your laundry and you don't say as a much as thank you. You have so many people eager to do things for you? You just go around looking angry. I had my fill from your father. I don't need it from you."

"I didn't know I was doing that."

"Well you are. Let me tell you this: either you get better to be around or you can find yourself another place to live."

"I didn't mean to be difficult." He wished she would find some sort of resolution without him and just leave him alone.

"You need to figure out fast what's going on with you. Is it the girl? This all started when you stopped seeing her."

"It was over long ago." This was the first time she had presumed to talk about Anna. He did not like it.

"Was it? Then why are you behaving this way?"

"I don't think I'm any different," he said defensively. "It didn't work out with her. That's it. That's what you wanted, isn't it? It's what you said in the letter. She read it. Then it was over."

"You let her read my letter? That was just a mother wanting the best for her son. You stupid, or what?" Carolina was outraged at the blame he was trying to assign her.

"What do you want of me? I don't know what you want of me."

"Something better than this. And don't you go blaming me because you couldn't make things work. It wasn't my fault. You didn't have to let her read the letter. You could have worked things out if it was so important to you. You're no good to me like you are."

"It didn't work. We both wanted to end it." Bill didn't like the idea that she was inquiring into the state of his soul again. What business was it of hers? What business had it ever been?

"Did you tell her you didn't want to end it? Or did you just sit there in silence with that look on your face?"

"What look?" he said angrily.

"The long-face look. The look that says I didn't try and don't blame me for messing up my life. It's what I do best. So what did you tell her?"

I don't remember."

"Let me guess, You said nothing." Carolina got up and threw dishes in the sink. "I don't want you here like this. Do us all a favor and do something about it. Either that or move out."

"She's probably found another boyfriend and forgotten me."

"So you have been thinking about her," Carolina said in triumph, "So you care. So go do something about it."

"I'll think about it."

"Well you think about it good, you hear? I want someone here I can live with. If you can't break the hold she has on you, you're no good to me."

Anna's name was still on the cluttered mailbox when he got there. An old house had been made into six student apartments, two-room conveniences with enough room for bare essentials and books. He almost wished she'd moved. He stood outside her door and heard Beethoven's seventh. She still liked classical music. He turned to go but stopped himself. Finally, he turned and knocked.

"Who's there?"

"It's Bill. Can we talk?'

"What do you want?"

"I want to apologize."

She opened the door and he could see right away that she was pregnant. "So?"

"May I come in?"

She let him in reluctantly but stood far away from him.

"How long . . . ?"

"The baby's due in September. I'm going back home next month after finals. I'm going to transfer and my mother is going to help me with the baby to allow me to finish school and support it."

"Is it mine?"

Anna looked as if she has been hit across the face. "Get out," she spat at him.

"I thought you knew how to take care of yourself. An older woman would. I'm sorry. I can't say anything right." He heard himself move from accusation to self-pity in a few seconds. He didn't feel proud although he couldn't help himself.

"It's long past saying the right thing. I want you to leave."

He hesitated. He knew if she shouted or screamed five other students would be on them in a moment. "This isn't right," he said quietly.

"No it isn't," she agreed.

"Anna, I have missed you these past months. I want to make them up to you."

He tried to take Anna by the shoulders but she stepped away and put the sofa between them. It was shabby and old fashioned but large enough to make an effective barrier.

"We don't need you," she said definitely.

"Well, maybe you don't need me, but the baby will."

"I told you I needed someone who wanted me for me, not for someone or something else. I'm going to be fine. I, we, don't need you."

"Anna, I never lied about being a romantic chap who can say the things you want to hear."

"I never asked you to say anything. I asked you to be there."

"I just couldn't do it."

"What makes you think you can now?"

"All I can say is I'm here and I want us to be together."

"I'm not buying," she said. "You need to leave and now." She walked past him and opened the door to the hallway. "Here's the exit. Get out while you can. No demands on you. No one asking more of you than you want to give. Get out."

"I'll go if you want me to. But aren't you being selfish?"

"Me? Selfish? God, you're a piece of work."

"I never said I was perfect. But you aren't either." He moved toward the door and stood inside the threshold watching her. "If you don't want the baby, my mother would be willing to take it."

"Your mother!" Anna's said in horror. "You think she's fit to raise my baby?"

"Our baby," he corrected her.

"I want this child," she said emphatically. "Neither you nor your mother is going to lay a hand on it."

"Are you such a fit mother?" he said nastily. "Maybe they'd say you weren't fit to raise it."

"I will deny you are the father."

They glared at one another in the doorway until Anna broke away and walked back to the sofa. When she sat on it the springs creaked and the cushion sank down into the frame. She started to cry. He came over and put his arm around her shoulders. He tried to hold her but she pulled back.

"I'm sorry," he said quietly. "I didn't mean it."

"Is this how you want me to spend the rest of my life? Listening to your outbursts?" She turned her head away.

"I'll try to be better. I'll be faithful. I'll bring you home my paycheck. You'll finish your education—I promise—as far as you can go. I'll take care of you. Isn't it enough?" He heard himself making the promises he had said he never would.

"I don't believe you. Why should I listen?" Anna had seen through his uncertainty.

"Anna, you'll have to settle for the actions." Finally, he began to feel solid ground. He could commit to taking care of her and this child without feeling that he had sold his soul. He did not understand why he felt that way and all he could do was hope that she would let him.

"Your actions so far have been shitty."

"Anna, I'm who I am. I don't love humanity. I don't love the world. I hate the vapid artificialities and hypocrisies. I'm no Prince Charming if that's what you're looking for. But I care about you."

She started to cry again, and this time she let him cradle her in his arms. This is insane he thought. She's never going to change her mind. He wanted to go outside and have a cigarette.

"I'm frightened," she admitted. "I don't want to do this all alone."

"You don't have to. I've said I'll be with you."

He pushed her away from him so he could see her face. It was swollen and her eyes red, but she no longer looked angry. Something in her expression made him realize she still cared for him.

"We'll be all right. You'll see." Not good, but the best he could do. She nodded her head slightly. He pulled her toward him and held her against him. He could smell her shampoo.

"It's been hard these past few months," she said. "I've been sick."

"Why didn't you tell me?"

"Why didn't you come to see me?"

He remained silent.

"What made you come here now?" She pulled back from him and looked at him intently.

"I missed you. I was dating someone and I realized it wasn't what I wanted."

"You were dating someone else?" He face contorted into a mask of shock.

"I thought we were broken up. You called it off, remember?" His tone suggested that if he saw someone else, she should consider that it was her own fault.

"Have you gotten her pregnant too?"

"No, she's older. She took precautions."

"What the hell do I need with you?" Anna stood up abruptly and walked back to the door and held it open. "Get out," she said.

"I'm sorry, Anna, obviously I've said the wrong thing again." He stood up and moved towards the door. "I thought I was being honest. We were split up and I thought it was over for good. But I've come back on my own and I realize I was wrong. I was miserable without you."

"And have you broken up with her?" Anna's tone was cold and accusing. "I will."

"So she doesn't know she's about to get the boot. God you are a shit."

"I know. " He smiled weakly. "I never made her any promises."

"So that makes it all right? You go through life making no promises and then no one can expect anything of you?"

"Anna. I came back because I want us to be together. I want us to get married. I want to make those promises to you and keep them. Please let's build a future together."

"I don't know why I am bothering to listen to you. You give me one good reason for me to see you again." She sounded disgusted and he knew her decision could go either way.

"Anna, I'm not going to pretend I know what to say. I've never seen a happy family. My parents certainly weren't. All I've ever seen is recrimination and manipulation. But I have to believe there is more out there and I want to have the chance to find it with you."

"Why are you so angry? Why do you say things designed to hurt me?"

"I don't know. I don't mean to. I don't like being put on the spot. I feel sandbagged."

"But it's OK for you to do it other people? You've been wounded so you're wounding others? Do you expect they'll say it's all right? What have I ever done to you to deserve this treatment?"

"I don't know. I'm who I am. I don't know what else to say. I think I've said all I can."

There was silence for several minutes. Bill had a strong desire to say forget it and walk out. But he stood in unaccustomed silence just looking at her.

"I don't know," she said. "Nothing's right. This is not how a relationship starts."

"How should it start?"

"With something other than take it or leave it, which is the sense I'm getting right now. You're treating me as if I've done something terrible and you can't forgive me."

"I didn't mean to give that impression."

"Bill, dishonesty is not your strong suit. You can't hide your thoughts."

"All right," he said, "take it or leave it, Anna. What are you going to do?"

"What I can't figure out is whether you were being honest or stupid when you told me about this other woman. Did you intend to tell me how little I matter? I don't know how long it will be before you get up and just walk out."

"I said I'm not going anywhere."

"And I'm not sure I believe you." Anna stared at the carpet. Her face revealed her conflict and dismay. Eventually she allowed her eyes to meet his as if she were trying to see into his soul. There was silence in the room as she weighed her feelings and her choices. When she finally spoke her voice rasped with disappointment.

"I know you've done the best you can. I also know you care. But can you overcome the past? It weighs on you. There's so much confusion in your mind I don't know if I can reach you. I'd be lying if I said I was comfortable about this. Part of me wants to run away and put an end to it, but another part says that I need to face the future with you. If we are to be together I have to accept you as you are. But the big question is what you are capable of becoming. Whatever it is, to be together we have to build something that is enough for both of us."

"I don't what you mean," Bill said uncomfortably. He felt he was being judged by someone who had seen too much into his soul for comfort.

"I know, and that's the problem," she replied. "You have this protective wall around you. I'm not sure if I can breach it."

"I promise I will do my best for you." The words were hollow, but he knew at that moment that a whole lifetime of hope depended on her answer. It felt karmic even though he had convinced himself that such concepts were nonsense.

Anna reached out her hand. "I know," she said sadly. She looked at him compassionately and watched his struggle.

"I don't know how open I can be. But I'm willing to try if you can show me what you want."

"Bill, I don't know if I can do it. But I do know that for some reason it's important that we try."

Bill did not know if he was relieved or disappointed. Her words suggested that she was accepting a destiny she would not have preferred. She was right, though. This was no way to start a marriage. But they had made a pact, and he knew they would have to live by it. He took her in his arms and thanked her. Nothing more was said. He was glad, for he had no words left.

"I have no idea what to tell my mother," she said at last. "She's expecting me to go home to have the baby."

"She doesn't have much to say."

"Yes she does. She's my mother."

"We'll have to persuade her." Bill's words were definite as if a new purpose had come into his life. He would be a husband, he would be a father, and it was meant to be.

. . .

Julia's reaction was as drastic as Anna had feared. She came down the coast immediately. setting herself up in a motel room not far from the campus and summoning them. Bill knew what to expect when she looked him up and down with disdain as they came into her room. She held her head erect, her shoulders stiffly back, and her mouth drawn into a tight, thin line. Her first words were confrontational. "What do you think you are doing, a man of your age with a girl not finished college?"

She did not invite them to sit down. Black hair, grey eyes, and a prominent nose, she looked formidable. "I wanted her to finish her education," Julia said angrily. "This girl has a destiny and I don't want anything to interfere with it."

"She will finish school. She'll go as far as she wants to. I'll see to it."

"How?" Julia was uncompromising in her opposition to him.

"Mum," Anna said, embarrassed and trying to break in.

"Don't interrupt," Julia said. "Let's hear this." Julia was in full sail. She reminded Bill of his own mother, Carolina. But where Carolina manipulated, Julia surged forward to confront.

"Anna will finish school. Nothing will change for her."

"After the child comes? What then? Do you even have medical coverage for her to have this baby?"

"I have medical benefits from my job at the telephone company. I'll keep the night job at the radio station as well. We'll find an apartment. We'll get married as soon as possible. At most she will miss one semester. There's no need for you to be concerned."

"Are you telling me to mind my own business? This is my daughter. You don't dictate terms to me."

"Wait a minute, Mum," Anna objected. "I'm not anybody's property. This is reality. A child is coming. I don't want to get married without your blessing, but this is going to happen. It's the way it has to be."

"I thought you wanted to come home to have this child," Julia said. "You said this man wasn't there for you."

"Things have changed," Anna said simply.

"Don't sacrifice yourself for him. He's not worth giving up your life."

"She wouldn't be," Bill broke in. "I'd never let her do that."

"How could you do this to me?" Julia's said to Anna. Her face was red and tight with anger. "Didn't I do a good enough job of caring for you?"

"I know you're disappointed in me," Anna said. "I didn't plan for it to turn out this way. But I promise I'll get the education you want me to have."

"This man will be nearing sixty when you are in your forties. Do you plan to be his nurse?"

"Mum, I'll get my education. We've promised. Anything else you have to trust to my good judgment."

"I'll never forgive you if she doesn't get her chance." Julia glared at Bill, her tone admitting her defeat. "I expect you to keep your word to her. This is a trust you're taking from me. It's been more important to me than my life. I want her to have her education and a future."

"She'll have it," said Bill, not angry but strangely moved by a sense of obligation to the pact he had made with Anna. "Of course, she will."

1:00 a.m.

*I*KEPT MY *word to Anna. I'm proud of that, although Julia never forgave me, even when Anna went on to earn one degree after another. I didn't see much of Julia over the years. Anna took Michael to stay with her each summer and she seldom came near me.*

I also arranged matters so Julia and my mother stayed apart. It was easy since they disliked one another on sight. But I soon saw they were not competitors for me. They were like two monolithic forces each claiming Anna and each jealous of the other. It was as if something had come between them that neither could forgive.

Like most things I didn't want to deal with, I left them to Anna. She managed them as best she could. She refused Carolina's invitation to religion just as she tempered Julia's confrontations. It was as if she had been born to do this while I stayed uninvolved.

Uninvolved. Yes, that was me. The cavern is not allowing me to ignore my failings. I can see it now: Like Aonio, I was selfish. But while he was selfish in the name of knowledge, I've been selfish in the name of avoiding responsibility, at least until Anna came into my life. Neither Aonio nor I are admirable, and the worst part is I can't see that either of us have left the world much better for our being in it. Is this realization of my own inconsequence all part of dying? Do we all have to take our turn in the cavern? Is this how we come to understood that we were part of something larger than ourselves?

Chapter 11

The Prison of the Inquisition, August 1569

A
FTER HE HAS been there for what Aonio reckoned must be nearly
twelve months, a new man came to see him. He wore a priest's
vestments with a heavy black cloak stretched across ample shoulders and
a prominent stomach that rested on his knees. With his close-cropped
hair and pugnacious jaw, he looked as if he might have come from a long
line of butchers. He sat down heavily on the one chair and left Aonio to
sit on the bed.

"I am Luca Marcucci. I have been appointed to be your lawyer."

"My lawyer?" Aonio raised his eyebrows and crossed his arms.

"You're entitled to have a lawyer." Marcucci made this explanation in
pained tones as if he were speaking to someone who should have already
known this.

"I need no lawyer. I am trained in law myself." Aonio felt indignant.
How could this man claim to be a lawyer and not know to whom he was
talking?

"Civil law, not Church law and certainly not the law of the Holy
Inquisition." Marcucci's patience was tested; he thought himself a
competent advocate, perhaps not in the same league as this imperious

academic, but much more practiced in the ways of the Vatican. He didn't warm to this man and his lip curled slightly. In his opinion, the prisoner would do well to remember who was on trial. "I would advise you to listen," was all he permitted himself to say.

Aonio frowned but was silent.

"The three inquisitors in your case are ready. When you appear before them, you have a choice. You can admit to the charges against you and throw yourself upon the Church's mercy, in which case the investigation ends and a report is given to the Holy Father. Or you can choose to deny the charges. If you deny, the investigation proceeds until the inquisitors have learned enough to write their recommendations. If you admit to heresy and renounce your errors, the sentence is usually life in prison. If you harbor heretical views and are found unrepentant, you face public execution."

"What if I am able to prove I am innocent?"

The lawyer raised an eyebrow and thought for a moment. "I don't believe I've ever seen it happen. Determinations of innocence are usually made long before a court is convened in Rome. You were interviewed in Milan, weren't you?"

"I spoke with Cardinal Marzoni, who came from Siena to examine me."

"Didn't you hear the result?" The lawyer shifted his weight on the chair. Had there been a problem with the paperwork? Such things happened but usually at the local level. The Holy Office at the Vatican was efficient in matters of heresy and trials.

"I wasn't told. All I heard was that Cardinal Ribena issued an order for me to come to Rome."

"Well, there was your answer," Marcucci said. "If the bishop had been satisfied, the case would have been resolved right then and there."

"But I was never told exactly what the charges were to be against me. How can I prepare a defense without that information?" Aonio felt exasperated. He was used to clarity and precision in the presentation of law cases. A clear statement of charges was always the first step in a properly conducted debate or trial.

"Your defense starts now," Marcucci said flatly.

"But with more time and direction, I could have prepared much better to make my case."

"Your case?" Marcucci let the words roll delicately on his tongue as if this was a totally new concept he was about to consider and discard. "What does that mean exactly? Are you criticizing the workings of the Holy Office? If you are, I must tell you that this is not a good way for you to start this matter."

"I mean no disrespect for the Holy Office. I am asking only whether my case has been treated with the customary procedures. But perhaps you might clarify for me what you will be doing in this case." Aonio backtracked politely. He had no need to offend this man more than he apparently already had.

"As your lawyer I can advise you on which questions to expect and how best to answer them. But I must inform the Holy Father if anything you say resembles a confession. I would save any admissions for a confessor."

"I have nothing to confess," Aonio said proudly. "But I would like to know how the inquiry will proceed."

"Usually, the inquisitors start by asking for an accounting of your life. It's best to be thorough because they will have reports from people who know you. Anything you leave out will be suspicious. They can ask questions about anything. They want to hear particulars, including names and places. The more you divulge, the more they will think you honest. Then they will move more specifically to matters of belief and faith. Since you have written a good deal, they will undoubtedly focus on your published works. But they may also draw upon the testimony of the witnesses."

"Who are these witnesses?"

"You won't know. The Church takes this precaution to protect them in case your friends should want to take revenge."

"So I must defend myself from unknown enemies who can say anything they wish?"

"Not completely. If the Inquisition finds they have perjured themselves, they can be imprisoned and tried themselves."

"Has that ever happened?"

"Actually, in one case I heard about. It ended with the Church seizing the perjurer's possessions and lands."

"I am glad to hear the Church is just."

The lawyer ignored the irony. "I want you to understand your position in this Inquisition. You may have mastered debate and words, but neither will help you here. Answer the questions simply and with as few words as possible. The fewer the words, the less the possible misunderstanding. I've seen cases where the inquisitors were inclined to be lenient until the accused talked himself into being hung."

"I respect your advice." Aonio nodded and looked at the floor. There was no need to reveal anything that could give advantage to his adversaries. "What else should I know?"

"I'll come by to see you regularly until your trial starts and see how you progress in your defense. I can advise you on how particular arguments have fared in trials before yours. I cannot, however, offer advice on what to say, only on how it might be received. I must also warn you that I have not worked with the particular members of the inquisition chosen for your case. In fact, they are strangers both to me and to Rome. The selection process has not been shared with me." Marcucci gave a slight raise of his eyebrow that implied this was not usual.

"It's difficult when I don't know the charges." Aonio looked directly in his advisor's eyes. "Usually in law cases, I know the charges and can prepare a speech to refute them."

The lawyer returned his gaze. "This is a different law, with different procedures. Also different evidence. If you want to give me names of those willing to testify to your good character, I can contact them on your behalf. They may or may not respond, but occasionally these intercessions have reduced the charges."

"Thank you," Aonio said quietly, noticing that Marcucci used the word *reduced* rather than *dismissed*.

"Your list will need to be sanctioned by the Holy Office, of course, but I have never seen such requests denied."

"I would like paper and my writing instruments to do this."

"If you give me the names, I will make contact on your behalf. The guard can collect the list from you and forward it to me when you're ready. There's been a delay in your case since one inquisitor had to wait until the Pope signed the order promoting him to bishop. It's my understanding they will be ready about eight weeks from now."

The lawyer rapped sharply on the door and stopped briefly as it opened. "I'll be by to see you next week."

The keys grated, the door creaked, a cloak rustled, and the man was gone.

"Anything you want?" the guard asked gruffly hoping for his share of Aonio's dwindling resources.

"Not at this moment, thank you." The man slammed the door, and Aonio settled back on the bed. The leather straps under him creaked as the headboard banged back against the wall. Eight weeks seemed forever, but at least the process had started. He would soon have his chance to debate his accusers and let the power of truth prevail.

On the appointed day, guards took Aonio along a dark narrow corridor and into a large room where the light was unpleasantly bright after his cell's dimness. He stood inside the doorway, blinking. It was a long room with windows set high in the walls that sent shafts of sunlight bouncing off the plain white walls and illuminating unremarkable frescoes in the ceiling. The three inquisitors were already there. One man sat at the head of a long, dark wood table while the two others sat on either side of him. Their high-backed chairs were brocaded with a pattern of wolves and raptors set against a dark green background of twisted trees and vines. A gold fringe along the chair bottoms did little to soften their slightly ominous effect. Off to the side, a hard-faced, impassive notary sat by himself at a table.

Aonio sat on a hard bench facing up to the men at the table. As he sat there, he noticed strange details. The twisted fringe was detaching from the bottom of one of the side chairs. The wood in the planked tabletop had raised in places; it was stained with water rings and had flat patches of aged candle wax in the middle, suggesting it had once been used for meals. Candle smoke had muddied the painting on the ceiling in certain spots; he had to strain to make out Judith displaying the severed head of Holofernes. He noticed flecks of dust rising and falling in a shaft of sunlight, which reminded him of Jacob's ladder. But overall, to Aonio's mind, the room felt dead with the weight of enforced belief and bureaucracy. He turned his eyes reluctantly away from the windows and the freedom they represented.

The men at the table were all younger than he. The eldest, the man at the head of the table, was a bishop with thinning blonde hair surrounding a bald spot. The man to his left was younger, with pale skin and cropped dark hair. Judging from the lines between his eyebrows, he had trouble seeing. The man on the right was swarthy and heavier. He kept his vestment wrapped tightly round him as if he were cold. Aonio studied them and remembered what the bishop told him in his garden—these would be hungry men, hand-picked by Rome for loyalty and ambition.

The notary's pen scratched audibly as he recorded the scene. Aonio looked at him curiously. The man was hunched over his work, his eyes focused down.

The blonde-haired bishop, clearly the one in charge, opened a large ledger and leaned across it to look down at Aonio.

"Aonio Paleario, do you understand why you are here?" His voice was authoritative and official, the voice of accusation and judgment.

"I was told to report to Rome," Aonio replied.

"You have been called before the Holy Office of the Inquisition to answer to charges of heresy." The bishop's voice was stern as he corrected Aonio. "We are tasked to examine your soul to judge the sincerity of your belief in the Catholic Church. It is important you understand fully what this inquiry will seek to determine, so I shall ask the notary to read the precise charges to you. But before he does so, the members of this Inquisition will introduce themselves. I am Umberto Locati de Piacenza. I was named Bishop of Bagnoreas this year. Previously I was Commissioner of Santa Uffizio." He cradled his fingers delicately and looked slightly patronizing as he nodded to the dark man seated beside him.

"I am Donato Stampa, Assistant to the Inquisition." The younger man did not look at Aonio when he spoke. He concentrated his attention on the papers on the table, keeping his head down close to the pages as if straining to read them. Aonio regretted being unable to make eye contact with Stampa; he had wanted to start off this trial with a strong show of his credibility and integrity. Only fearful or guilty people avoided meeting gazes. He did not want anyone to think that of him.

"I am Vincenzo Donzelli, Vice Commissioner of Mondovi," the swarthy man said without being asked. When he let his eyes fall sideways, Aonio had the feeling this man might be uncomfortable in his role. Perhaps this was his first Inquisition. He at least had looked directly at Aonio before looking away, a weakness that Aonio was glad to be aware of and might be able to use later. Donzelli also had the mannerisms of someone long at the Roman court—a slight self-conscious movement of the hands as he spoke and the tendency to glance at his companions for agreement.

With the introductions over, the bishop turned to the notary and, without asking him to identify himself, directed him to read the charges. The notary cleared his throat and read them from the side table where he sat.

"Aonio Paleario, you have been charged with the following offenses against the Holy Roman Church. First, you did cause the publication of writings without the permission of the Vatican censor. Second, the publication of said work contains a set of fatal errors, namely the denial of purgatory and commendation of the forgiveness of sins through justification of faith alone. Third, you have denied the Pope's position as the vicar of Christ by attacking the representatives of His Holy Church."

"Serious charges," said the bishop. "Aonio Paleario, how do you plead?"

"I am not guilty." Aonio spoke distinctly and clearly despite the rasping from the dryness in his throat.

"Very well," said the bishop. "By custom we will examine these charges point by point and judge their merits. You are commanded in God's holy name to speak the truth in everything you say."

Aonio nodded. He would have liked to make an opening argument, but he saw that he had no power to set the rhythm or the calendar. Despite this, the way was clear before him: he would admit nothing and try to determine from their questions what they knew. He would give no names and offer little information with the potential of exposing others. Then, he would seize whatever opening there was to define heresy, prove that it did not apply to him, and expose the shallow evil of those who had accused him. In this, of course, he was going against the advice of his lawyer Marcucci, but Aonio felt free to do so. It was his trial and his life and he would do what he felt he must to make his case.

The bishop drummed his fingers on the table. "You were late in responding to the orders of the Holy Office. We know that you were called to appear twelve months before you finally presented yourself. You were aware you had been called?"

Aonio felt surprised. He had not expected that they would start the proceedings with the timetable of his travels. He offered the only explanation he could. "The Milan city fathers requested a delay to allow them to receive the services for which they had paid me. When the winter storms came, I was too ill to travel. My doctors sent a letter explaining my condition."

The bishop was not impressed. "If you had not delayed, your health would not have been an issue."

"I meant no disrespect to the Holy Office."

"The father Inquisitor was not pleased when he heard you tried to have your case moved to Milan."

The bishop's tone was pompous and Aonio realized he was repeating what he must have heard from his superiors. The three inquisitors couldn't have been inconvenienced since they hadn't been appointed. It had to be the higher ups in the Vatican who were annoyed.

"I made that request only to accommodate those who might be willing to testify on my behalf. Those would be people who have known me for the past twenty years or more. They are older as I am and would find travel difficult. In addition, I no longer know anyone here in Rome."

"For this the Father Inquisitor was forced to wait?"

"No disrespect was intended," Aonio repeated.

The bishop shrugged. His point had been made and all had been recorded by the notary; he was ready to move on. "Your lawyer tells us that he has advised you of how this tribunal will proceed, so you know that it is usual in these proceedings to ask for a brief accounting of your life until you received the order to consult with Rome. Give this to us now."

The room was silent. The dark haired assistant finally looked up and stared shortsightedly at Aonio; the swarthy vice commissioner settled back into his chair. The room waited for Aonio to begin.

Aonio drew breath and tried to relieve the pressure on his lower back. He nodded to indicate his readiness. "I was born Antonio della Pagliara in Veroli in 1500," he began. "My parents were Matteo della Pagliara and Clara Jannarilli." He stopped to take a breath and heard the scratching of the pen as the notary recorded his words.

Stampa used the moment to break in accusingly. "This is not the name you go by. You do not use the name with which you were baptized."

"No," agreed Aonio, "I was called Antonio at birth. As I grew older, it was fashionable to adopt more classical names. Aonio sounded Greek."

"It has been suggested," Stampa said nastily, "that you removed the tee from your name to remove any reference to the crucifixion."

"Never," Aonio said passionately. "I would never deny my savior. I love Jesus Christ with open and complete heart."

"Go on with your life," said the bishop.

It took Aonio a moment to settle down and even then he frowned at the place where Stampa sat. "My mother was a member of a well-known Veroli family who had lived in that town for many generations. My father was from Salerno and related to the Prince of Sanserevino. My parents were devout and pious, particularly my mother, and they were well respected in the town."

"Who provided your first religious training?" Donzelli asked.

"My mother did initially. Her uncle was a canon in the Veroli church and the whole family was truly committed to the love of God. Afterwards, my father arranged for his friend, Ennio Filonardi, the Bishop of Veroli, to instruct me on doctrinal matters."

"The Bishop of Veroli was a good and revered Churchman," Donzelli said to the others in case they had not heard of him. "So," he continued to Aonio, "you would say your first instruction in the Catholic faith was careful and orthodox?"

The bishop leaned forward slightly. The questions were establishing an important point of order. Ignorance of doctrine was one thing, the deliberate repudiation of it quite another. The prisoner could be making an important admission.

"The bishop was an excellent teacher and well respected. He taught me to love God and truth."

The bishop leaned back. Aonio had carefully sidestepped the question of instruction in doctrine. That would have to be established later.

"What about your education?" Stampa asked.

"My father entrusted my education to his friend, the solicitor Giovanni Martelli. From him I learned a love of language. He was a fine poet and taught me Latin and Greek. He was my master until I was seventeen. When my parents died, I sold the family house and used the money to continue my studies in Rome."

"What year did you come to Rome?" Donzelli asked.

"It must have been in the1520s, a long time ago." Aonio could not remember all that well anymore. He generally remembered dates by the age of his children, but they had not been born when he first came to Rome.

"So you were in Rome during the sack of the city?" Donzelli sounded interested. He hadn't been born when it happened.

"I joined the household of Cardinal Cesarini. But at the time of the siege in 1527, we had moved to his country villa. We escaped the terrible destruction brought by the German and Spanish troops. But it still affected us since many fine scholars were killed and their libraries destroyed."

"Wasn't there trouble involving you when you were in Cardinal Cesarini's household?" Stampa had been consulting what Aonio realized must be notes on his life that others had provided.

"The cardinal's stewards became jealous of my closeness to the cardinal," Aonio said disdainfully. "I was working on an index to the works of Livy. They accused me of stealing one of the cardinal's manuscripts with the intention of plagiarizing the index system for my own work. But index systems cannot be interchanged. It was a ridiculous charge as anyone who had any education could see immediately."

"Tell us how that was resolved," Stampa demanded.

Aonio looked at his interrogator. Was he this aggressive and arrogant when he was a student at the university? He assumed he must have been, for this is the way of youth, and he was hungry for knowledge and advancement when he left his parents' house. Things seemed to matter in different ways then and everything had a magical urgency.

"Because of the stewards' lies, I decided it was time to leave," Aonio said proudly. "I heard about the excellent scholars in Padua and Perugia and I was determined to find them. I packed my belongings and went to Padua."

"So you left in disgrace?" Stampa seemed to relish this interpretation.

"Some may think so. I disagree. I made my case to the cardinal who was wise and gracious enough to accept it. I chose to leave because I felt I had been conspired against by jealous, ignorant louts. I was offended that anyone had listened to them. I went to Padua because I wanted to study Aristotle in the original Greek with Professor Lampridio. I went by way of Siena at the invitation of friends."

"How long did you stay in Padua?" Donzelli asked.

"I stayed long enough to be impressed by the professors engaged in new theories of writing history; otherwise, the faculty and students were engaged in translations, an activity I found interesting."

"Tell us about what happened in Siena on your way to Padua," Stampa said.

Again, Aonio was not surprised by the question. He had suspected that the enemies he had made in Siena were behind this latest attempt to discredit him. As he looked back, in fact, he realized that was where the trouble all began. Would this tribunal believe it was about a trial over six barrels of salt? But that would be the truth.

"My friends were charged with transporting salt without paying taxes. The punishment was death. I was able to prove they were not guilty. Those who lost the case became my enemies."

"Did they not denounce you for heresy?" the bishop asked.

"My enemies lied about me. But the charges were shown to be untruthful and the matter dropped."

"Isn't it true," Stampa said triumphantly, "that those charges were not pursued because the Bishop of Venice intervened on your behalf and had them quashed?"

"I was blessed," Aonio replied, "that wise and thoughtful men saw the injustice of those accusations and saved me from those who tried to harm me."

"What happened next?" The bishop did not want to lose control of the inquiry. He determined to keep matters moving forward.

"I spent some time at the university in Padua and then I left." Aonio said it simply as if there were nothing more to say on the subject.

"What about Erasmus of Rotterdam?" prompted Donzelli. "What of him? There were many exchanges between people in Padua and him were there not? We have evidence concerning you in particular."

Aonio paused to arch his back and tried to get comfortable while he thought. What evidence did they have? He couldn't be sure they weren't just bluffing to trick him into revealing more evidence to use against him. He answered cautiously. "I met Erasmus when I traveled to Switzerland. While I was at Padua, Cardinal Bembo shared letters he was exchanging with him. Cardinal Bembo hoped Erasmus would lead the German reformers back to the Church."

"Who else was in contact with this Erasmus? Were you involved in this?" Donzelli asked. "Was there discussion of his works and letters?"

"Not to my awareness," Aonio replied. "As I said before, I prefer to work alone."

"Are you telling us that there was no discussion at all?" Stampa said incredulously.

"Certainly there was. During those years we translated much of Erasmus' writing. I worked with such fine scholars as Bembo, Vergerio, Contarini, and Servetus. But any discussions we had were directed to the challenge of translation from Latin into Italian or to understanding history and government."

"All dead," Stampa snorted. "These works of Erasmus, were they not works banned by the Holy Office?"

"Not at that time," Aonio reminded him.

"We have been told about your often expressed admiration for these German reformers," Stampa continued.

"I have respected many people for the excellence of their scholarship," replied Aonio. "But I have also admired many Greek philosophers and no one has suggested I have adopted Greek beliefs. I can admire fine scholarship in others without adopting their viewpoints and philosophies."

Stampa leaned forward. His dark eyes glinted. "Do you then admit you respect views contrary to the official position of the Church of Rome?"

"You put words in my mouth that I do not speak. I respect scholarship. That does not mean that I agree with it. I am a deeply religious man. I have no quarrel with the Church of Christ." Aonio braced his shoulders from his discomfort.

"Do you then say that you consider the Church of Rome to be the only Church of Jesus Christ?" When Aonio said nothing, Stampa sat back in triumph. "See, his silence condemns him."

"I believe," replied Aonio, "that the law says that words prove guilt; silence proves only assent."

"That is the general interpretation," the bishop agreed.

Stampa's face knotted in frustration. "Don't you think we have heard it all? The feeble attempts at saying nothing while appearing to answer questions? The dancing around the issues? How much can I say without imperiling my soul and still mislead these inquisitors? Do you think us fools?"

There was a heavy silence marked by the scratching of the scribe's pen.

"You said you made enemies in Siena. What was the outcome?" Donzelli's voice was slightly conciliatory, his tone implied contempt of Stampa's rash impatience. For a strange moment, Aonio and Donzelli become co-conspirators in changing the direction of the questions.

"My enemies prevented me from gaining a professorship at the University of Siena, so I went to Lucca. I was asked to teach their young men and to give several public orations in Latin each year as well."

"What did you talk about?" Donzelli asked.

"I spoke about patriotism and the power of oratory to guide men to virtue. I spoke also about law, my own profession, as public speaking worthy of study and honor. My last oration was about happiness, which I showed resulted when life was lived virtuously through contemplative wisdom."

"Did you speak publicly about faith and the Church?"

"No. None of my public orations concerned faith. I said that was matter for the Church to address since it was beyond logic."

"Who were your associates? Did you discuss matters of faith with them?"

"I worked alone on my own studies. It is not my habit to collaborate with others."

The notary's pen scratched away at the transcript of the proceedings. The inquisitors were restless and shifted in their seats. It was starting to be clear that this trial was going to last longer than they had hoped.

"How long were you in Lucca?' Donzelli continued.

"About ten years, if I remember correctly."

"Why did you leave?"

"I was ill and I missed my family. I went home for a time to be with my wife and children. But I could not rest for long as the bills mounted. I was invited to apply for a position of professor of eloquence at the University of Milan. I was successful and have been part of the faculty in Milan until I was summoned to come to Rome."

"What topics have you talked about in Milan?" the bishop asked.

"My primary focus has been criminal law."

"What writing have you done? With whom have you shared it?"

Aonio answered carefully. He did not know what the inquisitors might have in their possession. "I have written letters to many people. I have prepared many orations for the university. It has been my privilege to make public presentations to the citizens of Milan. I have worked with fellow professors and scholars at the university but it has always concerned the nature of rhetoric and interpretations of the classical authors."

"Which people have you written to?" the bishop asked.

"I have written to scholars all across Europe. Too many to name."

"On what topics?"

"I have shared my thoughts on subjects such as justice and ethics."

"And evil, apparently," interrupted Stampa. "You have been heard talking about it in your cell. Have you been practicing what you would say here? Why should we believe anything you say?"

The bishop stared at his younger colleague with a look that told him he was not following the prescribed order of the inquiry.

"These things will come out in their own good time," the bishop said. "Is there anything further you would like to add to these proceedings at this time?"

Aonio shook his head.

"Since we have completed the opening requirement of this inquiry," the bishop concluded, "I propose we adjourn."

The notary opened the door and the guards took Aonio away to his cell. He sagged onto the mattress, exhausted. His voice was hoarse and his back tightly constricted across his hips. Slowly he bent one leg to relieve the pressure. His knees felt numb and the soles of his feet hurt.

Just when he thought he might drift off to sleep, the cell door opened peremptorily and his lawyer Marcucci entered.

"You did not follow my instructions," Marcucci said sharply. "I told you to answer the questions honestly and directly."

"I thought I did."

"The committee is displeased with your performance."

"My performance?"

"They felt you were withholding information, particularly the names of those you have conferred with."

"Most of them are dead."

"You know, this is the fast way to the rack. They want names. They want to know how far heresy reaches into the fabric of the universities."

"I have nothing to give them."

"You'd better think hard. They think otherwise. They want to know about your associates in Padua and Siena and particularly in Milan, and about any priests who have taken your confession."

"What is it they want to know?"

"What you have talked about. Who has talked about Church matters with you. Anyone who receives letters from German reformers and who writes to them."

"Why don't they ask me these things directly?"

"Because for your soul's salvation they want you to offer these things. They can extract information from you later if necessary."

Aonio was silent. The man continued with his directions about what should happen the next time. Aonio soon ceased to listen and the lawyer left. Aonio was glad of the quiet. He had a larger problem than worrying about the next part of his trial. He had spent most of his money and must be prepared to live on what the prison was willing to supply. He was most upset about wearing dirty linen and he knew he would present a sorry picture when he was called before the inquisitors again.

When the cell door grated open, he assumed it was the guard come to take away his bowl of watery soup. Instead it was Calla.

"How are you?" Calla asked with his birdlike flutter, but he did not wait for a reply. "I have something to tell you."

Calla swooped toward the table and put down a bundle of linen. He wrinkled his nose as he did so, and darted quickly back toward the door. Aonio assumed he must smell bad from the man's expression of distaste. Calla stood at the door for a few moments with a prim smile on his face.

"From my family?" Aonio asked. The bundle appeared to be fresh clothes.

"I'm told the man who brought it didn't say. He said he'd been asked to bring this to you and then he left without giving a name. There was no other message with it."

Aonio frowned "He must have been well trusted."

"Oh, this happens all the time," Calla said airily. "Most people prefer not to give their names at the Inquisition prison. They usually get someone else to make the delivery. The good news for you is that the man brought money with him. This has been placed into your account. I assume you would like to have your clothes laundered and something better to eat?"

Aonio nodded in surprise.

Calla called for the guard and waited while the key was turned.

"Someone will come to you. By the way, I understand the inquisitors will call for you again tomorrow. The arrival of this money is well timed."

A swish of robes and the grate of the door and Aonio was alone again. He opened the bundle of clothing and laid the items on the table. There was a loose, coarse shirt, several pairs of under linens, and used but serviceable britches. He felt profoundly grateful as his current clothes were badly soiled and the seams were pulling apart.

He wondered how Marietta had managed to get this bounty to him. It had to be her for who else would have done this kindness? Or perhaps Fedro had managed to make it happen. They hadn't forgotten him after all. He felt they were letting him know that they understood his task and supported him. But was there anything in the clothes to let him know? Eagerly, he unfolded the clothes, looking for anything that could give him a clue. He was disappointed when he initially seemed to find nothing. Then he turned the clothes inside out and ran his fingers along each seam. It was then that he found a slight rise in the seam around the inside of the collar. It seemed that there was a loose extra seam concealed inside. He picked at the threads until it opened and a tiny piece of paper fell out. It was only the width of his finger. Eagerly he read it. "Things are well. We pray for you. PG." Pterigi Gallo. Aonio felt his eyes sting. His old servant had not forgotten him. There was life and kindness outside these walls and he had forgotten about it in his isolation. Pterigi. Not his wife, not his children. But someone tied to him by bonds of friendship. He choked back tears as he thought of him.

With the new money, he sent his old clothes out to be scrubbed and was able to clean himself. He sat at the table in his new shirt and underwear while he ate a bowl of stew. His hair was long and scraggly now, but there was nothing he could do about it. He had not seen his face for over a year. He knew his beard had become matted and stained, but his appearance didn't matter much to him anymore. Where once he took care to trim his beard and hair and wanted to wear clean linens, he was content to be fresh and not smell of urine or sweat. They had brought him water from time to time to clean himself, especially before his lawyer or the priest came to see him. But washing from a bowl was not the same as wearing clean garments. He had lost several more teeth, but these dropped out on their own and he found them on the bedding when he woke in the morning.

"Tell us more about what happened in Siena," the bishop said when the Inquisition resumed.

The room was set up exactly as it had been during the first meeting. The three inquisitors sat in the same seats. Aonio had to clear his throat several times before he could form intelligible words. His voice sounded like a rattle.

"Wasn't there a question about friars in Siena?" As usual, Stampa asked his question tersely.

"A pair of friars visited my friend's aunt and stole money from her. The money was never returned, but everybody knew what the friars had done. I publicly exposed them."

"These were men of the Church who swore that they had been falsely accused. They deserved respect for what they represented." It was a statement not a question. Aonio looked directly at the assistant but did not reply. "They were Franciscans," Stampa explained to his fellow inquisitors. "You knew who they were, didn't you?" he said to Aonio.

"They were thieves who had no right to represent a God of justice." Aonio coughed and his shoulders heaved with the exertion. It took time to remove the irritation in his throat. The notary gave him a drink of water.

"I want to go back to your time in Padua," Donzelli said. "You said you met Erasmus in Switzerland and we know you were translating his books. What were your letters to him about and have you been in contact with other German reformers?"

"I discussed with him the great advances being made in scholarship in Germany and France. We exchanged a few letters before he died, nothing more. It all took place nearly forty years ago."

"What recent dealings have you had with German reformers?" the bishop asked.

"Very little."

"Except you receive regular letters from Basle and Geneva. Would you kindly explain." Donzelli leant back against the chair back and cradled his fingers expectantly.

Aonio did not know who had told the Inquisition of these letters. He wondered whether they had intercepted some he had never received.

"I have colleagues located in France and Germany, Switzerland, and England. We share our work with one another and keep each other apprised of our interests."

"What exactly are those interests?" The bishop asked.

"We translate books we believe will advance our understanding and provide commentaries on difficult passages."

"Give us examples," said Donzelli.

"I have been working on commentaries on Livy and Plutonius."

"You want us to believe all the letters you have received over the years have dealt with ancient historians?" Donzelli sounded incredulous.

"No. There have been many works of interest to me. I have commented on texts on criminal law and philosophy and rhetoric."

"You maintain," thundered Stampa "that you have never discussed the Church or freedom of conscience with these people you corresponded with in Germany?" He made a disgusted face and snorted.

They have no proof Aonio thought. They have no letters, but they know I have received them. I burned every one after I had read it.

Someone has told them I received them. Is it the spy in my household?

Aonio sat silently while the bishop regrouped the questioning.

"We'll come back to the matter of the letters. While you were in Padua, you wrote a poem about the immortality of the soul?"

"I did."

"What did you say about it?"

Aonio looked squarely at the bishop. He had the feeling this poem is where the Inquisition has been headed all along.

"About the absolute joy of the soul being rejoined with the Maker who places a spark of eternity in every human being."

"What happens after the end of mortal existence?" the bishop asked.

"The soul returns to God."

"What is the role of purgatory?" This question came from Donzelli.

"I do not deny the possibility of its existence."

"Do you believe souls who die in God's grace but still have unrepented sins must remain in purgatory for a period of cleansing?" Donzelli had obviously been appointed to pursue this question.

"I do not deny the possibility." Aonio looked from one to the other of his examiners. It was then that he noticed that Stampa had before him a copy of his poem. It was heavily underlined with notes in the margin. He could see they planned to go through word by word. He inwardly sighed.

"Do you believe in the power of prayer to raise souls out of purgatory?" Donzelli asked the question slowly and emphatically.

"I do not know."

"Purgatory is not human logic. It is a basic teaching of the Catholic Church reconfirmed and authorized by the Council of Trent. To say you do not know is direct disobedience to the Church fathers. They have told you that it exists." Stampa's voice rose as he leant forward.

The bishop again silently reprimanded his younger colleague. Stampa noticed the rebuke this time and sat back in his seat.

"Ah, yes," Aonio nodded, "The Council of Trent."

From where he now sat in this interrogation room and looking back in time, he saw it had been naïve ever to have thought faith could be decided by open discussion. Or to believe the Church would ever willingly surrender the power to govern religious observance. Yet Aonio had hoped that reconciliation was possible between the reformers and the Church. The Council of Trent, slowly but surely, had killed those dreams.

"Have you ever ordered prayers to be said for departed family members?" The bishop tried to find common ground between the inquisitors and the man they were examining.

"When vandals attacked my parents' grave in the Church at Veroli, I sent money for it to be rebuilt."

"But did you order prayers for them?"

Aonio frowned. "I do not recall."

Stampa made a note on his papers and turned scornfully away.

"What about this book published in Germany without approval?" the bishop asked.

"It was a reissue of an earlier, approved work," replied Aonio. "Nothing in it was new. The printer did not correct the pages properly, however, and many errors slipped in despite his having a fair copy from which to work. Among his many errors was his failure to include the page showing the license from the Vatican censor. The earlier book had received this approval. This was a serious and unfortunate oversight."

"We have been told," said the bishop, "that you wish to study the Bible and determine its authenticity. Is that correct?"

"Those are not my views."

"Would you tell us how you would describe your views? What is it you are looking for?"

"I wanted to study God's words in the original languages of the texts."

"To what purpose?" Donzelli asked

"I wanted to learn the exact words of God so that I could honor Him."

"And you don't believe that what the Church teaches is sufficient and correct?" the bishop said.

Aonio was exhausted. He knew what was coming next. They would ask why he did not trust the Church. Why had he placed his intellect over the judgment of the Church Fathers? Didn't his words reveal a desire for a personal relationship with God? Didn't he therefore sympathize with the German Reformers? How could he deny his heresy? He closed his eyes and sat with resignation as the preordained structure of the Inquisition played on around him.

2:00 a.m.

*I*CAN SEE *the inquisitors want to be done and go on to their dinner. Their minds are made up as they were before this charade started. They want Aonio's trial to appear fair and legal to prevent him from becoming a martyr. The Vatican wants any punishment to come from the civil authorities of Rome so the Church can claim never to have condemned anyone to death. The Roman authorities will want to appear independent, even if the Vatican sends a coded message indicating what they want done. Questions and answers must be properly documented and the procedure scrupulously followed so no one can be held responsible. All the inquisitors want to hear from Aonio is his admission he is wrong and the Church is right. Nothing else he has to say is of any interest except to him. Only Aonio has any illusions about the power of his personal oratory.*

I can hear Anna playing the Russian Easter Overture now. The orchestra rises in the opening crescendos and I feel myself relax and smile. I am proud I kept my word to Anna. I should have said so many things. It was the issue of our marriage and it was the issue between Michael and me. The boy needed a father and I wasn't there. Why is it people who need affirmation so often choose people who can't give it? But I already know the answer. The cavern has taught me. It is because we are born to overcome those limitations.

How difficult it is for us to learn the right pathways. Everyday life gets in the way. Our lives and purposes are trial and error, and there are no road maps or a compass. The cavern tells me in the end we are responsible for ourselves. No amount of prescription or teachings can save us—and, as I have learned, everyone enters the cavern alone. That's what will happen to Aonio. I can see it coming. He will be a hero and a devout Christian in his own mind, but in the minds of the others around him, he will be a nuisance. What an ambiguous thing to lose one's life over: a power struggle over who holds the truth about something that cannot be proved because no one has returned from death. From my vantage point, it's like putting people to death over whether UFOs will disgorge little green men or purple teddy bears, and yet, people will go to their deaths proclaiming one or the other only because it is believed by the group they belong to. Humans are a very strange species.

The cavern undulates around me. I know it's a call for me but I'm not ready. You can't take me now, I say to it. Already I feel changed and I hardly recognize what I have become. I want to debate the truth now and the answer is important to me. I seek the answers to the questions I denied myself the chance to explore during my life. Something has come alive in me. Let me go back to my own life or to that of this Aonio Paleario. I don't care which as long as it gives me the answers. I want to understand why Anna came into my life. She's the only one I don't understand so far. Why did she come to me and why did she stay?

Chapter 12

Colle de Val d'Elsa, August 1569

CECILIANA WAS DRIFTING off to sleep. She and Beatrice had been banished to their shared bedroom at the top of the house. "Take Beatrice up to her room," Marietta instructed. "We have family things to discuss." Ceciliana wondered as she heard this. The girl was fifteen, surely old enough to be included, but she shrugged and asked Beatrice to come help her wind wool.

The upstairs room was like a small attic that opened onto a flat roof. It had been the older children's nursery but used for storage once they were grown. When Marietta became pregnant, it was pressed back into service. She wasn't pleased to find herself expecting another child at the age of forty, a time when she had reasonably thought that part of her life was done. Her pregnancies were difficult, and after the last one she'd been reluctant to sleep with her husband in case she got caught. As the years passed with no product, she became careless. Beatrice was the unwelcome result, as was the need for a wet nurse since Marietta had no intention of feeding the child herself.

Ceciliana proved her worth many times over since she also had cooking skills, but the discovery of her further talents came later. She was available because an overturned cart and a runaway horse had ended her husband's life, leaving her six months pregnant and without any prospects. In fact, when she lost Luigi she lost her home, means of support, and companionship. He was good-looking, with blue eye, dark lashes, and sexual authority—just the way she liked her men—he also made her laugh, and thought she was all he had ever wanted in a woman. His death was the type of accident where there was no one to blame. These things happened, people said. The local landowner, Luigi's employer as well as the landlord from whom she and Luigi rented their house, took pity on her because it was his cart and horse that Luigi was driving. He said that Luigi had been a good man so he was willing to help. He and his wife took Ceciliana in, and when the wife realized that Ceciliana was not afraid of hard work, pregnant or not, she took a liking to her. Ceciliana learned to cook in that household and eventually gave birth to a child she called Maria. The little girl had long eyelashes, turquoise blue eyes like her father, and blond hair.

"You sure she's yours?" the cook laughed as she looked at Ceciliana's dark hair and vibrant but otherwise plain features.

"She'll be a heart-breaker for sure," Ceciliana said proudly.

"Don't get too certain of things," the cook warned. "God takes the good ones."

"Not my girl," Ceciliana immediately objected. "I'm going to be the best mother in the world. She's all I've got."

God had other plans. When Maria was six months old a man in the village came down with a fever and died. One by one the other villagers caught whatever it was. They ran a high fever, could keep no food down, and those who were not strong to begin with quickly succumbed. Ceciliana caught the fever and survived. Maria did not. She gave one gulping gasp and died in her mother's arms. Lost in grief, Ceciliana buried her in the church yard next to Luigi, refusing to be comforted by any ministrations about God's will. She knew she would never recover from her feelings of bitterness and betrayal by life. Her breasts ached with her milk, and when she heard that a family in nearby Colle needed a wet nurse, it seemed a godsend. She applied for the job by expressing her milk into a cup so that Marietta could taste its sweetness. When Beatrice was laid in her arms and suckled easily, Ceciliana made a silent plea to God: I will take care of this child as my own if you will forgive me for whatever sin it was, unrepented of, that led you to take Maria from me. It was thus that Ceciliana tied her destiny to the future of this small, dark-haired baby, whose mother seemed indifferent unless something was not to her liking. It was the father, Signor Paleario, who took more personal interest as the girl grew older. But he was seldom home, so it was possible for Ceciliana to fantasize that she was the girl's mother and not just her nurse.

Ceciliana now sat in a carved chair between the beds, the wool she had Beatrice had been winding fallen into long loops across her lap. Beatrice watched as Ceciliana's eyelids flickered and her head drooped onto her chest. The girl was no fool. She knew what was happening downstairs, and she intended to overhear if she could. Biding her time, she waited until she thought Ceciliana had fallen completely asleep and began to tiptoe toward the door. She froze when Ceciliana's head jerked back. Ceciliana looked at her through blurry eyes, smiled briefly without registering anything much and closed her eyes again. Almost immediately, her breathing deepened once more and her hands released the wool, letting the entire bundle settle onto the floor at her feet.

Beatrice crossed quickly to the door and carefully inched it open to avoid making the hinge creak. As soon as it was wide enough to squeeze through, she gave one more glance back at the sleeping Ceciliana then slipped away to the head of the narrow stairs leading down to the main hallway. She went three steps down to where she could hear the family's conversation but not be seen. At first it was just a murmur of voices but by concentrating, she could make out what was being said, particularly when someone was angry and raised his or her voice. Judging by the volume, the discussion was heated. She could hear her brother Fedro's voice the best, while her mother's voice was more indistinct.

"My house is small and with the baby, there is no room for her," Fedro said.

"Well, I can't be without someone to help me. Do you expect me to be without any servants?" Marietta sounded indignant and petulant.

"You'll be hardly alone with my wife and our servant. You can make do." Fedro sounded cold and unsympathetic.

"We've been saying all along that she should go into a convent," Caterina's voice was distinct and angry also. "You are being unreasonable, Mother."

Beatrice puzzled for a moment. Who were they talking about? Was it Ceciliana? She felt horrified. Ceciliana had always been the loving broad breast she could run to when she was afraid. She could not imagine her mother letting her go. Surely they would find a way to keep her.

"Would you want to go into a convent?" Marietta sounded defensive and accusatory.

"I'm a married woman. I don't have to make those kinds of choices. But what's her alternative? " Caterina was using her I-know-what's-best tone, the one that announced she was the only reasonable person alive. "So you tell me what to do about her. There's no house for her to live in and soon there'll be no money to support her. If she wants to eat, she'll have to find a place willing to take her."

"You're talking about her as if she's a piece of furniture," Marietta said although she didn't sound very upset at the comparison.

"I'm talking sense. Sentiment has nothing to do with this. She has become a burden."

"Who's going to care for me?" Marietta's voice now had a self-pitying whine.

"I told you," Fedro said impatiently. "You will come to live with me and my family."

"What if I don't want to? What if I would rather go to a poorhouse? I won't be the mistress of my own house anymore. Your wife will be the mistress. I'll have nothing to say and no position in your house. What am I supposed to do with myself?"

"It can't be helped. Look at this realistically, Mother. I have a house but it is not large enough for more than my wife, my children, me, and now you."

"I can tell you right now that my husband's family will not take her. It's bad enough I'm related to a heretic. They won't tolerate two." Caterina's voice was steady and distinct.

"You need to sell this house, and we'll hide what we can from the Inquisition," Fedro agreed.

"Fedro's right," Caterina said. "You have to sell this house and let the family spread out. Beatrice's future is the convent. Even if she had a dowry left after the Inquisition is through with us, no one in his right mind is going to choose a wife from this family. She's the heretic's daughter. If I were unmarried, I should be facing this as well. It's reality. We have to deal with it, so must she."

Beatrice's heart skipped a beat. They were talking about her.

"You're probably right," sniffed Marietta, "but have you considered what this means for me? You're all busy with your lives and families. If I go to live with Fedro, I am not in my own house. I am a guest at his wife's pleasure."

"We've already been through this. How many times do I need to assure you, we will do everything we can to make you comfortable." Fedro's black eyes flashed with impatience. "Having you is not the issue here. It's what to do with Beatrice."

"I always expected to die in this house. I've lived here since before you were all born."

"Well, father has taken care of that. He turned out to be a selfish, arrogant snob."

"Fedro!" Marietta sounded shocked.

"It's the truth, Mother. He didn't ask us if we wanted to be in this position. But we still end up paying for his folly."

"So what do we need to do? What is being proposed here?" Caterina cut in with customary clarity.

"First we sell the house for as much as we can get." Fedro jabbed his finger in the air as if he were arguing a case before the civic elders. "Then we lie low and distribute the money among ourselves."

"You'd leave me destitute as well as alone?" Marietta sounded appalled.

"Of course not, Mother," said Fedro. "Any money from the house is yours. We have to make it difficult for them to find."

"What happens if the Inquisition tries to seize the house from whomever buys it?" Caterina asked.

"We must assume that will happen," Fedro replied. "Whoever buys the house must understand the possibilities. But we know the law. He hasn't been executed yet. Our defense is he was not a convicted heretic when we sold."

"What else can they take from us?" Marietta asked, wondering whether her few pieces of jewelry were safe.

"Everything," said Fedro curtly. "If they want to, they can go back and try to reverse all exchanges of money and property. They can seize any farm equipment or animals, so we'll sell everything immediately. They'll take furnishings, even clothes, if they can find them. We can take a stand on everything predating your marriage, Mother, including your dowry. We'll argue that your family money never belonged to your husband since you have always handled the household finances. Your dowry was used to buy this house and pay for additions. We'll argue you were within your rights to sell it. Your family can testify. We'll argue that Caterina's dowry was paid years ago when she was married and has long been spent. The Holy Office will have to pursue the case locally. We'll have an advantage there. But don't think for one moment that anyone will stand by us—not with charges of heresy."

"Oh, my God, my God," Marietta wept. "How could it have come to this?"

"What about Beatrice?" Caterina asked. "What's been decided? When do we make arrangements to move her?"

Beatrice didn't remain to hear more. The only home she had ever known was now unfamiliar and unwelcoming. She was a burden. Even her family said that. She rose from her hiding place and tiptoed back into her room. Inside the room, Ceciliana was still asleep in her chair, her mouth open and her head flung back, exposing an expanse of neck her over ample breasts. Beatrice was glad of that. She walked to the window, pushed aside the shutters, and climbed out onto the roof.

It was past sundown and the air had stilled into a dusk; it was that time of day when the things of daylight yielded to the dark. Of course her family had to make sensible decisions and couldn't be sentimental. She knew Fra Pietro had told them her father's trial was about to start; that meant there was no hope that the charges against her father would be dropped. She'd wondered what that might mean for her since she was the youngest, but she had not been prepared for the calculating way they talked about her. They were as unemotional as they described her as a liability, born when Fedro was thirteen and Caterina eleven, just one more mouth to feed and a further division of the family inheritance. She knew how they felt because she had survived by listening and observing them all.

Most of all, however, she had observed herself. This quality of self-awareness made her seem much older than she was, a quality that delighted her father who undertook to educate her. She happily learned all he was willing to teach, even when it brought her into conflict with Caterina and her mother. But even he held back certain ideas, saying they were not appropriate for young women to study. She could not convince him that learning should to be open to all who sought it.

She crossed the roof, passing where the laundry flapped on washdays, and stopped at her favorite spot on the parapet. It was the place where she watched for her father when she knew he was expected home. "You be careful there," Ceciliana would call anxiously when she saw Beatrice sit on the wall and dangle her feet over the side. "We don't need you getting hurt." Beatrice would laugh and reassure her, but she would not come down. It was the place where she could look across undulating hills on all sides, the fields green against the darker spires of the cypress trees, and carpeted with red once the poppies came into bloom. She could see to the hills of Colle and up north to the towers of San Gimigiano.

Now, she watched as the clouds glowed turquoise on the horizon and became extinguished with the suddenness of night. One by one the stars came out. It was a magic time of night for her. It always had been the time she reflected on life.

"Papa," she whispered to the stars. "They want me to go to a convent. Mama is always angry now and Caterina is worse. They don't think I know the nature of the charges against you, but I do. They say you're a German reformer who believes in individual conscience. But all that means is that you want to come on this roof at night and speak to God directly. It all seems so pointless to persecute you. Don't we all respect the same God? They say you may be executed. But for what? Fra Pietro says that salvation is freely available to all as long as they believe in Christ, and no one I know has ever believed more faithfully than you. You speak of the crucifixion with tears of gratitude in your eyes. But what has this devotion brought you? I know you will be upset with me, but I am now questioning your faith. I can no longer believe in the censor and incense as a way to salvation. Not when they do this to you. I think it is much better to look at the stars hanging over the dark hills in the distance than to listen to sermons on original sin. The hills are where God is. But what kind of God demands people to love Him through fear. He should be horrified at killings done in His name. I cannot believe, I will not believe, in a God without compassion. If we are flawed, it must be because He made us so. The Church has no right to torture and condemn in His name."

She squinted at the stars as she stared at the night sky. There were no lights to blot them out and they stretched out like an infinity of trailing sparks from a dying fire. Surely the God who made such beauty could not be the vengeful killer of His own creation. Her father was right. The Church must be wrong. The Church was wrong.

Silently she stared to the heavens and challenged God to send her some sign of his presence if He disagreed with her. Each passing moment of silence strengthened her defiance. "Yes," she said out loud. "I am the heretic's daughter. And I am proud of it. I see Fedro's contempt for our father. I see Caterina's need to dominate and control. I see Mama's superstitions and emotional overreactions. Mama said I read too much and my head was stuffed with silly ideas. She took away the books when Papa wasn't home. But learning things wasn't silly and I could have told Fedro where he was wrong about beauty that evening when he talked with Fra Pietro, but no one would have listened to me because I am a girl. The beauty Fra Pietro was talking about was not just simplicity, but about things done so perfectly that we see them in new ways. I see beauty all around me, whoever or whatever created it. Papa said as much except he chose not to explain his words. Education was wasted on Fedro because he saw it only as a way to earn a living. He never had an original thought in his life—how could Papa overlook my yearning and reward Fedro's laziness? How can they justify denying education to a girl and then blaming her for growing into an ignorant woman?"

Footsteps sounded on the narrow stairs leading up to the attic bedroom. From the heavy tread, she assumed they must belong to Fedro. They must have made their decision down below and sent him up to announce her destiny. He was the last one she wanted to hear it from. It would be only a short while until Fedro woke Ceciliana; then they would look for her. She looked up into the night sky and spoke directly to the stars. "My life is my own and I am free to do with it as I will." Resolutely then, and in complete control of herself, she gathered her skirts around her knees and looked down into the courtyard. The fountain with the nymphs was empty of water as usual, but she knew the ancient fauns and pagan deities meant more to her than the pious pontifications of the

Church. "I curse the Church that has done this to my father," she said. Then, as she heard Ceciliana call out of the bedroom window, asking if she were on the roof, Beatrice leaned forward and deliberately fell into the courtyard.

3:00 a.m.

IREACH OUT *to stop her fall. It is an instinctive and futile gesture because neither I nor anyone else can change the cascade of events we call history. She died long ago, but some impulse deep within my soul makes me want to protect her. Once she has fallen into the darkness, I cannot bring myself to look down at her crumpled form in the courtyard below. I hear Ceciliana call for her with increasing alarm. Then a search is mounted through the house until Fedro curses loudly as he finds her.*

Marietta starts screaming when she hears, but she seems more concerned with what the neighbors will say. "We're cursed," she wails. "First a heretic in the house and now a suicide." Caterina tries to drag her mother away from the body, telling her to keep her voice down about any suicide. "Let them prove it," she says. When Marietta sees Ceciliana, who is in copious tears, she attacks her and calls her a slut for not watching the girl more closely. "On my heart," Ceciliana sobs, "I love her as if she were my own." The scene is destined to become even more chaotic and noisy until Fedro steps in between Marietta and Ceciliana and brutally tells them both to shut up. His lawyer mind takes over. He makes them all go into the house and wait while he carries Beatrice to the upstairs bedroom.

"She fell," he says when he comes back down. "She was out on the roof and it was an accident. She often went out there by herself." "How could she do this to her family?" Marietta moans. "Why did she do this? First her father, now her. Who's going to believe it was an accident? We are ruined." "We're already ruined," Caterina says, "What's the difference?" "Enough," says Fedro firmly. "Why she did it doesn't matter. We are wasting time. We need to come up with a story."

I cannot agree the girl's decision was correct, but I understand it. Perhaps she had more of Fedro's pragmatism and Caterina's absolutism in her than anyone realized. She made her decision rationally, a remarkable thing for a young girl, but Aonio had clearly taught her to think and once that is done, one can never return to ignorance.

But regardless of what philosophers might argue, her choice was not as free as she thought. Choices come with the price tag of consequence. If we cannot predict or anticipate this consequence, it finds us nonetheless as we are taken prisoner by experience. What happens happens, and without self-awareness all we can do is learn from it. I see Beatrice's suicide as the first consequence of Aonio's decision to pursue truth at any cost. I doubt her death was what he intended or expected. Yet he should have known that every choice has an equal reaction even if it is not immediate. The open question, though, is how much she realized that, like his, her choice would also have consequences. It seems she was indeed the heretic's daughter.

I wonder what I am supposed to take from watching this family drama. I suppose I should take a closer look at my tendency not to decide because I can see now that undeciding is a choice as well. In fact, the decision not to decide is the one I used to make the most. If the sound of a frog jumping into a pond reverberates around the world then a suicide must also have an impact. Under the right circumstances, we know that individual lives can change the course of history, so the only conclusion I can draw is that we have no right to think ourselves insignificant. As human beings, we are the heroes of our lives, and those lives inevitably impact others'.

Anna and Skipper thought we spend our lives with the ones we are meant to know. Is this the universe asking the same questions about meaning as I am? Do we return with the same people looking for answers to this question of what it means to be human? Do we make collective mistakes that we try to correct? But if so, where is all this headed? I'm not sure yet that I can accept the idea of recycling souls. And yet even I can see that to be fully human we need to be the mystics of our own lives.

When we drove into the mountains that day, Anna asked me about the seven dwarfs. I thought her question just a distraction to take my mind off my illness. But she was serious. She was asking about meaning. The seven are some of life's simple things that woven together make up the tapestry of our lives. Anna would be proud of me now. I've remembered one of the two I missed. Sleepy. I was willing to allow myself to sleep through life's possibilities and connections. In this I am not alone, and the trouble for us all is that we don't know it until something wakes us. For most, as it has been with me, we awaken only when we must confront our own mortality.

Anna's playing Beethoven's Ninth Symphony now. I lie back to listen. I am not afraid of the cavern anymore. It has become familiar, even comforting. I glimpse familiar shapes hovering outside my ability to see them clearly. I know they have come for me. I am grateful. I know why you are here, I tell them, but, please, not yet—there is more for me to learn. Show me what happens to Aonio.

Chapter 13

Inquisition Prison, October 1569

AONIO HAD COME to think of his cell as his haven. It had been his so long he missed its familiarity when they dragged him away. When the door slammed behind him on his return, it signaled the quiet when he could think himself far away.

He was in worse pain than ever. Yesterday they told him he had been found guilty of heresy, but he might yet find mercy if he was willing to recant. When he replied that he had nothing more to say, they came and took him to the room of screams in the bowels of the prison.

Calla led the way, praying for Aonio to return to the true Church's teachings and asking him if he were ready to accept the pope as the true vicar of Christ. Aonio said nothing and clenched his teeth as they strapped him to the rack. Will you return to the Church for the sake of your immortal soul? Still he said nothing as they tied the ropes around his wrists and ankles and started to turn the capstans at the top and bottom of the table. As the ropes tightened. his arms were pulled above his head and he could feel his ribs stretching and snapping. Still he said nothing. Another turn of the wheel and he blacked out. They threw water on him to revive him and then turned the wheel another quarter turn. Will you accept the teachings of the Church? Again they turned the wheel. There was pain and terrible feelings of things pulled apart. He was dizzy and sick. He felt his hips start to pull out from their sockets. A terrible pain seared through his body. "Anything. Anything," he screamed. Then everything went black.

He lay crumpled on his bed now, more a sack of human refuse than the proud man he once was. He felt ashamed that he could not bear the rack and was sickened by the joy his captors expressed when they told him he had recanted. Above all he was distraught because the inquisitors had given him no chance to present his arguments. They had silenced him when he asked to speak. His journey to Rome, his hope to present truth, all was now gone and all was wasted. He wanted to be alone to grieve his own weakness, but the clank of keys told him he would not be allowed to. Fra Pietro was let in and sat down on the chair at the table. The priest took a few moments to study the crumpled man on the bed.

"I am sorry to see you in this place," Fra Pietro said.

When Aonio did not reply, the priest continued.

"The Father Inquisitor gave me permission to visit you. He says you have recanted and wishes you to make a public confession."

"Or they will torture me?" Aonio gave a sardonic snort.

"Sometimes it is necessary to use harsh means to heal the soul." The priest tried to sound consoling but managed instead to sound condescending.

"How do you know about my trial?" Aonio tried to sit but was forced to hunch over to protect his broken ribs. His breathing was shallow because of the pain.

"I work for the Bishop of Colle now. I was asked to Rome to provide character testimony for you."

"How long have you worked for the bishop?" Aonio ignored the priest's self-importance and wondered if whatever testimony Fra Pietro had offered was the price for his advancement.

"Some months since." Fra Pietro was deliberately vague. He didn't want to let Aonio know that his promotion had come through shortly after Aonio entered through the prison's door.

"So you have seen my family?"

"I left your wife in good health but much distressed."

Aonio did not respond. He hoped the priest would say more without trying to bargain knowledge of Marietta and the children for the public statement they wanted him to make. Fra Pietro appeared torn by indecision and there was silence in the cell for several minutes.

"Marietta has sold the villa. She is living with your son Fedro. The Office of the Inquisition has made no move yet against your property."

Aonio nodded. He was sorry to hear that Marietta had lost the villa. But perhaps that was for the best. It was old and needed upkeep. "How is Caterina?"

"She is well, but she and her husband have also moved away. His family was disturbed by the talk in the village and offered them property closer to Siena. They requested her not to admit she is related to you. I'm sorry to be blunt, but consequences follow everything we do."

"And Beatrice?"

The priest hesitated and did not meet Aonio's eyes. "There is bad news," he said finally.

Aonio started and banged against the backboard. This was the last thing he had expected. "What kind of news? "What has happened in God's name?"

"I'm sorry, Aonio. She is dead."

"No." Aonio fell back and groaned loudly. It was several minutes before he could control himself. He wanted to believe the priest was lying, but he could not ignore the serious, sad look on the man's face. He was forced to realize the man had spoken what he believed to be the truth.

"How?" Aonio's already raw voice had become an anguished croak.

"I was called to your house. It was late. Fedro came to fetch me and was to lead me back on foot with a lantern. There has been a terrible accident, he told me. Beatrice has fallen from the roof onto the courtyard below. As I put on my cloak, I asked if he had called the doctor. He said it was too late. There was no breath when they reached her. I asked him what kind of accident it was as we were hurrying along the road. I had to consider how it would be possible to be accidentally out on the roof and then accidentally fall from it. All your windows have shutters. What would she be doing on the roof? It was my duty to ask these questions. Your son told me they didn't know. He told me that the family, by which I assumed he meant your wife, was blaming Ceciliana for not doing her duty of watching Beatrice. When I got there, I saw Marietta with my own eyes beat Ceciliana and call her a worthless slut. 'Control yourself, Marietta,' I told her. 'This is not helping.' But privately I wondered how Ceciliana could be responsible for watching a girl who was almost a woman. Many her age already are mothers.

They took me up to her bedroom where they had laid her on her bed. From the side, it seemed as if she were asleep. But when I approached, I could see she had hit her head so hard that nothing human could have saved her. Marietta went into hysterical crying once she saw her again while your daughter Caterina tried to calm her down. Marietta finally asked me to conduct a service for her since she said that the family needed no further trouble from the neighbors. That's when it struck me that something was very wrong. 'Wait a minute, I said. I have to be sure this was an accident.' They looked at one another then, and I could tell they had the same question themselves. Perhaps they hoped I would not notice. "

"Suicide? They thought she'd taken her own life?" Aonio moved restlessly on the bed. It creaked and groaned under his weight. He felt nauseous.

"We have to investigate I said. We took the lantern to the roof. If we could find a broken tile or something to indicate that she had tried to save herself, we could justify a finding it was accidental and therefore not an offense to God. But we could find no such evidence. For her to have fallen into the courtyard as she did, she had to open the window to the roof, cross a flat section, and climb over a wall. We can look at this again in the morning, I said, but it looks to me as if she meant to go out on the roof. 'Can't you find it an accident?' Fedro asked. I told him I wished I could, but unless he could bring me further proof, I would have to consider her death a suicide. I spent the night comforting Marietta and saying prayers. Marietta was frantic at what the neighbors would say and started to suggest that Beatrice must have been sleepwalking and that if Ceciliana had only been more alert this would not have happened. But there was no one who could confirm she had any history of sleepwalking. The night was dry, the roof not slippery, and she had to climb over a waist-high ledge to fall.

Next day, the bishop is contacted and based on the facts has the same questions I have. Suicide is an abomination to God and in the old days it would have been justification for torturing her body, burning it and scattering the ashes. We do not encourage such practices these days, but given the situation, burying her in Marietta's family plot was impossible because it was on hallowed ground. I said I'd try to keep the facts as quiet as I could, but naturally there was much talk among the neighbors what with you not there and now this happening to your daughter. There was even talk of curses. Beatrice was secretly buried two days later in the woods on your former villa grounds. They had recently dug a grave for your old dog, Bruno, there, so the ground had been disturbed already and would call no special attention to the site. There was no marker to attract malevolent spirits. I'm sorry, no matter how hard the Church tries to suppress the old superstitions, people still believe in them. It was the best we could do."

Aonio stared stolidly at the ceiling, tears trickling down both cheeks. "Dear God," he said to himself, "is this the price, the sacrifice for finding truth and wishing to honor You?" He felt elemental anger with Marietta and Ceciliana for not protecting her and for this bumptious, arrogant priest whom he believed had used his family and his daughter for his own ambition. How could Beatrice have one this to herself? Hadn't he taught her better than this? Where was Marco and his promise to watch over her?

"Did anyone say why she might have done it—if she did?" Aonio asked, barely managing to contain his anger.

"There was discussion, but you'll understand it was not in front of me. I think your family concluded she had despaired."

"What role did you play in this?" Aonio's words dripped with accusation.

The priest saw his expression and shrank back in surprise. "Me?" he managed to blurt out.

"Tell me you didn't ply her with innocent seeming questions. Has your father received any letters lately? Did he tell you about them? You can tell me, I'm your family priest. I hear your confessions. I am quite safe. Has he had any visitors, strangers perhaps?"

The priest stood up so quickly he knocked over the chair. The man on the bed looked like a coiled snake that was ready to strike.

"Are you all right in there?" the guard called gruffly through the slit in the door.

"Yes," the priest replied. "It's all right."

Fra Pietro turned to look at Aonio with burning eyes. He remained standing and spoke with cold precision.

"I have never discussed you with Beatrice. I baptized her. I respect her mother and her mother's family. Look at yourself, Aonio. Ask your own role before you accuse someone else."

Aonio fell back weakly and stared at the cracked and dirty ceiling. He could trace the outline of the mildew stains. They looked like dirty clouds.

"If not her, who? It had to be you who told the Inquisition about letters sent and received. Where did you hear it? If you want me to believe you did not use and betray Beatrice, who in my house was your spy?"

The priest picked up the fallen chair and sat down. He studied Aonio carefully, wondering at the wisdom of complying with the request. In the end he shrugged.

"All right. In a few days you will address the cardinals and the pope. Did they tell you? The emperor wrote to His Holiness and asked for the charges to be dropped against you. The Vatican said you had been found guilty and heresy was not negotiable. But out of respect for the emperor, His Holiness agreed that the cardinals would hear you make your case. Tomorrow, you will address them. It will change little since you have recanted. If you plead well, you may escape execution when the civil authorities determine your punishment. But it doesn't matter much now. So you want to know? I can assure you it was not Beatrice, or Marietta, or your other children. It was far different from what you imagine. I did not plan on any devious spy network. I didn't need to. Once a month, your servant Pterigi drove the horse and cart into the village. He brought Ceciliana with him to visit the local market. Pterigi visited various women in the region and would be occupied for several hours. This allowed time for Ceciliana to gossip as women like her do. She is proud of you. Her professor she calls you. She chattered away as she wandered among the stalls. Nothing went on in your house without somebody knowing. I didn't need to ask. All I had to do was listen."

"Ceciliana?"

"She just wants to feel important. She started talking one day about the letters coming to the house. I don't imagine she saw any harm in this at all. She is quite proud of working for a famous man. It is the nature of women like her."

"But Ceciliana can't read."

"She didn't have to. Remember, she would be the one who took tired, hungry men into the kitchen for a plate of spaghetti and a glass or two of wine. They would talk, one servant to another. I've come from Basle; you should see the weather up there. The emperor's man and I rode over the pass together. Idle servant talk, boasting in many instances, no intention to betray, but very interesting when it's put together by someone who knows what is happening beyond Colle."

"Why should I believe you?"

"Because you have no reason not to."

Aonio lay still on his bed. The priest waited his moment to accomplish what he had been sent to do. Now was the moment. He took a deep breath.

"Aonio, I have a document I would like you to consider signing."

"What is it?" Aonio did not move his eyes from the mildew stains on the ceiling.

"It's a public recantation of the heretical beliefs identified in your writing. It also affirms your confession of faith, accepting the pope as the vicar of Christ and your belief in the Bible and the Church fathers."

"Why should I? Wasn't the torture enough?"

"Because it may save your family. If you make a convincing public confession tomorrow and are sentenced to life in prison, you may spare them the confiscations and the ignominy of your public execution."

"You ask me to choose between my faith and my family?" Aonio turned bloodshot eyes on the priest.

"Or is your pride involved here?" Fra Pietro repeated here what he had overheard one of the inquisitors say.

Aonio remained silent.

"Read it," the priest urged. "Ask yourself if you have ever said prayers for someone's soul. If you have, you believe in purgatory. If you sign, it will show you do not sympathize with the German reformers. You have already indicated your willingness to disavow the claims to individual conscience. Come back to the welcome arms of the Church for your soul's safety. I urge you to read and sign this recantation, so you can be moved from this prison to a better place and you can have your books and papers and your scholarship. The Church is prepared to be a tolerant mother if you return to her."

"And you guarantee this?" Aonio wondered how Fra Pietro had gained such stature to make promises of forgiveness on behalf of the Church.

"No one can make such guarantees. But I showed this document to the bishop who investigated you and he thinks it a sincere and welcome statement."

"You showed this to the Inquisition? They thought I had written it?"

"No. I merely asked what he would think if this document or another like it were to be presented to the Holy Office. The authorship did not come up."

"You thought this would help?" Aonio rose on one elbow and twisted his body as if he would get up. The priest stood again and backed away.

"I thought it would help a grieving mother who has buried a child, your other children, and—yes—you as well in avoiding a terrible and public death."

Aonio lacked the energy to swing his legs over the bed and fell back. The priest lay the document on the table, drew his vestments round him, and banged on the door. "You can tell the guard your decision, but you don't have long."

When the door slammed behind the priest, Aonio's first impulse was to tear the document to pieces. His grief grew as he thought of his daughter buried in an unmarked, unblessed grave. He would never forgive the ones who should have watched her. Exhausted and in pain, the tears rolling down his cheeks and into his matted beard, he wrapped the blanket around him, rolled onto his side, and fell into a fitful sleep.

4:00 a.m.

I ROLL OVER on my side as far as the catheter will let me. But my mind is not asleep. The bishop asked Aonio if he had reached the point where faith had become obstinacy. I don't think it was faith. I think it was truth. He was obstinately pursuing his idea of truth. To a degree, I admire him. If everyone who didn't agree with prevailing "truths" just went along, learning would cease. We need people willing to stand up for their beliefs. But who determines truth and how it can be tested?

How strange it has taken me a lifetime to see that abstractions like justice and truth are merely fashions; yet people give their lives for them. Absolute faith does not exist either. Human minds construct them all and all share the same weaknesses—and strengths, let's not discount that—as any other human endeavor. How can a truth that purports to be evidence of God's love cause death and torture? Aonio asked that question but could offer no solution except to study the original texts—as if they were any less the work of human beings. His truth was academic, to be revealed by whittling away additions and accretions to the word of God. But he never asked how reliable those scrolls and documents were to begin with.

I am not Aonio, willing to give my life for an idea. But watching Aonio has already taught me my cowardice. I never accommodated to my mother's church but lacked the guts to say so. I never took a stand. It was easier not to face my mother and her priests. I would now, and I know that if ever I have the chance again to speak, I shall not make the same mistake.

Chapter 14

Castel Sant'Angelo, November 1569

T HE NEXT DAY, very slowly and painfully, Aonio dressed himself in preparation for his oration. Scornfully, he threw Fra Pietro's proposed confession down the sewage hole. He stood as proudly as he could, knowing that God had given him the chance to speak the truth.

The guards dragged him down narrow streets from the prison to the Castel Sant'Angelo. There he was deposited in an opulent room that had gold-tinted frescoes on the ceiling, and heavy tapestries hung along three walls, depicting the acts of various historical popes. On a dais at the front of the room was a long, wooden table with incised panels along the front and coiled carving traced around the edge. The table looked official and intimidating, with feet carved to look like lions' heads. Behind the table were ten brocaded chairs five on each side of a larger golden chair. For now, these chairs were empty. The guards took Aonio to a small, latticed wooden chair beneath the dais before stationing themselves along the wall behind the prisoner.

Aonio looked at the imposing portraits of former popes displayed as a group on the one bare wall behind the dais. There was Clement, whose ineptitude brought on the siege of Rome. There were the three popes who came and went between Clement and Caraffa. Paul III, a Farnese, who said he wanted to reform the Church—they all said that—but couldn't combat the entrenched Vatican bureaucracy. Julius III followed, a compromise candidate who simply left Spain and France to fight things out as long as they let Rome alone. Then came Marcello Cervini, who took the name Marcellus. Poor Marcello was pope for three weeks until he caught the Roman fever. Most recently added to the wall was the portrait of Caraffa, the most hated man in Europe as he himself admitted.

After a while, a door opened and the cardinals came out talking with one another and paying no attention to Aonio. One by one, they sat down in the brocaded chairs. At a signal, the guards came forward and roughly lifted Aonio to standing position. Aonio's pain was dulled by his distraction as the cardinals all rose and fell silent. Caraffa then entered and walked to the golden chair in the center of the dais. Even though his hair was grey and his face hatched with lines, Aonio could see he was the same Caraffa except that his mouth slashed his face even more severely and his stocky build had thickened into menace. Caraffa seated himself, wrapped his cloak around him, and placed his feet on a small stool in front of his chair. The cardinals then sat down, and several moments passed before anything was said. Caraffa looked bored and displeased as if he thought this business with Aonio should have been over long before now. He gazed contemptuously at the unkempt old man below him on the chamber floor.

Aonio looked up at Caraffa, savoring the idea that before all these cardinals, he would prove that Caraffa had squandered his opportunity to build the Church on God's word.

Caraffa scowled as he shifted uncomfortably in his robes, his large hands dwarfed by the ceremonial brocade of his sleeves. He nodded peremptorily to the cardinal on his right who rose to address the prisoner.

"Aonio Paleario, the Holy Office has found you to be a heretic and the Church is ready to refer your case to the Civil Authorities for sentence. Before doing so, we understand from the Holy Office you have recanted.

His Holiness is willing to hear those words from your own mouth. You are commanded to be brief. Begin."

Aonio stood as straight as he was able, clinging to the back of his stool for support. He was thankful not to be told to sit because he wasn't sure he could have risen again. He cleared his throat and tried to stand firmly on both feet. It was difficult as his joints still ached from the rack and he felt one of legs start to shake from the strain of standing. He cleared his throat and had to restart his speech several times before he had enough momentum to continue.

> Lords of the Church, I have been told I should confess my faith and explain the circumstances bringing me here today. I am given to understand those men who investigated me have already presented their report. I do not know what they told you. I find myself with few defenders alive who will step forward and risk the wrath of those in powerful places who have accused me.

The cardinal interrupted him. "We know the particulars of your history and the people you consorted with. Discuss the heresy."

Aonio cleared his throat again and continued.

> Once before in my life, I was accused of heresy. After close examination and a proper public hearing at which I had the chance to speak, I was absolved of the charges. I said then and I say now that I have never followed the Germans anymore than I would follow the Spanish or the French in matters of faith and truth. I choose to follow only those whose judgment is supported by scholarship and God's revealed words.
>
> I stand accused of wanting reform within the Church. I have been very honest in this regard. I said that I could find no justification for some of the rituals. This does not mean that I dispute them. It means only that I believe we need further examination of

the original texts. And I am not alone in calling for reform within the Church. Many have made such calls, including some of the most saintly holders of the papal tiara. It has been my lifelong hope that through scholarship, we could become once more a unified community of believers committed to the will of God.

Now, let me emphasize further that I agree that I have spoken throughout my life against hypocrisy and ignorance among those who betray belief in the name of the Church. I will certainly accede to the fact that I have denounced certain monks who presented falsehoods to the ignorant who have no way of judging the truth of what they are told. Until the Council of Trent prepared the guidelines for training priests, there has been no commonly accepted education for them. That means that many have been allowed to perpetuate their ignorance on those they would lead. This is a betrayal of a sacred trust and makes them evil men.

Outraged conversation rumbled among the cardinals at this point. Caraffa raised his hand and there was immediate silence. Aonio cleared his throat and continued.

You may well ask what I mean when I use the word *evil*. There are two types of evil. One is evil directed toward God such as disobedience to His commandments. The other is evil directed toward people, that is, using falsity, hypocrisy, and violence intended to harm others. Evil is undertaken by vicious people who subvert their power to do good. But there are degrees of evil and it is my contention that the most evil is committed by those who have the most power, but the greatest evil is committed by those who not only have power over people but do it in the name of God.

We can all agree that the action of soldiers who slaughtered the innocent citizens of Rome was evil. We can further agree that the imprisonment of His

Holiness Pope Clement in the Castel Sant'Angelo was
further evidence of inhumanity and horror. But those
soldiers bore no particular malice to the people whom
they slew. They were ravenous dogs without moral
conscience; they had no power over Rome except the
force of arms. I contrast that with my own situation
as I stand before you. I have no power over others. I
have caused no harm to people's belief in their Creator.
Yet I stand here accused and now found guilty of
being evil in an affront to God. This I do deny.

Am I a hypocrite who preaches what I do not believe?
How can this be when I see everywhere Churchmen
who are not virtuous and provide an evil example to
those they are meant to teach? I stand accused and yet
these men are the ones who do not uphold the teachings
of the Church they represent. I stand accused of not
following Church laws and yet there are priests even
among the highest, who openly maintain households
and in fact marry off their sons and daughters to
political advantage as if they were kings or emperors.

"This is no recantation," loudly exclaimed the cardinal at the Pope's
left. "Who is this man to denounce others. He is a heretic. Why is His
Holiness subject to this filth?"

The pope made a slight movement with his hand to quiet the cardinal
and pointed to Aonio, who took it to mean that he should go on. Caraffa
smiled slightly. It made things easier for the Inquisition when the
prisoner condemned himself.

You may well be saying this man is unrepentant
and a fool. But am I? I see about me the Church's
pervasive falling away from its own ideals. Is this
how mankind behaves in a Christian society? Is the
Church to be the instrument of oppression against
those who wish only to be pious and honor their
God? These are not the teachings of the Christ I
have loved and honored throughout my life.

> I have been told things may go better for me if I repeat
> today what was extracted from me through torture.
> This I refuse because I have been motivated by love of
> my God and by love of the truth that the creator has
> granted to us. I will not renounce the truth, neither
> for the fellowship of man or the Church nor for the
> lessening of any mortal pain inflicted on my body. And
> I say this now. I will not accept the pope as the vicar
> of Christ because he has allowed the power granted to
> him by God to be subverted to harm the people that
> God created and loves, and because of this I say he is
> an evil man for he has no obedience to his maker.

Caraffa smiled again as Aonio drew in his breath to continue with his oration: The cardinals stared down at him with hatred. They were restless in their seats and looked as if they might attack him. Aonio drew in his breath and made his final pronouncement.

> I stand here as a man of faith and truth. I confess to
> my faith in God and my devout belief in His son, Jesus
> Christ. I do deny the Church has any power to control
> my thoughts or drive me away from personal knowledge
> of my God. I do deny that of which I am accused.

"A damnable reformer," one of the cardinals yelled loudly.

"Let this be over," the cardinal next to him agreed. "There's no repentance here. The man has not recanted."

Aonio let his eyes sweep around the raised pageantry of the colorful robes and hats lined up before him. The pope still sat as he was. The cardinals either stared at Aonio or looked to the pope for guidance. The room was silent. Their outrage with him was reflected by how rigidly they sat. It made Aonio think of Da Vinci's mural of the Last Supper on the wall in Milan. He felt shaken with the intensity of what he had declaimed. His hands felt wet, he shivered, and his head felt heavy. But he felt proud of what he had done.

Caraffa turned to the cardinal on his right and the man leaned forward. The cardinal's scarlet sash reminded Aonio of a parrot he once saw in the palace at Milan. The bird charmed all who saw it with its bright black eye and long blue and red feathers. But the servants quickly learned its capacity for malice as it bit unwary fingers and destroyed anything within its reach.

He heard someone talking and realized that the parrot has risen from his chair.

"Aonio Paleario, you were invited to speak before His Holiness and the cardinals of the Catholic Church in order to judge your professed return to the Church. By your own words, we can see you are not sincere and, in fact, you have obstinately relapsed into your former errors. This body finds ample evidence to justify the charge of heresy and you will be remanded to the civil authority for the final disposition of your life. The Holy See orders all copies of your writing whatsoever to be destroyed and your name removed from any public records. Your existence is an abomination to Christian believers and they shall turn their backs on you."

Caraffa and the cardinals then left the hall. When they were gone, the guards dragged Aonio back to his cell to await the civil judgment, which was a foregone conclusion. Aonio would be put to death, although it was as yet unclear how and when.

5:00 a.m.

I WATCH THEM *pull him away, a man broken physically but with a burning fury strong enough to defy Caraffa. He gave the oration that he wanted to, but I have to shake my head.*

The fact the Church is hypocritical and intolerant hardly needed proof—most human institutions are one way or another. Aonio knew they intended to execute him before he went to Rome and he knew what they would do to his family.

I agree that a man must be what he believes in and be willing to speak out and take the consequences. That is accountability, but accountability is individual. Is he a man of honor when he forces others to pay the price of his personal conviction? Did he have the right to choose his family's destinies for them? I cannot see where Aonio ever understood this. He took away their choice without understanding that choice is what makes us human.

Aonio's works will not survive except in a few hidden copies, and his name will be excised wherever and however long the Church has means to reach. The Inquisition will continue. Protestors will not flood the streets because he has been executed. Yet these are the things he gave his life for and he will be forgotten—at least until Anna and a few other scholars looking for research topics come across him. But perhaps that is all any of us can ask for in this life, to have someone remember and speak out our names.

Chapter 15

The Inquisition Prison, July 2,1570

THE MISERICORDIA OF San Giovanni Decollato were called to Aonio's cell in the late afternoon on the day before his execution. These kindly priests, who hid their faces beneath white cloths, were allowed to provide comfort to the condemned. They brought pen and paper and asked Paleario if he would like to write letters to his family. He said he would. While the priests remained by his side, Aonio wrote two final letters in his jagged printing—one he hoped would comfort his wife, another to his son. He sounded out the words as he laboriously wrote the letters.

> Dearest Wife:
> Do not be sad for me as I leave this earth. I have no
> regrets and look forward to the happy union with my
> maker. Draw the family around you and give them
> comfort, for you are the only one left who can do this
> for them. I am an old man and the world will not
> miss me. I hope Fedro will be virtuous and honorable.
> May God the Father and Jesus Christ be with you.
> Aonio Paleario, Rome, July 3, 1570.

To my beloved son Fedro:
I write through the kindness of the Misericordia
who assure me this letter will be sent to you. I know
things must seem hard and bitter to have taken
place against someone who has loved his maker as
much as I. But such is the will of God and I ask you
to accept it as I have with all humility. I have little
to leave you, but I take pride that I leave no debts.
Do not let believe anyone who claims otherwise.
Take care of your mother. It will soon be time to
go, so I ask God to console and protect you.
Your father, Aonio Paleario.

The Misericordia took the letters and left him for his final night on earth. They would return in the morning and stay with him until his execution. Aonio sat on the bed with his head bowed. He began praying.

6:00 a.m.

*I*FEEL AN *upsurge of impatience with this man. Enough of this hypocrisy and denial. It's time he faced the truth and did his time in the cavern as I have.* "Why did you let her think she is your beloved wife?" *I say out loud. I expect no answer, only the emptiness of my own frustration.*

"Because she is" *he replies.*

I stare at Aonio in shock. This man can hear and understand me? After all this time of watching him, this man can hear me? I lapse into astonished silence.

Seeing no one to account for the voice he has heard, Aonio's face freezes in disbelief. His eyes become wild and his hands shake. For a moment I am afraid he will die on the spot. But I do not feel compassionate. In fact, I have a malicious desire to smother his smug belief in his own nobility. "She didn't bother to see if you could be helped," *I say nastily.* "How supportive of her." *My voice is hard and accusing.*

Aonio flattens himself against the wall next to his bed, his pale face distorted by fear. I watch as he crosses himself. He still looks as if he is about to collapse from shock.

"Why didn't she help you?" I ask more gently. It's not totally his fault that she wanted to distance herself from his predicament. Marietta and her conniving son always were more about themselves even though I cannot blame them.

Aonio gets up from the bed rapidly, letting the headboard spring back against the wall. Then he goes to the door and looks for me through the grate as if I must be on the other side. When he finds nothing there, he turns to stare blankly at the window and at the few pieces of furniture in the room. Defeated when he finds nothing, he huddles back on his bed and closes his eyes. He shudders as if he is in the presence of Satan.

"Why?" I prompt him again. I feel rather powerful in my invisibility.

He opens his eyes and rakes the room once more. Then he puts his head down in misery and wraps his arms around himself protectively.

"It's a long way and she's an old woman," he says.

"The priest, whatever his name was, could have brought a message." I know he won't like my pointing out that he is making excuses for her.

"She has a lot on her mind. She has to care for the family and secure the property." Those few words tell me everything. He also knows Marietta's faults and propensities. All along he has known where her focus will be.

"Mostly taking care of herself," I realize that I am acting on my own dislike of Marietta.

Aonio's head snaps up in indignation. "I won't hear bad things about her. She gave me children and she was a good mother. This is my last letter to her, why should I speak unkind words? She is as dear to me as my own life."

The passion of his defense surprises me for a second, but then I realize that he needs to maintain some semblance of being a gentleman. "As your *own life?" I repeat mockingly. "Considering where you are and how you got here, that doesn't seem to say much. And, by the way, what was it you thought you were accomplishing? You certainly weren't doing it for your family. It looks to me like wasted effort."*

Aonio shakes his head vigorously and clenches his fists. I can see I have touched a sore point—perhaps even his greatest fear. His voice shakes with emotion. "If I believed you, I should despair. I do not despair. What I have done will make a difference."

"To whom?" I reply nastily. "To Beatrice?"

"I don't know what happened to Beatrice. I have only the word of a self-serving priest."

"Who was there."

"I do not believe him."

"You must believe him. I saw it happen."

"You saw it happen?" Paleario looks around the room for me again. His face is contorted with anger. "How could you have been there?"

"Spirit is everywhere." My reply is ambiguous because I don't care to get into an argument with him over the nature of the universe and his theories of immanence. If I don't know how I have been watching his life, then I certainly can't explain to him.

"This is against all human reason," he says. "You're either my imagination because I face my death tomorrow or you are a devil sent to tempt me. Either way, be gone from this place. I do not believe in you. You are not real." He raises his arm and makes a large and deliberate sign of the cross.

I chuckle. It will take a lot more than the sign of the cross to drive me away. "None of this may be real," I reply dismissively. "Isn't that what the Greek poet Pindar said. You must have read him. You probably translated his work. Life is but a dream of shadows, he said. But let's say life is real. Didn't you think your actions would affect your family and your descendants?"

"Why would they? I am sorry for Marietta and the children, but they will find their way and they will understand the importance of what I was working for."

"Your family's issues and sorrows will not disappear merely because you think they are important. Your daughter died thinking of you, you know. Your wife, the one you write loving letters to, and your other children were the immediate cause of it."

"What do you mean?" Paleario's mouth goes slack with shock. His defiance of a few moments ago crumbles as I watch. He is not as dismissive of his daughter as he is of his wife.

"Your wife wanted to keep her as a servant. Your children didn't want the cost of supporting her after you beggared them, and they won the argument. They planned on sending her to a convent. Incidentally, they blamed her death on your woman servant and you rather than themselves."

"Ceciliana?" He frowns. "But she was always fond of Beatrice."

"More like a mother to her?" I add nastily. "Well, your wife beat her, called her a slut, and threw her out. They said she hadn't watched your daughter closely enough."

"I'm sorry she was blamed, but I am more sorry Beatrice made that choice. A suicide pains me more than anything. She should have chosen life, even in a convent." A tear rolls down Paleario's face.

"As you have chosen life?" Now I have him. I've caught him in a major inconsistency and I savor my moment because I know he has no answer. He knows it too.

"Go away. You bring me no comfort. I know you are evil."

"Not yet." I keep my voice steady. "I want you to understand that your decisions affected not just those around you but also those who follow.

Your choice did violence to you and caused immense suffering to everyone else as well."

"Who have I hurt? Tell me their names. If Beatrice despaired, I am disappointed in her."

"Beatrice did not despair. That was the only way Fra Pietro could explain it to you. Beatrice went to her death defying the Church. In fact, she called herself the heretic's daughter before she jumped. Her only regret was that you had limited her education because she was a girl. She thought you had wasted your time with Fedro."

"She learned eagerly," Aonio agreed. "But I am disappointed in her mother and the others for not protecting her. I curse Marco who said he would watch over her."

"I'd be careful with the curses," I caution him. "You sound close to despair yourself. Now let's talk for a moment about your ideas. You seem to believe that there is such a thing as absolute truth and that you own it."

"Of course there is absolute truth," Aonio says indignantly. "Truth is what God tells us."

"And what if God decides to trick or test us?" I try to sound innocent as I say this.

"God is perfect," Aonio thunders. "He does not lie to us. He has made the word perfectly for His creations."

"Isn't that faith rather than truth?" I'm being coy. But this is becoming interesting.

"Faith and truth are the same when we interpret correctly what God has revealed to us."

"How do you know that the Scriptures have accurately reported what God revealed?" This is a question that has always intrigued me. I want to hear how he deals with it.

Aonio does not seem to have an answer. He shifts ground to avoid answering my question. "I have devoted my life to studying the ancient texts. God's word is sacred."

"You miss my point." I say calmly. "I'm not challenging your reputation. I'm pointing out that those texts you studied were written down by humans—what happens if they got it wrong or if they only imagined that they heard God's word? This is the point where faith takes over from truth. If you ask me, those texts are the foundation for faith but a shaky basis for truth and destroying people's lives."

"I have never destroyed lives. The Inquisition does. Corrupt priests do."

"You miss my point again," I reply. "What if nothing can be proved? What if everything is the product of flawed human reason? What if people have been killed over false ideas that only parade as truth?"

"Truth is beyond reason. As long as the texts are accurately translated, they are the only proof we need of the truth of God's word."

"So you're telling me that the Scriptures are self-evidently true as long as they are properly translated. What about interpretation? What makes your interpretations more reliable than the Church's?"

"Now I know you are a devil. You have been sent to make me abandon my savior." His voice rises in self-righteous annoyance, and I realize with a smile that Aonio Paleario is not above changing the subject when he doesn't want to answer. I decide to tweak him.

"I wouldn't have thought a rational man such as you would believe in devils."

"Who are you? I challenge you to reveal yourself."

Now it is I who changes the subject. "You believe in the soul's immortality, don't you? You should. You wrote about it."

"What about it?"

"What do you think happens when you die?"

"I believe in a forgiving God who will be with me in death and my soul will go back to where it came from. I think He will be proud of me because I have fulfilled His mission."

"So you understand what God wants?" I look at him in surprise. Defiance I expected, but not arrogance at this point. Doing God's will is the Church's self-justification and that's arrogant enough. "You expected a reward for harming others" I ask him. "You thought if you destroyed others around you, you would stand better with God? Or did you think inflicting pain was merely the price to be paid for your freedom to read old texts (which, incidentally, history is going to prove don't agree with one another), and then develop your personal version of the truth?"

"It is not my version of the truth. It is The Truth." Aonio's voice rises again.

I sigh. I think he hears me and he jerks his head up. His lips are set and his face is pinched with anger. He is back to defiance.

"Let me ask you something," I say bluntly. "Tell me the difference between you and Caraffa and his Inquisition."

"How can you ask me such a thing? He and the Inquisition have destroyed untold lives."

"So it's a question of degree? He's injured many more people than you have, so you are more correct?"

"I fail to see the comparison." Aonio's voice is cold. He turns his back to where he thinks my voice is coming from.

"Let me tell you what I see," I say mercilessly. "Both you and Caraffa have theories. Notice that I use the word "theories" and not "faiths." I don't know how sincere Caraffa is in believing his. But he has the Church behind him and, except for you, not many people willing to oppose him. You have ideas you think truer than the Church's, and you want your ideas proved right. In the name of those ideas—whether yours or Caraffa's—you both trample the little people around you. Neither of you is interested in helping these people find their own pathways to a relationship with God. You want to impose your ideas on them."

"But when people are caused to believe in lies, they are misled." Aonio's voice has risen to an anguished scream. He turns around and stares blindly at the ceiling.

"That's what the Church says. Why can't you and Caraffa trust people to find their own way?"

"Because they might believe in dangerous things."

"I fail to see how the ideas they form for themselves can be any more dangerous than what the Church or you propose."

"You judge me. You question all the things I hold sacred. You accuse me of vile things. Who are you to talk?"

I stop for a moment to think. Who am I? Right now, that's a rather good question. Am I alive? I don't know. Am I dreaming of shadows? If I am, whose dream is it?

"I hope I have learned we are here to learn compassion for ourselves and for others who choose to share our lives with us."

"Then how are you to be judged?" he demands. Although he has no idea why I am hesitant, he is skilled enough in debate to recognize the shallow evasion of my answer and to press his attack.

"I judge myself by the same standard that I use to judge you—by consequences," I say. "What difference have you and I made by having been alive? What has your pure reason contributed to the world? Tell me what good things you leave behind?"

"I am not to be judged by consequences," he shouts at me. "I am to be judged by the consistency of my commitment to the truth." He sounds pompous and professorial, as if confessing to some minor flaw confirms his innate superiority. His tone irks me.

"So Beatrice died because she wasn't perfectly committed to your idea of truth?"

"No. I see where you are leading me. You want me to say she paid with *her life because of my dedication to seeking truth."*

"A good start. At least you didn't blame it all on the Swiss printer as Marietta wanted to."

"I don't know how else I could have lived my life and followed God's wishes."

"Let's leave God out of this," I reply. "It has to do with what you owed the people around you. It wasn't death."

"I did not willingly cause anybody's death. I am no murderer. I will not believe my life has been in vain. My name will be recalled one day as someone who was devoted to his God and chose to die rather than live in an unjust world."

"You are relying on history to justify you? You believe that those who follow you will revere you? They won't even recognize your name. Trust me. No one knows how we will be judged, but just because you are convinced of something does not make it true. Did you think Europe would go up in flames because you had been arrested?"

"You don't understand."

"Make me." I throw out the challenge realizing that the five hundred years between us are an impenetrable barrier. I know things I can never explain and hope for him to understand. I wait in the ensuing silence for him to speak.

"I believed my example could help reform the Church," he says. "By removing abuses we could again become one congregation of believers. We could unite to seek the truth of the Scriptures."

"Did you think the pope, the cardinals, the bishops, all grown fat on the abuses you mention, and all the little fish whose livelihood depends on keeping them in power, would willingly allow you to change everything?"

"I hoped the truth would prevail." He sounds sad as if he is starting to understand the failure and inherent tragedy of his life.

"You know what I think," I say equally sadly. *"I think you have too positive an opinion of the power of human reason. Stack words and ideas against money and power, and guess which one always wins. I also think that Beatrice was indeed the heretic's daughter, your daughter. Neither one of you had any thought for consequence. You because you were too self-centered and she because she was too young."*

"I think you are too cynical." Aonio's voice has taken a magisterial finality. *"We who know the truth are required by the ages to speak out for it and for the future of mankind. When we use reason to seek truth, when we clear away the errors of the past, we hold in our hands the power to make a difference. It is our duty to speak out and take action against abuse and falsehood."*

"This is not one of your orations," I reply tartly. *"This is your life and the consequences aren't theoretical. You can't just talk your way out of this."*

"I am not a heretic."

"I didn't say you were. The Church did. But was your daughter's death worth your chance to tell Caraffa you thought him wrong?"

"Her death doubles my sorrow."

"Aonio, I am asking you about the consequences of your decisions. You can blame the Church for repression all you want, but the Church is human and was merely reflecting the people it represented. You were part of a movement but not the blazing beacon you wanted to be, and it was your family that paid for it."

"I love my family."

"I disagree. Your work was to love other people and not everyone can."

"I disagree with you as well. I have loved people too."

"There are many who will call you noble for standing up for your beliefs, Aonio. But you are just as flawed as the rest of us. You have lost your connection to the community of beings around you. The German reformers

worked together and created new forms of faith. They were the ones who prevailed. Not you with the single, flaring fire of your self-sacrifice."

"I am no German reformer," he thunders.

"Yet you have behaved no differently from the Church that is putting you to death," I thunder back. "Only except the Church's interest is power and yours is knowledge. When it came to the people around you, you've treated them no better."

"You have no right to talk to me like this."

I can see him slipping away from me, retreating back to his reputation and the comfort of what he has believed in all his life. I let him go. What we have to offer one another has been given. I have learned what I needed to. It is time to tell him who I am.

"I am the lessons that you leave behind you, Aonio. I am the future that you set in place. As you say, we come from spirit, we return to spirit. All we have is our capacity to learn and develop our own moral consciences. That is how we must all live our lives."

"Begone. Stop torturing me. Leave me to my thoughts and prayers."

"Aonio, you can banish me, you can ignore me, but you cannot deny me. Every choice you ever made in your lifetime is part of what has followed, and you live on not through your books but through your tattered family and ultimately through the example set by your actions."

"I had to live my life in the present. I can't live in a future I don't know. I cannot be responsible for what happens after I am dead."

"I am the proof we all are. I have spent my life hiding from decisions like yours. You might have had reason to think only of yourself. But I should have known better. I do now."

"I will die tomorrow. I will not accept I have anything to do with you."

"You do not need to accept me," I tell him. "I have learned this lesson for us both. Nothing else matters."

Chapter 16

Castel Sant'Angelo, July 3, 1570

IT WAS DAWN on the day he would die. Aonio had spent a restless night, awoken by a repeated dream whenever he drifted into sleep. He was on a hillside, lying on the ground among bushes and rocks. Others were with him. One man was dark with black, unreflective eyes. Another was a slight, nervous man who fluttered his hands in a strange bird-like way. This man kept talking about trying not to fall asleep. "We must be faithful," he kept repeating. "We must not sleep." But everyone other than the three was sleeping. A slight breeze rustled the leaves.

In the distance, Aonio could hear soft prayers but could not make out the words. Someone called out below. Feet tramped up the hill. Swords clanked and the voices came closer. He knew what these feet and voices meant and was afraid. The dark man was angry and shouted out defiantly. He called for Aonio and the nervous man to stand firm. The nervous man started sobbing while the others awoke in confusion. In the darkness, Aonio pushed himself through the bushes and away from his fellows. When the marchers reached them, he was hunched behind a rock with his heart pounding. He heard triumphant calls, "They're here," and sounds of a struggle. He heard the dark man call his name in a mixture of anger and anguish. Then there was a heavy thud and the nervous man cried out. Gutteral voices issued orders. The voices echoed down the hillside as the prisoners were taken away.

Aonio remained trembling in his hiding place. He waited considerable time before he made his way down the trail. At the bottom, a rough voice demanded if he was one of the people on the hill. With a wavering voice he denied it. He was asked again, and again he denied it. Then he was allowed to pass.

In the end Aonio was too afraid of the dream to sleep. He kept hearing the dark man call his name, and he knew he had betrayed his fellows. He watched the dawn come through the slit of window in his cell and heard the familiar chink of the keys as the Misericordia came into his cell. There were three of them, wearing large red crosses on loose white robes. Their eyes showed beneath the facemasks under their pointed headgear. They entered and lined up across the doorway, two guards behind them. The murmur of their prayer sounded like the insistent humming of bees. One approached Aonio and made the sign of the cross. He turned and motioned Aonio to follow. The other two joined in behind them. One guard led the way while the other followed the procession.

Aonio was unsteady as they went down the stairs and through the twisting passages. The human misery stored away in the side cells was silent. When they came to the inside corridor behind the prison gate, the guards dressed Aonio in the cloak of shame. It was painted with the flames of hell. He was then put in the back of a cart. The three masked priests took up their positions in front and the first one hoisted up a wooden cross. Soldiers walked behind. As the door opened to the outside, he could see a crowd had gathered, jeering and jostling to see who was being led away to die.

The Misericordia began their solemn chant, "Forgive, forgive, our God, receive this penitent and hear his plea to you to die a good Christian and fit to enter heaven. Forgive, forgive, our God, and hear this man who believes in the Holy Roman Church and who has made confession."

If Aonio heard the words, he did not react. He had been warned not to speak on his way to execution. If he did and it was deemed to be blasphemous, they would drive a stake through his cheeks and tongue and another vertically through his lips to form the sign of the cross. Thus they would silence him in the name of the Holy Church. He did not believe all the beliefs of the Roman Church, but the time for debate was over.

He looked at faces as the cart bumped over cobblestones and ruts. It was not far down the road from the prison to the Castel Sant'Angelo. A light rain fanned across his face and those of the people watching him. Paleario saw a butcher with a bloody apron leaning with crossed arms against a wall. A boy with bright red hair stared at him blankly, his open mouth revealing missing teeth. A middle-aged woman with a tight scarf around her head looked frightened. "Of me?" Aonio wondered. People hung over the sills of windows along the street. Street urchins taunted him and threw stones until a soldier chased them away. He heard laughter and someone called out the word *heretic* before spitting with a loud hawking sound.

The cart lunged on through the light summer drizzle until it came to a platform where the gallows had been erected on the river's bank. Heat shimmered from a bonfire, with pops and snaps sending green wood twigs twirling through the air. The black-covered hangman stood impassively on the wooden platform while Paleario was handed down from the cart and led up the stairs. The crowd flowed in and massed at the base, peering upwards at him and held back only by the soldiers. Aonio tried to hold his head up proudly, but he was too tired. His side hurt and blood pounded in his ears. He tried to pray but all he could say over and over in his mind was "My God be with me. My God be with me." They put the noose around his neck. He turned from the blurred faces and saw the mighty golden dome of St Peter's. He smelled the smoke from the fire below and the woody scent of the rope they put around his neck. He heard a hush when they placed the hood on his head. Then there was the crack of the trapdoor beneath his feet and he was hanging.

7:00 a.m.

I STRUGGLE FOR *breath, and something rattles in my chest. The cavern has taught me that all beings look for their spirit selves. Finding personal meaning is the responsibility of being born and people cannot walk away from it by letting others tell them what is true. I feel a rush of happiness at knowing. It feels like a soft spring rain washing away the darkness of winter and bringing the promise of new growth.*

I remember the name of the final dwarf. Happy. I picture that dwarf, always smiling, making the most of who he is and clear-sighted about what he really needs. I see the prior's lovingly described tapestry of life, in which every one of us is a thread in many pictures. I feel a joy that reaches out to everything around me and opens up my long-trapped feelings. I no longer feel the need for self-protection. I want to shout out loud the things I've learned and flood the world with the light of my new understanding. I am made fresh like a giddy child.

Thank you Skipper for your friendship through the lifetimes. Thank you Carole and Caterina for your level-headedness both then and now. I am sorry, Michael, that I was not a better father. It was because I had not learned to trust you, and I hope you will one day understand. Thank you, Anna, for staying with me. I am proud of your quest for knowledge and I would have despaired had I lost you once again, but I ask you to move beyond being the heretic's daughter and find peace for yourself alone. I am sorry that I was emotionally stillborn and could not give you and Michael the kindness and love you deserved. I hope, Julia, that you laid to rest the haunting fear that you were responsible for that suicide.

I am sorry that I was not able to see the aching beauty of this life even with its misapprehensions and misunderstandings, even with our failures to see who we really are until the realization comes creeping into our lives just before we are to leave them, even with the poignant failures as we try to reach out to one another without recognizing that one pebble can create a sea of waves, and even as we try to impose our theories and ideas on a universe far beyond our ability to comprehend, let alone control.

I am sorry for the sadness that resulted from my decisions. I am sorry for the decisions I did not make but should have. I am sorry Fedro that you and I could not find resolution. Perhaps one day you can forgive me. I am sorry Carolina, mother, I did not see how religion was your shield against the sorrow and violence around you. As Marietta might have tried, you wanted to force me into conformity for my own safety. But I was right too—belief is not the same as truth, and horror follows when people cannot see the difference. You wanted assurances and guaranteed ways into Heaven, but no such ways exist. If they are offered, they distract from the hard work of learning for yourself. At the same time, we are also part of a vast community of spirits looking for the light.

I hear Marion whisper to Anna that I am going and she should say goodbye to me. I brace myself for the final snuff out, the blackness at the end of my lifetime, but, instead, a blazing light has driven away any darkness. The shapes I saw before are waiting to help and welcome me. I feel their kindness. Thank you for coming for me, I tell them. They smile. I am no longer afraid only amazed at recovering what I thought was lost. Held in Anna's arms, I take one final deep, gasping breath and move joyfully toward the figures and the light.

Epilogue

A ONIO PALEARIO WAS hanged on July 3, 1570, still maintaining human beings can be responsible to their maker only if they are free to know Him. His body was taken from the gallows at the Castel Sant'Angelo and burned. The ashes were scattered in the Tiber River. The Catholic Church placed his works on the Index of Prohibited Books and Authors and destroyed every edition they could find. In time, no one remembered him in his native land, but he was codified among the Protestants as a martyr for the freedom of individual conscience, a designation he would not have liked.

Donata Stampa, assistant to the Inquisition, the dark young man, was named Bishop of Nepi and Sutra soon after the committee finished their investigation of the heretic, Aonio Paleario. The vice commissioner, Vicenzo Donzelli became Bishop of Valva and Sulmona.

The Holy Inquisition continued sporadically until the last execution for heresy took place in Spain in 1834. The Index of Prohibited Books and Authors was not abolished until 1966.

The Paleario family survived as best it could. The della Rena family, into which Caterina had married, conveniently forgot to include her maiden name in any family documents or on any monuments. Her children were never told what had happened to their grandfather. Fedro

Paleario was forced to live quietly, although his daughter Cosima created a stir at the Medici court because of her stunning beauty. Nothing more is known of any descendants except for members of the Pagliarii family to this day living in Veroli who claimed to be related to Aonio Paleario once it was safe to do so.

Marietta and her son mounted a vigorous campaign against the appropriation of their property. Seven years after Aonio's death, officers of the Inquisition came and confiscated all their possessions and property, including inheritances long paid to the children's spouses. The magistrates later found the agents of the Inquisition had exceeded their authority. Restoration was ordered of Marietta's and Caterina's dowries. The sale of the villa was found to be legal, and the Inquisition was forced to drop charges against its new owner. Marietta died in 1585, fifteen years after her husband, and his exact age to the day. She had lived the last part of her life with her son Fedro.

Fra Pietro was not reassigned to Rome, nor did he obtain Aonio's writing desk. Fedro gave the desk to the Bishop of Colle for his assistance in protecting the family's estate, and from there it traveled to Florence to adorn one of the new villas springing up in the hills of Fiesole. Eventually, it was sold to an American collector. It ended up in Albuquerque, New Mexico, in a land that Fra Pietro could know nothing about. It is still as loved today as when Paleario and Pterigi packed it on a cart to travel between Colle and Milan.

Anna del Vecchio continued to teach and write and found her own way to say farewell to her husband through her poetry. She sent part of Bill's ashes to Carolina, and scattered the rest on Guanella Pass high above Georgetown. Her breakthrough poem was said by her critics to be the first promise of her later work. Her words were about Bill and her reaction to his death.

Stone Fences
Guanella Pass, March

Today I have brought your ashes to free them
Into the mountains beside the road from Georgetown.
There is snow here, ridged beside the car,
And Guanella Pass is a grey-buffalo
Shrouded by paper clouds that still promise snow.

Yet, around me are the signs of life returning.
The jay's cry echoes amidst the rustling pines,
The melting snow glistens sparkling blue silver,
The creek runs with melt beneath the winter ice.

At the top of the pass, I shall commit you
To a Druid ring of rocks still buried by the snow.
Here I shall brush away the sky to make
Room for you amidst the hills you loved.
And I shall incant the farewell sung by every generation
The song of the unknowingness of death
And the hope that there is something more.

Tonight, I shall dream of flying with you
Over the town of Georgetown
Out to where infinity begins on the grasses of the plains.

Without Bill, Anna and Carole drifted apart. By intuitive mutual agreement, Anna never spoke again with Carolina who lived out her life, finding comfort in the knowledge she had tried to come to her son as he was dying.

With time, Michael built his bright professional future and became the man he was always meant to be. Anna saw him on the usual holidays. But it was understood something broken had been repaired, something long dead had come back to life.

Among Bill's papers, Anna found poetry written in his jagged upright printing. One poem in particular startled her:

> Fire, the efficient destroyer.
> It renders unto God
> Only smoke and ash
> And their pitiable baggage
> Duplicates around the globe.
> Humans are nature's error.
> I am not a Sunday agency
> Dispensing brotherly love
> Pulsing with love
> Oozing nonsense
> Oozing hate.
> Only the wind and snow
> Never neglect the graves.

She stared at the poem for a long time before placing it back among his papers. After several years of maintaining the old house and land, she sold it and moved to a warmer place. One day, she took out Bill's novel and sat down to read. He had written about traveling through space to find a new home out among the stars, one where there would be tolerance and peace. She hoped that those dreams had brought him comfort as he wrote them. Then she started to form his pages into a coherent book.

With his death, the waters closed over Bill's head and his existence was marked only by his son and the memories of those who had known and loved him. But it was enough.

Afterword

A onio Paleario has been described as a martyr for individual conscience. He was denounced as a protestant reformer, tried by the Catholic Church's Inquisition, and executed because, in the face of the terrible destruction of the fall of Rome in 1527 (the 9/11 of its day), the Church preached that only pure conformity to dogma and teachings could protect the world from God's anger.

Paleario went to his death proclaiming his devotion to Jesus Christ but also claiming that the practices of the Roman church were not based on the Bible. He was right, but still to be just as dead. The list of those responsible for his death and the many others who suffered a similar fate stretches from his own home town of Colle di Val D'Elsa into the Vatican itself. The Vatican has never released the details of his trial although, to be fair, that may be because they can't find them.

Aonio Paleario's life and death is the genesis of A Dream of Shadows. But I must hasten to add that I have used history to my own ends. There was an Aonio Paleario. He was born around 1500 in Veroli, outside Rome, and he was a lawyer as well as a professor of rhetoric and speech at various universities. He married a woman named Marietta Guidotti, with whom he had children and the usual worries about raising them. The Roman Inquisition executed him for heresy in 1570. He left letters and writing in Latin, although there is disagreement about whether he wrote some of them. He is remembered primarily for his law career, a series of controversial trials, and his martyrdom. Some scholars claim he was an Italian protestant because he asked for individual freedom to do research; one went so far as to call him a Lutheran. My impression of him is that he was not a reformer as much as a scholar seeking academic freedom during a time when theology controlled all forms of thought. Everyone can agree, however, that he lived in difficult times and—in modern terms—tempted fate by standing against prevailing and arbitrary Catholic doctrine. This makes him closer to being a modern man, generations ahead of his time.

Like Paleario, Clement VII and Cardinal (later pope) Caraffa, and the Sack of Rome are historical. Clement VII (1523-34), was arrogant, narcissistic, clumsy, and politically inept, surprising given his Medici family pedigree. Like most high-ranking churchmen of the time, religion was a career, a means to political power for him as well as advancement for his family. Clement alternated between being drunk on his own importance and relying on his supposed Medici cleverness to neutralize some of the most contentious and warlike powers in Europe. It didn't work. During the siege of Rome, he wound up starving in the Castel Sant'Angelo along with everyone else until he paid ransom to the occupiers of Rome. But even then, the lessons were soon forgotten. Once rescued, he went back to his old practices and tried politicking his way out of the mess he had created. Scholars such as Paleario who questioned the rational basis for the Church's teaching and the excesses of popes such as Clement were at best inconvenient because they raised difficult questions and at worst a threat to the Church's security as well as the stability of the countryside itself since the Church was the only entity capable of keeping peace.

Caraffa, on the other hand, was worse than Clement. As the head of the Inquisition, he had opportunity and motive to persecute, and he did. Enthusiastically. He was described by the Venetian ambassador as ill-tempered and intolerant of any opposition, quite unsuited to lead the Church; the ambassador said Caraffa loved the Inquisition so much he would have got up from his deathbed to go to work. Even Caraffa was surprised when he was elected pope because he knew the level of hostility he had aroused. Given Venice's generally sardonic tolerance of Vatican power because of its attendant patronage, the ambassador's assessment was straight talk indeed. As usual in times of transition, Sixteenth Century Italy was the best of times for certain people and the worst of times for nearly everyone else.

Despite these correspondences between history and the modern experience, this book pretends neither to be a history of 16th Century Italy nor a biography of Aonio Paleario. I have, in fact, conflated two papal reigns for the sake of the story and I have taken liberties as well with the little we know of Paleario's personal life.

Anyone who wants to learn more about Aonio Paleario can consult the two-volume biography by M. Young entitled The Life and Times of Aonio Paleario (1860), although Young presents Paleario as a martyr for the Protestant cause. Salvatore Caponetto provides a more modern account in Aonio Paleario (1503-1570) e la riforma protestante in Toscana (1979). Paleario's letters survive but are available primarily in eloquent Latin, the language of scholarship during the Renaissance.

Garry Wills' Papal Sin: Structures of Deceit (2000) shows the endurance of calls for papal reform—Vatican criticism is its own tradition, the most recent being Eric Frattini's The Entity: Five Centuries of Secret Vatican Espionage (English edition 2008). Those interested in the Roman Inquisition will find a description in Edward Peters' Inquisition (1988).

The descriptions of the Mantua tapestries are based on Clifford Brown and Guy Delmarcel's Tapestries for the Courts of Federico II, Ercole, and Ferrante Gonzaga 1522-63 (1996). The account of shipbuilding relies on Frederic Chapin Lane's Venetian Ships and Shipbuilders of the Renaissance (1934), which is reprinted now in paperback. Salt trials are historical and not confined to Siena: Mark Kurlansky's fascinating book Salt (2002) is a study in monopoly for something we take for granted today but was once absolutely vital in preserving food. For those interested in theories of spiritual rebirth, Shepherd Hoodwin's The Journey of Your Soul, based on the Michael teachings, provides one of the most organized explanations. Accounts of near-death experiences include Elizabeth Kubler-Ross's seminal study On Death and Dying, as well as books such as James Van Praagh's Talking to Heaven and Sam Parnia, What Happens When We Die (2006), which attempts to document near-death experiences.

The End